DRONE
GAMES

PRAISE FOR *DRONE GAMES*

"*Drone Games* is a well-written work of fiction that is very believable. Drones and UAVs are hot topics in the airport management community today. Our concern has been focused on unintentional collisions between airliners and unmanned aircraft. However, after reading Mr. Narlock's book, we now need to consider the possibility that drones can also be used as weapons of terrorism."

—PETER HORTON, *Director, Key West International Airport*

"As I prepared my 777 for departure from Heathrow Airport in London to Dulles International, I found myself scanning the perimeter fence lines for drones! A fascinating and realistic novel that really got me thinking!"

—JOHNI CHRISTIANSEN, *US commercial airline pilot*

"What truly makes a thrilling novel, no matter how well-written, is how realistic and true to scientific facts and logical conclusions it is. Joel Narlock has captured this timely, frightening phenomenon in *Drone Games* to a tee. I highly recommend it to any reader, with the warning that you may have second thoughts about the next airline flight you take."

—JERRY SANDERS, *Colonel, US Army, retired; US commercial airline pilot; certified flight instructor*

DRONE GAMES

JOEL NARLOCK

SWEETWATER
BOOKS

An Imprint of Cedar Fort, Inc.
Springville, Utah

ISBN 13: 978-1-4621-1487-0

Published by Sweetwater Books, an imprint of Cedar Fort, Inc.
2373 W. 700 S. Springville, UT 84663
Distributed by Cedar Fort, Inc., www.cedarfort.com

LIBRARY OF CONGRESS CATALOGING-IN-PUBLICATION DATA

Narlock, Joel, 1954- author.
Drone games / Joel Narlock.
   pages cm
   ISBN 978-1-4621-1487-0 (perfect : alk. paper)
 1. Drone aircraft--United States--Fiction. 2. Terrorism--United States--Fiction. I. Title.
PS3614.A696D76 2014
813'.6--dc23
                              2014013414

Cover design by Kristen Reeves
Cover design © 2014 by Lyle Mortimer
Edited and typeset by Melissa J. Caldwell

Printed in the United States of America

10 9 8 7 6 5 4 3 2 1

Printed on acid-free paper

THE LORD will bring a nation against you from far away, from the ends of the earth, like an eagle swooping down, a nation whose language you will not understand, a fierce-looking nation without respect for the old or pity for the young. . . . They will besiege all the cities throughout the land. . . . If only it were morning! Because of the terror that will fill your hearts and the sights that your eyes will see.

—Deuteronomy 28:49–50, 52, 67

IT HAS become appallingly obvious that our technology has exceeded our humanity.

—*Albert Einstein*

I ALWAYS say my biggest worry is an attack on a plane.

—*Robert Mueller, FBI Director 2001–2013*

FOREWORD

ROBERT C. MICHELSON

HIGH SCHOOL English was never one of my favorite subjects. In fact, I learned more grammar rules by studying Spanish. But I did enjoy creative writing. As an aspiring engineer, creativity was essential, so it was natural that my creative bent would be expressed in terms of technical stories, especially science-fiction short stories. Who would have guessed that my career would thrust me into cutting-edge research, essentially creating new things and demonstrating capabilities that had never been done before? While others were reading science fiction, I was living it.

My career has had very few limits. If I could get an idea funded, I could implement it without regard for company product lines or corporate bottom lines. Such was the nature of full-time research at one of the world's top university-based research institutes.

I started out designing remote sensing systems but later gravitated to aerial robotics. Unmanned aerial vehicles (UAVs) combine aeronautics with IT. Give a UAV the ability to "reason," and you have an aerial robot. That was my passion. A flying robot that could act intelligently on its own—as if piloted by a human—but with no human intervention.

My first attempt at building an aerial robot was actually in high school. I took a control-line model airplane and removed the control lines, replacing them instead with a series of weights and using gravity for stable flight. It was a horrendous failure for reasons that are quite obvious to me now, but it was a beginning.

Over the years, I worked on various UAV programs for the US government and taught at Georgia Tech and internationally. While America focused on large fixed-wing UAVs such as the General Atomics Predator and Teledyne Ryan's Global Hawk, my attention turned to biologically inspired machines with flapping wings and small size—the kind that were perfect for covert operations. I developed and patented the "Entomopter" (*entomo* meaning "insect" as in *entomology*, and *pteron* meaning "wing"; thus it's an "insect-winged machine").

I suppose I'm a purist when I bemoan the media's use of the antiquated term *drone*. During the Vietnam War, US drones like the Ryan AQM-91 Firefly flew reconnaissance missions to waypoints and simply returned to base. Far from intelligent machines. We've come a long way since then. In the 2013 International Aerial Robotics Competition, a Chinese autonomous aerial robot covertly entered a building and, without any prior knowledge of the floor plan, created a laser-scan map while reading directional signs in Arabic as it moved. Upon locating the correct room, the aerial robot retrieved a flash drive from a box on a desk and then deposited an identical flash drive to delay detection of the espionage-related theft. It then used its map to exit the building—all in under ten minutes. That is the future. An advanced aerial robot that thinks for itself. Not just a "drone," and certainly not fiction.

Purism aside, a swarm of sophisticated, fun, mysterious, and fascinating flying machines is about to invade our skies. A new species. The next new thing. Their functions, uses, flight paths, and silhouettes will soon become commonplace, embedded in our psyche and day-to-day culture just like that of microwave ovens and cell phones. Perhaps in five years, we'll all own one. It's 11:00 p.m. Do you know where your drone is?

So, that brings us to Joel Narlock's fictional story, *Drone Games* in which an Entomopter plays a central role. The Entomopter, as with all technology, is neutral. It is a thing, neither good nor bad. It has beneficial uses as well as nefarious ones. Much akin to a gun that can be used to feed a family or kill a family, the misuse of a drone such as the Entomopter emanates from the dark heart of its user, not the inanimate object itself.

Drone Games tells a story of homeland terrorism. The potential has existed for years but is rarely talked about openly. It poses a classic scenario: What if an otherwise benign drone fell into evil hands for an evil purpose? What kind of havoc could be wrought?

To be sure, *Drone Games* is not a how-to manual for the misuse of drone technology; rather, it is a scenario designed to entertain the reader. It should also provoke thoughts on how to defend against someone who might actually attempt such tactics, and rightly so. We can always use good security forethought. The world is already a dangerous place, and sadly, many security operations are purely reactive. A shoe bomber attempts to bring down a passenger airliner, and now we must all remove our shoes at airport checkpoints. Why were we not scanning or removing footwear prior? It is naïve to think that evildoers do not already possess the ability to create aerial robotic weapons. Many terrorists and their collaborators are trained at the world's finest universities.

Human beings, educated or not, who are bent on committing evil will use every high-tech tool available. *Drone Games* explores one such scenario in which a harmless flying device is used to terrorize America and cripple its economy. It is an entertaining novel that can be appreciated by readers on several levels, from those who love suspense and the unfolding of a crime investigation, to the geek in all of us who is intrigued by an evil protagonist's technically plausible schemes.

I pray that the plot stays fiction.

ROBERT C. MICHELSON
Principal Research Engineer, Emeritus
Georgia Tech Research Institute
Adj. Associate Professor (Ret.)
School of Aerospace Engineering
Georgia Institute of Technology
President & Principal Research Engineer
Millennial Vision, LLC

EXPLOSIVES ON passenger aircraft . . . hidden in shoes and under-wear—tactics that had failed miserably when Richard Colvin Reid and Umar Farouk Abdulmutallab had tried to light theirs on fire.

There *must* be another way.

This was on Ali I Naimi's mind as he sat with his comrade, Georgia Tech Professor Faiz Al-Aran, in Fishawy's Café, a foodless coffee and teahouse that, barring world war, had been serving customers 24/7 since 1771.

Naimi's vintage white linen suit, wire-rimmed glasses, and brown leather saddle shoes suggested a diplomat or a seasoned grandfather— the antithesis of the battle-worn mujahid in a pakol beret and ammu-nition vest who once led guerilla raids against Soviet Special Forces in Afghanistan. A salt-gray beard and nicotine-stained mustache hid the shrapnel scars on his face.

Too old for field operations, Naimi was now the head of al-Qaeda's majis al shura, a council that discussed and approved major terror opera-tions. The importance of this position was based in the Holy Qur'an:

> *Those who conduct their affairs by Shura are loved by Allah. (42:38)*

It was late afternoon, and the usually bustling café was eerily calm. A group of students from the Royal Danish Academy of Fine Arts compared their sketches of the Jawhariya Madrasa-Mausoleum, a sacred monument from 1440 that Denmark had helped to restore. A few locals debated Egypt's future. Their civil discussion quickly turned into an argument, and then stopped. When it came to solutions, no one dared show support for either Western democracy or the outlawed Muslim Brotherhood. Even the waiters were jittery. The café itself had received a bomb threat. This was a troubling time for everyone.

It was perfect for plotting jihad.

Naimi opened the *Wall Street Journal* and quoted from an article, "Al-Qaeda leader Ayman al-Zawahiri calls for more 9/11-style terror attacks inside the United States."

Publicity such as this in a major Western newspaper gave him comfort and hope. Al-Qaeda needed a victory. Something to rally around and be proud of again. He wanted to stand and shout, but he tempered himself. *On the night they killed Osama bin Laden, the Americans danced in the streets and performed their disgusting fist pumps*, he recalled. He would not celebrate this headline. Not yet.

Naimi set the newspaper down. "The FBI calls us radical jihadists. Perverters of Islam. They say we are emboldened and still a dangerous threat. Perhaps they have discovered your plans, Faiz. Attacking fifty-six targets is bold and dangerous—for them and for us. Some on the council are questioning your tactics, especially this business of crashing three passenger planes with a flying toy. Frankly, I have concerns."

"Four passenger planes," Al-Aran corrected in English without looking up, his face buried in a small spiral notebook, his eyes alternatively shifting from the notebook to a game board on the table. He stroked his black, trimmed goatee as he studied a series of attacks against enemy positions, probing for weaknesses. Seeking maximum damage. There were several options: Frontal, diagonal, and even flanking and L-shaped attacks. Al-Aran shook his head in disgust. The pathways were blocked, the targets impenetrable. The only option left was mass suicide against enemies that he termed the *white faces*.

"The Americans are like children," Al-Aran said. "Frightened and paranoid of hirabi. They see terrorists in their dreams. Allah has always shown us the path to victory. If Zawahiri seeks larger targets, then he will be pleased with my operations. Great risk brings great reward. My tactics are sound."

"I hope you are correct," Naimi cautioned. "Day after day the Americans increase their security. I suspect now that whenever Arabs attend a marathon race or walk through a shopping mall, even their smallest children carrying stuffed animals will be harassed and searched. Years ago, we carried nitrocellulose through airports in Madrid, Heathrow, and even New York, thanks to that spiced aftershave with the ship on the bottle. Now even water is forbidden.

"Did I ever tell you that Zawahiri was only fifteen when he planned to overthrow the Egyptian government? We played together in the same suburb of Maadi just six miles north . . ." Naimi peered over his glasses. "Are you even listening to me? Look at you. Your concentration is weak. You have lost originality and surprise. You telegraph every intention. You study that notebook until your eyes swell, and for what? Your soldiers are still slaughtered like sheep. I think you have become distracted by that computer always at your side. Too much conversing on the Internet with the students at your Georgia Technical Institute. Next you will invite the American NSA into your classroom."

Al-Aran accepted the scolding because he knew Naimi was right. Something had gone terribly wrong. His reputation as al-Qaeda's best operational strategist was at stake. Now even he had doubts. *How can I have been so stupid?* he wondered. Frustrated, he spat at the notebook and swept it off the table.

Naimi politely retrieved it. He thumbed the pages, chuckling at the nonsensical maze of lines and scribbling. All for a simple game. A separate section caught his eye. It had no scribbling. *Hogeschool van Amsterdam, Domein Techniek: Analyses of Boeing 777 Landing Gear.*

Al-Aran sat back in his chair, massaging his balding scalp with both hands. The situation was hopeless. His attack force had started with fifteen men and one woman. A lopsided ratio, but the woman was extremely powerful. Her skills equaled those of the men combined. Now even she was dead.

Those accursed white infidels.

3

He gave Naimi a vengeful glance, then surrendered the game with the lip of his teacup.

The black king tottered over onto the chessboard.

"It seems I am too clever for you, Faiz," Naimi said, inserting his pipe snugly into the corner of his mouth and drawing several deep puffs. The tight brown ball flamed orange. "The secret of chess, win or lose, is knowing that you have caused severe and repeated damage to an enemy. That itself is quite gratifying. Your plans will reignite a war that we once started but never fulfilled. Terrorism is a morally demanded duty. America is like a house that a snake has entered—a house filled with children. Who among us would not step forward and kill that snake? If you are successful, the world will know your name and your face. It will be prudent for you to disappear."

"With a band of masked horsemen into the mountains of Pakistan?" Al-Aran grumbled, recalling the last rumored sighting of the ghostlike Zawahiri.

"Portugal," Naimi answered. "The *Abuzenima* is an Egyptian vessel that sails the Saharan coastal routes. My brother has been captain for many years. I'll speak with him. His name is Riad, the peaceful one. He has a farm sixteen kilometers east of Aljezur. He raises sweet potatoes, peanuts, and broad beans. A mysterious animal visits his garden each night and leaves a calling card. He believes it is a mongoose, but I think not. When you meet, you must tell him that it is an Iberian lynx. He will know that you are a friend. Then you will no longer be hirabi, but retired terrorista. The fertile valleys of Aljezur are beauti—"

"*Kysse, kysse, kysse, kysse, kysse, kysse . . .*"

The men turned.

Two of the art students, goaded by the daring group chant, put on an even more sensuous exhibition that included bumping and grinding. The vulgar display ended with a raucous cheer.

Al-Aran turned to Naimi. "There is Egypt's future—a new democracy, one that accepts the culture of Western filth. Infidels were never allowed here. Now even women come and do as they please, and good Arab men say nothing."

"Times change, even in old places," Naimi said, stirring his tea. "Tell me more of this flying toy."

Al-Aran produced his pipe and slapped the bowl vigorously against his palm. His dark eyes burned angrily at the students.

"It is a sophisticated drone, not a toy. Remotely controlled and four years in development. I supported the design team. The drone's inventor is my colleague in Atlanta. I have his trust and confidence. And remember, liquefied nitrocellulose is still common lacquer. Clear and highly combustible, yes, but US airport scanners will detect explosive liquids even when they are mixed with a harmless companion."

"You are not worried?"

"I do not intend to fly through their security lines," Al-Aran stated with a hint of sarcasm. "The drone will carry solid explosives in quantities more than sufficient to severely damage an aircraft."

"I thought you abandoned Semtex because of its chemical signature."

"I did abandon it," Al-Aran answered. "Semtex has always been a wonderful plastique in both availability and power. Unfortunately, it is too easy to identify and follow. The Americans know it is our weapon of choice."

"Then what will you use? RDX? PETN?"

"Potassium chlorate," Al-Aran replied. "At one thousand meters per second, it cannot match the detonation velocities of other high explosives, yet it will still produce enormous damage. But more important, it will quickly dissolve in water, making the spent residue virtually untraceable. And that is key. The first aircraft explosion must be bathed in uncertainty. Deciding how to acquire and transport potassium chlorate is a nonissue. We can make it ourselves with no worries of sabotage or compromised supplies. The way to defeat American airport security is to avoid it entirely. Let them search forever and waste time and resources scanning passengers and protecting an aircraft's interior. I will attack the exterior. If Allah once allowed us to successfully carry chemicals through airports, he will bless my plans."

Naimi removed his pipe. "The travel routes for your students are safe?"

"Foolproof," Al-Aran replied. "Some of my best have come through our new northern crossing. They rent fishing boats on a Canadian border lake and drift to isolated points on the American shoreline. Not one has been challenged or even approached. They reach Minneapolis without the slightest concern. America's Homeland Security demonstrates the height of its ignorance, from senior management to the lowest levels. Unqualified employees in key positions are rarely fired for even the gravest incompetence. I know a middle-aged woman who worked for our campus payroll administration in Atlanta—a scatterbrained peahen. Now she parades back and forth as a TSA supervisor in baggage and x-ray security at Hartsfield-Jackson Airport. Hired to meet a gender quota. America's border is a wineskin with gaping holes. Think of it—a country's security entrusted to peahens! There is continual chaos in US immigration. Even the American Congress continues to avoid the issue for fear of offending Latino voters. And now, thanks to Cale Warren and his amnesty, Allah has opened a window of opportunity."

"The American president is not stupid," Naimi countered. "He boasts that he can place an agent every thousand feet on their borders. He would not propose something as foolish as amnesty without recourse. Perhaps it is an elaborate trap?"

Al-Aran scoffed. "Ten thousand miles of trap? I could personally drive a herd of camels from Mexico into Arizona and the immigration patrols would tip their hats and point me to water." Al-Aran smiled, but then frowned at Naimi. "Why are you laughing?"

"I am sorry, Faiz, but that is a sight I would pay to see: my best strategic planner high on a camel, clutching the cantle horn, a quiet voice singing in the moonlight."

"The voice you hear will neither be mine nor the Bedouin," Al-Aran warned. "It will be the voice of the American economy in its death throes."

"Al Jazeera made a television report on this Arizona," Naimi recalled. "The US government will acquire and uplift its own fleet of drones. Do you know for what? Aerial surveillance of endangered sheep."

"Praise Allah for their environmental priorities."

"So you have the explosives and the tactics," Naimi said. "Who will operate this drone?"

"Akil Doroudian," Al-Aran answered. "Born and raised in Montreal. His father, Reza, and I served together in the People's

Mujahedin during the revolution. Reza was wounded on Black Friday and fled to Canada."

The Iranian Revolution of 1979 deposed the Shah of Iran, a secular, lavish, and brutal dictator widely viewed as a puppet of the United States. Black Friday was named after the protests that occurred on September 8, 1978, in Zhaleh Square in Tehran. Government tanks and helicopter gunships killed eighty-nine demonstrators, including three women.

"Even in difficult times, our victories have been great," Naimi announced. "Do you trust this Akil?"

"Akil's parents are dead, but they left a child of Allah," Al-Aran said. "He is young but disciplined. Unknown, with an average face. He blends well. A typical Western youth. He will not draw attention."

"Akil . . . one who uses reason," Naimi translated the Sunni name. "Where is he now?"

"Posing as a university student in a city in Midwestern America."

"He has adequate resources?"

Al-Aran smiled slyly. "You forget that I am a tenured professor who travels. I have a healthy expense budget. We have safe arrangements."

Naimi fondled his pipe bowl. "Discipline is a fine quality, but is Akil committed to our success?"

Al-Aran folded his arms. The skin below his left eye twitched. It always did that whenever someone questioned his judgment. "A difficult term."

"Commitment or discipline?"

"Akil is the most cunning soldier I have ever trained," Al-Aran said. "I wish I had ten thousand like him. His tongue is smooth, and his ability to think on his feet is quite remarkable. He is resourceful and intelligent, with a clean identity and background. His mind constantly searches for opportunities. His talent with electronics is excellent, and he is also a chemical genius. He will not make a fool of himself like that idiot Jdey."

The FBI had recently posted a video on its website of Abderouf Jdey, a Saudi National from Yemen, performing a maniacal machine gun dance and screaming death to infidels. He was widely suspected of providing the explosives for the 2009 Christmas Day bombing (Amsterdam to Detroit), the October 29, 2010, cargo plane bomb plot (Yemen to the United States), and the May 8, 2012, passenger plane suicide bomber plot (Yemen to the United States). The FBI also believed that he fashioned and delivered the materials used in the Boston Marathon bombing, an action that was unsanctioned by Naimi's council.

"Chemical knowledge is an ugly skill," Naimi said. "But one that all of our soldiers must learn and exploit. Jdey is an excellent technician who can design anything. Unfortunately, he has become, shall we say, an exuberant liability. He is established in New York City. You may use him as you see fit."

Al-Aran knew what that meant. Jdey was a carryover from another age and time, a lone-wolf jihadist who thrived on brute force—and lots of it. The US military prison at Guantanamo Bay was filled with them. Jdey routinely balked at organizational planning and tact. Naimi believed he had become uncontrollable.

"Akil knows this drone?" Naimi asked pointedly.

"He has studied the design."

"Studied but never operated?"

"The training will come easily," Al-Aran said. "In that respect, it is a toy."

Naimi frowned at that. "Dispersing a liquid or powdered chemical into a lake or a city street, yes. Flying a remote-controlled toy in a straight line is not difficult. But for your airline operation . . . we are not speaking of a straight line."

"The drone is easy to fly and maneuver. There are many vulnerable areas on an aircraft wing, especially near the inboard ailerons and flaps. It should work."

Naimi narrowed his eyes "We have known each other too long, Faiz. You are not confident. Why?"

Al-Aran drew in a breath, then let it out. "I cannot guarantee success. Even a large hole in a wing might not destabilize a plane. The bond of airfoil and fuselage is simply too strong. The timing for pilots to complete their preflight checklists is also unpredictable. Sneaking the drone onto a runway and then chasing after a moving aircraft may indeed be too difficult. I am sorry, Ali. I may have to rethink the tactics."

"Neither of us is perfect," Naimi said, brushing the apology aside. "We all must rethink from time to time. What sets Allah's people apart is our ability to adapt and survive under adversity. Allah gave you a mind that easily marries technology to strategy. I have no such skill. You told me that this drone can follow coordinates to a general area and then be delicately guided to its target by a distant soldier. I believe you, and I trust you. If you have discovered an opportunity with aircraft landing gear, then I will support it. And you seem to have everything in hand," Naimi continued. "I understand the drone is a finalist in a science competition in Rome. If it wins, then the entire world will notice."

"Notice what? A flying assassin that can kill an aircraft or a harmless surveyor that collects rocks on Mars?"

Naimi considered the point and had to agree. "Your colleague, the drone's inventor . . . where is he staying?"

"The award ceremony is at the Sheraton Roma. He is at the Atlante Star near the Vatican. Suite 400." Al-Aran's eyes swept the café. He lowered his voice. "America is asleep, Ali. We can stab a knife in her heart. On her own soil. I have the right soldiers, the right plans, and it is the right moment in time. We must act before she awakens. Her economy staggers next to a cliff. All we need to do is push. Ours is no longer a military war, but a war of economics. My operations will bring unparalleled suffering to four sectors of the US economy: airlines, consumable meat, stored water, and standing forests. Air, earth, water . . ." A waiter approached. Al-Aran waved him off. ". . . and fire. Four passenger aircraft will fall from the sky. Twenty-seven cattle feedlots will be infected. Nine reservoirs will be poisoned, and sixteen forests will be set ablaze. The targets are spread throughout America, each selected to achieve the widest impact. Akil himself has gone to great lengths to establish four different identities, one in each airport city. He has found access to every target runway. I have never seen such vulnerability."

"Where are these airports?"

Al-Aran arranged four pawns on the chessboard. "San Diego International, New York's LaGuardia, O'Hare in Chicago, and Milwaukee, a mid-sized city on a Great Lake. It will begin there. The runway proximity is excellent."

Naimi opened the newspaper with a sharp snap.

"What do you ask of the council?"

"Permission," Al-Aran answered, booting his laptop. "The acts I propose to commit against America's homeland will encourage others across the world to join our faith and our cause. We will show a unified struggle by undertaking all operations at once. We will strike with a fist forged by Allah. I need only to finalize locations and dates with each of my lead soldiers."

"Over the Internet?" Naimi whispered angrily. "Target locations, dates, and naked information? Our most sensitive plans displayed for all to see? You are aware that President Warren and his NSA collect Internet messages and even phone records of American citizens, news organizations, and even journalists with impunity?"

Naimi was forever fearful of computers and their so-called secure networks. He believed they were listening devices used by American intelligence agencies—something that was actually proven to be true.

Al-Qaeda thrived on publicity, the fuel that bred passion. Zawahiri, Osama bin Laden's replacement, advocated using all forms of modern media to call for America's destruction. The recent rollout of the Shamukh al-Islam website, used by members to communicate and issue propaganda statements, had just activated its first Twitter account with twenty-nine tweets.

"You forgot foreign allies," Al-Aran said smugly. "The president is under severe criticism for doing so. The people have turned against him. One report suggests that there will be official censure and perhaps even impeachment. He has just announced a plan for complete surveillance reform."

Naimi wanted to laugh. "Take caution in your political conclusions, my friend. Especially with the propaganda that flows from the American news media. I doubt if they have read the US Attorney General's brief in defense of the matter. Mr. Warren will clearly demonstrate that he has the power and authority to continue these so-called 'data intrusions' under the guise of national security."

Al-Aran shrugged. "It makes no difference. They will never discover us. Can't you see, Ali? We will never compete with America's military or technical might. The NSA can unravel the encryption that millions of Internet users rely on to keep electronic messages confidential. Their newest data center in the state of Utah is capable of collecting and analyzing every security camera video, every email, text, or voice message ever created. They are dealing in volumes of storage called zettabytes—trillions of megabytes. The entire United States produces 3.2 zettabytes of data each year. The Utah facility alone can store over five zettabytes. So what good does it do to try and hide?

"My communicating on the Internet is simple and appears in plain sight. Your own council uses Internet websites to boast of victories and recruit soldiers. But you neither trust nor understand the technical workings and efficiencies of modern social media and the simplicity of electronic mail. I do. Anyone on Earth may participate. Each day, billions of messages travel back and forth from usernames and identities that are completely obscure. If we avoid obvious flags and keywords and profess Western cultures and lifestyles, then detecting and interpreting our messages is impossible. It is as simple as showing a desire to eat or drink that which is forbidden.

"Let them monitor. How would they find a single cup of water in the oceans? More important, why would they want to? No intelligence team of humans or supercomputers would have reason to suspect anything. You must trust me, Ali. The Internet is everywhere, even in old places. Using it to communicate works perfectly when one thinks and speaks like an infidel."

Naimi nodded thoughtfully as he took all this in. "Air, earth, water, and fire. Which operation will bring the most death?"

"Death cannot be our only objective."

"What do you mean?"

"We must change the way we think, Ali," Al-Aran said. "Our targets must be economic. Bin Laden knew this, and now Zawahiri has also reached that conclusion." He leaned forward. "Look at the attacks in Boston and Kenya. What do we gain if a soldier with a backpack manages to break through the defenses in a US airport? A few hundred dead and perhaps one aircraft. The Americans will grieve, their president will predictably speak of healing, and then they will assess and bolster their front-end security. A completely shortsighted victory.

"But when multiple aircraft begin to mysteriously explode in flight, the Americans will have no choice but to close their skies and their airports. The financial impacts, even for a few days, will be fantastic. Imagine five days, or ten. What if we could clip the wings of seven thousand passenger planes indefinitely?"

The two men contemplated that for a moment—the legs of a major transportation sector broken. The economy of the United States brought to its knees once again by al-Qaeda.

"We have always known that America's airlines are a golden target and worthy of sacrifice, but there are others. I have a soldier poised in London, a courier who has devised a completely foolproof and undetectable way to carry fifteen kilograms of dried meat—meat that is infected with bovine spongiform encephalopathy—from Heathrow to Miami, on a passenger aircraft, no less. His team will mix it with common feed pellets and then harmlessly sightsee across America, visiting cattle feedlots, pastures, and even family farms. Or perhaps he could use drones? Within a month, the raw fear generated by hundreds of confirmed and pervasive outbreaks of mad cow disease will bring the US beef industry to ruin."

Naimi turned back to his newspaper. This was precisely what Zawahiri had been advocating in recent jihadi blogs produced by their media wing, as-Sahab: to bleed America's security and economy as punishment for the continuous war on Islam and Muslims.

"When would the first aircraft fall?"

"In nineteen days," Al-Aran answered. "Monday, May 18. Akil has selected a morning departure. I need only your approval."

There was an extended silence, as if everyone in the café had knowledge of the conversation and was waiting for the pronouncement.

"The earth, water, and fire operations must wait," Naimi calmly ordered. "You may attack America's airlines. If Akil succeeds, we will see about their meat."

"Those who happily leave everything in Allah's hand will eventually see Allah's hand in everything," Al-Aran whispered. "I leave for Atlanta tomorrow."

"It is in his hands," Naimi agreed. "But the destruction of four passenger aircraft will require four drones."

"Six. One will be tested, and one will be kept for future . . . assessment." Al-Aran smiled. "There are twelve waiting in a Georgia Tech research lab next to my office."

"I wager two or three will achieve success," Naimi said, folding the newspaper under his arm and rising from the table. "Guard yourself, Faiz. May Allah bestow his blessing upon young Akil and this flying technology."

Al-Aran methodically tapped his keyboard. A Gmail screen appeared with an interactive chat box. There was one contact name in the list, online and available. Al-Aran typed out a message.

> **PartyLuvr30308:** Dude, the party is set for the eighteenth of May. I'd like to finalize things around noon on the fourteenth. I really have a taste for some good barbecued pork.

The return message came moments later.

> **Toothdoc2b:** Sweet. Sounds like fun. I know a restaurant where the meat falls right off the bones. Can't wait! C U soon. Best.

2

AKIL DOROUDIAN closed his laptop.

He lowered the window of his 2003 Toyota Camry and peered across the parking lot. Satisfied that the East Layton Avenue address matched the one in the newspaper ad, he shut off the engine. The stiff spring wind was making his eyes water. A tear ran down his cheek. A rare event—he never cried for anyone or anything. He wiped it away.

Akil lifted his Milwaukee Brewer's baseball cap and finger-combed his lengthy, red-brown hair. He drew out a small white book from his jacket and rubbed his thumbs lovingly across the gold-leaf lettering. He pulled on the end of a thin cloth ribbon, and the Holy Qur'an split open. Transfixed, he digested the text with passion, as if he were rededicating himself to some lover or deep cause. In essence, he was.

Surah 9. Repentance, Dispensation

1. *A declaration of immunity from Allah and His Messenger, to those of the Pagans with whom ye have contracted mutual alliances:*
2. *Go ye, then, backwards and forwards, as ye will, throughout the land.*

3. *And an announcement from Allah and His Messenger, to the people assembled on the day of the Great Pilgrimage, that Allah and His Messenger dissolve treaty obligations with the Pagans. If then, ye repent, it were best for you; but if ye turn away, know ye that ye cannot frustrate Allah. And proclaim a grievous penalty to those who reject Faith.*

4. *Then fight and slay the Pagans wherever ye find them, and seize them, beleaguer them, and lie in wait for them in every stratagem of war; but if they repent, and establish regular prayers and practice regular charity, then open the way for them: for Allah is Oft-forgiving, Most Merciful.*

Akil kissed the book and tucked it away.

He dialed his cell phone. After four rings, an answering machine picked up. A female voice spoke.

"You've reached the Russian Star Tattoo Parlor. We're located at 2460 Kettner Boulevard just off West Laurel Street across from San Diego International Airport. We're open from noon to ten o'clock. Remember, no matter who you are, you must be special to wear the Russian Star." *Beeeep.*

Akil looked at his watch. "Hello. This is Eddie Ginosa again." His voice was young, confident, educated with a Midwest American accent. "I left a message yesterday. I just want to make sure you got my deposit check for the apartment. I'm in Milw . . . Minneapolis doing some last-minute packing. I'd like to move in a few days early to clean. If it's all right with you, I'll even pay for paint. I'll try and call late—"

"*Hola* . . . um, hello," a soft-spoken Spanish voice answered.

"Who is this?" Akil asked.

"Marissa. It's early here, *señor.* Everyone is asleep. Can you call back?"

"You're not sleeping," Akil said flirtatiously.

She yawned. "I know. My kids woke me up. They're hungry."

Akil frowned into the phone. "Is this the Russian Star?"

"*Sí.* I mean, yes. I work here, but I also live here. It's just temporary. I don't exactly have my own place."

15

"That's cool," Akil said. "Um, I need to leave a message for Viktor Karkula. I mailed a money-order down payment for an apartment. Do you know if he got it?"

"Viktor is the owner. I think he did, but I'm not sure. You'll like the place; it's right above us. The last tenants weren't real quiet, so Viktor made them leave. He gets really mad when people party and make noise. He has a bad temper."

"Thank you, Marissa. That's good to know."

"Don't mention it. I hope it works out for you. Maybe I'll see you when you get to California. You sound like a nice guy. We don't get too many around here. Bye-bye."

"Wait—I am a nice guy. And I really like kids," Akil said. There was silence on the other end, and he realized he was talking to no one.

He dialed a second number.

"Cohen Commercial Leasing," a receptionist answered. "May I help you?"

"Dennis Cohen, please," Akil replied. The transfer rang once.

"This is Denny."

"Hey, Denny. John Ghoacci. I wanted to follow up on my lease?"

"Johnny, baby," Cohen sung. "My Paisan. How are you? Or more importantly, where are you? Still in Minneapolis? I heard you got snow. Hey, listen . . . the owner signed the lease at eight bucks a square foot for twelve months. We got your deposit, so you're good to go on the first. O'Hare Aerospace Center Office Complex Suite 200 West. You have a really great view of the airport sunsets. We just opened a new fitness center. You need housekeeping?"

"Not right away," Akil lied, "but I'd like the option."

"No problemo, Paisan. You can sign up anytime. When ya comin' down?"

"Next week."

"That'll work," Cohen assured. "Always a pleasure to have a new tenant. The lobby code is the two-digit current month and year. You'll get your office door code in an email. You need anything else, you call me, okay? And, hey . . . no more Twins. You're a National League Cubbie fan now. Have a good one."

"You too." Akil clicked off and dialed a third number.

After eight rings, a woman picked up. Her voice was grandmother-sweet.

"Kenny? By the saints, are you still in Minneapolis, lad? How is your poor mother?"

"There's good news, Mrs. Timmons," Akil announced. "The pneumonia's under control. She's home now and resting. I need to stay a few more days."

"Take your time, lad. I won't run away . . ." There was a loud rumble in the background. ". . . Oh, that LaGuardia," Mrs. Timmons cursed. "It's near to the end of the world with those jets. As sure as Jesus rode a donkey, one day they'll take my hearing, and I'll sue that airport for its millions. Then and only then will I go back to Ireland. And this old neighborhood will be the sadder for it. The colored are taking over anyway. I should've given this place up after poor Dermott passed. My brother Bernard is here. He's come all the way across the Atlantic to finally visit that Statue of Liberty. He's the only thing I've got in the world now. I sure hoped the two of you might meet."

"I'll try, Mrs. Timmons. Bye now."

Akil got out of his car and approached the Legion's entrance, giving a wary glance to the full-size M-60 tank and Apache helicopter guarding the building's flanks. Across the street to the south, Mitchell International Airport was layered in fog. An unseen jet thundered into the air. He could just see the top of the control tower, and for a moment it reminded him of the Makkah-al-Mukarramah Mosque.

When she was alive, his mother, Sonia, painted Montreal's cityscape as a hobby.

Akil had neutral feelings for the female that had resided in his home. She seemed to be a doting woman-servant who cooked, cleaned, laid out his clothes, and constantly hugged him. A pale-skinned, short, and dowdy Czech with drawn, chubby cheeks and auburn hair, Sonia worked as a clerical assistant in downtown Montreal's La Tour IBM-Marathon Office Building. A shy introvert, she rarely offered anything about her life or family unless it was about her beloved son. When coworkers questioned her husband's occupation, she said she didn't know. When pressed, she said she thought he bought buildings, and they ridiculed her even more. Cruelly, they labeled her as mentally slow.

Her husband, Reza, lived an ultra-conservative Wahhabi Sunni lifestyle and trained his son in that course, controlling every facet of Akil's upbringing, including a special school—a daily Tahfidh Qur'an (Holy Qur'an memorization). He taught his son a well-known rule: memorizing when young was like engraving on stone, and memorizing when old was like engraving on water. Reza also taught Akil that Islam had three enemies in the world—Shiites, Israelis, and Americans—and anything that he did to harm them was favorable in Allah's eyes.

When Akil was eight, Reza took the boy and disappeared, giving no warning, itinerary, or contact information. For reasons unknown, Sonia never called the authorities—only a former IBM supervisor who offered no help. Four days later, distraught and near zombie-like, she arrived at work, pried open a window on the forty-seventh floor, and leaped out. For his part, Reza returned to Montreal with Akil thirty days later, satisfied that his pilgrimage to Mecca had forged the solid foundation of a young religious zealot. He purged their home and Akil's memory of Sonia's existence and never mentioned her again.

Akil stared suspiciously at a vintage pineapple hand grenade cemented to the Legion's door and pulled the pin. A return buzzer sounded, and the door popped open. A musty stench filled his nostrils, and he immediately felt sickened. Akil believed that of all the Satanic beings Americans worshipped, alcohol was equal in power to their god of sex.

He recalled the teachings of his cultural mentor. An Egyptian writer and educator, Sayyid Qutb (pronounced Koo-Toob) was the father of modern Islamic rage against America. In 1949, he studied at what would become the University of Northern Colorado. What he witnessed prompted him to condemn America as a sinful, materialistic hell devoid of morals and thus unfit for any Muslim.

Qutb determined that America was obsessed with alcohol, sports, body perfection, and open sexuality. America's women were seducers who relished dancing, exposing themselves, and enticing men with desire. Qutb taught that the world consisted of two groups: those who followed Allah and those who followed Satan. Believers versus infidels.

As such, jihad was a total and complete duty to be carried out by all Muslims—men and women, young and old. All infidels in any community, group, or race were to be confronted, fought, and annihilated by any means possible.

Qutb returned to Egypt and rose to power as the leader of the Muslim Brotherhood movement. In 1966, he was convicted of treason and executed for plotting the assassination of Egyptian president Gamal Abdel Nasser. Qutb's writings formed the core beliefs of modern radical Islamic groups, including al-Qaeda.

Akil drew one more breath of fresh air. "Hello? Marianne?"

"She's off today, and we don't open 'til ten," a raspy male voice sang out. "Who wants to know?"

"Michael," Akil said, stepping inside. "I spoke with someone named Marianne last night about renting an apartment. Was it your wife?"

"Not unless you called heaven. She's been dead four years."

"Sorry, I didn't mean—"

"Sorry for what? Everybody dies sometime. Marianne's one of our bartenders. Pleased to meet you," the man said, tucking his black POW-MIA T-shirt into Marine utility fatigues that hugged a trim waistline. He extended his hand. "I'm Jerry Watts, but you can call me Chief. Sit down. Be with you in a minute."

Akil straddled a stool. He surveyed the long, dim room. An elevated stage, a side alcove, a pool table. The solid wood bar top held a collage of foreign coins and heroism medals embedded in a thick layer of clear varnish. The walls were covered with camouflage netting, military photographs, flags, rifles, and handheld weapons. A shoulder-fired missile launcher hung from the ceiling. Next to the cash register, an empty 155mm artillery shell collected tips.

Watts returned with a rental application tucked in his back pocket. "What's your name again?" Watts asked, studying Akil's face.

"Waleu," Akil answered. "Michael Waleu. I'm from Quebec."

"You sure look like Sean Penn, that Hollywood commie actor. You're a lot younger, but you got that same kind of baby-baboonish, monkey face."

"Excuse me?" Akil bristled. "Did you just call me a monkey?"

"Relax, kid. I didn't mean anything. I was a police chief for twenty-seven years. A heckuva lot of people look like animals. I used to tell my officers to identify suspects that way. Let's see . . . long hair, clean hands, backward ball cap, and worn blue jeans. I bet you're a college student with a little hippie mixed in. University of Wisconsin?"

"Marquette Dental," Akil answered, irritated, but also impressed by the man's perceptiveness. "I got accepted right out of high school. It's a new seven-year program. Two more years, and then I move into orthodontics. I have a crazy schedule. My girlfriend goes to Winona State in Minnesota, so I'm gone a lot. You know how that is."

"None of my business," Watts assured. "You come and go as you please around here. Nobody keeps tabs except at the bar. Case closed."

"Is it still available?" Akil asked.

Watts carefully added three scoops of horseradish to a large plastic jar filled with red liquid. He tightened the cover and shook it vigorously. "The apartment? I've been trying to rent that sucker all year. It's just an efficiency, but today's your lucky day. I'll throw in the utilities and give you half the garage if you take it. You want a drink?"

"No thanks," Akil said. "Can I see the apartment?"

The two men walked through the bar, into a hallway, past the restrooms, and up a narrow set of stairs. The bottom three creaked. Watts opened the apartment door and sniffed. Thankfully, there was no stale beer odor.

"There's another entrance in the kitchen off the porch. Doesn't bother me which one you use. Four hundred a month including utilities and appliances. But I'll be honest, with all the planes coming and going, it's not real quiet for studying. Not to mention us veterans can get pretty rowdy, especially with live music. I gotta warn you, my birthday's coming up, and I'm throwing a heckuva bash. This place'll be rocking like crazy."

"Really? How old?"

"The big six-oh. I can't believe it myself."

"That's awesome, Chief. When's the party?"

"May seventeenth. Karaoke starts at eight sharp."

"That's a Sunday night," Akil said, hiding his disappointment. "I suppose all your police buddies will be here?"

"Nah, the Legion's a private club. Just vets and their wives." Watts raised the window blinds. "I'll take care of you, pal. I'll make sure you get tucked in if you drink too much. Another nice thing up here is the view—if you're into flying, that is. That runway is only a stone's throw away. Jets line up for takeoff just beyond that fence. There's a radio in the kitchen. You can hear pilot chatter on 88.5 FM."

Akil briefly glanced outside and then turned away, seemingly more interested in the cleanliness of the bathroom.

"It's yours if you want it, but I'll need an answer today," Watts pressed. "I'll even give you a break on meals. We cook some good chow for a bar. Where else can you get homemade soup for two bucks a bowl? Tomorrow night's dollar tacos. What do you think?"

"I love Mexican," Akil admitted. He walked into the kitchenette and observed a chained door that led onto a small porch. A rusted barbecue grill hid the fact that half the railing was missing. He opened the refrigerator and turned the cooling dial to high. The compressor kicked in with a mild hum. He reached into his pocket. "You got a deal, Chief. Here's May's rent plus a deposit. I'll just need a receipt."

"Sold," Watts announced, stuffing the keys and the rental application into Akil's hand. "You can move right in. I've gotta get ready to open. We'll do the paperwork later."

Akil listened for the stair creaks and then returned to the front window. He lifted a pair of binoculars. The departure point on Mitchell's Runway 19R was just five hundred feet away. The morning traffic on East Layton Avenue was mild. It would be less traveled at dawn. The proximity was more than excellent—it was a gift from Allah.

He knelt on the floor.

Surah 84. The Sundering, Splitting Open

19. *Ye shall surely travel from stage to stage.*
20. *What then is the matter with them that they believe not?*
21. *And when the Qur'an is read to them, they fall not prostrate,*
22. *But on the contrary, the Unbelievers reject it.*
23. *But Allah has full knowledge of what they secrete in their breasts.*
24. *So announce to them a Penalty Grievous.*

WASHINGTON, DC
NATIONAL TRANSPORTATION SAFETY BOARD
OFFICE OF AVIATION SAFETY
MONDAY, MAY 4

TOM ROSS, NTSB acting division chief of Aviation Engineering, squinted at his reflection in his computer screen. He licked his palm and tried to smooth down an unruly hair lump. Ross was tall with sandy-blond hair and a fair complexion, and his face blushed every time he felt embarrassed. His female coworkers teased him unmercifully. They said he looked like a boyish Harrison Ford.

He reached into a drawer for a small red bag of Indian brand pumpkin seeds that he had ordered online from a vintage candy site. The white coating fed his salt addiction and, in some quirky way, methodically eating the seeds one by one lowered his stress level. That's how he rationalized it. The medical facts disagreed. He didn't want to think about that.

Ross opened a thick document stamped *Courtesy Copy* in his in-basket. He shook his head at the eleventh revision of the latest Department of Homeland Security organization chart. Thankfully, the NTSB wasn't part of it. There weren't many advantages of working exclusively for and under the scrutiny of the United States Congress, but this was definitely one. He wondered how many DHS employees

22

would be physically transferred and on which effective date. Relocation was always rough, especially on families.

Family. Like a powerful magnet, the word pulled his thoughts back to a quiet neighborhood in Arlington, Virginia, a connected two-story duplex, and a relationship with Marcia Davies that he had once thought might lead to a family. His first wife of eighteen years had been a kind, small-town Ohio woman with traditional down-home family values. She'd undergone a delicate female operation and, while recovering at home, had died suddenly from a blood clot.

Ross had been devastated by the loss and buried himself in work just to survive. He'd met Marcia at a technical aviation conference in San Francisco and was immediately smitten. He had no clue that behind her sexy smile and her degrees in engineering and accounting lay a brash, spoiled daddy's girl raised in country clubs, fur coats, and fine Southern estates.

The marriage happened quickly on a luxurious and private Caribbean island. Two years later, Ross knew that he'd made a terrible mistake. His sweet Southern belle had grown into a self-centered, nasty stranger skilled in tantrums and manipulation. Her penchant for materialism grew out of control. She regularly berated him publicly and openly flirted with any male who'd pay attention. Ross had worked up the nerve to divorce Marcia but not the heart to ask her to leave. He simply drifted back into the escape of work.

Marcia continued to live in the upper flat while heading up Deloitte's Audit Division on 12th Street Northwest in Washington, DC.

Ross was on rotational duty as the investigator-in-charge of the NTSB's "Go Team," an elite group of specialized experts, ready to respond to catastrophic aviation accidents at a moment's notice. During their assigned tours, Go Team members were on call 24/7, expected to arrive at the accident scene as quickly as possible, analyze what happened, and ultimately provide a safety recommendation so it never happened again.

All members understood that nothing short of death or Armageddon should stop them from responding. No personal commitment was unbreakable. Disciplinary measures were routinely threatened and meted out. During 9/11, the US Justice Department took the investigatory lead of the airline crashes, while NTSB provided advice and support. Nevertheless, Ross worked for months on four hours of sleep per night. He took one precious day off for a funeral, only to have it remanded when Flight 587 crashed on November 12, 2001, in Rockaway, Queens, New York.

Field Specialist Ron Hollings poked his head inside Ross's office.

"Guess where we found the file on that 747 that crashed near Madrid in 1976—the one with the wing failure?"

"The men's room storage closet," Ross replied offhandedly, his tongue locked in fierce struggle with a stubborn pumpkin seed fragment.

"How'd you know?"

"It used to be a pre-archive holding room, but no one followed up. Boxes just started accumulating."

Hollings glanced at the pumpkin seeds—a solid stress indicator. True to his gender (no matter what reality TV writers scripted) Ross, like most men, wasn't comfortable talking about personal relationships. Hollings knew he needed a shove.

"Did you ask her to leave?"

"No."

"Why not?"

"I will, I promise. I just don't have the energy."

"You look tired, Tom."

"Thanks. I know."

Hollings closed the door and sat down.

Ross rose from his desk and gazed blankly through the windowpane. "Marcia's always been high-strung. She blames her job. Public accounting firms are ruthless. She drags herself upstairs every night, and I can tell she's physically and mentally exhausted."

"Stop rationalizing a nasty situation," Hollings said firmly. "Marcia's a nasty ex-wife and a nasty tenant. You need to do two things: tell her she needs to go, and then find a new renter. Someone nice. *Then* worry about a new relationship. They're out there; I guarantee it. Maybe even on one of those dating sites."

Ross made a painful face and spit a seed hull at the wastebasket. He flipped through his calendar. "I need to think. Tell Jenna I'm taking the rest of the—ugh! Is today the fourth?"

Hollings nodded.

"Another Homeland Security presentation?"

"Yep."

"I can't win," Ross said softly.

"Nope." Hollings glanced at his watch. "Ten minutes. I saved us front-row seats."

Ross opened his office door. Employees were already making their way to the conference center.

"I can't win," Ross repeated, reaching for a notepad. "Just what I need, another boring security consultant. I've heard enough of them to last the rest of my career. What's the warning this time, anthrax-laced toilet paper?"

"I'm not sure, but Barrens arranged it personally. I don't think the speaker's a consultant. I think he's one of their directors. He's definitely got Secretary Bridge's ear. Barrens wants everybody there. It's another departmental edict."

Ross stared at the calendar for a few moments and then defiantly reached for his briefcase. "What could be important enough to bring the Secretary of Homeland Security to this place on a Monday morning? Screw it. I'm leaving anyway."

"Tom, that's not a good idea. This is a mandatory meet—"

Ross cursed, slamming his briefcase to the floor. "This job has sucked every living drop of energy out of me, and now they want my soul. Well, guess what? I'm not giving it."

Hollings let his boss vent. He knew it would pass. Ross rarely showed this kind of emotion, especially not since his promotion to acting division chief. His workload had doubled with the responsibility. It was both sad and somehow reassuringly human that, when faced with mounting personal and professional pressures, even the best people had breaking points.

Ross rested his forehead against the wall. "I'm sorry, Ron. I'm not sure I can handle another motivational speaker telling us how far to bend over during a Washington terrorist attack. I've heard it all before. I'm just sick of it."

"Hey, I understand," Hollings reassured. "If it makes you feel any better, this guy's spiel is supposed to be pretty good. A friend of mine over at Justice heard it and said it really woke him up. Your friend Ms. Petri has publicly challenged the content. If she's there, we might see some fireworks."

Nancy Petri was an Illinois congressional representative and special liaison to the NTSB's Office of Public Affairs.

Ross rolled his eyes. "Petri runs her office by the book and nothing but. If this guy gets cocky I wouldn't want to be in her sights, but whatever. Let's go. And mark my words—I will get my life in order."

He slid into his suit coat and strode out the door.

THE NTSB used a state-of-the-art underground conference center adjacent to its headquarters building at 429 L'Enfant Plaza Southwest in Washington, DC. The center consisted of a theater-style auditorium for 350 people, 1,682 square feet of flexible space, and two aisles wide enough to accommodate even the largest of public press venues. Every seat was filled.

"Good morning," Roger Barrens, the NTSB's Managing Director, announced from the center stage. "We're excited that the Secretary of Homeland Security, Samuel Bridge, could join us this morning."

The room gave out strong applause. Bridge waved. Barrens produced a fact sheet.

"The speaker you're about to hear is Jack Riley, Director of Homeland Counterterrorism. Mr. Riley hails from Georgia, where he graduated from Emory University with a degree in mathematics. He served in the United States Air Force, achieving the rank of captain. In Desert Storm, he was in charge of placing, encrypting, and synchronizing all satellite-to-ground voice communication links. He's a third-degree black belt in Tae Kwon Do and also has, dare I say, the unique honor of reporting directly to Secretary Bridge and is therefore allowed to ignore . . . er, bypass all those evil undersecretaries."

This drew a mass chuckle. Barrens's brother carried that title in the DHS Office of Intelligence and Analysis.

"Mr. Riley also has a rather quirky fetish for stuffed animals that's well-known in the intelligence circles. I'll let him explain that. His presentation today is called "Komodo." The president has seen it and was so impressed that he ordered it be taped and delivered to all federal, state, and local law enforcement agencies in the nation. That about sums up the gravity. Secretary Bridge has also expressed strong support for the theory based on its, and I quote, 'on-target significance.' With that, let's begin. Mr. Riley?"

The audience applauded warmly.

The spitting image of a youthful Sidney Poitier sprang from his chair next to the Secretary and approached the podium. He appeared physically fit, with a strong jaw line, symmetrical facial features, a touch of temple gray, and an unusually grim visage. He clipped a wireless microphone set to his belt and necktie but had apparently forgotten to turn it on. His midnight blue suit gave off a subtle metallic flash as he walked regally down the center aisle. He carried an olive-gray, black-blotched stuffed animal the size of a football under one arm. It was a fish.

"Thank you, Roger. Good morning. My Christian name is Prince—Prince Jackson Riley. I'm neither Irish nor next in line for the British or any other throne. My mother named me *Prince* because she thought I looked like African royalty when I entered this world. My friends still call me that. You may call me Jack.

"As Roger pointed out, I work in DHS counterterrorism, and I have one heckuva job. I get to snoop around, ask questions, assess and alert other agencies about potential gaps in defenses for current terror threats, and also share what I consider to be potential future threats to the homeland, no matter how far-fetched they may seem. I suppose you might consider me terror's point man—specific or potential, imminent or elevated; bombings, cluster-cell identification, motorized incidents, weapons of mass destruction—you name it.

"But don't let the impressive title fool you. My extremely skinny staff and I work in the trenches hand in hand with every federal enforcement agency. It's all about teamwork. For some strange reason, my boss doesn't believe in letting dedicated, loyal, and hardworking human beings take time off. He just keeps piling on the assignments." Riley turned. "How long has it been since I've had a vacation, Mr. Secretary? Three years or four?"

"Write your senator," Bridge responded to a throng of laughter.

It had been four years. A day here or there was fine, but Bridge had finally allowed his senior staff to take an extended vacation only after bin Laden had been killed.

Riley shook his head and turned back to the audience. "Perhaps we'll meet somewhere in an official capacity, but I hope not. Terror is never a pleasant thing." He pointed to the large US flag standing in the corner. "Take a good look at the symbol of American freedom, people. It might be the last time you'll ever think that."

A slide appeared on the room's two ten-by-twelve-foot projection screens.

> You can't defend against the unthinkable
> without thinking about it in the first place.

"And now, the unthinkable."

A photograph of two adult Komodo dragons appeared, mouths agape, spaghetti-like streams of saliva dangling disgustingly. The title said: *al-Qaeda*.

"Before we get started, I've been working real hard to clean up my language and apologize in advance if I slip," Riley announced. "I tend to get emotional about terrorism and more than a little colorful. I'd also like to find out where your heads are." He held up the stuffed toy. "This is Shaitan. In Arabic, that means 'Satan.' He represents an evil black grouper that I've been chasing around the Florida Keys. I've hooked him several times, but he's always managed to slip away. My daughter taught English in El Salvador and shared my fish story with some villagers. One was kind enough to hand-sew this little guy. Who among you is smart enough to catch Shaitan?"

Several hands went up. Riley flung the fish across the room in a wide arc. It landed in a woman's lap.

Riley strolled toward her. His eyes took a snapshot of her name tag and appearance. African American, thirties, medium build, short hair, attractive. "Patricia Creed, NTSB Aviation Operations. You look familiar. Nice to meet you."

"Nice to meet you. I prefer Tricia."

"Okay, Tricia. You win the prize. What do you do?"

"I support aviation accident investigations. Mainly interviews with principals, survivors, relatives, and other witnesses. Usually face-to-face, but not always."

Riley nodded, impressed. "What's your vision of the next 9/11?"

"Excuse me?"

"The next large-scale terror attack on American soil."

Creed straightened in her seat. "Well, I'm not exactly familiar with terrorism tactics. Um . . . what about blowing up Amtrak trains or poisoning food at McDonalds?"

"Yikes, that's scary," Riley said, extending his arms. "I always did like their French fries. Do you like my fish?"

"It feels like a beanbag," Creed noted, squeezing it thoroughly before tossing it back. The audience chuckled nervously.

Riley tucked it under his arm. "Those are red beans, Tricia. One more question before we move on. Where does our freedom come from? How is it guaranteed?"

"Um . . . the Constitution. Speech, liberty, the pursuit of happiness. Our freedom is guaranteed by the US Constitution, specifically the first ten amend—"

"*No!*" Riley's voice boomed into the microphone. The volume was so loud that several people jumped in their seats. The audience gave out a collective murmur.

"Words on a piece of paper do not guarantee a thing. Ms. Creed, you are a highly trained investigator in the field of American aviation, yet thirty seconds ago you admitted that you're not, what was the word you used . . . familiar with terror tactics? The first thing you need to know is that we *all* need to be familiar with terror tactics. Second, paper documents, rules, regulations, and all that political correctness are totally meaningless. More important, relying on them as some kind of all-protecting shield will kill you and innocent Americans. Freedom against terrorism is guaranteed and maintained through physical force, or lost for the lack of it. A society that clings to a list of paper rights without force is doomed. Most Americans don't have a clue about what it will take to protect our freedom."

Riley stared at the ceiling theatrically.

"Our frontline military and law enforcement personnel are doing a great job defending us against terrorism, but they need help—your help. It's time for homeland civilians to step up. From this day forward, I want each and every one of you to start thinking critically about your jobs, your day-to-day activities, and about every situation or human you encounter. Now, don't do anything crazy or weird. Just give a little eyebrow raise to the *potential* that whoever or whatever you come across may have some type of terror linkage or relevance. Think on it briefly, file it away, and then move on with your lives. And by all means, if something doesn't feel right or you hear a little voice, report it. The bad guys out there are getting smarter; they hate us, and they want us dead. Period. Sorry, folks, but I didn't create this environment. That's just the way it is. Ms. Creed, you may not believe this, but thank you. Burgers and trains are interesting ideas for terror strikes. Let me share three of mine."

Riley made his way to the front of the room and placed Shaitan on the podium. He definitely had everyone's attention.

"On a warm June evening, there'll be a break-in at a fireworks factory. Small town, no alarms, no guards. The perpetrators will steal forty-eight crates of large air-bomb fireworks slated for the upcoming Fourth of July gala. The crates contain 512 cylindrical cardboard tubes, four inches in diameter. Each air bomb is slightly larger than a baseball. The tubes have no distinguishing marks, but they contain significant amounts of powdered aluminum. There'll be a brief newspaper article, people will be pissed, and everyone will blame teenagers. Four months later, on a brisk Sunday morning in November, two jihadists will drive into an unguarded private hangar at a quiet US airport and overtake a corporate jet that's waiting to fly three senior executives to a quarterly governance board meeting. After killing them and the pilot, they'll load and dump 2,800 kilos of the powdered aluminum onto the cabin floor. One jihadist will strap on a high-explosive booster, a pyro detonator box, and a base canopy parachute. The other jihadist, a trained pilot, will conclude his interaction with departure control and fly that jet out.

"Once airborne, the pilot will claim some type of mechanical failure, descend to a few hundred feet, and then continue off-radar at four hundred knots. After just eight minutes of flight, the pilot will climb to seven hundred feet and then kill the engines and all electrical power. At the apex of that climb, the parachutist will be able to safely bail out. The pilot and the jet will quietly glide down and crash smack in the middle of an open-air football field. Sixty thousand NFL fans, plus millions of television viewers mesmerized by the crash, will see some unknown type of mist or dust cloud fill the stadium. And in a deadly, effective encore, that parachutist will float into that cloud, flip a switch on the box on his belt, and detonate. And that, my friends, will ignite a secondary event called a thermobaric fuel-air explosion.

"The mix of oxygen and explosive aluminum dust will create the fuel and framework for a blast hundreds of times more powerful than conventional explosions. A fuel-air bomb's power has been compared to that of a nuclear weapon without radiation. Temperatures will reach 4,500 degrees Fahrenheit. The blast wave overpressure will be so great that eardrums will rupture and internal organs will be sucked out of people's mouths, along with all the air in the stadium. Thousands will perish from asphyxiation. The final fatality counts will reach numbers unlike anything the United States or even the world has seen since the large-scale bombing campaigns of World War II. Victim identification alone will take weeks. The physical carnage will compare to Hiroshima. And we're not done yet."

Riley guzzled half a bottle of water. "What I'm about to show you is a fuse—one that will ignite the mother of all terrorist actions. More than twenty-three times deadlier than 9/11. You can count on it. My friends, this attack will be short, unimaginably brutal, highly coordinated, and most of all, purposeful. It will have extreme significance, and it will involve the smallest military invasion force in history—one hundred and forty soldiers to be exact—who in just thirty minutes will attempt to destroy the freedom of the United States of America. And they will succeed. Why? Because we're vulnerable. And more important, because our Constitution guarantees it."

Riley motioned to the projection screens. A list appeared.

KOMODO ONE

Disney's Animal Kingdom—Lake Buena Vista, FL
Six Flags St. Louis—Eureka, MO
Kings Island—Mason, OH
Universal Orlando—Orlando, FL
SeaWorld—San Antonio, TX
Disney's Hollywood Studios—Bay Lake, FL
Busch Gardens—Williamsburg, VA
Six Flags Great America—Gurnee, IL
Epcot Theme Park—Lake Buena Vista, FL
Six Flags Over Georgia—Austell, GA
Playland Amusement Park—Rye, NY
Disneyland—Anaheim, CA
Six Flags Over Texas—Arlington, TX
Magic Kingdom—Lake Buena Vista, FL
Universal Studios Hollywood—University City, CA
SeaWorld—Orlando, FL
Six Flags Magic Mountain—Valencia, CA
Luna Park, Coney Island—Brooklyn, NY
California's Great America—Santa Clara, CA
Six Flags Darien Lake—Darien Center, NY
Six Flags New England—Agawam, MA
Knott's Berry Farm—Buena Park, CA
Worlds of Fun—Kansas City, MO
Cedar Point—Sandusky, OH
SeaWorld—San Diego, CA

"Twenty-five theme parks. You know these places. You've packed up your families and traveled there. Perhaps you've even seen some identified as potential terror targets. But you've never imagined the tactics.

"On the perfect date, let's call it K-Day, one hundred guests across the United States will simultaneously enter these theme parks. Did you catch that? Not terrorists, not soldiers, not enemy combatants . . . guests. One-zero-zero. Four in each park. And trust me, none will comply if asked to hand over the weapons strapped under their clothing. One MP-5 machine gun, two automatic handguns, and one thousand rounds of .40 caliber ammunition in fast-load magazines. For those of you who at this very moment are so anal as to want to calculate the ammo weight, I'll save you the trouble—approximately forty pounds. Easily concealed and carried. Two pairs of shooters in each park. One pair protects the other. At a precisely coordinated time, they'll open fire and continue until all ammunition is spent. Ever hear the expression 'shooting fish in a barrel'? These fish will include women and children, young and old. At the end of this random killing spree, seventy thousand Americans will be dead or wounded."

A new list appeared.

KOMODO TWO

Wrigley Field—Chicago, IL
Fenway Park—Boston, MA
Yankee Stadium—New York, NY
Oriole Park at Camden Yards—Baltimore, MD
Coors Field—Denver, CO
Progressive Field—Cleveland, OH
Turner Field—Atlanta, GA
Dodger Stadium—Los Angeles, CA
Safeco Field—Seattle, WA
Rangers Ballpark in Arlington—Arlington, TX

"Precisely timed with the theme park attacks, forty fans will enter these ten baseball stadiums. Four-zero, same weaponry. They'll take seats near the home and visitor dugouts. They'll enter the field of play, calmly open fire at both bench and active players, and then continue targeting general stadium fans until their ammunition is spent. You can add another ten thousand to the casualty list . . ." Riley paused. "And twenty major-league baseball teams will cease to exist."

The audience sat stunned.

Riley stayed silent for a full fifteen seconds.

"The shooters will drop their gear and disappear into the chaos, and believe me, there'll be chaos. Authorities will never be certain of their exact number. Within the hour, al-Qaeda will publicly reaffirm their February 23, 1998, declared fatwa calling on all Muslims to kill Americans wherever they are found. K-Day. It will be quite historic, for at that precise moment, we'll all need to sign up for Yiddish class. America will have become Israel on steroids, complete with military curfews, roadblocks, checkpoints, and religious persecution. Anyone with dark hair and a suntan will feel racial mistrust and bigotry so severe it'll make slavery in the old South seem like, well, Disney World.

"In the aftermath, Americans will start making life-altering decisions to avoid major cities in a rationalized attempt to live and raise their families in terror-free environments spelled r-u-r-a-l. People will establish virtual safety zones, and any outings beyond those zones or into crowds will carry overwhelming tension and suspicion. Fear will bear on every decision involving congregating in large numbers or traveling, and millions will simply stop doing either. For how long is anyone's guess.

"In the next segment, we're going to examine why K-Day will happen, why we won't or can't stop it, and why the incomprehensible violence and subsequent threat of open warfare in our beloved country are only a means to an end. Remember, I said Komodo is only the fuse. I haven't explained what it leads to. But first I suggest we all take a break. Based on your facial expressions, it looks like some of you could use one."

MILWAUKEE, WI
GENERAL MITCHELL INTERNATIONAL AIRPORT

MILWAUKEE'S AIRPORT was quiet, filled with only a handful of business travelers, a few young people, and a custodian and his cart. Shop lights flickered on. The terminal smelled of fresh-baked goods and coffee mingled with an occasional wisp of jet fuel that had sneaked through the jetways. The TSA security lines were empty.

Sitting at a Starbucks kiosk, WITI local Fox 6 News reporter Neela Griffin booted up her laptop and opened a Microsoft Word folder named *Carly Simon*. She scrolled through the document list and opened *YoureSoVain.doc*. She stared blankly at the 1973 hit song lyrics and sipped her extra strong Americana. Her senses steadily improved, and she spotted her camera operator, Terry Lee, at the checkout counter. He was rolling his T-shirt sleeve over his bicep, exposing a new Celtic sunburst tattoo to a young female server.

Lee was twenty-eight years old, with rugged, dark features, and his unshaven beard and unkempt hair rang GQ. He had natural on-air confidence and occasionally expressed interest in the opposite side of the lens. Sadly, the average news viewer might never get past the body ink.

Lee's official union title was Remote Broadcast Specialist, a new breed of electronic news gatherer. His oversized, cable-free backpack could capture and transmit live news video over cellular networks, completely eliminating the need for a typical HD satellite truck. Finished with a shot, correspondents could manipulate a scene themselves via laptop or upload the raw footage for studio editors.

Lee set his breakfast on Griffin's table and flopped into a chair as though he had been slapped. He held a bottle of apple juice up to the light and shook it vigorously.

"Are there any normal babes in this world?" he lamented. "I asked where she hung out, and she said she's in hot water a lot. The last thing I need is somebody with a criminal record."

Griffin chuckled. "For your information, Hot Water is a dance club on Water Street downtown. It's rated as Milwaukee's best."

Lee stared at his coworker. "I hate mornings. My head hurts, my arm is sore, and everything just feels out of sync."

"I'm surprised you had any bare skin left. How many tattoos is that now?"

"Nine," Lee said, peering at Griffin's laptop screen. "I think I'll do my name next. A letter on each knuckle like my cousin. Then I'll be obsessed too."

"I am not obsessed," she shot back.

"*Riiiiight.* That old tune is all you think about."

"I'm trying to unravel a mystery."

"I know. You've told me a hundred times," Lee said. "Why don't you just let it go? Everybody knows that Carly Simon wrote *You're So Vain* about Mick Jagger or that prune-faced, old Playboy dude."

"Wrong."

"Whatever," Lee said dismissively. "Nobody knows or cares about any of those old farts, so why should you?"

"Because it's still a huge media secret," Griffin said. "I'm not positive myself, but I've done enough research—newspapers, political issues, media stories, especially from the early seventies. I had to experience the same events, influences, and lifestyles that Carly Simon encountered when she wrote that song. Anyway, I think I got into her mindset. I found eleven confidence indicators. I call them pointers—eleven unknown facts that all pointed to the same guy. It was incredible. He's such a perfect fit I'm surprised no one has ever suspected him before. I'm ready to go public."

"Public as in a news story?"

"Uh-huh. I have an outline for the whole segment. I just need to convince Gillespie to let me produce it my way. If I'm right, it'll mean national exposure."

She spun the laptop.

You're So Vain
Alternate Title: Who are you, Mr. Vain?
By: Neela Griffin

Pointer #1: Son of a gun

The whispering introduction of "You're So Vain" was a tribute to Joey Bishop, your close friend, fellow gang member, and opening act. Joey had this trademark phrase sewn onto his bathrobe.

Joseph Abraham Gottlieb, a.k.a. Joey Bishop, was an early television comedian, entertainer, and talk-show host. Lee had never heard of him, but he nodded thoughtfully, trying to hide the confusion on his face.

"Look, it's none of my business, but there's more to life than song mysteries. I'm serious about my cousin. He's a cool dude and definitely not a wife-beater. You should start seeing people."

Griffin stared into her cup. Lee was young and inexperienced, especially with committed relationships, but he meant well. Nevertheless, the comment hurt. Her brief, abusive marriage was over. Her life and spirit were finally healing, and she was gaining both physical and emotional strength.

At thirty-eight, Griffin had been forced back to school at Independence University. The classes were hard and bitter, and she wondered if she could ever trust another man again. She closed the laptop.

Lee gulped the last of his juice and let out a muffled belch. "So tell me again: why am I out of bed this early in the morning?"

"A man named Brett sent me an email about a hole in Delta's security," she answered. "Ticketing and passenger boarding."

Lee frowned suspiciously. "What's he look like?"

"He said he'd be wearing a Green Bay Packer jacket, but not green and gold. We've never actually met."

"Brett? Green Bay Packers? Neela, you're freaking me out. This could be a complete hoax, or worse, the guy could be a nutcase. People report fake news tips like this all the time."

"His story could be big. It might have a terrorism angle."

"Great." Lee threw up his arms. "Like when you called the FBI about a suspicious white van at the federal courthouse—the window-washing van?"

"Someday I'll break a major news story, mister, and you'll be begging to film it."

"Nutcase," Lee mumbled through a mouthful of bagel. "Just trying to get on TV."

Griffin had her own reputation at Fox 6. Supporters labeled her investigative style "aggressive" and "bold." Jealous detractors called it "lucky ignorance." She managed the station's "Crime Stoppers Tip Line," a position that afforded maximum face time in a major news market, but one that also saw her career path running parallel to and well beneath the anchor desk instead of intersecting with it.

She lifted a cheese-filled croissant with both hands. Pausing in mid-chew, Griffin spotted a man browsing in the gift store next to the entrance to Terminal D. He was of average build, balding, and in his mid-forties. His black leather jacket bore a tone-on-tone Packer chest emblem.

He pretended to read a magazine, but Griffin could feel him peering. She was used to stares. Stunningly attractive, her body was thin and muscular. Her long, jet-black hair and white complexion were considered black-Irish. But attractiveness had a downside. A consultant's report showed that male television viewers lost a full seven seconds of comprehension of opening news content while evaluating female commentators.

She nudged Lee. "Get your camera. Try and get those TSA screeners in the background."

Lee gave a frustrated look as he unzipped his backpack. "Some anonymous guy sends an email and you grant him a taped interview. You have no idea who he is, and the topic is airline security. And you want this to run on Wednesday's nine o'clock segment? This is a huge prank."

"There's a gun involved."

"*What?*"

"A hidden gun."

"C'mon, Neela. TSA employees have been shot at and even killed at airports. You can't bring that up in here. I need to know where this is headed or I'm gone, and so is my camera."

Griffin made a fist at Lee and then approached the man. "Brett Marshall? Thanks for coming. We're setting up now."

Marshall casually surveyed the area and noticed a sheriff's deputy beginning to take an interest. "Do you have to use my real name?"

"This lighting sucks," Lee sung from behind the viewfinder. "Try moving left."

Griffin noted that Marshall's voice had a slight lisp, but his tone was deep and would carry well. She clipped a microphone to his collar. "Your name is essential to the story, and by the way, that's my assistant, Terry Lee. He's actually a talented professional when he keeps his mouth shut and acts like one." She flashed a brief smile. "We'll edit the rough spots. Viewers will concentrate more on the subject than your name. Just relax and start at the beginning."

"Do I tell the truth?"

"Yes, of course." She nodded to Lee. The camera turned on. "Mr. Marshall . . . tell us what happened to you last week as you boarded a flight in Fort Lauderdale."

"I walked up to the Delta Airlines ticket counter and told the agent that I was flying to Milwaukee. I also mentioned that I had a gun."

"You attempted to take a gun on a passenger aircraft?" Griffin asked. "What kind of gun, and for what reason?"

"A Beretta 9mm handgun," Marshall said. "And no, ma'am, I didn't try to actually carry it onto the aircraft. I just said I had one. You're supposed to declare that so it can be inspected and tagged inside your checked luggage. That's the law."

"What happened next?"

"Well, the ticket agent looked at my name, and then she gave me a form that allowed me to carry the gun on the plane."

"Why would Delta Airlines give that form to you?" Griffin asked.

"I have no idea."

"You signed it?"

"Yes, but I didn't read it thoroughly, and that was my mistake," Marshall admitted. "It's a five-part form with extremely small print. I thought it was standard procedure."

"What were you supposed to do with the form?"

"She told me to take it to the boarding gate."

"Are you a police officer?"

"No, ma'am. I'm an accountant. I figured she got confused with my name and thought I was one, you know, a federal air marshal."

"What happened next?"

"I walked through security, and I handed the form to the gate agent as instructed. He looked at it briefly and then told me to take a seat. A few minutes later, a flight attendant walked over and handed me this pink copy. She whispered that the captain had signed it and then reminded me that I couldn't have any alcohol."

"Okay, I'm trying to see an advantage here," Griffin speculated. "Let's play this out in a worst-case scenario. You're in the air on a passenger aircraft, and the flight crew believes that you're an air marshal naturally carrying a concealed loaded firearm. You're not really carrying, but they *think* you are. If you were a terrorist, you could probably create panic, especially if you jumped out of your seat and started waving a toy hand-gun, but it's only a bluff. Ultimately, to cause real harm to the passengers, crew, or the aircraft itself, you'd need a real weapon."

"Or have access to one."

Griffin gave him a quizzical look. "Access how?"

"Law enforcement officers and federal air marshals on the same flight are quietly introduced to each other before takeoff so they can study each other's appearance and learn where they're seated. That way if something happens, like an attempted hijacking, they'd know where help is. It's a professional courtesy thing."

"Okay, so if there was an air marshal on board, you would have been introduced to each oth . . ." Griffin's voice trailed off. "You'd know who's carrying a real firearm on the aircraft and where they're sitting."

"Yes, ma'am," Marshall said. "There's your terrorist advantage. Get yourself a simple pack of permission forms—forms that no one veri-fies—and keep boarding passenger aircraft pretending to be in law enforcement. Eventually, you'd be introduced to someone who has a real weapon. Someone you and your accomplices can overpower. Maybe you can even gain control of the plane. I'm not an aircraft engineer, but shooting a gun inside a pressurized cabin probably isn't good. Take it one step further—if no one is introduced to you, you can safely assume there's no air marshal on board. My friend said that flights at Reagan National in Washington, DC, always carry two marshals, and they always whisper who they are to the flight attendants in plain view of other passengers, and they always sit in first class."

"Did you contact Delta?" Griffin asked.

"I emailed their Consumer Affairs group and told them there was a firearm security hole in their boarding process. Seven days later, a woman called back and accused me of being the problem. She said that the ticket agent who gave me that form was a newbie and that it was a simple training mistake. She said the situation would never have turned dangerous unless I was dangerous. I also emailed the facts to the Chairman of the US Subcommittee on Aviation Safety. He never got back to me at all. I was sort of upset about that. I figured somebody should know."

Griffin faced the camera. "For those of us who fly, especially in today's aviation environment, this is a very scary situation. Stay tuned for an exclusive follow-up with officials from Delta Airlines and the Department of Homeland Security. Reporting for 'Crime Stoppers Tip Line' at Mitchell International Airport, this is Neela Griffin, Fox 6 News."

The camera stopped.

Griffin unclipped Marshall's microphone. "This is great material. Thanks for coming forward. It needs to be told. I'm actually leaving for Italy tonight on special assignment, and I'd appreciate it if you wouldn't talk to any other stations, okay? I think we can do at least two more segments after we confirm a few facts."

Marshall shook Griffin's hand and headed down the airport corridor.

Griffin walked over to Lee. Her face carried an obvious smirk. "You were saying something about a nutcase?"

"Italy?"

"Sorry. I wanted to tell you yesterday, but I forgot," Griffin apologized. "Gillespie assigned me to it personally. I'll be back Tuesday."

6

JACK RILEY waited politely as a few stragglers hurried to their seats. There wasn't much talking.

"Okay, why is K-Day so powerful and so perfect for a terror attack? Two reasons. The first is obvious, and it once cost a US president a general election. Anyone? George Bush Sr.? Bill Clinton?

"One of the best ways to significantly hurt the United States of America is to hurt the economy. With respect to America's resolve and the US military's campaigns in the Middle East, terrorists have learned that entangling countries into lengthy war hurts both physically and economically. Therefore, terror will become drawn out forever, and it will turn both high-tech and guerilla lethal.

"One more thing. In my humble opinion, I believe our intelligence agencies are being fed information for no other reason than to burden our security forces and keep true motives hidden. Two young and inexperienced wannabe jihadists managed to shut down the entire city of Boston, including its transportation systems. One anonymous phone call threatening a chemical or explosive attack in New York's tunnel or subway system will alert 25,000 defenders and cost twenty-four million dollars. Think about that: one incredible call. And that's just one alert in one city. How long can any budget hold out under that kind of pressure? Questions?"

"Mr. Riley, I think you and your entire presentation are preposterous," Illinois Congressional Representative Nancy Petri spoke up. "A Congressional Report on Terrorism showed that cities can survive even the largest calamities. We concluded that 9/11 was more a human tragedy than an economic one. The attacks were simply too small and too geographically concentrated to make a significant dent in the nation's economic output. And it certainly didn't cause any recession. The Bush economy was already in its third consecutive quarter of contraction no matter what individuals in your political party may say. You do remember that after closing for just four trading days, our financial markets opened and operated without a single major problem? The American people have an uncanny ability to rebound."

Murmurs sprang up around the room, and buoyed by the sound, Petri continued.

"And you're obviously either misinformed or haven't done your homework on theme parks. Just last week, my family and I attended the pre-season opening of Great America in Gurnee, Illinois. They unveiled state-of-the-art metal detection equipment that every one of us had to walk through. In addition, they hand-searched purses and even baby strollers. As far as your baseball scenario, I highly doubt that such a thing could ever happen. Our enemies wouldn't dare. Think about what that would mean to the country's psyche. Besides, we have top-notch security in place to stop those actions. I personally resent even hearing such nonsense."

Jack Riley held back a smirk. "My ideas aren't preposterous, ma'am; they're devastating. Terrorists don't give a rat's rear end about what we hold in esteem, including sports. In fact, the more we idolize a cultural icon like baseball, the higher it moves on the target scale. The truth is, we don't like to hear reality. Americans tend to live in a figurative world where everything—and I mean everything—is taken for granted with respect to open freedoms.

"The ramifications of target vulnerabilities are just starting to emerge, and they are crushing. September 11 cost New York City eighty-three billion dollars and sixty thousand jobs. We estimate that the sporting event we used to call America's pastime would be completely shut down for two seasons. The forecasted economic losses to cities with host baseball stadiums are in the hundreds of billions. Three small-market teams might never recover. They'd simply be lost to history.

"But it's more than that. The psychological impacts would last for years. And, of course, we haven't discussed the date. That, my friends, is utterly unthinkable. The explosion at the end of the fuse. K-Day is a fixed secular holiday, a national celebration, and a time when citizens go about their daily lives having fun and enjoying traditional summer activities. Want to permanently imprint a terror tattoo right on America's forehead? Destroy the sanctity of her birthday. That's right. The Fourth of July would signal the beginning of the end of our precious open society.

"The major cities within the US would become military guard posts. With respect to those theme parks, every single one schedules an evening fireworks celebration. The crowds will be enormous, unconcerned, and anticipating noise. If you think 9/11 damaged the airlines, Komodo would sound that industry's death knell—especially on routes to those locations.

"And to prove that, let's talk for a moment about travel. Annual theme park attendance is over three hundred million, a number that's expected to increase steadily. Can anyone here spell *target-rich environments*? After K-Day, an entire generation of prime spenders will never take their families to a theme park again, no matter how safe the physical conditions become. The mere potential that something so horrific and violent could happen again will be enough to dissuade travel.

"But don't miss the point, people. Americans are resilient, and we would no doubt grow stronger. This isn't a forever thing. Time would heal the effects of even mass carnage, but by then the damage would have been done in a beautiful and complete fashion. How long can any business survive after losing an entire generation of customers? The US economy would flirt with the country's second depression primarily because people would be in an extended state of shock and fear. And for those of you who need financial gravitas, we hired the Cato Institute to model the economic impacts.

"Relative to Ms. Petri's statements on the strength and resiliency of our financial markets, she's right on point. All I'm suggesting is that we not get complacent with our open freedoms. I won't bore you with details, but after the events of K-Day, the Dow Jones Industrial Average would snowball downhill for thirteen consecutive months. That'll make the 401(k) pain caused by the housing collapse seem like Christmas. We call it the Komodo Effect. This small, slow, but dangerous reptile waits in ambush for prey many times its size. With a single bite, infection starts immediately, and is always fatal."

Petri rose from her seat. "Mr. Riley, point taken. But I certainly don't have any more time to sit here listening to speculative, rambling propaganda about lizards. You of all people should put a little more faith in our homeland security defenses, sir. If you'll excuse me?"

Flanked by two aides, she stormed out.

A man in the front row spoke a word under his breath. Riley strolled over and peered at his ID badge.

"I agree with you, Mr. Tom Ross of NTSB Aviation Engineering. It is unbelievable. You're an airline guy. Tell us about the skies and what you think about our open freedoms. Are we vulnerable or not?"

"Well, first, I'm not TSA," Ross announced the point loudly. "So I don't have my finger on the pulse of air travel security if that's what you're asking. Second, Nancy . . . er, Ms. Petri offered some good points. Frankly, if it was your objective to scare us today, I'd say you accomplished that. It's true we're all seeing more stringent security rules being implemented for electronic devices on planes, especially for passengers traveling to the United States."

"And why is that, sir?" Riley surveyed the audience. "What are they looking for, people? It starts with a B."

"Bombs," a female voice responded.

"Yep." Riley nodded. "Carried on and undetectable. It's like an addiction. They're still trying to sneak explosives on aircraft. One of so many potential vulnerabilities."

Riley gave Secretary Bridge a stealthy glance and noticed him glance at his watch. Riley returned to the podium and tucked Shaitan under his arm. "I'd like to end things here and leave you with one final albeit sickening thought: if any of the K-Day terrorists are

captured and found to be American citizens, they'll be eligible for con-
stitutionally afforded defenses. And you can bet that we'll vehemently
try and enforce those rights. Good grief, it took four years to convict
Major Nidal Hasan for the mass killings at Fort Hood. That miserable
son-of-a . . . er, individual admitted he murdered thirteen people, and
we'll be feeding him breakfast, lunch, and dinner every day on appeal
for the next fifty years."

Riley glanced at his watch. "No part of this presentation is confidential. In fact, Komodo needs to be shown and publicized to as many
people as possible. But, as you just observed, that's a tall order, especially when entrenched bureaucrats have their heads stuck up their . . .
well, in the sand.

"They don't want to know. Why? Because they don't believe in
taking either preemptive or drastic measures to stop potential threats.
They claim it tramples on the Constitution. Many don't have the funds
to do anything about it anyway, even from a planning perspective.

"Secretary Bridge and the president have already listened to my
'scare tactics'—twice. It's one of their top priorities. Needless to say,
they're already receiving plenty of heat from people who share the
congresswoman's opinion that I'm indeed crazy and that such events
could never happen. Just the other day, five thousand law enforcement
officers in San Francisco went on alert after someone saw a suspicious
rubber boat puttering around the Golden Gate Bridge.

"Anyway, I'll be at the Martin Luther King Federal Building in
Atlanta on May 11 and the Peck Building in Cincinnati on May 18. If
you have contacts in those offices, I'd appreciate it if you'd give them
some feedback. My video should be finished by then. It's free.

"My best advice to you today? Be safe, be alert, and start thinking
about the unthinkable. And since Congresswoman Petri brought it
up, I'll say one more thing about top-notch security and trusting your
family's freedom and safety to state-of-the-art equipment: Six Flags
Great America at Gurnee, Illinois, has an employee entrance with no
detection equipment at all. It's staffed by a seventy-year-old security
guard named Fritz. He's had two knee replacements, and he's addicted
to caramel corn. Have a safe day."

ROME, ITALY
SATURDAY, MAY 9

GEORGIA TECH Professor Michael Robertson stood up from a kneeling position in front of the commode. He was in the men's restroom at the Sheraton Roma Conference Center. He braced himself inside the stall until everything stopped spinning.

He listened quietly, almost able to hear echoes bouncing off the red-black marble walls. It was both humorous and frightening that a forty-year-old human being could make such outrageous noises. Thankfully, he was alone.

Noting the pungent smell on his breath and hands, he twisted the door latch and gingerly made his way to the sinks. His face was still warm, and his heartbeat was elevated, but his gag reflex had slowed, indicating that for the moment what little was left in his stomach had opted to stay.

He swished a mouthful of water from cheek to cheek and spit. He envisioned the lead story in the Atlanta Constitution: "Hometown Finalist Pukes at Pirelli International Technology Awards Ceremony."

Didn't that happen to someone else at a foreign banquet? he wondered. *Yes. President George Bush Sr. Right next to the Japanese Prime Minister. Wonderful.*

The scarlet towel draped over Robertson's shoulders made him look like an escapee from some princely barbershop. He patted his face with more water and examined the outline of his month-old beard. It had filled in nicely. His wife was right—he did look more European. Every little bit helped.

Robertson folded the towel and then his hands. He wasn't overly religious, but he occasionally chatted with the Almighty whenever he needed help. This was such a time. "Dear Lord . . . you know how I feel about winning. In the meantime, please make the food disappear, and please . . . don't let me get sick in front of two thousand people and world media. And if I do, then please let it be on the Germans. Amen."

Robertson returned to the banquet room and his seat at the head table. His entrée had been whisked away.

One prayer answered.

It had started with the appetizer, bread piled with tomatoes and thin-sliced meat soaked in olive oil. He should have known from the stench that something was wrong. Ham wasn't supposed to be translucent blue. It had obviously outlived an expiration date.

No one else complained, which meant it was either a conspiracy against Americans, or the Italians had simply developed a tolerance for sunbaked pig. Then the main course—oily, deep-fried sea-something with an odor of catfish stink bait. After two bites, his stomach went over the edge.

Linda Robertson bent for her purse and caught a whiff of her husband. "Oh my, did you throw up?"

"Throw up?" he squeaked. "Why would you think that?"

"Your knees are dusty, and I do have a nose," she quipped. "Michael, look at me. You did, didn't you?"

He grimaced. "The fish had a funny aftertaste."

Carlo Burno, the master of ceremonies, was making his way down the lengthy table, greeting each of the ten finalists and their spouses.

Linda checked the time and tore open a roll of antacids. "Do you want to lie down? There's a lounge upstairs."

Robertson's only response was a sour belch.

"Professor, I'm your wife, and I love you." She turned his head. "See that saxophone player? If you make a scene at this table, I'm going back to the hotel with him. Chew."

"You barely ate anything," Carlo observed as he reached their table, massaging Robertson's shoulders. "Perhaps we should have prepared something a little more American. I hear y'all are partial to fried chicken." The remark drew a table chuckle.

"It's the competition," Linda spoke up. "He's a little queasy. He'll be fine."

Carlo smiled sympathetically. "Parasites. Sometimes they hide in the suction cups. It's rare, but it happens. Let me know if there's anything I can do. I'm reminding all the finalists about the press conference. The winner will have a few minutes to address the media. With so many reporters here, we might as well take advantage of the publicity. Good luck."

Suction cups? Robertson felt his stomach undulate. His mouth filled with saliva. *Focus. Concentrate on the audience . . . no—read something.*

He snatched the ceremony's program booklet. Candidate biographies. The inflow of information successfully routed his brain away from suction, stomachs and food. He had never seen his name in gold leaf before. He flipped to the back page and an English version of the menu. His eyes widened:

> *. . . remove eyes, outside skin, and intestines . . . cut off head and tentacles . . . combine ingredients into cavity and sew closed . . .*

"I'm sorry I missed such a delicious meal. Calamari imbottiti is an Italian tradition," a heavyset man announced in a thick German accent. "Good to see you again, Michael. I'm so pumped I really don't feel like eating. The world's most prestigious technical competition can ruin an appetite, even in Rome."

"Hello, Gerhard," Robertson said, setting the program booklet aside and closing his eyes again. "I thought Germans were always prompt?"

"I was trimming my acceptance speech. It was much too long."

"Gerhard Bender, this is my wife, Linda."

"Ah, the kindergarten teacher." His eyes roamed boldly over her body. "Somehow I thought you'd be younger. I represent Innovation Technologies."

Linda crossed her legs and pulled her skirt taut. "I represent Decatur High School," she clarified with a nasty look. They shook hands.

He pulled her face closer. "Forgive me, but I'm so pumped. I insist on a dance after the minor formality of winning." He glanced over her shoulder. "Your husband won't mind, will you, Michael? Michael—wake up. Are we boring the king of the flying bugs?

"Are you and your British friends at Cambridge still staying up nights peering into a microscope and counting the wing beats of the hawk moth, or are you now collaborating with those zookeepers at MIT who train rodents to search for earthquake victims? What was that project again? Ratbot?

"You know, working with animals is not that difficult. Neither is flight. Birds have been doing it for years. Flap a wing, and into the air you go.

"Speaking of that, it's a real shame you came all the way to Rome just to go back with nothing but air. But I suppose you can always say you gave it a good American try."

Linda had an uncontrollable urge to slap Gerhard, but she feared his cheeks might burst. She fondled a dinner knife. "And what exactly is your entry?"

"My *winning* entry is a concept called 'FreeNet.' A completely digitized and paperless society. Free Internet access, monitor screens, and print capability for everyone. We've tested a Berlin market for over a year. All paper media is cloud-based. Magazines, newspapers, business and legal documents, advertising, every piece of mail—all digitized. You decide what you wish to read and print. It will transform the world.

"We even sent a team to interview your American postal service. Unfortunately, when they understood FreeNet's ramifications, things got a little hostile. Innovation always has a winner and loser. And trust me, they would be big losers. The projected cost savings gained by eliminating all the human mail carriers was huge. We haven't yet extrapolated the benefits to the global environment by saving all those trees.

"A little more practical than a flying bug, isn't that right, Michael? I'm so pumped." He lifted a glass. "To FreeNet and the end of junk mail."

The room's lighting dimmed.

Robertson cautiously felt his stomach. He'd never won anything in his life except a disappointing white ribbon in a fourth-grade spelling contest.

Perennial . . . p-e-r-e-n-i-a-l.

I'm sorry, son, but we needed two Ns.

Linda squeezed her husband's hand. "How much is 250,000 euros in US doll—?"

"Shhh," he interrupted. "That's bad luck."

Conversation in the room quieted. Overhead spotlights beamed onto a podium in the center of an elevated stage.

"Ladies and gentlemen," a voice boomed in English through the speaker system. The room went silent. "Pirelli Managing Director of Research and Development, Carlo Burno."

Applause.

Carlo strode to the podium and gently adjusted the microphone. "We'll begin with a most appropriate quote from someone who helped liberate our country from the Nazis in World War II. 'For over a thousand years, Roman conquerors returning from the wars enjoyed the honor of a triumph, a tumultuous parade.'" He turned to the head table. "On behalf of General George S. Patton and Pirelli International, I welcome you, the modern-day conquerors who have left your own research wars to be with us this evening.

"One of you will indeed enjoy triumph. Not by means of a victory over a traditional enemy, but rather a victory over technology. You are here not by chance but by skill, dedication, and, most important, design. We at Pirelli believe that design excellence must be recognized and rewarded on a world scale.

"As you know, the Pirelli Award favors a diverse scientific culture and is a further testament to research and development, especially when humanity benefits from new ideas and technologies. Our international jury has evaluated over one thousand entries and culled them down to you, a select group of conquerors. I should also mention, while it's not a guarantee, all six previous winners went on to a certain Scandinavian capital to solidify their achievement in science. But such triumph tends to arrive suddenly with much fanfare and leave just as unexpectedly. Cherish this moment and remember: all glory is fleeting."

Three giant overhead screens lowered, framing the room.

Carlo turned to a group of nine men seated at a table off-stage to his left. "Has the jury made a selection?"

"We have," responded Ilya Frigogine, jury coordinator and former Nobel Laureate for Chemistry. He approached the stage and transferred an envelope.

Carlo calmly sipped water from a stemmed goblet before breaking the seal. He took another agonizingly long ten seconds to examine the contents and then placed the envelope onto the podium. He smiled at the head table.

"Ladies and gentlemen, as part of a manned mission to Mars—" Robertson buried his face in his hands "—planned for a future United States NASA endeavor, I present to you a truly wonderful and revolutionary device that can operate beyond the boundaries of atmosphere. One with the ability to both fly and crawl. It is my privilege to announce that this year's winner of the Pirelli Award for best new technology in any school, college, university, or research center worldwide is . . . the Entomopter drone, created by Professor Michael Robertson and his team from the Georgia Institute of Technology, USA."

The room erupted. Guests rose to their feet. Media cameras whirred as the overhead screens showed animation video of two mechanical creatures fluttering above a terrain rover that was rolling across the Martian landscape. Each creature alternatively set down on a platform on top of the rover and picked up a slender tube before flying off.

Still seated, his skin prickling with excitement, Robertson opened his eyes. He never felt Linda shaking his arm and shoulder almost violently.

News correspondents hurried forward.

Temporarily blinded by the spotlights now trained on him, Robertson's walk to the podium felt dreamlike. Unbelievably, he had completely forgotten about his stomach. Adrenaline was apparently a great antacid.

Carlo presented Robertson with a mahogany plaque fitted with a large gold medallion. After an admiring glance, Robertson set it aside and waved to the crowd appreciatively.

The video screens now showed a field-level view from inside Georgia

Tech's Bobby Dodd football stadium. A pony-tailed technician stood on the midfield grass, extending one arm. The drone appeared and gently set down like some trained mechanical parrot. Bending at the knees, the man heaved it skyward like a falconer. It sailed through the air toward the end zone, passing between the goalposts. Circling back, it deftly perched sideways on one of the uprights.

The audience applause grew to a crescendo.

Robertson produced his glasses and notes. The audience sat.

"Thank you, Carlo. I want to express my appreciation to the members of the jury, the Pirelli family, our Italian hosts, my distinguished colleagues, my wife, Linda, and especially the other finalists and their respective teams who also put forth tremendous effort and resources."

Robertson cleared his throat and motioned to the overhead screens. "Instead of a football theme, we considered flying into a soccer goal. Unfortunately, insects don't take too kindly to nets."

The audience chuckled.

"We scientists tend to lean toward the introverted side of the gregarious scale. People say that I fit somewhere between boring and bullheaded because I tend to make unilateral and sometimes wrong decisions. I respectfully disagree. For example, the last decision I made on behalf of my drone team was to either allow or not allow my research assistants to travel to Italy and attend tonight's ceremony. I simply determined that most young, single men would prefer to hang out in a campus laboratory rather than cavort through wine-filled Italian taverns with beautiful women and the most gracious people in Europe. I freely admit that I may have been wrong."

The remark drew a generous laugh.

"It is fitting that our drone is recognized in Europe. The very name *ento* for insect and *mopter* for split-wing originated here. I accept this award on behalf of Georgia Tech and my brilliant, dedicated research team. Before we get into questions, and in keeping with the tradition of this award, I would like to reaffirm my personal and professional commitment to using our drone to benefit humanity. I pray that its ultimate owner—and I certainly hope it's NASA—will honor that same commitment. Thank you again. I'm humbled and very grateful."

The audience stood and offered another long ovation.

Robertson had no idea that his drone would generate so much excitement or be accepted so well. For a moment, he regretted not bringing one along and perhaps even flying it over the crowd. But live demonstrations either hit home runs or left poor impressions, especially with new technologies. He had concluded it wasn't worth the risk. He figured the world would see it up close soon enough.

It was time to begin the Q&A session. He nodded to a youthful correspondent.

"Thank you, Professor Robertson," the reporter said. "Darren Beel from Reuters. I don't think many of us have ever seen or heard of your Entomopter drone before. Would you mind giving us a brief rundown on its specifications, capabilities, and significance to a space project?"

"Certainly. As Mr. Burno alluded to in his remarks, it's all about a planet's atmosphere, or lack thereof. The Martian airspace at ground level is like Earth's at 100,000 feet—unstable and extremely difficult to fly through, linearly speaking. Ground rovers are a first step, but they have limitations.

"The most efficient way to explore Mars is from the air. Unfortunately, a conventional fixed-winged aircraft would have to fly 250 miles per hour just to stay airborne. That makes landing, collecting samples, and mapping virtually impossible.

"On the other hand, when insect wings flap through the air, the low-pressure vortex created above the wingtips gives it tremendous lift. Our drone is a multi-mode vehicle with spring-tensioned legs, which means it can be hand-launched, fly slowly over rough terrain, and can literally cling to whatever it lands on. It can collect or deposit samples, recharge, communicate, and even download data before returning to its original launch point. As far as physical design, think of a dragonfly with antennae in two sets of wings—a dragonfly the size of a pigeon. Yes, on the left."

"Thank you. Judy Chin, China Sun Group. Can your drone walk, and do you plan on offering it for sale in the retail market?"

"It can't really walk, but the legs can clamp together and hold it in various positions. They can also pick up light objects. The capability is especially useful for grasping, transporting, and releasing things, like tools or rock samples, for instance." He looked at his notes. "I'm sorry, Judy. What was your other question?"

"Can I buy one?"

"Um, sure . . . assuming we get to that point. I suppose NASA's not the only one with interest, but there are patent and ownership considerations and, frankly, we haven't worked all those out. I'd have to get back to you with a better answer. Yes, ma'am."

"Debra Vaser, Forbes Innovation and Science. Two questions: How is your drone powered? And how much has NASA—I assume it's NASA—appropriated for program funding, and what effect, if any, does the overall drone controversy on spying have on your project?"

Robertson paused to write. She had actually asked three questions. He couldn't remember if the budget number was proprietary. "First of all, it's not really a machine because there's no stored or combustive power source. Without getting too technical, we developed a liquid propellant that flows to a muscle-chemical reciprocator, or MCR. That's the drone's real claim to fame. The MCR consists of two parallel shafts that, when forced by propellant and catalyst gases, push pistons in opposite directions and move both the leg and wing sets. Suffice it to say that it's not powered by a traditional engine or motor, but rather by a chemical reaction. A reaction that not only allows the wings to flap, but also creates enough electrical energy to power a few sensors. A smartphone-like camera, for instance.

"With respect to the reaction, we combine polynitrogen, which is a hydrocarbon similar to kerosene, and a catalyst. I'm sorry I can't be more specific about the composition; we do need to keep some trade secrets. I'm certainly not a spokesperson for NASA or the military, but I think it's simply coincidence that the Institute for Advanced Concepts and other Pentagon agencies like DARPA have invested heavily in their own robotics programs. You really should ask them."

"Sir, for the record, it says here in the program bio that your full name is Michael Charles Robertson," a British correspondent spoke up. "Would that be accurate?"

This drew a suspicious frown from Robertson. "Um, yes. But I think they've turned some of my work history around."

"Just to follow up, Professor. I heard that your university considered shipping you off to the military. And seeing that your NASA is a tax-payer-funded body, can you be more specific about similar unmanned drone venues and projects? And was it also a coincidence, sir, that your drone's claim to fame, this MCR apparatus, carries your initials?"

Robertson smiled slightly, his ego exposed. He knew when he coined the term for the muscle technology that he might pay a price. He spotted the reporter's ID. *Arrogant BBC.*

"Caltech's Microbat team built the first battery-powered, flapping wing, micro-aerial vehicle small enough to fit in the palm of your hand," Robertson said. "Then there's Berkeley's micro-mechanical flying insect, a ten-millimeter device capable of autonomous, programmed flight just like true flies.

"For years the Massachusetts Institute of Technology tried to combine the flight mechanics of insects with neurobiology, structural engineering, and aerodynamics. It's a difficult challenge. Even the most brilliant scientists are learning that it's one thing to build an airplane and quite another to build a bird.

"Work on unmanned drone technologies is exploding all over the world. The US Naval Research Laboratory just announced that their fuel cell–powered Ion Tiger unmanned aerial vehicle flew for forty-eight hours using liquid hydrogen fuel in a new cryogenic fuel storage tank and delivery system."

Robertson poured a glass of water. "No one is shipping us anywhere near the military. In fact, it's just the opposite. We're completely separate from the research groups that traditionally test unmanned drones out of Fort Benning. And we're not part of robotics either, which is another huge technology sector. Those folks are developing machines to help medical patients with caregiving tasks such as housework, feeding, and walking.

"Quite frankly, I believe that Georgia Tech doesn't know where to put us. Right now, we're off-campus at the Technology Square Research Building in downtown Atlanta. We've turned one of their conference rooms into a test lab. I have a standing policy to welcome any organization that wants either an up-close demonstration or a friendly visit. Unfortunately, there has been a general loss of enthusiasm for space ventures with all the funding cuts, but I'm confident that NASA can rekindle public excitement. President Warren certainly supports aggressive space exploration. As for the MCR initials, these were pure coincidence."

"But if NASA can't or won't accept your invention, wouldn't that suggest that your drone might be available for other, perhaps darker applications—including those in law enforcement or even the military?"

Robertson frowned. "I really don't know," he said. "We built the drone to explore planets. The beneficiaries are NASA and Georgia Tech's bank account, in that order. There are plenty of other drones that can handle private or military surveillance. Our first priority is strictly planetary. Yes, ma'am, in the front row."

"Neela Griffin, Fox Cable Business Tech. Is your project classified?"

"Good question. Let me be clear. My drone is not classified. In fact, you've already seen the preferred test site. Our stadium has lots of camera angles. The system components are modular and almost toy-like in design. They're very easy to control and very sturdy. They have to be because of all the Martian rock structures. Even if the wings bump into something during flight, they're designed to snap off and be easily replaced.

"The most aggressive drone aviators are under age twelve. My two sons learned to fly in less than an hour. It uses a handheld wireless controller-transmitter with toggles and buttons just like modern video games. If any of you or your organizations want a crack at being a drone pilot, come see me. I'll be more than happy to make the arrangements."

"Could your drone be used to deliver a weapon of mass destruction?" Griffin blurted.

A hush spread through the room. Even the waitstaff who were quietly collecting the tableware paused.

Robertson peered over his glasses. "The drone was built to survey Mars and collect samples. I don't think it would do very well in a military proj—"

"That's not what I asked," Griffin said. "On February 5, 2003, Secretary of State Colin Powell made an absolute fool of himself in front of the United Nations and the world warning us that remote-controlled Iraqi drones outfitted with spray tanks and biological weapons constituted an ideal method for launching a terrorist attack. Many people believed that potential pushed us into the Iraq war. So, could a terrorist use your invention as a weapon of—?"

"No," he shot back. "We're not interested in destroying humanity. We're interested in improving it."

The audience applauded.

Carlo gently interjected himself. "Thank you, ladies and gentlemen, but we're running a little behind. This concludes our official program. Please join us out on the terrace for an evening of romance with the Riccardo Perrici Ensemble. You'll also find a delicious selection of wines and desserts. Tonight's specialty is Zuppa Inglese, or the Italian Tipsy Cake. We hope it lives up to its name. *Buon appetito.*"

LINDA ROBERTSON sat on the edge of the Jacuzzi, gently sweeping her hand through the 102-degree water. She stared, dreamlike, out of the window at the surreal sight of St. Peter's Basilica to the southwest. Rome's setting sunrays had formed a golden halo around the dome just like so many artists portrayed around the radiant face of Christ.

Robertson eased into the tub, moaning from the pain in his intestines.

Linda kissed his forehead. "Know what I think I'll do?"

"Find a new husband? One who doesn't ruin a wonderful vacation in the world's most romantic city? We should cancel dinner. I'm really sorry. I feel terrible."

"There's always room service," she said, drying her hands and setting the towel within his reach. "There's a gift shop downstairs. Do you need anything else?"

"I'm fine." He drew her hand to his mouth. "I'll just sit here and sulk. Be careful."

She dimmed the room lights and left.

Robertson submerged until his mustache met the water. His finger touched a button. Soft water jets rolled up and down his back like an undulating snake.

There was a knock at the door.

Now what? Robertson wondered. *Great—she forgot her key card.* He stood slowly and snatched a towel. Dizzy, he carefully made his way across the room and reached for the dead bolt latch. He never considered the security peephole.

"Professor Robertson?" Robertson quickly covered himself. Ali Naimi removed his hat and respectfully averted his eyes. "My name is Ibrahim Al-Assaf. I apologize for the intrusion, but I was unable to attend your award ceremony last evening. I heard it was most interesting. We have a mutual friend, Professor Al-Aran. I believe he is a colleague of yours. He mentioned that you were staying here. May I?"

"Um, sure." Robertson turned to verify that his wife was presentable, then remembered that she wasn't there.

Naimi hesitated. "This is inconvenient. Perhaps tomorrow would be better?"

"No, please. Come in," Robertson said, noticing the man's rugged complexion and lifeless, black eyes. He motioned to an upholstered chair by the window. "Excuse me for just a minute."

Naimi sidestepped a suitcase on the floor. It was stuffed with T-shirts.

Robertson emerged from the bathroom in a white terrycloth robe. "May I get you something?" Naimi declined. Robertson opened a small bottle of Perrier. "Faiz and I share office space at Georgia Tech. Sometimes we even cover each other's lectures. How do you know him?"

"I work for the Minister of Petroleum and Mineral Resources for the Kingdom of Saudi Arabia." Naimi sat back. "If I may speak freely? There is a certain business proposition."

Robertson frowned deeply. "Proposition?"

"Well, you may know that our Kingdom produces one quarter of the world's oil, with new resources being discovered faster than current reserves can be used. Our field at Shaybah is already the fourth largest. We are also very proud of the fact that at one dollar per barrel, our production costs are three times less than the world average. Dr. Al-Aran is currently assisting us at Shaybah with an Arab-Exxon development venture. He is in charge of laying out new airport runways. I'm afraid the desert is quite inhospitable."

"Faiz has a PhD in operations research from George Washington University," Robertson noted. "He's an expert in that area. What's it got to do with me?"

"We wish to evaluate a new form of surveillance at some of our strategic production sites, including security cameras that are reliable, highly mobile, and easy to operate. These flying drones of yours—when Faiz described the project, it piqued my curiosity."

"You want to use drones for security?"

"Evaluate," Naimi quickly corrected. "On a platform, literally. We need something that has the ability to position itself atop strategically placed platforms and observe production operations. We wish to determine if your drones can accomplish this."

"What kind of platforms?"

"Observation stands attached to existing equipment and framing. Derrick steel, for example—both flat and round. We wish to evaluate the possibility of deploying a series of moveable sentries that can quickly reach certain high-risk areas and monitor our assets. Not only in Shaybah, but potentially all our fields. But this must be done very quietly and without drawing attention."

"I'm confused," Robertson said suspiciously. "What's wrong with traditional options like good old security cameras?"

"Intolerable," Naimi said with a dismissive wave. "Far too permanent and thus vulnerable to sabotage. And I'm afraid a human military presence is also something we cannot afford."

Robertson misinterpreted the comment, and his frown grew even deeper. The Saudis weren't exactly known for frugality.

"What about planes or helicopters?"

Naimi smiled politely. "Professor Robertson, I appreciate your suggestions and concerns, but you don't understand. The Royal Family is committed to solving this rather delicate problem of wide-area security in the quietest way possible. We cannot abide armed patrols or the engine noise of military aircraft littering the skies above the Kingdom. It's an extremely sensitive situation, particularly with the current value of petroleum.

"You must know that the Saudi government, under the leadership of the Custodian of the Two Holy Mosques, his Royal Highness King

Abdullah, must manage the region with the utmost reverence. It is related to appearance, but frankly, there is another reason. One that is somewhat unpleasant.

"You may think it unusual for Arabs to be concerned with terrorism, but certain organizations have made repeated threats regarding Saudi oil. Some believe it is the largest prize in the world for the West to capture and terrorists to destroy. We must take these threats seriously. Dr. Al-Aran has explained that your drones have some dexterity as well as a small profile?"

Robertson sipped his water thoughtfully. Now he understood. This man was referring to the surge of Middle Eastern government overthrows, a.k.a the Arab Spring. The Royal Family was running scared.

"Very limited dexterity. But we're already negotiating with NASA. I wouldn't be able to look at any other offers until our position with the space program is finalized."

"Completely understandable," Naimi acknowledged. "But certainly you would be agreeable to a trial evaluation for a brief period—say, thirty days? Something that would allow us to see these drones in action."

"I'm not sure that's possible," Robertson countered. "I'd have to talk to my university. They would have to approve something like that."

"I mean no disrespect, Professor, but there is a sense of urgency in this matter. And with you here and unavailable for conference, well, Dr. Al-Aran has already conversed with the appropriate trustees. They were most enthusiastic in expressing preliminary support for such a trial. Arrangements have already been made on your campus in Atlanta for us to acquire the necessary system components. If we like the results, then—"

Robertson's eyebrows went up. "What did you say?"

"We've arranged for a point of transfer."

"No, before that. You said something about trustees. What trustees?"

Naimi gently stroked his mustache. "I recall the name Garton. Yes, that's it. Professor Al-Aran has had direct conversation with Dr. Winford Garton. He was most enthusiastic about the prospects."

He would be, Robertson thought. Garton was Vice Chair of Georgia Tech Research Corporation, a non-profit entity that secured and managed research funds. He was also the drone project's primary sponsor. He'd sell freshmen on the black market if it meant a grant commitment.

"Okay, let's back up. You apparently don't need my permission, so why are you even here? It's obvious that this is a done deal."

Naimi joined his hands, prayer-like. "Michael, we need your expertise, or that of your program staff, particularly with technical nuances and hands-on training. We prefer to borrow, say, four or five drones for a very brief period, evaluate them on site at the Shaybah location, and make a final decision. We certainly wish to keep you in the loop, so to speak, at least in the short term.

"Of course, there will be compensation made to your campus research facility. An initial down payment. If we like the system, we will make a second payment that will constitute a full purchase. You will obviously retain patent rights and may serve as a general advisor during the trial. The Kingdom is very flexible in these matters. If we decide the drones are not feasible for airborne security of our oil fields, then we shall return them immediately, and you may keep the deposit. In any event, your university gains ten million US dollars. Five million have already been issued."

Robertson lifted the Perrier to his lips but didn't drink. His mind was trying to comprehend what he just heard. The sudden gasp of air brought on a coughing gag.

"Dollars? Just to perch a flying camera on an oil rig? Are you craz . . . er, serious?"

Naimi thrust his hand between the window sheers and peered outside. "Again, you must forgive me. I am an honorable man and do not wish to appear condescending. Saudis are taught at a very young age never to boast of wealth. At current trends, our Kingdom's net oil export revenue for the current production year is projected at 300 billion in US dollars. I can assure you of two things: the monetary aspects of this arrangement can be compared to a purchase of"—he glanced at the suitcase—"a vacation souvenir. It is indeed trivial, and I am indeed not crazy."

"I didn't mean it that way," Robertson apologized. *Ten million dollars still isn't trivial.* "You mentioned a transfer point?"

"Dr. Al-Aran has attended several US OPEC conferences. Members of the Royal Family feel comfortable with him, but more importantly, they trust his judgment. As an Arab, he understands the eccentricities of our business culture, not to mention the language. We wish to have him take the lead in this matter. He has informed us that he is knowledgeable enough with the drone's design to transition and even operate the system. Do you share that assessment?"

Robertson cursed to himself. His colleague was literally stealing his project. "I do not," he said flatly. "The good Dr. Al-Aran might be well advised to consult with me, or at least my research assistants, before making any more commitments. I need to speak with him before this goes any further."

"Of course," Naimi said, tapping his watch and casually lifting it to his ear. "That reminds me . . . how many drones are currently in existence?"

Robertson's head was spinning. "Huh? I'm sorry. Um, ten . . . no, twelve. I think we have twelve assembled and ready to fly. We can make more on site right from our own lab. All the parts are modular. How many units did you say you'd need?"

Naimi pursed his lips thoughtfully and then shrugged. "If I recall correctly, Dr. Al-Aran has stated that six drones should give us more than enough insight to make a decision. We've worked closely in the past. He understands the Kingdom's rather straightforward methodologies." Naimi rose from his chair. "Then it is agreed. Six units. May I presume that we have your tentative support?"

Robertson recalled his award ceremony and that Fox reporter and her question about weapons of mass destruction. Could she have had a point? Would the federal government consider his drone project to be classified research?

It had high enough visibility now with the Pirelli Award. All Robertson had to do was raise the question. An International Trafficking in Arms Regulation (ITAR) roadblock would nip this whole transfer idea, or at least slow things down. The law certainly applied to colleges. Georgia Tech conducted its research at the highest level. The campus Security Department would never let his drone float into the hands of foreign nationals without going through a lengthy ITAR approval process. The whole idea would die on the vine. Best of all, it wouldn't be his decision.

Robertson smiled. "An off-site transfer might require some special permission, but overall, I don't think there'll be any opposition, especially if it's a temporary thing. I suppose my team could help make it a smooth transition."

"It has been a pleasure, Professor Robertson." Naimi offered his hand. "Enjoy Rome. Travel safe on Wednesday, and congratulations again on your technical award."

Robertson locked the door and returned to the Jacuzzi. He let his head submerge completely before turning on the jets. He felt like he could throw up, but he was too angry.

What is going on? His drones being relocated to some oil field in the desert? Robertson couldn't stand Dr. Winford Garton III. He was a sixty-five-year-old, condescending, Southern-born, aristocratic salesman. The term snake oil came to mind. Though married, Garton was also a campus womanizer, who had been reprimanded twice for sexual misconduct—specifically, improper touching.

Robertson wanted to pick up the phone and stop this whole ridiculous desert surveillance idea. The patent issues had never been resolved, and if push came to shove, he really didn't know who owned what.

Is the drone my invention or Georgia Tech's? he wondered. They handed him a research team and told him to develop something that could fly on Mars. *Am I that expendable?* Funny how word of the drone had spread so quickly, but after all, the Pirelli Award was an international event. This was probably the first of many weird offers. And this Al-Assaf character and his Saudi money. Talk about weird.

It really wasn't a proposition at all, Robertson recounted. Propositions meant you had a choice. The Saudis were known for dangling huge sums of cash in front of academia when they wanted something, and knowing an insider like Faiz certainly helped.

Rome or not, now Robertson was even more anxious to get home. He spit a stream of water upward like a fountain. He wondered vaguely, as he sank into the water again, how Al-Assaf knew that his flight left on Wednesday.

9

ATLANTA, GA
TUESDAY, MAY 12

KEVIN JONES set his guitar—a Taylor acoustic six string—next to an open window in the fourth-floor robotics lab of Georgia Tech's Technology Square Research Building. He reached for a pair of binoculars and rolled his fingers over the focus dial until a Domino's Pizza delivery car on Fifth Street came into view. Target acquired.

"Yo, Zee. Pavlov was right."

Roman "Zee" Zibinski stopped trimming the rough fiberglass edge of a newly molded drone wing and cocked his head thoughtfully. He'd heard the name before in some distant class and associated it with canines, but it, along with a gazillion other lecture facts, were sound asleep in his head, refusing to awaken. He visualized Cesar Milan, the Dog Whisperer.

"Who's Pavlov?"

"The father of stimulus-response," Jones replied. "When Ivan Pavlov rang a bell, his dogs knew they were going to be fed and started to salivate. When I see a pizza delivery car, I start to salivate. Pavlov was right. It's an involuntary reflex."

"You're always salivating," Zee quipped. "It's either food or girls. We've had pizza three nights in a row. I'll pass."

"Did you hear that Domino's wants to use aerial drones? What a great idea. No traffic lights, hot food, and you don't have to tip the driver."

"Are they hiring?" Zee asked halfheartedly. "Maybe I could be an unmanned delivery technician."

"Hang tight," Jones said, reaching for his instrument. "You'll get a job offer. Even I figured I'd have to play and sing at a local bar to pay the bills before I won the lottery. They'd call me Pavlov with a guitar—guaranteed to make women salivate."

Zee stretched a rubber band and snapped it across the room. Amazingly, it clung to the back of Jones's shoulder-length mane. "You are truly disturbed. You can't hang around a research campus strumming old Simon and Garfunkel songs forever. Instead of playing 'The Sound of Silence' all day, you might want to learn the sound of scissors and get a haircut. Seriously, what are you going to do?"

"Put it in a ponytail."

"I mean your future," Zee clarified. "The drone project is finished. There's nothing more to do except negotiate with NASA, and neither of us has any say in . . . wait, you won the lottery?"

Jones slowly picked each note of a D chord and heard a slight off-key wave. He gently twisted the tuning knob of the stubborn B string and set the guitar in its case.

"Yep. I get to move to a place where I can work on my tan and sing for the women. Someplace warm and sunny with the Padres and Chargers."

Zee set the drone wing down and put his glasses on. "Space and Naval Warfare Systems Center Pacific? In San Diego?"

Jones smiled. "I'm in."

"Why didn't you tell me? Dude, congratulations. That's awesome. Which one?"

"The New Professional Program," Jones replied. "I wanted to tell you, but I felt guilty. I was hoping there were two openings."

"I'll be fine," Zee said, the disappointment obvious on his face. "What project?"

"Robotics and marine mammal research."

"I'm proud of you, man. You earned it," Zee said, hugging Jones tightly. "That's Christy Liepmann's team. One of her dolphins found that Howell torpedo. I'm really happy for you."

A US Navy dolphin looking for mines off the coast of San Diego found a museum-worthy, nineteenth-century torpedo on the seafloor. The brass-coated torpedo was invented by Lieutenant Commander John Howell in 1870. The Howell torpedo could travel four hundred yards at twenty-five knots and carry a one-hundred-pound warhead that detonated on contact. Only fifty were ever made.

Jones gave his friend an impish smile. "I'm happy you're happy. Pick a color."

Zee froze suspiciously. "Kevin Jones, don't you dare."

"Relax. Just pick one."

"Kevin, no. You might not think so, but we carry a certain level of prestige on this research team. Not to mention working our butts off. We can't afford a negative background check. We could get in a lot of trouble, especially with your new job and now with this Pirelli exposure. I need things to look good on my résumé."

"Please?" Jones begged. "Consider it operational training for one last pizza. I'm leaving tomorrow forever. You gotta give me one more chance."

Zee exhaled a deep breath. "Black."

"You chose wisely, my son."

Zee cursed to himself. "I hate it when I do that."

Jones walked to a large metal cabinet and turned a combination dial. He slid a plastic case from a shelf and brought it to the table. Inside, twelve colored drone frames rested between forty-eight sets of matching wings: blue, yellow, red, and black. He lifted a set and turn-clipped four together, twisting each pair into locking slots on the rear and front sections of the drone's thorax. Next, he inserted four pliable legs coated with rubberized silicone into the frame's underside. Each leg tip had a textured pad that, when pressed toward its counterpart, locked into position to grip and hold.

Assembly took less than a minute.

Jones placed the drone upright on the table. It looked like some evil queen hornet. He plucked a thin plastic cartridge from the case and held it up to the light. Next, he inserted a syringe into a container of bright-orange liquid labeled "polynitrogen propellant" and drew back the plunger. He injected the liquid and snapped the cartridge cover shut. He turned the drone upside down and removed a thin plastic shield from the tip of a camera lens. Finished, Jones inserted the fuel cartridge. The wings twitched once, twice, then instantly blurred.

Zee opened a laptop and connected a USB cable. "I need you to focus."

Jones gently tossed the drone into the air and quickly moved a toggle on the controller-transmitter. When he rolled the toggle's tip between his fingers, the drone obediently turned, pointing its camera at Zee.

Zee's screen showed his fuzzy image sitting at the laptop. He adjusted the picture quality and then raised one thumb.

"Okay, it's time for the Georgia Tech slalom," Jones said, approaching the window and surveying Fifth Street below.

The drone had flown this street course autonomously as programmed by a flight control algorithm. The record was one minute and eleven seconds. Jones had come close to beating it manually before but had never succeeded.

He positioned the controller firmly on the window ledge. "The bet is one large cheese and pepperoni pizza. The course is eight streetlights, four up the block and four back. The drone must circle each pole. When it reaches the last light, it must dock on the upper banner arm and then return through this window and back to this table. Seventy seconds or less."

"Without losing a wing," Zee said.

"Without losing a wing."

Zee set a stopwatch on his phone. "Ready . . . go."

Jones raced the drone forward into the night sky, gliding it downward against the building's façade, around the first aluminum streetlight, expertly approaching and then looping around the second, third, and fourth lights like some Olympic downhill skier. It was missing the pole shafts by mere inches.

"I can't believe we're doing this," Zee sung, noticing several pedestrians pause on the sidewalk and scramble for their phones. "You've got thirty seconds."

Video game–like, Jones contorted his body with the controller as he guided the drone across Fifth Street and through the backstretch, winding around streetlights five, six, and seven, and then deftly setting the drone onto the upper-most of two horizontal banner bars on street-light number eight.

"We have surface locomotor grip," Zee's voice proclaimed in an official tone.

Jones pressed a control button with his thumb, and the insect's legs released.

"Twelve . . . eleven . . . ten . . ."

Hovering free, the drone streaked for the fourth floor, narrowly missing the treetops on the grassy perimeter below.

"Six . . . five . . . four . . ."

Jones centered the drone at the window, took a split-second to eye the path and angle, and then eased the drone over the threshold and back into the lab. It skidded to rest on the table next to Zee's laptop. The wing beats petered out.

"One," Zee announced. "Unreal. You made it."

"*Yee-hah!* Mission accomplished, sir!" Jones, shouted, raising his arms. "I ought to be in the military. Precision drone pilot extraordinaire."

"That was pretty cool," Zee admitted, removing the drone's fuel cartridges and wings. "If Robertson ever knew about this, he'd have a stroke."

There was a loud knocking on the lab door.

Jones quickly disconnected the laptop cable. He slammed the window shut an instant before the door clicked open.

"Who is in here?" The voice was male and stern. It wasn't maintenance. "Mr. Jones? Mr. Zibinski? Why is this door locked?"

"Dr. Al-Aran, sir . . . um, we were just finishing," Jones squeaked, standing guiltily at attention. "It's been a long day. How are you? Locked? Um, no particular reason, sir. We just felt better about security with the project and all."

Al-Aran gave the room a general glance. Satisfied there were no hidden women, he tucked his security SmartCard away. "You might be interested to know that your drone was named top Pirelli prize winner. Professor Robertson sent a departmental email. Your research budget just got a quarter-million dollars richer."

Al-Aran walked to the room's refrigerator and popped open a Coca-Cola. He spied the drone on the table.

"I suppose we might bend a few rules tonight," he announced, lighting his pipe and dropping his match into the can. It sizzled briefly.

"Gentlemen, you should be proud. You've come a long way with your little flying gold mine. Did Professor Robertson ever mention that I helped design the wings for the first prototype? We cut them from containers that held Atlanta's world-famous soft drink." He tapped the aluminum can. The drone's original name had been *The Coke Roach* until their lawyers intervened.

"They're on the wall in Professor Robertson's office," Zee said. "But we're way beyond that now. Everything's synthetic." He lifted the drone from the table and offered it to Al-Aran.

"I remember it being heavier." Al-Aran set his pipe down. "But that was some time ago. Can it still carry its own weight?"

"More than double," Jones answered.

"How long is the average flight time?"

"Fifteen to thirty minutes."

"And then what?"

"Not much," Jones said. "One fell from three hundred feet, and the frame was fine. It's a pretty rugged design."

Al-Aran made a mental note. "Who is most qualified person to provide technical answers regarding flight performance?"

"Robertson," both answered.

"But I probably know as much as he does," Jones added.

"One more question. How long would it take for a novice to become proficient at controlled flight, including maneuvering up to a structure and landing on, say, a vertical metal tube or shaft?"

Jones thought for a moment and shrugged his shoulders. "Half an hour, tops. Zee made a really great online training video that walks through everything from boot up to fuel to modular part replacements. Why do you ask?"

"I need you to gather six drone frames and all related components. We're lending the system out for a while."

"Huh?" Jones asked incredulously. "To who?"

Al-Aran relit his pipe and shook his head. "Six years of higher education should have taught you something about the use of subjective versus objective pronouns. To *whom*, Mr. Jones. A Saudi evaluation

72

team is considering trialing the system. They're interested in controlled flight maneuvering in and out of derrick rigs and grasping and holding onto metal structures to film and observe desert operations. It's called asset monitoring."

"Are you serious?"

"Arabs are always serious about security, particularly when it involves oil."

"Don't we need some kind of permission?" Zee questioned.

"You're absolutely right. I almost forgot." Al-Aran reached in his pocket and flashed a piece of paper.

The first thing Zee noticed was that the check was drawn on the Bank of Riyadh. But then his mouth dropped open when he spied the dollar amount. He had no clue that it was a complete fake.

"And this is only the down payment. If our drones perform well, there'll be another just like it. I know it's late, but I need you to have everything packaged and in my office before you leave. Do me another favor and print out a detailed set of operating instructions. Something that's complete but easy to follow."

"Sure, but what about Professor Robertson?" Zee asked. "He won't be back on campus until Thursday. Shouldn't we at least let him know? Who's going to explain the system?"

Al-Aran folded the check and tucked it away. "I am."

AKIL SAT with his feet propped on the kitchen table in a brick, two-story, side-by-side, rented flat near the corner of Ditmars Boulevard and 81st Street.

He finished his second Big Mac and made a point to recover the last French fry from the bottom of the bag. He lifted his shirt. His stomach was expanding nicely.

He scanned a flyer that some protesters handed out at the McDonald's drive-thru exit. LaGuardia's Runway 4/22 was just four hundred yards away, and area noise pollution was a constant thorn in the sides of the residents. The concrete noise reduction wall across the street somewhat muffled the airport's ground activity, but it did little to quiet airborne traffic.

The flyer showed Akil's house centered in the photo along with his Toyota. Thankfully, no other meaningful identification was apparent. He crumpled the flyer into a tight ball and buried it in the trash can. There was work to do.

Akil retrieved the last two plastic gallons of bleach from ten cardboard cases in the bedroom. He filled a measuring cup with potassium chloride granules until the needle on a small vegetable scale read sixty-three grams.

He poured one bottle of bleach and the granules into a large metal pot on the gas stove and turned the burner to medium-high. The liquid reached a slow boil in six minutes. He dipped a battery-charged suction tube into the mixture and watched the plastic balls float upward to the full-charge calibration line. He turned off the heat and set the pot in the refrigerator next to two others. Each was labeled with masking tape to indicate rotation en route to a final cooling temperature of thirty-three degrees. A heavy crust of crystals had formed around the rim of a pot at the front of the production line. Akil gently scraped the excess into a 1-cup gun mesh funnel from a local paint store and tapped the filtered material into a drinking glass. It was already half full. He carefully measured out fifty-six grams of crystals and added them to a container of one hundred milliliters of distilled water. This he also boiled and cooled into a secondary crystallization process.

After another round of gentle scraping, this time with a plastic spatula to avoid sparks, a white powdery substance finally appeared— potassium chlorate. Akil placed the powder in a flat pan and heated it to drive out any moisture. Next to that pan, he heated an even ratio of Vaseline and wax melted with a small amount of white camping kerosene. He poured that mixture over 90 percent of the potassium powder and allowed the kerosene to evaporate. He kneaded the now gooey gray-brown matter together and pressed the finished product into a rectangular plastic tray separated into six-ounce cubes. Finally, he poured a layer of melted wax over the tray until each space was waterproof.

He updated a label on the container with the name and the birth date of each charge—a charge with the explosive power of one stick of dynamite and a room temperature decomposition lifespan of four days.

Akil dug deep in his pants pocket and unfolded a single sheet of paper.

KILLING MADE EASY
PREPARATION OF POTASSIUM CYANIDE (KCN)
Heat ammonium formate crystals by flame in an environment containing as little oxygen gas as possible. The ammonium formate decomposes into formamide ($HCONH_2$) and

further into hydrogen cyanide. Condense the gas given off in a rubber, plastic, or glass tube that has one end immersed in a beaker containing a solution of potassium hydroxide (KOH). Position the tube so that any liquid in it will run off into the beaker of potassium hydroxide. The hydrogen cyanide will quickly react with the potassium hydroxide to form approximately 65.1 grams of potassium cyanide crystals. Hold your breath and dilute 900 to 1000 mg in any drinkable liquid. Victims will fall into comas almost immediately. Timeframes depend on stomach contents, but death generally occurs in less than two minutes. KCN is virtually untraceable, and its symptoms mimic heart failure. Antidotes, even if administered directly after ingestion, often cause severe and irreparable brain dam—

The front-door handle began to turn, followed by a squeaking of metal hinges. Akil reached for his Glock 23 Gen 4 .40-caliber pistol and flattened himself against the refrigerator. The door continued to open, stopped only by the latch chain.

"Kenny, are you in there, lad? I thought I fixed that doorbell, but I guess it won't work."

Akil crept into the bathroom and twisted the tub spigot.

"I'm in the shower," he shouted.

Mrs. Timmons pressed her face into the door crack. "When did you get in, lad, and what's that smell?"

"This morning. I was cleaning."

"Now, don't you fuss. You come next door when you're finished and meet me brother before he leaves. We're conversing in the living room. You'll need to hurry because the taxi man is on his way."

"I'll be there in a few minutes," Akil answered. "Should I bring anything, Mrs. Timmons?"

"Just that Scotch and Soda coin trick you promised from that mall in Minneapolis. And even though I'm your landlady, there's no need to be so formal. You might refer to me as Mary."

Akil heard the door slam shut. This was a problem. Mrs. Timmons was a petite Irish-Catholic in her late seventies with a constant smile and hosiery balled at her ankles. Her husband had passed away a year ago, leaving her to manage the rental property. She was thrilled with the extra income, but obviously ignorant about New York tenant law—barring an emergency, it was illegal to enter a residence without cause or advance notice. Akil was becoming the son she'd never had. He couldn't tolerate such uninvited intrusions, especially if he wasn't there.

—

Next door, Mary Timmons flopped onto her sofa and filled a glass from a jug on the coffee table. She raised a toast to her brother, who was sitting in a chair across the room. "Bernie, I really like that kid. If I were fifty years younger, I'd go for him myself. He's only been here a month, but I can tell he's a good one. And a worker too. What other young man would clean that whole apartment, so you could lick the floor and not taste a bit of dust? Wouldn't let me pay for a thing. I never in my life saw so much bleach. He must have carried in a hundred gallons. What in the world was he thinking? But then, the place was filthy. The Olsons, who lived in there before, were as near to pigs as pigs could be. Their mongrel dog did his jobs on the upstairs carpet until there was a ring around the whole bed—left his filth for the whole world to see! Can you fathom a stench like that? How could people with working nostrils tolerate such a—?"

"Mrs. Timmons?" Akil's voice spoke through the screen door.

"Come right in, Kenny. I've been swearing up a storm about the previous tenants when I should be thanking the Savior for who I have now." She tried to rise but gave up. "Kenny, this is my brother, Bernard Sloan."

Countryside Irish, Bernard was a hairless clone of his sister, complete with rosy cheeks and perpetual smile. He stood and extended his hand.

"It's a fine pleasure to meet you, Mr. Wory. Me sister's told me quite a bit about you and your sick mother, and I surely hope that she's making good progress back to the world of the healthy."

There was a moment of awkward silence as Akil struggled to comprehend the fast monotone. He noted the strength in the little man's grip. It was icy from caressing a huge glass of beer.

"I've never been to Ireland, but I hear it's beautiful."

"Oh, it's far more than that. So many think the populace lives in the bigger towns, but there's a whole 'nuther world out there among the greens."

"What part of Ireland?"

"Greencastle County Down, right along the coast of the Irish Sea, about an hour's drive to the south of Belfast. We can see the ferries making their way up to Ulster. Been a lobster man all me life, but that's only for six or seven months of the year, so then I try and get a good price for the shellfish."

Akil nodded. For a moment he thought the language was some form of old Gaelic. He managed to hear the words *lobster* and *fish* in the diatribe and correctly concluded that the man had something to do with the sea.

"Greencastle is a medieval fortress that sits on the hill behind our old homestead," Mrs. Timmons said. "Would you believe that Bernard and I used to play up there when we were just six years old? The Normans built it all from stone in the thirteenth century. We could see all the way down to the cellar through the holes in the floors. We'd jump across without any fear at all. Bernard would hide and then scare me half to death with his screams. Pigs stayed in that place, and they'd chase after us. What I wouldn't give to hear them snort again. But that was ages ago."

"It sounds very nice," Akil said, noting the time.

"Kenny's a bartender, Bernard. I'm sure the two of you would've hit it off," Mrs. Timmons continued. "And he's a trickster too. But only at night. In the daytime he attends the university."

Bernard nodded curtly, tipping his glass.

"That's a fine place to start out now, as long as you know what you're wanting to study."

"It's gadgets," Mrs. Timmons said. "He tinkers with everything. And that reminds me, Kenny. Why in the world would you have so many of those tiny little telephones all lined up on your sink? Plugged into the wall sockets like kittens drinking their mother's milk. The other day, I think there were five. God rest his soul, Dermott used to say they were the toys of the devil himself."

Akil smiled broadly. "I . . . um, gifts. They're family gifts. They were on sale."

"You're a thoughtful one, Kenneth. Are you able to join me for dinner tomorrow? I bought a beef roast fat enough for the whole neighborhood."

"I'm really sorry, but I can't," Akil said as though in pain. "My mother's been asking for me again. I have to leave in the morning. I should be back in about a week."

"Well, that's a shame, but family comes before all else in this world. Godspeed to you when you travel. And speaking of travel, did you happen to find that spare set of Scotch and Soda in the stores?"

Akil grimaced. "I completely forgot. I promise I'll bring it next time."

"Do you have yours, then? I know you never go anywhere without it."

Akil reached in his pocket and produced a plastic case the size of a cigarette pack. Scotch and Soda was a brilliant vintage coin trick that made a quarter literally disappear from a person's closed hand. Mrs. Timmons's father had dabbled in sleight-of-hand when she was a child. She had been enamored by Akil and his magic coins since the day he'd rented the flat.

Akil completed the trick with his usual flair and tucked the little case away.

A vehicle horn beeped twice.

Bernard hugged his sister in a long embrace. He wiped his eyes with a handkerchief. "I guess I'm just not used to that odor comin' from next door."

"Now don't you try and blame Kenny and his hundred gallons of bleach, you old crier," Mrs. Timmons chided through her tears. "Even though he's got enough to scrub the whole neighborhood. I'll miss you too."

One bullet per head, Akil thought. *They'd fall together onto the sofa in some final act of macabre embrace. The basement and heavy plastic would easily mask the odor of two bodies for perhaps ten days.*

"Somebody call a cab?" a voice shouted from outside.

"You ring me when you get home, or I'll worry through the night!" Mrs. Timmons shouted above the roar of another aircraft.

Bernard walked to the curb, shook Akil's hand, and blew his sister a kiss.

The taxi sped off.

Akil returned to his flat and peered through binoculars from his upstairs bedroom. The planes on LaGuardia's Runway 4 were backed up and averaging four minutes of hold time between departures.

He opened his Qur'an.

Surah 48. Victory, Conquest

1. *Verily we have granted thee a manifest victory.*
2. *That Allah may forgive thee thy faults of the past and those to follow; fulfill His favor to thee; and guide thee on the straight way.*
3. *And that Allah may help thee with powerful help. . . .*
4. *And that He may punish the hypocrites, men and women, and the polytheists, men and women, who imagine an evil opinion of Allah. On them is a round of evil: the wrath of Allah is on them. He has cursed them and got hell ready for them, and evil is it for a destination. . . .*
5. *We have truly sent thee as a witness, as a bringer of glad tidings, and as a warner. . . .*
6. *Verily those who plight their fealty to thee do no less than plight their fealty to Allah. The hand of Allah is over their hands: then anyone who violates his oath, does so to the harm of his own soul, and anyone who fulfills what he has covenanted with Allah, Allah will soon grant him a great reward.*

DECATUR, GA
THURSDAY, MAY 14

LINDA ROBERTSON sat up in bed, jarred awake by footsteps in the hallway. The clock on the nightstand suggested dawn, but the room was nearly black, thanks to the room-darkening window blinds. There had been a recent string of morning break-ins in their normally crime-free suburb ten minutes northeast of Atlanta. Her mind raced to remember if she'd activated the alarm system. She slithered her hand under the covers and tapped her husband. Michael didn't respond. A pinch produced a mild snort.

The noise in the hallway stopped.

"Someone's in the house," she whispered.

Michael sat up, and when he did, he felt instantly nauseous. His eye sockets throbbed as he squinted across the room. Incredibly, the French door handle began to turn. He watched helplessly as light and something long and slender eased inside.

The unmistakable outline of a rifle barrel.

Michael felt as if he was living an out-of-body experience. He could see and comprehend what was happening, but he couldn't move a single muscle.

"That's far enough, buddy," he managed to say. "If you come in this room, I'm going to tie you to a tree outside and squirt you with the garden hose."

Ignoring the silly threat, the assassin calmly approached the bed and took aim.

Helpless, Michael did the only thing he could to save his life.

He whipped the covers off his wife.

Linda screamed, taking hits to her arms and chest. She jumped out of bed, fled into the bathroom, and slammed the door.

Unmerciful, the assassin turned his weapon back to Michael.

"All right, that's enough!" Michael laughed.

Stuart, their six-year-old son, dropped the Nerf gun and proceeded to turn the bed into a circus trampoline.

"You didn't wake me when you got home," he pouted.

Linda opened the bathroom door. "You were sound asleep," she said. In seconds, she had tackled her son to the mattress and caressed him tightly. "Mmmm, I missed you. Where's your brother?"

"Playing video games on his computer. Did you bring me anything from Eye-taly?"

"Italy," Linda said. "Did you behave?"

"*Mom*," he protested the obligatory parental question. "We always do. You can even ask Aunt Tina. Did she go home? We played a game called Molopoly Junior, and me and Christian were a fast race car, and we had all the houses, and Aunt Tina was a iron. She said that's the one you always pick. We won because we bang-rupted her. Did Dad win? What's a morgadidge? We saw a cool black snake outside."

"Yes, your father won, but he doesn't feel well." She handed her son a fistful of Nerf darts and gently pointed him to the door. "A mortgage is a piece of paper that says you own something and have to pay for it. Aunt Tina left last night. Time to shower up, please. School today."

Grumbling, the assassin shuffled off.

Linda ran a brush through her hair. "Are you going to campus?"

"I have to," Michael said, twisting his neck from side to side.

"You don't look very well. Do you want me to call the doctor? I'm sure he could give you something."

"Nah, I've just got a funny feeling. It's probably nothing."

"Your stomach?"

"NASA, what else? Or, to be more specific, NASA's budget.

Everything in that agency is about money. If they can't make a commitment, my drone project is screwed and so am I."

"Professor, stop worrying," she ordered. "I'm sure it'll work out. And if it doesn't, then you'll just have to find someone else who's interested."

"Sure. There's all kinds of companies planning trips to Mars. Maybe I could write to Steven Spielberg."

"What about that oil field security thing with the Saudis?"

He frowned. "The flying cameras? I'll find out more about it today, but I guess it's moving forward. Faiz is arranging an on-site trial for some delegation. I'm not giving it much credence. The drone wasn't designed for security. I didn't want to burst any bubbles, but I've got a feeling they'll take a close look at the mechanics and pack the system right back up. It's not that sophisticated."

"You're angry, aren't you?"

"Not at all. I like being kept in the dark about my own project."

"You like being in control."

He smiled at his wife's perceptiveness. "I don't like being irrelevant."

She kissed her finger and touched his chin. "Stop fretting, and stop selling yourself short. You just earned a huge award. It's something you can be proud of for the rest of your life. No one can ever take that away. Your drone is a great invention. Whatever happens, I love you."

"*Daaaad*, could you come here?"

Michael placed his hand on his stomach and gingerly walked upstairs.

"Hey, bud."

"Hey," ten-year-old Christian Robertson acknowledged, his eyes fixed on the computer screen. "Josh lent us Spider-Man. Check it out."

The boy's thumbs and fingers expertly pressed buttons on the game controller. In synchronized rhythm, the screen character sprang sideways, from building to building, simultaneously shooting streams of webbing at an array of menacing attackers dressed in black camouflage and brandishing automatic weapons.

Michael nodded. "That's pretty good, mister. How about your reading?"

"Spider-Man can stick to things sideways just like your drones," Christian said. His fingers made a final series of clicks on the controller.

The video character leaped to a flagpole high above the cityscape and then raised both arms in victory. Music filled the speakers and a voice offered congratulations at defeating level three of ten. "Do you think I could fly one again sometime?"

"Sure. *If* you improve your reading grade." The sound of running water flowed through the wall. "Okay, Spider-Man. Hop downstairs and say hello to your mother, and then hop in the shower after your brother."

Michael picked up the controller and casually examined the buttons. He pressed one. The video game came to life. A swarm of attackers appeared, weapons blazing. He frantically tried to rouse the motionless hero. Streams of bullets easily found their mark. The game ended abruptly with a demonic laugh.

"Sorry, Spider-Man. You lose."

KENOSHA, WI

FAIZ AL-ARAN pulled his Kia Sorento into the Brat Stop Restaurant's parking lot at the intersection of I-94 and State Highway 50. He shut off the engine and yawned deeply, arching his body until his fingers touched a fiberglass suitcase in the backseat.

Someone tapped the passenger's window.

Al-Aran unscrewed the cap on a thermos before unlocking the door.

"Nice to see you again, Professor," Akil said pleasantly, sliding inside. There were customers milling outside the restaurant, so the men refrained from traditional greeting kisses. "Follow the road behind the restaurant and turn left on—"

"Patience, my young *lutador*. We will sit a moment and talk . . . in English." Akil folded his hands on his lap. "In four days, America will feel a devastating wind, yes? You are prepared?"

Akil nodded once. "Everything's cool."

Al-Aran smiled, pleased with Akil's Western demeanor. It was both refreshing and comforting to know that his best operative had adapted so well in a culture he was seeking to destroy. "Are you learning from the Internet?"

"There's a boatload . . . er, hundreds of sites and videos of remote-controlled drones," Akil said. "I found one that lets me practice with a simulated joystick."

"You are comfortable with your surroundings?"

"My landlord here likes me a lot. He's offered me a bartending job. He's a disgusting alcoholic, and it will be a pleasure to end his life. My LaGuardia lady trusts me like I'm her son. Both locations have perfect perimeter access. O'Hare may be tricky. The runway is near a huge FedEx building. It's always busy, but I think I can maneuver around it."

"And San Diego?"

"I'm working on a traveling partner," Akil said with a thin smile. "She's a Latina with kids."

"Your MoneyGram is arranged. All you need is a reference number and ID," Al-Aran said, handing Akil a white envelope. "You're gaining weight."

"Nearly ten pounds," Akil said, tucking the envelope into his jacket and exposing his Qur'an. "Why didn't you fly? And what's a *lutador*?"

"May I?" Al-Aran extended his hand toward the Qur'an. Akil passed him the book, and Al-Aran thumbed the worn pages. "*Lutador* is a Portuguese word for 'freedom fighter.' Flying means airport scanning machines and surveillance cameras—all baggage opened and inspected by security is photographed. No one must see our toys. And no one must see this." He kissed the Qur'an and handed it back. "The tactics have changed. Have you set the Milwaukee timetable?"

"Yes."

"And the aircraft selection?"

"As you ordered," Akil replied. "Delta. MD-90 series. Two fuselage-mounted engines. A morning flight to Atlanta. Changed how?"

"Suffice it to say that you will not have to maneuver underneath or even near the flaps." Al-Aran started the ignition and turned on the heater. "You will fly the drone to the front of the aircraft and attach it to the vertical shock strut of the nose landing gear. It will be swallowed inside like poison."

"You mean the main landing gear?"

"The nose," Al-Aran calmly repeated, seeing the confusion on Akil's face.

"But there's no fuel in the nose," Akil protested. "We should attack the center tank. If we destroy the front wheels, an aircraft can still land safely."

"There are many vulnerabilities on an aircraft," Al-Aran said. "The older designs use steel cables and hydraulics to control everything. Aircraft with fly-by-wire systems transmit commands from the cockpit via electric wires to actuators on the control surfaces themselves. You must trust my plan. Tell me about the explosive."

"I made twenty-four hundred grams," Akil answered. "Enough to cut each aircraft in half."

"That's exactly what I don't want," Al-Aran said firmly. "The first plane's failure must raise doubts about the cause. We need uncertainty. We need the infidels thinking and discussing. I want you to use a measured amount of explosive so that the entire cockpit is not destroyed. How large is each charge?"

"Approximately 150 grams."

Al-Aran paused to calculate. He knew that just 250 grams of high-energy PETN and Semtex-H destroyed Pan Am 103, a 747 flying over Lockerbie, Scotland, in December 1988. The detonation velocity was nearly five miles per second. That charge was placed in the forward cargo hold and detonated at 32,000 feet. It literally severed the cockpit from the rest of the plane. The pilots were found still strapped in their seats. Potassium chlorate, however, was one-fourth as powerful.

"Use two charges," Al-Aran ordered.

Both men froze as another vehicle pulled alongside. The Wisconsin State Patrol deputy gave them an unconcerned glance and continued to the restaurant.

"Three hundred grams," Akil confirmed.

"Everything you need is in that case. Controller, Web access to a training video, and five drones. One drone is expendable. There are two types of plastic cartridges: fuel and catalyst. How long before the Delta explosion?"

"It'll happen quick," Akil predicted. "If my timing is right, fifty to sixty seconds after takeoff. I'll set a longer delay for United's. How many grams for that?"

"Six hundred," Al-Aran replied. "A delayed detonation is good. Let it get up to cruising altitude."

"If the harness fails or falls off, I'll have to carry the explosive between the drone's legs. The potassium can't tolerate friction or pressure above fifty-one pounds per square inch. I need to know the precise grip strength of the legs and also the maximum radio communication distance."

Al-Aran mused softly to himself. He scribbled something on a piece of paper. "This man was a lead member of the original project team. When you contact him, speak directly on my behalf. Make up whatever you like. He plays an instrument—a guitar—and enjoys music. Have you arranged a field test?"

"There's a small rock quarry ten minutes away," Akil answered. "A farmer owns the property and never goes there. If the drone has to grasp and hold onto a vertical landing gear strut, then I have a perfect test target. If we park on the quarry's access road, no one else can enter."

"We will not park anywhere," Al-Aran said. "You will test the drone alone. The risk is great whenever two or more of Allah's people appear together. I will eat a meal and be on my way. Atlanta is a long ride."

Akil examined the note. "Why two names?"

"Jdey is a soldier of Allah. I have already contacted him. He knows nothing about this operation except that he is to serve you. Use him at any time and in any manner you choose. He is loyal and completely fearless. I have arranged for him to meet you. He is also a small arms expert. He claims to have valuable information about a federal firearms dealer who has a large weapons cache not far from here."

Akil's jaw muscles flexed and his eyes gave off an evil twinkle. "That could be useful when the time is right."

"We will not speak in person again—only Gmail."

He paused. "Four days. Allah will bless the tactics."

13

AKIL DROVE his Camry west on Highway 50 to County Highway J and then turned south on Quarry Road for another mile. The site was nothing more than an abandoned dump surrounded by gravel mounds and littered with shredded tires and rusted appliances. Broken glass was everywhere. He parked in the middle of the access road and dialed his cell phone.

"Hello?" a young male voice answered.

"I am attempting to reach a Mr. Kevin Jones, please?" Akil said in an exaggerated Middle-Eastern accent.

"Speaking."

"My name is Omar Yassin. I am calling from Al Hufuf, Saudi Arabia. Are you hearing me okay?"

Jones was in his San Diego apartment, perched on a stool in a spare room that he'd converted into a makeshift recording studio. He reached over a microphone stand and paused a portable audio recorder. "Yeah, I can hear you fine."

"Excellent," Akil replied. "I am engaged in a project with Dr. Faiz Al-Aran. He gave me your name as a knowledgeable contact for the device called the Entomopter drone. I apologize for the interruption, but I have a few technical questions."

"Not a problem. I was just jam . . . er, playing some tunes. No big deal." Jones slid off his guitar strap and shifted the phone. "How can I help?"

"Well, at this time we have three issues. I determined that you might save us time and effort if you've already encountered them. The first is environment. Can you give me any insight regarding the machine's tolerance with airborne particles or debris?

"If you're talking about a desert environment," Kevin said, "sand is no problem at all. We logged sixteen hours in a wind tunnel at category three hurricane strength and added silica to the airflow. The wings held up fine."

"Good! Second, with respect to the legs, do you recall the precise amount of grip pressure exerted when picking up an object? We certainly could calculate it ourselves, but I thought you might save us the trouble."

"I can't recall the exact number, but it was no more than forty-four pounds per square inch. The compression springs are completely removable and should retain stable tension for eight months."

"That's exactly what I needed to hear," Akil said.

"What's the third issue?"

"Oh, yes . . . maximum distance to receive radio signals from the wireless controller?"

"Line-of-sight signal will degrade at around a thousand meters."

"Perfect," Akil said, almost gleefully. "I am jealous. Dr. Al-Aran tells me you have exceptional musical ability. When I was young, my father would take me exploring in the desert. I would sing by the fire. My voice was so bad that the Fennec foxes would howl. I often wonder what it would be like to be an American rock-and-roll star who plays at various . . . how does one say it? Gigs? Sometime you must give me a lesson."

"Anytime, Omar. I'm not famous yet, but if you're ever in southern California, look me up. I just got out here. Singing in the desert with Fennec foxes sounds pretty cool to me. You take care, okay?"

"Thank you, Mr. Jones. You as well. Nice talking to you."

Akil clicked off.

He exited the Camry and walked another fifty yards. The air carried a sour stink from surrounding cabbage farms. He retrieved an old kitchen table and propped it next to a prairie-like field to the south. He scanned the far perimeter with binoculars and gradually focused on an abandoned car three hundred yards away.

He opened the case and removed a drone frame from its foam cradle. It was the first time he'd ever physically touched one. He noted the unevenness in the seam glue. It was lighter than he expected.

Akil inserted a front and rear set of wings into the body slots and then flattened a single piece of paper onto the table with numbered instructions. Next, he reached for his laptop and removed the battery. Inside and to the left of that compartment was a small hollow space framed by two memory chips. He tilted the laptop sideways until four fully assembled switches dropped out. Akil examined the soldering while the laptop rebooted. He inserted the program control disc and connected the USB cable to the controller. He read the next instruction and chuckled at the terminology. *Verify tension on surface locomotors.* He pinched the drone's legs together and then pulled them apart. Satisfied, he opened a Radio Shack bag and spilled out a handful of 555 timer integrated circuit chips. He opened his wallet and unfolded a hand-drawn schematic, written in pencil and labeled: *computer memory board layout.* Of all the times that airport security screeners had removed the laptop battery, they had never questioned the excess chips.

The 555 timer was simple yet elegant. It had one backup relay to guard against premature ignition. When fully assembled, the device consisted of ten watch batteries taped and wired in series, two switches, one capacitor, one resistor, one relay, and a three-inch long circuit board. A pocketed nylon harness held the potassium charge. The contraption resembled a pony express mail delivery system, complete with one small saddlebag draped over a giant dragonfly instead of a horse.

Where is the fuel? he wondered. After a few moments, he spotted a separate compartment inside the case and pulled the Velcro flap. He plucked out two plastic cartridges and laid them on the table.

Next, Akil gently lifted one potassium cube from a static-free container in his jacket. He tore off a strip of clear duct tape and wrapped one fuse packet to the cube, leaving two exposed strands of wire dangling from the tiny circuit board. He scrolled a clock timer on the laptop's screen until it reached 00:06:00—six minutes.

He carefully inserted the two wires into the clay-like potassium and packed the entry holes tight. He snapped the fuel and catalyst cartridges into place. The wings immediately responded, and he heard an audible tone indicating the unit was communicating properly with the laptop.

He tossed the drone skyward, where it hovered motionlessly above his head. He clicked the screen's timer button one last time. The seconds began counting down. He clicked the *go* button.

The drone flew off across the open field. It quickly became too small to track visually, so Akil glanced down at his screen, following it through the camera and watching the car looming larger. In less than a minute, the drone had reached its target and gone into a stationary hover, awaiting further commands.

Akil manually maneuvered the drone over the vehicle's hood. Unlike practicing online, operating the physical device itself was difficult. Between the camera's limited field of view and the drone's quick response to commands, Akil found himself overcorrecting, but he reasoned that his skills would increase with practice. Allah would see to it.

Akil looked at his watch and then gently eased the drone through the open windshield, hovering it above the dashboard. He touched the controller again, and the drone's legs clamped firmly around the steering wheel shaft. The shaft's circumference was thinner than that of a commercial aircraft's landing gear strut, but for this test, the placement motion would be the same. The drone predictably rotated sideways, clinging upside-down. Three wings snapped out of their socket joints. The harness with the potassium explosive held firmly.

Akil lifted the binoculars.

A split second later there was a powerful but muffled explosion.

The violent blast blew the car doors off their hinges and tore gaping holes in the trunk and roof. The steering wheel sailed high into the air like some jet-powered Frisbee.

The fourth drone wing fluttered harmlessly to the ground.

MILWAUKEE, WI

WITI FOX 6 News general manager Bud Gillespie sat at his desk, grim faced. His station had placed last in southeastern Wisconsin's April rating sweeps conducted by Nielsen Media Research. That made eight periods in a row.

Neela Griffin poked her head through the doorway.

"You wanted to see me?"

Gillespie pointed to a chair. He removed his glasses and stared at her. It was the same stare a father would give his honor-roll teenage daughter after bailing her out of jail for shoplifting.

"You had quite a trip to Italy, young lady."

"I can explain."

"Fine. You can start by giving me your definition of the word *ethical*." He sat on the edge of his desk. "Ms. Griffin, I'm going to be frank. I like you. We all like you. Your tenacity and reporting skills have stayed above average even with all your personal problems. I, for one, had serious doubts as to whether you could maintain your professionalism through a public divorce and that unfortunate spousal battery mess. But you did, and I'll admit here and now that I was wrong. Additionally, your on-camera demeanor in this market still portrays trust. That's something important to me, your coworkers, and this station."

His wording was a veiled compliment to her physical appearance, but he knew that he had to be careful. He'd recently reassigned another female employee from the anchor desk, and she immediately filed a discrimination suit. Management claimed it was due to poor performance. Everyone else figured it was due to excessive weight gain.

"However, your Ohio State journalism degree does not give you the right to run around Europe posing as a foreign affairs correspondent for a national cable network. We sent you to Rome to investigate a suspected theft ring of Harley-Davidson motorcycle parts. How did you end up at some science award ceremony bringing up Colin Powell and weapons of mass destruction? Correct me if I'm wrong, but you did introduce yourself as someone from Fox Cable? When exactly did you make that career move?"

"I thought that there might have been a big story—"

Gillespie pounded his fist on the desktop. "We're all looking for a big story, but you're not paid to freelance. Now I have to write three apologies. One to this Georgia Tech professor, one to the Pirelli Consortium, and one to our owners, who, by the way, will be ready to chew my head off after seeing our ratings. Neela, I'm not a reporter any longer, and I hate typing."

"It won't happen again. I promise."

"What was the name of that entertainment piece you were developing to identify a mystery person in some pop song? Something about narcissism or vanity?"

"'You're So Vain,'" she said halfheartedly.

"Yes, now there's something newsworthy."

"That's not exactly the kind of story that'll benefit society," she gently protested. "I have a new lead that exposes a security hole at a major airline. A passenger can gain access to a firearm on a commercial aircraft just by having the right form—a form that no one is cross-checking or verifying. Delta has refused to respond or even comment and—"

"Stop," Gillespie said, exasperated. "Will you please tone down the drama and keep a lower profile? So far, none of our competitors have picked up on your little Italian stunt. I hope for your sake it stays that way. We'll wait and see. I'll give you one more chance. I know we talked about weekend anchor, but I've decided to keep you on the tip line and out of trouble. No more special assignments and no more travel. I want you working local and nothing more. It'll help you learn a thing or two about patience."

15

PROFESSOR MICHAEL Robertson unscrewed the cap from a bottle of non-drowsy Dayquil and guzzled a hefty swallow. He flopped into his desk chair and reached for a wad of Kleenex.

His landline phone chirped.

"Welcome back, son," the voice of Dr. Winford Garton III said. "I suppose, now that you're famous, you'll want your own building?"

Don't call me "son." You sold me out. "We're comfortable right where we are," Robertson said, sniffling deeply.

"I heard you weren't feeling well. We were quite concerned."

You don't care a whit about me or my team. "I had a bad case of the flu, and now I think it's just a bad cold. I'm about seventy percent, but thanks for asking. The Association of Unmanned Vehicle Systems International is hosting their annual Symposium in DC next month. They've asked me to be their keynote speaker. They'd like me to debut my drone."

"You mean Georgia Tech's drone," Garton quickly corrected. "Go ahead and do all the speaking you'd like as long as we lock down the second half of this Saudi thing. I'm sure you know that we've finalized a deal with Mr. Al-Assaf. Dr. Al-Aran has made all the arrangements. Good grief . . . all we have to do is let them fiddle

96

with your bugs for a few weeks, and we get a windfall for the university. I repeat, I want you to make sure Faiz has everything he needs to satisfy their requests. Five million dollars is a heckuva down payment, son. After all those hours of dedication—a tangible and fitting reward. You should be proud."

They're not bugs, Robertson wanted to scream. Instead, he said, "I'm not an expert on desert oil reserves, but this Shaybah field is about as hospitable as the planet Mercury. Winds routinely reach fifty miles per hour, dunes stretch one thousand feet high, and the field itself is forty miles long. The drone can't possibly cover such distances with its current signal strength. This whole idea is an unqualified disast—"

"Nonsense," Garton interrupted, unconcerned with the technical limitations. "Not another word. Dr. Al-Aran can work through any minor shortcomings. He has everything well in hand."

"I'm sure he does," Robertson said through clenched teeth. "Where is Faiz?"

"Why don't you take a few days off? You've certainly earned it," Garton said. "I'd love to chat, but I have another commitment. And by the way, we mustn't forget NASA. That's my favorite kind of project—fat and federal. Between the Pirelli Award and the Saudis, your bug has managed to bring five and a quarter million dollars into our coffers, not to mention keeping Tech's good name in the spotlight. I know it, and so does the board. That brings solid credibility. If this Saudi venture pans out, perhaps our next research center might bear your name. Look me up next week. We'll do lunch. That is, if you can stand lowly American food again. I hear the Italians really know their cuisine."

Garton clicked off.

Robertson Research Center. He envisioned the exterior lettering.

When his digestive system got back to normal, he would eat a cheeseburger for lunch. A large American cheeseburger with fries.

There was a knock on Robertson's office door.

"Have a seat, Mr. Zibinski," Robertson said, waking up his desktop computer and clicking the Skype icon.

Kevin Jones's face appeared.

"Morning, professor. Welcome home."

"You settled out there?" Robertson's voice was curt.

"Sort of. San Diego's a great music town. I signed up to play guitar at an open mic session at Seaport Village next to the harbor. I'm really nervous."

"That's awesome, Kev," Zee spoke up. "Wish I could be there to cheer you on."

Robertson blew his nose in a loud honk, and the room turned awkwardly silent.

"I know you're upset, Professor," Jones finally spoke. "I swear we wanted to call and keep you informed, but Dr. Al-Aran said he'd take care of everything. He just took control. What were we supposed to do?"

"Whoa, why would I be upset?" Robertson said sarcastically. "Someone literally overtakes my project without my knowledge or permission, and you two simply let it happen? But wait . . . maybe I'm overreacting. After all, I only invented the thing."

"Hey, Zee?" Jones's screen face was distorted. "Didn't Al-Aran say he'd keep everyone in the loop, especially about the hotel demo?"

Robertson raised one eyebrow. "What hotel demo?"

"The Swissôtel," Zee said. "In Buckhead. I guess one of the Saudi people leased a meeting room for some sort of demonstration. Meal service, private waiters. I think his name was Ibrahim-something. He and Dr. Al-Aran were even talking about making a video."

"Faiz took my drones off campus and is flying them in a hotel?" Robertson checked his watch. "When?"

The Skype video connection failed, leaving Jones's face frozen on the screen.

"Um, Dr. Al-Aran said he didn't need us," Jones said. "He figured he could handle everything himself."

"People have gone to jail for this kind of thing," Robertson seethed.

He recalled a Tennessee professor working on plasma actuators for Air Force drones. The US government considered the actuators to be controlled technical data, and thus sharing it with foreign nationals even inside the United States was prohibited. The professor was convicted on eighteen counts, including charges that he provided controlled defense technology and defense services to University of

Tennessee graduate students who were nationals of the People's Republic of China and the Republic of Iran.

"When does it start?"

"I'm not sure," Zee admitted. "I think they changed the schedule."

Robertson's face flooded red. He dialed his phone. "Buckhead, Georgia . . . the Swissôtel."

Administrative Services Supervisor Sharon Tillman cracked the office door. "Excuse me, Professor Robertson. Sorry to interrupt, but there's a Mr. O'Neill from NASA on hold. He says it's urgent."

Robertson slammed the phone onto its cradle. "Sharon, would you find Professor Al-Aran for me? I don't care where he is or what he's doing."

"I'm sorry, but Dr. Al-Aran is out of the office on vacation. He's on a cruise for the next three weeks."

Robertson sat, stunned. *This can't be happening.*

"Do you want to speak to Mr. O'Neill, or should I take a message?"

"Huh? No, it's fine." Robertson touched the speakerphone. "Stuart?"

"Michael, there's no easy way to say this, so I'll get right to the point. We're trying to make numbers work, but our whole program is under severe scrutiny. Everyone is running for cover. The Mars mission is still alive but with certain reductions. I'm afraid your project has been impacted. We're releasing the official announcement shortly. I wanted you to know before I called Garton. I'm sorry."

Robertson's face turned ashen. He sat motionless, staring across the room at the set of red-and-silver, Coca-Cola Entomopter wings pinned inside a glass display case.

"Impacted how?"

"The sub-project has been canceled. Funds have already been reallocated to the moon project. Looks like that's a go. You need to put all your schedules and any other work in progress on hold indefinitely."

"What about future planning? Couldn't we at least continue to test the—"

"Don't you understand what I'm telling you? We just don't have the funding for your drone. I wanted to tell you myself."

"The moon project is the dumbest idea I've heard this year. We've already *been* to the flipping moon."

"Michael, I don't know what else to say. I'm sorry."

"Stu, we've known each other for years. We roomed together in college. I named my kid after you. Help me out here."

"I'm sorry."

Robertson leaned into the speaker. "You're sorry? Tell that to the students on my research team who turned down other highly sought-after appointments to meet *your* time frames. Tell that to benefactors who donated the funding just to satisfy *your* needs. Tell that to the Pirelli Foundation, who just became the world's biggest fools for giving a golden plaque to something that's already been canceled. Exactly where would you like me to stick that?" Robertson heard a dial tone. "Hello? Stuart?"

16

"I JUST think it's best," Tom Ross said quietly into his phone.

"You think?" Marcia's voice screeched. "Let me tell you what I think: I think you're a failure, and a miserable one at that. A failure to me as a partner, and a failure to yourself as a human being. You haven't got the faintest idea of how to treat a lady, to buy her things and take her places and hold her on a pedestal. That's what a real man would do. You haven't got the guts. The only thing you're good at is whimpering on and on about losing your precious Amy. She's gone, so get over it. Nothing you do will ever bring—"

Ross clicked off and slammed his phone on the table.

The waitress appeared with a coconut shrimp appetizer.

"Are you okay, mister?"

"Bring me some scotch, please," Ross said, opening a bag of pumpkin seeds. "Good stuff. I saw a bottle of seventeen-year Balvenie Doublewood. Lots of ice."

"Little family dispute, eh?" A man's voice spoke through the wooden slats in the next booth. "I couldn't help overhearing."

Ross was about to politely tell the eavesdropper to mind his own business, but he recognized something about him.

101

"This is really embarrassing. I'm sorry you had to hear that."

"We all go through it, pal," the man said, standing up and boldly taking a seat at Ross's table. He extended his hand. "I'm Jack Riley."

"Tom Ross. I was at your presentation on the fourth. I really enjoyed it."

"Most people do." Riley opened his cell phone. "I thought I recognized you. NTSB, right? I hope you don't mind. I like to have a broad range of contacts."

They exchanged data.

"Nancy Petri was wrong," Ross said.

"I'm used to it." Riley smiled, eyeing the appetizer. "Politicians give me a headache. Do you mind?"

"Help yourself."

Riley dragged a shrimp through the plum sauce. "What's with the nuts?"

"Pumpkin seeds." Ross flicked one across the table. "I got hooked as a kid."

Riley frowned at the morsel, then touched it to his tongue. He made a pained face and placed it on a napkin.

"A little phone argument?" Riley ventured. "Your wife?"

"Ex-wife. It's complicated," Ross said. The waitress brought a fresh cocktail. He took a hefty swallow. "So, did you fly for the Air Force?"

"Nah, I'm not a pilot. I was in charge of Gulf War technical teams that trekked out into the desert and set up satellite receivers. We were based out of Langley. We made sure everybody could sync up with whiz-vee."

Ross paused thoughtfully. "That's a military radio communication system."

"Wideband Secure Voice is *the* avionics radio communication system. ARC-164 is a UHF frequency hopper that's totally uncrackable. Every aircraft we fly has it. We tried to upgrade once, but it was too perfect. It's the same system the president uses."

"Hmph. Sounds impressive."

"Impressive and top-secret. After the war, several units mysteriously appeared inside some Saudi F-15s accidentally installed by some of our own incompetent contractors. I irritated the chain of command and probably ruffled the wrong feathers. I never was very tactful with bureaucracy. After that, I figured my chances at reaching major were nil, so I got out."

"And now you've got your own bureaucracy at Homeland Security."

"Not exactly." Riley chuckled. "One secretary and two assistants."

"You're joking."

"Apparently you weren't listening very well during my presentation. I evaluate threats and point the appropriate federal enforcement agencies in the right direction. I'm the guy who makes sure that everyone and everything gets plugged in. Other than traveling my butt off day and night, it's a great job. I get to work alone and still carry a pretty big stick."

"Besides attacking football stadiums and theme parks, what else do you think al-Qaeda might do? Be honest."

"You don't want to know," Riley said. "Trust me."

"I do," Ross said adamantly. "Tell me the truth."

"With all respect to Jack Nicholson, you can't handle the truth."

"Try me."

Riley shrugged. "They'll make a statement. A very poignant statement."

"Like what?"

"Well, Mr. NTSB . . ." Riley swallowed his third shrimp and washed it down with some water. "I'm torn. I used to believe that terrorists were dead-set on getting educated on everything from chemical to nuclear warfare. Now I'm not so sure. After 9/11, we've ramped up our defenses and our security coordination to the point of mega-overkill. They're the best in the world. I'm starting to think that terror groups know they'll never match our capabilities and will simply fall back on what they do best: plain old-fashioned, senseless murder. The kind that makes a huge statement and simply can't be stopped. Here's a good one. Ever been to Arlington National Cemetery to watch the changing of the guard at the Tomb of the Unknowns?"

"Sure, many times."

"Ever been searched on the way in?"

"No."

"Me either," Riley said. "On the hour, every hour, a sergeant brings a replacement guard out to relieve the active guard. At one point during that solemn ceremony, all three are standing together, front and center. If I wanted to make a statement, I'd step over the flimsy rope line, walk right up, and detonate myself. What a despicable yet effortless way to completely disgrace the entire US military, huh? Or how about ordering my US sleeper cells to pick random but prominent members of congress? Shadow them day in and day out. Memorize their routines and schedules. Learn their neighborhoods, homes, and patterns. Then, on a given date at a given hour, execute them and their families in a horribly brutal way. Chop their heads off and send the video everywhere."

Ross was visibly taken aback. "You're really sick. I'm sorry I asked."

"Get a grip," Riley snapped. "And get ready, because that's exactly how terrorists operate. Do you think we're dealing with a bunch of punks in some make-believe game, or that our own homeland is some-how immune? Israel has been dealing with these monsters for years. A woman will board a bus or walk into a restaurant in downtown Tel Aviv and blow herself up along with everyone else. Or worse, she'll send in her kid. Those two numb-nuts in Boston did horrific damage to other human beings, but they were rank, unsanctioned amateurs. Sure, they got lucky with timing, but that's about it. They were untrained loners pretending to be jihadists. The next really coordinated statement will be so public and so shocking that it will be incomprehensible to every civilized human being. The United States is a huge hunting ground, and terrorists are cold-blooded predators, period. They prey on the weak and innocent. Life, to them, means nothing. They thrive on making their enemies as angry as possible solely for a reaction. They'd like nothing more than to whip us into a state of murderous revenge. It's all about keeping the cycle of fear and violence alive."

"Do you think something like Komodo could really happen?"

"Do you know any radical Islamic jihadists?" Riley volleyed back. Ross shook his head. "How about enemy combatants?"

"I know who they are. Soldiers who fight against us, right?"

"Captured soldiers," Riley clarified. "Like those interned at Guan-tanamo Bay. The worst sit in their cages down there and do three things: eat, sleep, and chant. Day after day, every waking minute of every hour. Know what they chant? Verses from the Qur'an. Every word in every Surah . . . er, chapter—and then it starts over. They're like broken records. Or worse yet, machines. Evil machines. Some live in a state of permanent psychosis—real Hannibal Lectors. The guards can't take their eyes off them for a second because they'll do anything to kill Americans. Most attended Wahhabi indoctrination schools, the kind where kids sit cross-legged all day long, rocking back and forth, reciting over and over until their minds are so fixated that they literally become religious robots. And you can bet they're not memorizing anything about 'love thy neighbor.' Wahhabi Islamic ideology teaches two fundamental principles: Israel has no right to exist, and America has no morals or right to rule and is therefore the central enemy of Islam. Fortunately for us, those robots aren't that smart. I mean, they don't have the ability to strategically plan attacks. They're more suited to ground work."

"You mean suicide bombings?"

"Especially suicide bombings. Granted, they're still completely brainwashed, but I'd rather deal with them than the super-terrorists that are coming."

"Super-terrorists?"

"Uh-huh. The next generation of terrorists will be born and raised in the West and will give their lives over to the dark side of Islamic jihad. They'll look and act just like you and me. They'll be hip and have the ability to drift in and out of their murderous mind-set at will. The super-terrorist will do everything possible to destabilize Western political, economic, and social conditions at any cost. So far, we've been pretty lucky in keeping things off our shores. Sure, we've had a few bumps, but on the whole, we've been pretty safe. When most Americans think of terror organizations, who comes to mind? Al-Qaeda, right? Maybe Hamas and Islamic Jihad? And now the ISIS jihadist army in this new Islamic state. But there's someone else who's figured things out, and they've done enough recon here to single out and attack public places, news groups, sporting events, government buildings, and military installations."

"That's great," Ross said. "Now that you've got me scared to death again, who is it?"

"Four letters, pal," Riley sneered. "I-R-A-N. The young members of Hezbollah and the Quds forces have been quietly spreading out into the West and assimilating into everyday life. And they've got one thing on their minds: dying with honor, either in open battle or by suicide. There's one verse in the Qur'an that they absolutely cherish. It's Al-Anfal 60: 'Prepare with all your armaments and force in your possession to confront the enemy so that your enemies and enemies of Allah will become fearful.' "

"Hold on," Ross said, raising his hand. "If they're so bad, then why didn't you mention them in your Komodo presentation?"

"You want me to start a nationwide panic? Besides, no one would believe three thousand targets. I have a hard enough time convincing folks that twenty-five theme parks are at risk."

"Three thousand targets?" Ross said incredulously. "I'm not sure I believe it."

"Believe it," Riley said. "The Iranians are the ones who first started in-flight probing of our commercial planes. They provided the intel to those kids involved in the attacks in London—the ten aircraft that were targeted for mid-air destruction. I can't tell you any more, but trust me; they're here, they're real, and they continue to operate today. They legally board US planes, cause some type of commotion, and then gauge procedural reaction and response. That's information that they plan to use against us in some form of terrorist attack. If they get real lucky, they'll expose an air marshal or some other law enforcement officer, and all we can do is give them a piddly wrist slap. The airlines are stuck too—no excessive questioning or racial profiling allowed. In fact, if they tried, the FAA would dole out fines. Hefty ones. The London carry-on bombers were either Iranian terrorists or trained by them."

"Fines?" Ross mumbled around an ice cube. "What idiot made that rule?"

"The Secretary of Transportation. Political correctness gone crazy. No airline can question or detain more than one person of Middle-Eastern descent at a time."

"So you're telling me that these Iranian super-terrorists can plot God-knows-what evil, and we can't do anything about it?"

"And the sad part is, we know for certain that they're testing US aircraft security to sneak explosives on board, assemble a device, and detonate it in-flight. The components by themselves are harmless and perfectly legitimate passing through screening systems. Israel would lock those guys up in a heartbeat, and we worry about violating their rights. Isn't the US Constitution great?"

"I'll be so glad when we finally win this war on terror," Ross said, sighing.

"Win the war on terror," Riley frowned, shaking his head. "The five dumbest words in the world. Why? Because it's impossible. It can't be done. Now, don't get me wrong. I'm one heck of a patriot, but that's the biggest line of political tripe ever. There is no such thing, yet everyone from the president on down speaks it. We're *not ever* going to win the war on terror. That's like saying we need to win the war on poverty or drugs or sickness. It'll take every ounce of our collective will and energy just to survive and control it. The war on terror is really an endless battle of attrition on a world stage fought against an endless army of pop-up killers who hate us and want us dead, period. And that hate just keeps rolling and gaining strength every day. No prisoners, no bargaining, and no peace. Dead."

"That's what I don't get," Ross said. "Where does it all come from?"

"The hate? Good question. Sometimes even I get confused. But beyond all the socio-political and territorial issues, Americans do stupid things." Ross bristled at that. "Easy, Sparky. I'll rephrase it. *Some* Americans do stupid things. Two examples: music and zombies. Music from the guards at Guantanamo is a rather unique way of gaining information."

"Music?"

Riley smiled. "You'd be surprised how effective a little rap music at prayer time can be. Especially the real raunchy stuff, like Ludacris or Lil' Kim. It literally drives the detainees nuts. Some have negotiated information for silence. Even the US military plays its games. But the highest level of hate is online. God only knows how they stay active or how the operators stay in one piece, but there are websites that have done more to inflame Muslims throughout the world than anything I can think of. They're probably not on par with occupying Saudi Arabia, invading Iraq and Afghanistan, or supporting Israel, but they're close. It's something you'll never hear about in the media."

Ross leaned forward. "Website atrocities?"

"Look, I may be a lowly government employee, but I have a basic understanding of what's happening in the current geopolitical world. Westerners in general and Americans in particular are not exactly in good standing with a lot of Muslims right now. I think the term is *infidel*? You do know that Islam strictly forbids anyone to draw or otherwise create, show, or depict a likeness of the Prophet Moham-med, right?"

Ross's mouth was already hanging open, but he managed a nod.

"Good. The reason we, the infidels, deserve a nonrefundable suite in hell is because we've done just that. We conceived ideas, we made videos, we wrote, drew, printed, unveiled, and even chuckled at pho-tographs. In short, we made fun of Islam. Case in point: remember what happened after a Danish newspaper published those eight car-toons? One hundred people were killed in riots in Europe, Syria, Leba-non, and Iran. Fast-forward to now. Muslims are surfing the Internet and watching YouTube videos like everyone else. Mohammed's once forbidden likeness is everywhere, from centuries-old art to comedic satire to utter filth. *Zombietime.com* has a click-and-view section called *Extreme Mohammed*. Check it out if you dare, but be advised. The content is far worse than any Danish cartoon of the Prophet with his turban morphed into a fused bomb. It's really disgusting.

"Once, at a White House press briefing, a news correspondent repeatedly asked US officials about the motivation for Muslims want-ing to harm us. Assassins were targeting Americans for death, and she wanted to know why. The answer is in that website, specifically in the *Email Response from Readers* section. It's really a titanic clash of two cultures. One touts its right to draw, publish, view, and laugh at virtually anything under the auspices of freedom. And the other cul-ture is absolutely outraged at how those rights are used to the point of blood violence. No disrespect intended, but it's the revenge, pure and simple. Why? Because a bunch of fools neither sees nor cares about the potential danger. Islamic jihadists are reigning terror upon humanity because their religion is under verbal and artistic attack. Sounds like reasonable thinking to me, but what do I know? I'm the crazy guy who cries wolf. Take a long, hard look at that site, Mr. NTSB. Infidels celebrate their free speech while Muslim extremists seethe. We must believe that their threats are serious. And a certain percentage will turn those threats into actions."

Ross stared into his drink. "I'm so glad we had this chat. I feel like I could throw up. Either that or move to a remote island . . ." Ross sat motionless, clutching his side.

"Are you all right?" Riley asked.

"Oh man . . . I hate that," Ross finally spoke. "Every once in a while I get a sharp pain, always in the same spot. It comes and goes. I'm fine. Where were we? Oh yeah, a remote island. You mentioned the Florida Keys the other day in your presentation. I heard it's a great vacation getaway. What's down there?"

"I can't tell you."

"What?"

"I'm not going to tell you."

"No terrorists, huh?"

Riley chuckled and shook his head. "Like I said before, a lone suicide bomber would blow up a kindergarten class and think nothing of it. But even that kind of 'damage,' for lack of a better term, is manageable. Sure, people usually die violently, but so does the terrorist. The super-terrorist will orchestrate the destruction of an entire city and then quietly and carefully move on to the next. That's the guy I fear. One time in Norfolk, I escorted four Saudi nationals to dinner. Radio technicians. They got in my car, and I politely asked them to fasten their seat belts. They refused. They said if Allah willed that they died in an accident, so be it."

"How did they get that way?" Ross asked.

"Okay, that's enough," Riley replied, wiping his mouth with his napkin. "Time for a culture lesson. Put that drink down and listen. No one knows how many radical religious killers there are in the United States. And that's including those who are Catholics, Lutherans, Methodists, Baptists, and so on. That's like trying to identify and count the number of people willing to murder. It could be fifty or fifty thousand. No one knows. But just nineteen individuals were responsible for 9/11. Twenty if you count that snake Moussaoui. And they all just happened to be Muslim—followers of the Islamic religion. All Muslims are not jihadists. If 9/11 were committed by radical followers of the Nordic gods Odin and Thor, we wouldn't condemn all blue-eyed, blonde-haired Scandinavians, right? The problem is, some followers of Islam are perfectly willing to use violence to get a point across. And no sane person would condone that. In America, a museum can display a painting of Jesus with his head covered in feces and the worst that'll happen is someone will try and revoke their tax-exempt status. If that were a portrait of Mohammed, I guarantee that the artist would end up with no head, and the museum would be set on fire. Religious fanaticism. You can't reason with it, you can't change it, and you certainly can't eradicate it. All you can do is keep fighting on and on and on. So, in answer to your question about stadiums and theme parks, as long as some radical human beings think we're a threat to Islam, yes, it can happen. And believe me, we're talking all-out war. You and I go about our daily routines following a life goal to some happy, peaceful end. Contrast that to Mr. Super-terrorist's goal—to destroy the enemies of Islam. And in case you're wondering, that's you and me."

"I think anyone who plans or commits violence in the name of religion is just outright insane," Ross said matter-of-factly.

Riley nodded repeatedly and twirled his index finger. "Now finish it."

"Huh?"

"Your testimonial. Finish it."

Ross swirled his drink and after a few moments, his eyes widened, and he blurted the answer like an enthusiastic schoolboy. "Anyone who plans or commits violence in the name of religion is outright insane and should be condemned and then stopped."

"Bravo." Riley smiled, clapping his hands. "It's easy to stand up at a podium and tell the media and the world that you condemn something. Our politicians do it all the time. But condemning something without physical action doesn't mean jack, and our enemies know it."

"So how do you deal with it?" Ross wondered.

"How do you deal with an airline crash involving hundreds of people?" Riley returned. "I can't imagine it, but then we both continue to fly, right? You and I have the ability to turn it on and off. Problem is, I don't believe most people can do that. Americans are simply too nice. We hold feelings high on a pedestal, as though they really mattered to terrorists. Wanna know something? They don't. Congressional rep Petri is a perfect example. Don't get me wrong. She may be a nice person, but sadly, she either can't or won't accept the fact that the world has dangerous people. And there are still way too many Americans who believe *we're* the problem. We need to remember history. Kinder and gentler just ain't gonna cut it in our future. The bottom line is this: if we don't or can't bring war to the terrorists, they'll bring it here."

"So what else do you do when you're not chasing the super-Iranians?" Ross asked.

Riley smiled slyly. "I already told you—the Keys. I have a small place on the water near Marathon."

"Aren't you afraid of hurricanes?"

"Hey, we're not talking about a New Orleans soup bowl. If a category-five storm hits the Florida Keys head-on, the coral and sand are still there. You rebuild. It's the chance you take to occasionally visit paradise and drive a thirty-two-foot Boston Whaler 305 Conquest with twin 225 hp Mercury OptiMax outboards. It's my one and only toy. Whenever I get the chance, I head down there and chase my grouper, Shaitan."

"Oh yeah," Riley said, smiling. "That's your fish that looks like a bass."

"Uh-huh. But Shaitan is much more than a fish. I named that ugly guy myself," Riley said proudly. "Satan the Grouper, the baddest of the bad. He's got a bad, ugly head with bad, ugly lips lined with bad, ugly hooks. My hooks. I figure he's at least one hundred pounds."

"One hundred pounds?" Ross asked skeptically.

"Groupers can get huge. The world-record black grouper is 124 pounds. Some Goliath groupers reach eight, even nine hundred pounds. The largest was twelve feet long and weighed fifteen hundred. There's an unofficial report that it ate a diver. Well, every time I hooked Shaitan, he's burned me. He hangs out in a series of underwater caves in a deep channel off Duck Key. Problem is, he never stays in one spot. He keeps moving to and fro on the Earth just like the real Satan. I've made it my life's ambition to catch that clever SOB, and when I do, I'm going to pack him on ice and introduce him to a new dark cave right in my backyard. It's called a Weber grill."

Ross chuckled at that. "So what's the name of your boat? Shaitan-Killer?"

"Not bad, but I named it after my island. Just-Duck-Key. Get it?"

"And where's home up here?"

"My wife, Kissi, and I have seventy-two acres outside of Middleburg, west of Dulles. She has five horses and boards two more right now. Horses are her thing. They don't like me, and the feeling is mutual. I'm too jumpy. They can sense uneasiness in certain people, and I guess I'm one of them."

"Kissi?" Ross chuckled.

"Short for Bhekisisa. She teaches economics and finance at Howard University. It's a long drive in, but we like our privacy. Her family owns a stud farm in South Africa."

"Big money in horses?"

"Don't go there," Riley warned, licking two fingers. "If you want to make a million dollars on horses, then start with two million."

"Any family?" Ross asked.

"Just one very smart daughter in first-year law. She wants to specialize in corporate real estate. You?"

"I live two miles from here, downstairs from, um . . . well, let's call her a difficult tenant."

The conversation abruptly stopped. Riley glanced at his watch. "I know you NTSB folks can't spend a nickel on meals, so why don't you let me pay for this?"

"No way. I appreciated the company. Even though you did give me indigestion."

Riley slid out of the booth and peeled off a few bills. "My boss may not let me take extended vacations, but he sure doesn't skimp on much else, especially when terror's involved. Don't tell anybody, but I can use his plane whenever I want. Someday you and I might have to conduct some official business in southern Florida. It's a G-1159 and plenty fast. Seats eleven. Two private passengers round-trip would cost twenty-five grand."

Ross recalled a recent media report about Homeland Security

lavishly overspending on employees at a local DC hotel. He wanted to mention that the NTSB also leased a private aircraft whenever rapid transport was required, but he let it go. It was a modest Learjet 25 that seated half as many people and cost one-third less to operate.

"Maybe I'll see you again sometime."

"If there's ever an aviation incident on your watch, you can count on it," Riley promised. "Fair warning—I can be a real pain in the neck."

"I'll try to remember that."

Riley nodded curtly. "Do me a favor and ease up on the salty white seeds. Next time you're online, check out 'diverticulitis' on *WebMD*. You got an umbrella?"

"Why? Is it raining?"

"Not yet." Riley patted Ross's shoulder. "But it sounds like your 'difficult tenant' is brewing one heckuva storm at your house tonight. Peace."

17

MILWAUKEE, WI
MONDAY, MAY 18
1:00 A.M.

NEELA GRIFFIN finished her Pilates-like stretching exercises and fell into bed. She reached for her phone and dialed her station's tip line. There was one recorded message from Sunday, May 17, at 9:00 p.m.

"Hello. My name is Dave from Mequon. There's a Pakistani guy who lives in a twenty-thousand-square-foot house on Pioneer Road. He lets his teenage son run around the property with an AK-47 assault rifle. They just spent $285,000 on landscaping, and the kid blew every one of the saplings in half. I've seen him shoot from the road. I heard that they've even got grenade launchers. You should check it out. If there's any kind of terrorist reward money, you can reach me at—"

She deleted the message and hung up.

—

AMERICAN LEGION POST 154

THE PARTYERS downstairs were still going strong. Akil's eyes watered from the tobacco smoke that had somehow, along with the blaring speaker music, drifted upstairs and into his room. He was nervous. Far too many critical factors were in play. Factors that, should

114

even one go wrong, offered little hope of success for his mission. He flopped onto his sofa and pressed the moisture from his eyes. *What if the Delta aircraft never comes to a complete stop at the departure point?* At least, in that case, the mission could be temporarily aborted. He could retrieve the drone and choose another plane. *What if the communication signal between the drone and the laptop is interrupted or lost?* That would be complete disaster. He'd have to pack up and leave the area immediately. The drone would fly aimlessly until falling, probably onto an open runway. Authorities would immediately discover it was carrying a timed explosive and then issue a terror warning to airports across the country. That would bring unbearable defeat to al-Qaeda and a resounding victory to the infidels—a crushing scenario.

Akil bolted upright at the knock on his door.

"Hey, Sean Penn Jr. It's Chief. Open up. One of the girls made you a plate of food—a fat ham sandwich. We're playing poker. We already got five. We need one more. You in?"

"I need to rest," Akil answered through a fake yawn. "I think I'm getting the flu. Just leave it by the door."

"You're no fun," Watts slurred, setting the plate down. "I'll check on you in the morning. G'night, Sean. Sleep tight, you little funky monkey."

Akil crept to the kitchen and tuned the radio to 88.5 FM, a rebroadcast of Mitchell Airport's tower frequency. He waited another minute before opening the door. He collected the sandwich plate and set it in the refrigerator. He double-checked the seal on a Ziploc bag isolated on a lower shelf, which imprisoned the bottle of potassium cyanide. He slid out a plastic tray. His watch said 2:00 a.m. *Good timing*, he thought. The potassium chlorate explosive needed three hours to reach room temperature.

—

MITCHELL INTERNATIONAL AIRPORT
5:20 A.M.

IT WAS ten minutes before general boarding.

Delta Airlines Captain Joseph Falk hurried down the passenger boarding ramp with a six large coffee cups. One cup was special. The

Starbucks ladies made a special blend of rich, dark cocoa for Falk and marked it with a distinctive red *X*. The early flight crews always flipped coins for breakfast. This was his third loss in a row.

A seasoned captain with 22,000 hours, Falk had flown since he was sixteen and had earned his commercial certification piloting trans-Atlantic cargo to Africa. Once, over the coast of Namibia, he drifted so low over a plateau that he could count the stripes on a herd of zebra. It was the only time he'd fallen asleep flying an aircraft.

The morning flight to Atlanta was routine. Still, Falk preferred westbound routes, and Denver, in particular, due to its pilot-friendly layout. No matter where a plane set down, it could reach a terminal without having to cross another inbound runway. Eastbound flights were the worst, especially Boston's Logan or New York's dreaded LaGuardia with its complex routing points, crowded skies, and temperamental controllers. Mitchell International was just the opposite. It was a quiet, well-run airport that was rarely congested, and the FAA used it to break in rookies. That meant by-the-book procedures and maddening distance spacing between approaches. It was a common joke among pilots that on a clear day, one could see training wheels at the base of Mitchell's tower.

First officer Tim Haas had never flown with Falk before and was eager to make a good impression. He reached for a clipboard that held one of three preflight checklists. He craned his neck briefly and noticed that the lead flight attendant had closed the cockpit door, a signal that the cabin was secure.

"So you're the one," Haas said.

"The one what?" Falk asked suspiciously.

"The pilot with the antique lunch pail. The other flight crews say it's a good-luck symbol. Gosh, I loved those old flicks, especially *Raiders of the Lost Ark*. Do you mind if I hold it?"

"A vintage Indiana Jones lunch box is hardly antique," Falk answered. "Sorry. You can look but not touch."

"Whatever you say, Indy. Do you wear a leather jacket and carry a whip too?"

"Only for unruly passengers." Falk laughed, setting the lunch box aside. "Okay, let's see if this old gal can still fly."

Boeing's MD-90 twinjet referred to a series of models certified by the FAA in 1990. Nearly obsolete, the MD-90 was best known for a quiet fuel efficiency that produced some of the lowest operating costs in the aviation industry. Only seventy-seven remained in US service, sixty-five of those with Delta. The Pratt and Whitney engines were fuselage-mounted.

"Where are we?" Falk asked.

"Before-start checklist. Hydraulic pumps on, fuel on."

"What's the volume?"

"Twelve thousand pounds. Navigation lights and rotating beacon are on. The maintenance log is on the aircraft." Haas scanned a dispatch release. "We are, in fact, flying to Hartsfield-Jackson. Oxygen system is set and checked. Pressure is set for elevation. The flight management computer is set and checked. Parking brake and pressure, checked. Rudder and trim set to take-off settings. Seat belt sign is on. We're all filled up, and the doors are closed. Before-start checklist is complete, Captain."

Falk spoke into his microphone. "Ground crew, how about a push?"

"Ready for push, sir," a tug operator's voice responded from outside on the tarmac. "Release your brakes."

"Delta 771 at gate D47 requesting clearance for pushback."

"DL771, you are cleared for pushback at D47," a ground controller's voice answered. "Advise ready for taxi."

Haas initiated the engine start-up sequence.

The tug pushed the aircraft back from the gate.

"Delta 771 requesting clearance for taxi," Falk stated.

"DL771, you are cleared for taxi on Bravo-Gulf-Echo. Proceed to runway 19R and hold for departure."

MILWAUKEE, WI
MONDAY, MAY 18
5:30 A.M.

THE POKER game at the American Legion had ended.

Chief Watts escorted the players to the parking lot. He turned back for the building and noticed a silhouette upstairs in an open window.

"I see you up there, you little monkey," he called to Akil. "I thought you were sick. What're you doing with those binoculars?"

"I can't sleep," Akil said. "Is everyone gone?"

"Yeah. With all my money. The only thing they left was a mess."

"Do you need any help?" Akil offered. "I could give you a hand."

"Heck, yes. And bring that sandwich if you didn't eat it. I'm starved."

Akil flew into his kitchen and pulled on a pair of nitrile gloves. He opened the refrigerator and gently removed the cyanide. He held a deep breath and delicately squeezed a full eyedropper over the ham. He carefully reset the bread and covered the now-lethal snack with a paper towel, exhaling down the stairs on his way to the bar.

Akil returned to his apartment and lifted the drone case onto his sofa. He removed the yellow frame and inserted a set of wings and legs. He reached for one timer assembly and tightly wrapped four windings of duct tape around the drone's body. A second layer of tape held the pouched circuit harness and two explosive potassium cubes, a total of three hundred grams, an amount capable of blasting a hole in a metal plate twice the thickness of the aircraft's skin. He pressed the sets of exposed wires into the cubes and then wound more tape across the entire assembly. It held together firmly. He removed the tiny cap from the front of the camera lens. He touched a toggle on the controller and viewed the laptop screen. The picture was clearly focused. Next, he glanced at his watch and set the laptop clock timer at 00:09:00. Finally, he snapped in the fuel and catalyst packets.

He tossed the drone into the morning sky and watched it flutter across East Layton Avenue and onto airport property, south across the public observation lot, and over a steel fence monitored by two security cameras. Both were angled down at the gate crossing.

Flight 771 was stopped at the end of the taxiway.

The drone approached the aircraft from the rear. Akil knew that the nose landing gear folded forward, so he had to maneuver the length of the fuselage to embrace the gear head-on. This he accomplished with relative ease.

—

CAPTAIN FALK spoke into his mouthpiece. "Delta 771 holding short of 19R. I still need a minute or so. Is it all right if we wait?"

"Roger, DL771. Hold short of 19R."

Falk turned on the cabin speakers. "Gooood morning, ladies and gentlemen. On behalf of the flight crew, this is your captain welcoming you to Delta Flight 771 with service to Atlanta. We are filled up today, and our flying time should be approximately one hour and fifty-five minutes. Atlanta has clear skies and a temperature of sixty degrees. We expect a smooth ride. Once again, thank you for flying Delta and welcome aboard. Flight attendants, prepare for departure."

—

AKIL EASED the drone forward, simultaneously pressing a button on the controller. The drone's legs clamped securely around the jet's front gear shock strut one foot above the wheels.

Akil activated a cell phone, dialed a number, spoke a brief sentence, and then turned the cell phone off.

—

5:59 A.M.

FALK TUCKED his clipboard away.

"Delta 771 ready for departure."

"DL771, you are cleared for takeoff on runway 19R. Climb to five thousand and turn left to one-seven-zero. Winds are calm."

The jet reached 165 knots and lifted into the air.

The landing gear folded neatly inside.

Fifty-five seconds later, the timer on the laptop screen reached 00:00:00.

19

FIFTEEN AND a half volts sparked into the potassium chlorate, and the explosive energy pushed a blast wave out at four thousand feet per second. The force sheared off the nose gear guide struts and retractable side braces, then tore through the gear bay bulkhead aft, destroying three twenty-eight-volt nickel-cadmium batteries, the main A/C power cable, and all hydraulic control points and tubing. The extreme heat melted every protected wire pack, the bus terminal block, and every connection inside the electrical equipment compartment. The blast also ripped through two $\frac{3}{16}$-inch braided steel cables that ran the length of the plane. The violent downward energy easily blew out both sets of gear bay doors, sending debris spiraling into the external airflow. The pieces were instantly sucked up and over the wing and into the left engine. The debris ripped through the engine's brittle titanium fan blades, destroying the vortex in the compressor that fed the combustion chamber and the fuel injectors.

The aircraft jumped as though hitting a speed bump and then gave a massive vibration.

"*Haas!*" Falk exclaimed. "What was that?"

"There's a problem, Captain. We're at one thousand feet! We need to climb," Haas pleaded. "Your control."

"My control," Falk confirmed. "Engine status?"

"Exhaust gas temperature is rising on the left. It's working too hard. We're losing power, huge. Left side."

"Mayday, Mayday, Mayday. This is Delta 771. We have an engine failure."

"Delta 771, what is your number of souls?" a tower voice responded immediately.

"One-five-two."

"What are your intentions?"

"We need to land, *now*."

"Roger, Delta 771. Runway 1L is clear."

"Negative," Falk replied. "I can't do that."

It wasn't that Falk *couldn't* turn back for the runway; he *wouldn't* turn back. He knew that at this altitude and speed, that was guaranteed to be fatal.

"Delta 771, can you make Batten? There is no conflict."

"We're unable. Heading zero-niner-zero. We need something flat. No obstructions. We may end up in Lake Michigan."

Batten International Airport's 6,500-foot concrete runway was short, but it would easily handle the emergency. Still, it was twelve miles away and south. The aircraft had drifted eighty degrees and was now heading due east.

"Seven hundred," Haas said.

"This is the Captain. Brace, brace, brace."

Falk steadied himself. He'd lost an engine just once before while aligned on Denver approach. This was different. Something was wrong. The controls weren't responding. His mind flashed back to his training. *Stay calm. If there's time, wait four seconds between decisions.*

When an aircraft engine failed, the remaining engine forced a turn in the direction of the failure. *Not here*, Falk reasoned. Side-to-side movement shouldn't be dramatic because the MD-90 engines were close together. Still, the aircraft was rolling, and he had to stop it. *Bring the wings level. Use right rudder.* He glanced ahead. Water. He tightened his grip on the control column and depressed the pedal.

Nothing. No response whatsoever.

"There's no rudder," Falk quickly announced.

Recovery logic raced through Falk's brain. *Think. Where was it? Gone. How? From what? Vortex shear? Had it been hit? By what? Was it even there?* His heart sank. He thought to use the ailerons to bring the wings back but remembered that was a classic rookie reaction. That would simply increase drag. Stalling would bring him down on terrain for sure, and on this path, that meant houses. He tried to compose himself a second time. The internal panic was too great.

A cacophony of voice and audio alarms from the Flight Warning Computer for engine fire, low altitude, landing gear, and electronic and hydraulic failure filled the cockpit. Falk frantically searched for a way out. A crushing pain suddenly gripped his chest, radiating outward and down his left arm.

The aircraft continued rolling in some surreal aerobatic maneuver gone wrong. The physics produced a 2-G pull toward the ground, one from the weight of the aircraft, and one from the reverse curve of the now inverted wings. At 180 knots, the plane quickly passed Lake Michigan's shoreline and careened toward the water like some giant twirling lawn dart.

Cocoa sloshed through the cockpit, soaking Falk's head and face. Some entered his mouth. Warm and semi-sweet, it was opposite of the liquid that was rushing toward the windshield. Upside-down, helpless, but no longer afraid, Falk closed his eyes and focused on the pleasant taste. Only half of his mouth worked. He managed one word.

"Starthucks."

—

THE JET'S low velocity and angled descent prevented it from exploding into the usual millions of pieces typical of a high-altitude crash. The tail's vertical stabilizer skimmed the water first, and then the left-side horizontal. The drag of a twenty-foot wide sea anchor split the tail cone's roof in a gaping crack. The plane briefly skipped back into the air high enough for a one-quarter turn. The right wing sliced the water and the enormous stress broke it away. Weakened by the underside blast, the nose section bent backwards like play dough. Moving in what had appeared to be slow motion, the aircraft now flailed wildly like some out-of-control gymnast, one arm extended, off balance and spinning on a great tumbling mat, somehow attempting to regain control via a clumsy maneuver, trying to make the best out of an awkward position. Completely out of its element, the jet did a final awesome cartwheel, coming to rest standing on end like a rocket preparing for liftoff. With both ends of the fuselage torn away, all buoyancy was lost, and the craft started to sink. The right engine, still roaring like some dying beast, finally choked out on massive amounts of water. The last sound waves raced to the shoreline in a deafening roar and were gone.

—

6:32 A.M.

NEELA GRIFFIN was half-asleep sitting up, a pen in one hand, a cordless mouse in the other. Papers were strewn everywhere. Each time her hand moved, the laptop's screen saver retreated into its secret hideaway and a Microsoft Word document appeared.

You're So Vain
Alternate Title: Who are you, Mr. Vain?
By: Neela Griffin

Pointer #1: "Son of a gun"
The whispering introduction of "You're So Vain" was a tribute to Joey Bishop, your close friend, fellow gang member, and opening act. Joey had this trademark phrase sewn onto his bathrobe.

Pointer #2: Your name has an "e" in it
And also an "a" and "r." These are Carly Simon's only public hints. She revealed your first, middle, and last name to just one person, NBC executive Dick Ebersol. He paid $50,000 at a charity function in August 2003. He signed a confidentiality agreement never to tell.

Pointer #3: "Your hat strategically dipped below one eye"
Your classic look. You loved your short-brimmed fedoras and wore them everywhere. Like your song lyrics, you and your hats went together like love and marriage. Or perhaps a

horse and carriage. "This I tell ya, brother, you can't have one without the other."

Pointer #4: "Your scarf, it was apricot"
So was your world-class Lamborghini Muira. Your favorite color was arancio (Italian orange). You had an excellent eye for those tones in your collection of French impressionist paintings.

Pointer #5: "You had one eye in the mirror as you watched yourself gavotte"
Gavotte—a lively French dance. You started your career as a fifteen-year-old singer/dancer. You learned to "swing" with the best.

Pointer #6: "And all the girls dreamed that they'd be your partner"
Perhaps your most (in)famous attribute. Crooning to throngs of adoring teenagers. Embarking on your solo career, you were once welcomed by five thousand swooning and screaming teenage girls at New York's Paramount Theater, shattering the previous attendance record.

Pointer #7: "You had me several years ago when I was still quite naïve"
A collective lament for all those immature, adolescent, and inexperienced virgins that you had "under your skin."

Pointer #8: "You said that we made such a pretty pair, and that you would never leave"
When you were young, you plastered walls during the day and sang at Irish political rallies and Democratic Party meetings at night. You jilted and betrayed many people by your shocking political shift from left-wing liberal Democrat to staunch conservative Republican.

Pointer #9: "Well, I hear you went up to Saratoga, and your horse naturally won"
Gambling was in your vain veins. You were appointed director of the Berkshire Downs Racetrack in Massachusetts

and regularly performed at Saratoga. You were forever
indebted to Las Vegas for resurrecting your failing career.

**Pointer #10 You flew your Learjet up to Nova Scotia to see
the total eclipse of the sun**

It was actually *over* Nova Scotia—twice. You named your
jet after your daughter Christina, and it was really a Grumman
Gulfstream equipped with a bed and bar. In the summer of
1972, you left America in a political huff and flew round trip
across the North Atlantic for England. The flight path followed the precise track of the famous July 10 solar eclipse.

**Pointer #11: "You're with some underworld spy or the wife
of a close friend"**

The FBI developed thousands of pages of testimony on,
from, and about you. You chummed with mobsters Lucky
Luciano, Sam Giancana, and Carlo Gambino. You even
shared women with your personal friend, President John F.
Kennedy.

Griffin's phone startled her. Early morning calls were always omi-
nous and usually involved family.

"Neela, it's Marty. There's been a crash at Mitchell. A passenger jet."

"Oh no," she said, putting her hand on her chest. "Bad? Which
airline?"

"We're not sure. We're hearing either American or Delta. Gillespie
just called and said he wants you there ASAP. They've shut down the
airport and . . . hang on. Someone's on the other line."

She closed her laptop and flew into the bathroom.

"Neela, that was Terry," Marty's voice returned. "It's Delta, and it's
bad. It went into the lake right over Grant Park. He's on his way and
said you should take Lake Shore Boulevard to 5th Avenue. He'll meet
you at that yacht club across from the water filtration plant. Don't
forget your phone. He'll call you."

"Thanks," she sighed but she didn't mean it. *Thanks for what?
Turning the rest of my day into one filled with horrific sorrow?* She'd
covered just one plane crash before—a small, single-engine type. A
pilot had taken his neighbor's kids for a ride in his Cessna. At three

thousand feet, the propeller shaft literally disintegrated, sending the blade twirling through the air. Oil covered the windshield. Luckily, he had enough skill to safely land in a hayfield, but that wasn't where his good fortune came from—it was the fact that the whole propeller had spun off. Otherwise, steering would have become aerodynamically impossible.

Griffin clicked the TV remote. There was breaking news of a Metra train derailment in Chicago.

20

EIGHT HUNDRED miles away, Tom Ross stepped out of the shower. He dried himself and turned on the TV. The screen showed Chicago emergency personnel. He managed to catch the end of the scrolling text that said something about a five-car, two-engine commuter train on fire with 125 injured. *What a way to start Monday rush hour*, he thought. Thankfully, no one had been killed.

His cordless phone chirped. He sat on the edge of the bed and picked up.

"Tom, this is John DeLane. How are you this morning?"

"Fine," Ross answered suspiciously. He knew immediately that something was up. He'd bet money it was a special assignment and that DeLane needed a volunteer. Dotted-line projects never flowed through the management chain. It made it virtually impossible for the victim to say no. In this case, the requestor was the department's director himself.

"Tom, are you aware that a major incident just happened in Central?"

"Uh-huh. It's all over the news."

"Good. I'd like you to handle it. Nothing against Chief Bowling, but his plate is full. And, frankly, you have the experience with crashes like this. I need someone with a good profile. Get your team on board and get out there, okay?"

128

Ross figured DeLane meant Central Chicago. Assuming there was no tampering with the rails themselves, the first point of concentration should be on area crossing switches and Chicago satellite photos. *But why is he considering this a major incident?* Ross wondered. He figured senior NTSB managers were so out of touch with the operational team members and skill sets that they often pulled in the wrong people. DeLane had to be stopped tactfully.

"Since there are no fatalities, I think Joe Scott over in Railroads should log in on this one."

DeLane paused. "What do you mean?"

"The train derailment. I'll be glad to speak to Joe about protocol and handling national media."

"Mr. Ross, we have a downed passenger plane. Delta Airlines in Milwaukee, Wisconsin. The Learjet is standing by at Dulles. I suggest you get cracking." *Click.*

Ross tore open a bag of pumpkin seeds and filled his mouth. His cell phone chirped. The ID said "Unknown Caller." There was a muffled hum in the background.

"Hello?"

"This is Jack Riley. Are you eating that salt again?"

Ross shifted the mouthful. "Sorry about that. What's up?"

"You tell me. I assume you know that a plane went down, so advise me. Who's in charge? The NTSB has a Central Region Chief, right?"

"Normally, yes."

"Who is it?"

"Me."

Riley digested that. "I need answers."

Ross put his phone on speaker and pulled on his socks. "What are the questions?"

"I need to brief Secretary Bridge ten minutes from now. Sorry, but that's his personal rule. He's real funny about airplane crashes. He'll want to know the number of casualties, how it happened, and if there's any possible terrorism connection."

"Jack, that's impossible," Ross said, the salty juice burning his throat as he swallowed. "That's the FBI. As far as cause, there's no way to tell anything at this point—"

"Mr. NTSB, I'm telling you that I need answers, and I need them now. If you don't know, just say so. As a precautionary measure, the FBI is already setting up HQ at a local hotel. I just left Cincinnati. I'll be on the ground in Milwaukee in . . . fifteen minutes. My job is to gather information from their case agent and the NTSB's investigator-in-charge. You just told me that's you. Three answers, please."

"I don't know, I don't know, and I don't know."

The line went silent. "When will you?"

Ross glanced at the time. "My team should be in Milwaukee in two hours and ten minutes. I'll call you. What hotel?"

"We're on approach into Mitchell, and I'm losing you. North end of the airport. It's the Courtyard Marriott."

The engine noise crackled out. The connection went dead.

Ross pulled a shirt over his head. *Riley, you are a pain in the neck.*

21

SOUTH MILWAUKEE, WI

THE WEATHER was unseasonably cool. Intermittent sun punched through heavy but fast-moving clouds. Light rain dusted Griffin's windshield. She made better time than she figured and noted that the other news stations and even the local authorities had the crash site wrong. They were too far south, almost to Racine.

Terry Lee had somehow managed to sneak himself and his camera equipment into the South Milwaukee Yacht Club's empty parking lot. When Griffin's Volkswagen Beetle pulled up, he kicked his leg in front of the remote sensor, and the electric gate drew open.

"There's a roadway that juts out into the lake about a quarter mile offshore," Lee shouted. "I can't believe the luck. There's no one here. The view from this harbor is totally open."

Griffin counted eighteen concrete block courses on the restaurant. She spied a rickety wooden stepladder and propped it onto a nearby picnic table. From the top step, she could just reach the edge of the building's flat roof.

Lee stared incredulously. "You're not going to do what I think you're going to do, are you?"

"Get your gear up here," she shouted over her shoulder. "We're going live."

The view was panoramic. Griffin stood mesmerized by the horrific scene of burning debris on the water. It looked like some flaming asteroid had exploded. Her hunch that there was no easy way for land rescue teams to access the shoreline except through this parking lot proved true. They'd have to come right past Fox's camera.

Advancing sirens confirmed that fact as the first official emergency vehicles appeared on Marshall Avenue. Authorities immediately established a perimeter and began diverting nonessential people and traffic. Shielding her eyes from the reflective glare of the now cloud-free sun, she saw that there was no sign of an aircraft—at least, in one piece.

"Twenty seconds," a producer's voice spoke through Griffin's earpiece.

Lee raised the camera to his shoulder.

Griffin adjusted her microphone. After coordinating the break-in sequence, the station informed her that the feed was being picked up nationally. She straightened the logo on her company jacket and gave her hair a few fluffs. She was facing west. Lake Michigan was in the background.

"Less than an hour ago, a commercial passenger flight . . ." she paused and touched her earpiece. ". . . we're confirming that it was Delta . . . crashed shortly after takeoff from Mitchell International Airport. What you're seeing behind me is exclusive live video of the crash site, and a debris field that appears to stretch from west to east. We are just now receiving preliminary information that there may have been over one hundred passengers and crew on board. We don't have any confirmation on that yet."

The voice of Fox and Friends morning news coanchor, Elisabeth Colby, interrupted. "I want to repeat for viewers just tuning in that we're speaking live with Neela Griffin from our local WITI Fox affiliate in Milwaukee, Wisconsin, at the scene of a Delta Airlines passenger jet that has just gone down in Lake Michigan after takeoff from Mitchell International Airport. Neela, has anyone given you any indication of the possible cause for the crash?"

"No, Elisabeth. It's too early. I don't see any of the federal officials who generally take charge of situations like this. Local emergency land and water rescue vehicles are just starting to enter the area."

Griffin noticed two men climbing onto the rooftop. Both wore dark blue windbreakers with yellow block lettering. She instinctively clicked off the microphone.

The first FBI agent rudely swept a finger across his throat. "Ma'am, you've got exactly ten seconds to pack up and get off this building. That goes for Kid Rock over there too. Tell him to shut down and leave now."

She walked briskly over to Lee. "Do what they say, and please don't give them any hassle. See if you can set up on that hill to my right. The first house on the point. The one with the flagpole. Be sure to ask permission. I'll try and get some statements. I'll meet you as soon as I can."

She'd had federal confrontations before and was experienced enough to know that their jurisdictional muscle-flexing was serious. Some agents even confiscated equipment and vehicles without warning or legal cause. The action rarely went to court, and the station always recovered its property, but only after bureaucratic delays that killed any chance of news exclusives.

A convoy of police-escorted vehicles appeared. The entire scene was quickly becoming federalized, which meant that media personnel would receive only limited information, usually from scheduled news conferences.

Griffin's brief moment in the national spotlight had ended. She stepped back from the camera and turned on her microphone. "Elisabeth, we've lost our video, and it looks like we're being asked to move to a safer location. I don't know how much longer we'll be able to broadcast. We'll try to check in later. Reporting live from a Delta Airlines crash site on the shore of Lake Michigan south of Milwaukee, Wisconsin, this is Neela Griffin, WITI Fox 6 News."

Griffin talked with the agents until she saw her partner drive away. She straddled the edge of the roof and then lowered both feet onto the stepladder. When she started down, the ladder suddenly twisted, sending her flailing sideways off the picnic table toward the pavement. Her tailbone hit first, and then the back of her head bounced off the concrete with a hard thump.

Three identical Ford E350 vans moved through the parking

lot. The lead van lurched to a stop. A man flew out of the passenger door.

"Lady, are you all right?" Tom Ross asked, noticing a circle of blood oozing from her hair. He stripped off his shirt and flashed his ID to an FBI agent. "Where's medical?"

"Straight ahead and left to the shoreline about a quarter mile farther, sir. They're setting up now."

"Do me a favor and call ahead on this, okay?"

"But she's a reporter."

"What difference does that make?" Ross snapped angrily. "She's injured."

Ross gently parted Griffin's hair and pressed his shirt onto her scalp. He raised his hand. "How many fingers?"

She stared at his blurred image incredulously and then tried to touch his cheek. Her eyes welled with moisture. "Daddy?"

"It's all right, ma'am," Ross assured. "Try and keep pressure on that, okay? We'll get you some help."

Griffin blinked her eyes repeatedly and noticed Ross's ID. She tried to sit up. "N . . . TSB? Would you mind if I asked you some questions? I really would appreciate an interview. It's the least you can do for trying to run me over."

"What? Nobody ran you over. You fell off a ladder. It was an accident."

"You asked me how many fing . . ." Her voice trailed off.

"Ma'am, it's a good chance that we've got well over a hundred fatalities to deal with out here," Ross said. "You're not making much sense right now, and I'm afraid I don't have time to try and figure it out. I'll give you an interview for ten minutes after you get treatment and after our initial press conference." He looked down and saw that she had fainted.

Ross noticed media gathering outside the fence and waved to his entourage. The vehicles moved on. He lifted Griffin and headed for his van. Her hair pressed against his bare chest and chin. It was mink-soft.

Ron Hollings helped Ross load Griffin into the middle seat, sliding a blanket under her head. The bleeding had slowed.

"We don't have a first-aid kit," Hollings said, starting the engine. "How is she?"

"She took a pretty hard hit, but she'll live," Ross answered, rifling through his suitcase. He pulled on a clean shirt.

The van rolled forward to a perimeter checkpoint. Ross pressed his ID against the windshield. A sheriff's deputy waved them through.

Ross gently wiggled Griffin's leg.

"Hey, no sleeping with a head injury. What's your name?"

Griffin sat up slightly and spotted a vehicle on a hill in the distance. A man was standing next to a flagpole holding a camera.

"Terry."

"Terry what?"

"Terry Lee," she said, still dazed. "He's trying to film—"

"Ron, meet Terry Lee. She's a reporter. Terry, if you promise to keep your eyes open, then I'll give you your interview. You can look me up at the Courtyard Marriott Hotel on South 5th Street. It'll probably be around eleven o'clock. That's the best I can do."

"Eleven a.m.?" Griffin asked, her head throbbing.

"No, p.m. I'll make sure I find you. There'll be a crowd."

The van pulled up to the medical station—a series of tents sealed off from the weather by heavy canvas—where two emergency paramedics were waiting.

Ross helped her onto a waiting gurney.

"Okay, Terry Lee. They'll take care of you from here. You'll be fine."

She motioned for him to come closer. "My name is Neela Griffin. Thank you. I'm sorry if I caused any problems." She wrapped her arm around Ross's neck and squeezed tightly for a long five seconds.

Ross didn't know why he closed his eyes, but when he did, his stomach flipped, over the crest of a thrill ride. He took a deep breath and gave his head a rapid shake.

The gurney rolled away.

"Are you going to stand there all day, or can we get back to work?" Hollings asked, frowning suspiciously at his boss.

"She hugged me," Ross said blankly. "Do you know how long it's been since someone hugged me? I forgot how good it felt. And . . . she smelled great. Like vanilla and cinnamon. I can't breathe."

"What in the world is the matter with you? Tom, I know you have problems at home, but you just met that woman."

"Neela," Ross said to himself. His smile quickly vanished when he saw the chaos out on Lake Michigan. Something in the water caught his eye—rectangular shapes rolling on the waves. He picked up a pair of binoculars. It was luggage.

22

THE NTSB and the FBI had leased adjoining room blocks. The hotel's largest meeting center was converted into a press site complete with a roped-off section separating media personnel from federal investigators. The NTSB followed the AIM (Aviation Investigation Manual), a thick, bible-like document with procedural rules on how to conduct, handle, and manage a major air accident. The rules specified everything from the bureaucratically absurd (how to prevent other agencies from drinking NTSB's coffee) to the serious (how to recover underwater wreckage). It even addressed how to designate restricted hotel entrances and exits so officials could come and go without having to pass through a phalanx of reporters or cameras.

Tom Ross stepped onto a makeshift stage followed by an entourage of local government, airline, and law enforcement officials. He tapped a microphone.

"Good morning. I apologize for the delay. Thank you for your patience and understanding during this very trying time. My name is Tom Ross. I'm heading up the NTSB's investigation of Delta Airlines Flight 771 along with our Go Team experts in flight and human performance, power, systems, air traffic control, and physical struc-tures. I'll share a brief status report on what we know at this point."

He produced several sheets of paper. "First, let me echo Milwau-kee's mayor, and city and airline officials, on how profoundly saddened we are at this tragic loss of life. In deference to the families, I will not be providing any names of passengers or crew; there are representatives here from Delta who will continue to address that." He adjusted the microphone. "Yesterday morning, at approximately 6:00 a.m., Delta Airlines Flight 771 departed Milwaukee's Mitchell International Air-port en route to Hartsfield-Jackson International Airport in Atlanta, Georgia. There were 147 passengers and five crew members on board. Approximately one minute into the aircraft's ascent to five thousand feet, the plane experienced a severe loss of both altitude and control, followed by a rapid descent into Lake Michigan two miles offshore. The main fuselage is partially intact and submerged in fifty-eight feet of water. This continues to be a search-and-rescue operation. There are rotational divers in the water, and those operations will continue. I am able to make the following statement: at this time we cannot confirm any survivors. That may change. There still may be air pockets inside the wreckage. We're working with Delta to obtain a verified passenger list. As for possible causes of the crash, it is far too early to speculate. As you know, with any water operation, recovery is made more difficult by depth and temperature. I regret to remind everyone that without insulated clothing, fifty-five degree water does not favor survivability over extended periods. I can confirm that we have located the general position of both the cockpit voice and flight data recorder, but they are under heavy debris. We have a good track record of recovering black boxes and are planning regular press updat—"

"Could this have been an act of terrorism?" a voice shouted from the audience.

Ross immediately stepped aside.

Walter Ford, Milwaukee FBI Special Agent in Charge, moved to the microphone.

"We plan on addressing those issues separately from the crash inves-tigation. A team of Special Agents from Homeland Security Inves-tigations is on site to help ascertain all the facts. That is a routine procedure. At this time, we have no evidence or indication to that end. We're in the early stages, and our priorities are with the families."

Ross returned to the microphone.

"We'll hold a follow-up Q&A session at this location. The NTSB's administrative liaison, Ed Roesler, will have information on an 800 number that Delta has provided for family members. He'll also distribute a media transcript. This concludes NTSB's remarks. I'm going to turn it over to Mr. Chuck Hill, vice-president of Delta Customer Relations. Thank you."

Ross spotted a woman seated in the back of the room wearing a Fox 6 News cap. He circled around the crowd unnoticed and pulled up a chair.

"How are you?"

"A little drowsy from the pain meds," Neela Griffin replied. "It took ten stitches."

"It's nice to see you again," Ross admitted. "I was a little short with you today, and I wanted to apologize."

"You're forgiven, but I have a confession too." She lowered her eyes. "When I was lying on the ground, you put your hand in front of my face and asked how many fingers there were. Did I say anything?"

"Nah, you were pretty out of it," Ross said, choosing to forego her "daddy" comment. "I think you were in shock."

"There were three fingers."

"That's right. So what's this about?"

"When I was ten years old in Cleveland, I fell off a porch and hit my head. My father took me to the hospital. He kept holding his fingers up and asking that same question. I stayed overnight while he went to work. He was a city firefighter. What you did brought back really strong memories. I guess I got a little choked up. Thank you."

"That's a nice story." Ross smiled warmly. "So what happened? Were you okay?"

"Oh, sure, I was fine. It was a routine—" Her smile suddenly broke down and she pressed a tissue to her eyes. "I'm sorry, I usually don't get emotional like this. It was just a bad time."

"Neela, what is it?"

She took a deep breath. "My father was trying to rescue a young child in a burning apartment building that night. The roof collapsed. I never saw him again."

Ross placed his arm around her and drew her close. She laid her head on his shoulder, closing her eyes to the sounds of family members in the room sobbing uncontrollably.

"I hate covering tragedies," she said softly.

"It's all right," he whispered, not wanting to let go.

Griffin was naturally attractive, but it wasn't that quality that drew Ross in. It was her sense of caring. This was a woman who felt for others. It was a quality he had always admired. He gently held her hand. She responded with an appreciative sigh.

"I'm supposed to eat," Griffin finally spoke. "Are you hungry?"

"I am, but I don't have a clue about the area. If you can drive, I'll follow you. It's got to be simple and quick and I could use something hot. Anything but fast food."

—

TWO MILES away and open 24/7, George Webb's was a traditional stool-and-counter restaurant and a Milwaukee landmark specializing in homemade soups and signature décor—two wall clocks synchronized down to the sweep of the second hand.

They ordered.

Griffin's eyelids drooped slightly, and she gave out a long yawn. "You know what's really frustrating as a local reporter? You wait for hours before anybody gives out any information. Everything's so secretive. Then the national network teams arrive and immediately get preferential access. I heard someone already asking family members how they felt. That really bugs me."

"That's bad," Ross agreed. "I'm not proud of this, but one time I got in a fight at a press conference. Some arrogant reporter from the Associated Press was badgering a woman who'd lost her son. The guy was actually demanding that she answer his questions. I grabbed the collar on his fur coat and yanked him outside." Ross sighed. "He was a real idiot, and it was ugly. I was a lot younger then and guess I took things a little too personal."

"He had a fur coat?"

"Yeah. Full-length rabbit or something. It really set me off."

The waitress arrived with two steaming bowls of chicken noodle soup. Ross reached into his jacket and tore open a small red bag.

Griffin wrinkled her nose. "Never saw anyone do that before. But I did hear that pumpkin seeds are a great source of protein."

Ross wasn't certain if she was being sincere or simply patronizing him and his quirky habit. He offered to share. She politely declined.

"How do you like working for Fox?"

"It's okay, I guess. I'm sort of on probation. They think I'm a problem child. I try and make an impact, but then I also try and do what's right. Sometimes the whole local news business drives me crazy, especially the corny coverage. Every time I suggest something, they tell me that it's either too politically sensitive or doesn't fit the station's image. I hate fluff. I can't seem to find a happy medium."

"How long have you worked there?"

"Funny you should ask. Tomorrow's my six-year anniversary and the official end of my three-year contract. I'm not looking forward to renegotiating. What about you? I suppose you were right in the middle of 9/11—*shoot*, I completely forgot. Excuse me." She dialed her phone.

"Newsroom," a youthful voice answered.

"Robby, this is Neela. Did Susan add any extra time for me tomorrow?"

"Hmmm, I didn't see her today. I don't think so, but let me check . . . nope, sorry. Hey, Neela? Nice job on the exclusive today."

She thanked him and clicked off.

The elderly white-haired man standing at the cash register couldn't stop his hand from shaking and dropped several coins. Griffin scurried after them. On her knees, she stretched under an empty booth. She returned the coins and then straightened one of the man's suspenders. He smiled warmly.

Ross mused to himself. He contrasted the scene with Marcia cursing angrily at a disabled man with a walker who couldn't move fast enough in a grocery aisle.

"What are you smiling at?" she asked.

"That was a very nice thing to do," Ross replied.

"He reminded me of my grandfather. I've always believed that we owe the elderly. They built what we have today. Sometimes I think that we treat them like a forgotten class of citizens. When's the last time you saw them marching for their rights?"

Ross was staring at her face again, mesmerized by the symmetry. Her eyes, nose, and mouth were perfectly balanced on her face, outlined by shimmering black hair. But his probing went beyond the physical. *Neela Griffin.* He didn't know a thing about her, but he still felt at ease. She was genuine. She was different. *But why?* he wondered. It was crazy. He'd known her for a total of two hours. Both Marcia and Neela were interesting, intelligent, and attractive women. *Why the difference? One has a caring heart, and the other doesn't. Could it be that simple?*

She waved her hand. "Hellooo, anybody listening?"

"Huh? Oh, I'm really sorry," Ross apologized. "It's been a long day. Um, the elderly. I guess I never thought about that before, but I tend to agree."

"Are you that tired, or am I boring you?"

Ross straightened himself. "You, my friendly reporter, are definitely not boring. I'm just . . . I was . . . I'm a little nervous."

"I make you nervous?"

Ross felt his pulse quicken and reached for his water. Three voices were screaming: one daring, one cautious, and one logical. *Go on, say it. Tell her how you feel. Tell her you like being with her.*

No. She'll think you're weird. Weird or desperate.

You just met. Wait for a better time.

No—you don't have any time. Just say it.

"I wanted to tell you that I—" His cell phone started to vibrate. He glanced at the number and turned it off.

Griffin noticed the time and opened her purse. "I'm really tired too. This is compliments of Fox, agreed?"

"Are you married?" Ross blurted.

"Not anymore," Griffin replied matter-of-factly.

"But you were?"

She pondered that. "Sort of."

"What does that mean?"

"Who's interviewing whom? This is my ten minutes. What about you?"

"Your time has expired. No comment."

"No way, mister," she said playfully. "You don't get away that easily."

"I don't want to get away. What's your cell?" Ross asked. They exchanged numbers. "Let's continue this another time. Please?"

She narrowed her eyes. "Why?"

"Because you owe me."

"For what?"

"A new shirt. I prefer dark-blue, collared polos with short sleeves and one pocket. How about tomorrow? We could celebrate your contract renewal?"

"I can't. I'm just swamped," she said. "And I'm sorry about your shirt. I think it got tossed."

"No big deal." Ross downplayed the obvious rejection. "Good grief, what am I thinking? I'll be lucky to see anyone for the foreseeable future."

Griffin produced a business card and patted his hand gently. "Thanks again. I need to go. You should too."

Ross escorted her to the parking lot and watched her speed away. His cell phone buzzed once. It was Neela. The text message said, *Shirt size?*

He smiled and turned for his van; then he stopped. The south wind carried an unmistakable smell. It was burnt jet fuel.

———

GRIFFIN DROVE west on College Avenue, north on I-94, and then merged onto westbound I-894, a bypass freeway that skirted downtown Milwaukee. At 3:00 a.m., the only other vehicle she saw was a lone county sheriff's cruiser tucked underneath an overpass bridge at 27th Street. The deputy was pointing a radar gun. She checked her speed and then lowered the windows. Awake for twenty-one hours, she needed fresh air. She opened her cell phone and dialed the station's tip line. She hadn't checked it all day. There was one message— Monday, May 18, at 5:59 a.m. The caller's voice was young, male, and distinctly foreign.

"Behold, America, Delta Flight 771. Allah has sent a devastating wind."

GRIFFIN SLAMMED on the brakes. The Volkswagen skidded sideways for fifty feet and came to rest facing the wrong way. She floored the accelerator and sped toward the freeway entrance ramp she'd passed a few moments earlier.

The sheriff's lights flashed on immediately.

She drove up the ramp, turned south on 27th Street, and headed east on Layton Avenue at seventy miles per hour. She ran two red lights.

A Milwaukee police squad joined the pursuit and quickly closed to within a few feet of her bumper.

The Volkswagen squealed onto South 5th Street and into the Marriott's parking lot, screeching to a stop at the main entrance.

Griffin lost her cap as she flew through the lobby toward a man in a suit talking on a cell phone next to the restricted room blocks. He had a badge ID clipped to his belt.

"Please help me. I'm with local Fox News."

One officer literally swept Griffin into the air and pinned her against the elevator doors. Another quickly snapped on handcuffs.

Bystanders watched with mild amusement as this obviously intoxicated female with a bandage on her head was escorted outside. They probably thought she was involved in some domestic dispute.

Griffin yelled over her shoulder. "I need Tom Ross."

"Wait, bring her back here," Jack Riley ordered from across the lobby, abruptly ending his phone call. The officers complied. "What did you say?"

"Please, do you know Tom Ross? It's an emergency."

"About what?" Riley asked suspiciously.

"Material evidence related to that plane crash. I'll only speak to him."

Riley conferred with the officers.

The handcuffs came off.

Riley escorted Griffin down the first-floor corridor and through a set of closed doors. The sign on a hallway stanchion said: *FBI Command Center.*

"What is this?" Walter Ford growled from across a huge table.

"She says she's a reporter," Riley answered.

"That's not what I asked."

"What time did that plane take off?" Griffin blurted.

"Get her out of here," Ford ordered angrily. "This isn't a press conference."

"The *exact* time."

Surprised by the woman's boldness, Riley held up his hand at Ford.

"Yes, ma'am. Anything you say. The wheels left the ground at *exactly* six-oh-one. Now, what else would you like to know?"

Ross entered the room. Griffin embraced him tightly.

"Tom, what's going on?" Riley demanded. "Do you know this woman?"

"Neela, what are you doing?" Ross whispered. "If this is about a story for your station, you can't—"

She placed a finger to her lips and leaned across the table for the speakerphone. She dialed the tip line's access number and turned up the volume.

The message played out.

Maintaining his demeanor, Riley put his arm on Ford's shoulder and walked him to the far end of the room. He bent next to his ear. "Walter, I don't want to tell you your job, but we need to contact Fox's communication carrier right away. I've got a hunch. Once that's started, I'll give you a few minutes to inform your chain of command before I call the Secretary. This is going to boil over *very* quickly. We need to stay calm and do the right things."

"What about her?" Ford peered at Griffin.

"She doesn't leave this room for the foreseeable future. Agreed?"

Ford nodded once and promptly lifted a phone.

Riley approached Griffin. "Ma'am, do you know which telephone carrier operates that tip line?"

"Sprint . . . er, wait. We just switched. I think it's AT&T now."

After several conversations and a flurry of orders, Ford returned to his seat and positioned two telephones in the center of the table. He dialed the residence number for Rand Harrington, the acting Deputy Secretary of National Cyber Security.

After a private conversation, Ford placed Harrington on speaker.

"Rand, we're all here. The reporter's name is Neela Griffin. She's with Milwaukee's Fox news station."

"Good morning, ma'am," Harrington's voice said. "This is an official investigation under the authority of the Department of Homeland Security. I need to inform you that you are not here as a suspect or person of interest but as a holder of potential significant evidentiary material related to a terror threat against the United States of America. You will not need an attorney present during this discussion because, again, you're not a suspect. However, we do need to ask you some questions. You may, at our discretion, be detained in order to provide us with that information so determined by Homeland Security. If you do not voluntarily cooperate, you may be held under abeyance detention in accordance with the authority granted to the DHS under the Patriot Act of 2001, as amended. We may or may not record this conversation. Do you understand?"

Griffin turned to Ross. He squeezed her arm and nodded reassuringly.

"I understand."

"Ma'am, you claim to have a voice communication message about an airline incident currently under investigation. Is that correct?"

"Yes."

"Why would anyone call you?"

"They didn't. I work for WITI Channel 6 News here in Milwaukee. We operate a crime tip line that anyone may call to leave messages on. It's available 24/7."

"We're confirming the call timing," Riley added.

"Who else has access to the messages on this tip line?" Harrington asked Griffin.

"Our voice and data support people at the station, but usually it's just me."

"Very well," Harrington said calmly. "Walter, I want you to contact Mitchell's departure control. I want two independent statements on the exact time that aircraft left the ground."

"We already have that," Riley spoke up.

"Re-verify it," Harrington shot back. "It was probably a cell phone, so let's get a trace started with AT&T's mobile switch people. If memory serves, that area has two wireless switches, a primary in the suburb of New Berlin and a backup on Milwaukee's north side. I want the subscriber identity and the origination and termination time slots confirmed. We should be able to compare them with the tower log."

"Sir, that's in progress too," Riley gently informed him.

"We need to play your message for Mr. Harrington," Ford said to Griffin.

She dialed the number. It played out on a second speaker.

There was extended silence.

"Has anyone else heard this?" Harrington's voice finally spoke.

"Just this room," Ford answered.

"Walter, pick up, please."

Griffin quietly rose from her seat and headed for the door.

An agent casually blocked her path.

"I'd like to take my medication and make a phone call," Griffin said to Riley. "Is that all right?"

"I'm afraid it's not," he said without looking up. "Please sit down. We need to sort some things out."

She glanced around the room. "You can't keep this quiet. That message belongs to a private business—a news business. That's why we exist. A terrorist blew up that plane. People have a right to know that the whole airline industry could very well be under attack. I need to call my station. This is the biggest news story we've ever had—the biggest *anyone's* ever had. I don't understand."

"Ma'am, calm down. Let us try and confirm the facts," Riley said. "We don't need to start shouting anything about the airline industry being under attack. And we certainly don't want to take away anyone's rights."

"May I at least use the bathroom?"

"I'm sorry. Of course." Riley nodded at a female agent. He leaned over the table and took Griffin's phone—an indication that he was serious. She didn't protest.

Another agent entered the room and handed Ford two pieces of paper.

"The official departure was logged at 6:01 a.m. Two minutes after the phone warning. And it was a mobile call. AT&T said it originated from a US Cellular tower at 5970 South Howell Avenue. That's on the south end of the airport. He was right there."

"Or very close," Riley muttered. "They're still in love with cell phones. After the Pakistanis tracked Khalid Sheik Mohammed to his safe house in Karachi, we all thought they stopped."

"Terrorists aren't stupid," Rand said. "They all know about cell phone tracing via SIM cards and won't fall into that trap again. They never stopped using cell phones at all; they've simply switched to disposables—throwaways. Probably a TRAC phone, prepaid and bought right off the shelf just about anywhere. No ID or credit card required. They'll use it once and then toss it. It's impossible to track or trace. We can fix a general radius from where a call originates, but it's wide and limited. It's a shame that disposables don't have GPS tracking ability, or we could narrow the owner's location down to feet."

Only if the owner is dumb enough to hang onto it, Riley thought to himself, slightly miffed that Rand beat him to the explanation. He rose from the table and pulled Ross into an adjoining suite. He closed the door.

"All right, who is this reporter and what is she to you?"

"This is nuts, Jack," Ross said defensively.

"This is way beyond nuts, pal. How well do you know her?"

"I swear we just met."

"Do you know that she's a constitutional time bomb? I'm talking unprecedented. She's a material witness with the ability to panic the country. All she needs to do is pick up the phone and boom—this story becomes world headlines. And I'm not sure we can legally stop it."

"You think she'd do that?"

"In a heartbeat. Some members of our beloved free press don't care about keeping information secret even if it aids our enemies. I don't care if we have to take that bandage off her head and wrap it across her mouth—I will not allow her to do that. The press isn't tipping our hand. Not this time."

"I disagree," Ross said firmly. "She's not that way. I'll talk to her."

Riley scoffed out loud. "Man, are you a dreamer. You just admitted that you don't even know her. Trust me. She's using you for one thing. Breaking news."

Ross massaged his chin. "So what are you going to do?"

"What are *we* going to do?" Riley corrected as he glanced at his watch. "I need to get back to Washington. I've got a fair idea where my boss will want this to go."

"A big, white house on Pennsylvania Avenue?"

"A big, white house." Riley motioned to a table in the corner of the room. "Have a seat, Mr. NTSB. As far as our little constitutional problem goes, there might be an alternative. I hope you're up for a special assignment. It's an extraordinary proposition, but these are extraordinary circumstances. I think it'll buy us some time."

24

MCLEAN, VA
5:25 A.M.

SECRETARY OF Homeland Security Samuel Bridge was a fifty-five-year-old veteran of war, politics, and, for a brief period, acting. A three-term ex-governor of Wisconsin, Bridge was a tall, square-shouldered man with a linebacker's physique. He had an angry face like that of a freight train's engine, which left his younger staff in a constant state of timidity and his older staff in a constant state of laughter at the younger staff.

Retired from politics, Bridge had been living in western Wisconsin on the bluffs overlooking the Mississippi River when the president proposed the DHS cabinet nomination. Bridge accepted under the condition that the administration let him secure the US-Canadian border. As a governor, he had championed the issue for years, but other than modest increases in state funding, little was ever done. In his final term, reports had surfaced about comments he allegedly made about becoming more of a friend to Wisconsin's Chippewa Tribe on the state's largest reservation at Lac du Flambeau. Something about sitting down with them "Indian-style," a gambling compact in one hand and a whiskey bottle in the other. He vehemently denied the allegations but chose not to seek re-election.

An avid Harley-Davidson fan, Bridge was in his driveway just about to leave on a week-long fund-raising ride in support of the Wounded Warrior Project.

150

"Sir, it's Jack Riley," an aide announced, handing Bridge a phone. "He's airborne en route to Reagan National. He says it's urgent."

Seated in full leather garb on his touring FLHR Road King, Bridge pulled off one glove and unsnapped his helmet. He still bristled at the thought of private aircraft being allowed into DC's airspace, even with a special transponder code and constant FAA radio contact.

"Mr. Secretary, it appears that we have a specific and credible terror threat," Riley's voice announced. "We just confirmed it."

"Confirmed how?" Bridge asked sternly.

"Someone called the news media and advised them of the crash two minutes before it happened. A warning like that suggests it was premeditated. Probably an onboard explosive," he theorized. "It appears to be a deliberate action."

Bridge immediately suspected in-flight explosion tactics similar to those planned by twenty-one London terrorists. Then he considered something even more sinister: Flight 587, which had mysteriously crashed in Queens, New York, sixty days after 9/11. The investigation suggested a combination of pilot error and vortex wind from another jet, but he wasn't convinced.

"Did you say someone advised the media?" Bridge asked. "On board how and where?"

"We're not certain, sir. Luggage, in-flight assembly, suicide . . . it's too early to tell."

"Jack, we can't move on guesses," the Secretary warned unnecessarily. "If you're telling me we've got a shoe or underwear bomber situation that's actually worked, then I'm going to personally find Darryl Nadler and serve up his head on a dinner plate." Nadler headed the TSA's Office of Security Operations, the group in charge of cargo and passenger screening procedures at all US airports. "What's your ETA?"

"Half an hour."

"Step on it," Bridge ordered. "I'm sending a car."

Riley clicked off. *Step on what?* he wondered. The G-1159's speed was already pushing 480 mph.

Bridge handed the phone to an aide. He checked his watch. "Get me Andrew Bard." He swung his leg over the Harley and walked it back to the garage, slamming his helmet onto the seat.

The aide returned the phone. "Sir, Chief of Staff Bard."

Bridge removed his other glove. "Andy, I've just been informed that the Milwaukee incident was premeditated. I'll need to speak to the president. I'm alerting OCP."

The Homeland Security Office of Operations Coordination and Planning was responsible for monitoring the daily security of the United States. It coordinated activities with governors, Homeland Security Advisors, law enforcement partners, and critical infrastructure operators in all fifty states and more than fifty major urban areas nationwide.

It was the information and decision-making nerve center that was missing during 9/11, and now it was the nation's best entity to respond to a homeland terror threat.

—

COURTYARD MARRIOTT

TOM ROSS approached a female FBI agent seated outside a room at the end of the hotel corridor.

"How is she?"

"She's stopped throwing things, but I don't think she's very happy," the agent answered. "We disconnected the room phone."

Ross gently tapped on the door, then opened it.

Griffin was sitting in a chair with her knees propped up to her chin. She was wrapped in a blanket and staring at the floor.

"Neela, it's me," Ross announced apologetically. "Are you okay?"

"Do I look okay?" she snapped.

He put his hand on her shoulder. She shrugged it away.

"Do you want to go to bed?"

Griffin gave a disgusted look and eyed Ross up and down suspiciously.

Ross blushed violently. "I mean . . . are you tired?"

"Just how many rooms do you people have in this place? The whole floor? What's next, a strip search?"

"Neela, what would you say if I asked you to become part of this investigation—an actual insider working hand-in-hand with the FBI and me? You get exclusive rights to the story and can report on any-thing you witness as long as it doesn't compromise the crash investiga-tion or national security. Other than some minor screening before it's released to the public, you'll have complete freedom."

Griffin raised one eyebrow. "Why would you and that Ford guy even consider allowing a news reporter to—what if I say no?"

Ross sat on the bed and folded his hands between his legs. "Neela, this is serious. You need to know that the FBI is looking at this from different perspectives. I want to be sure that you don't get into—"

She flung off the blanket and stood up. "Into what? What exactly are you trying to say? I didn't do anything wrong here. What perspectives?"

"The Patriot Act. Specifically, sections 212 and 213. They deal with electronic and voice mail communications. You need to know that Fox's *Crime Tip Line* has already been seized and is being monitored. No one has access. You can't reveal anything to anyone, not even to your station. If you do, you could be detained indefinitely as a material witness. I don't want anything like that to happen."

She tried to process what she just heard.

"Are you telling me that I'm some kind of hotel detainee?"

"No, you're not any kind of detainee. But I did tell Jack . . . er, Mr. Riley, that I would talk to you and that you'd listen. Neela, I think I must be crazy for even saying this. I don't know anything about you other than I like you and I hoped that you and I might get to know each other socially. I think this whole thing is unfortunate. I just don't want you to get in trouble."

She wanted to believe him, but she sensed a red flag. It was her own defense mechanism, and warning that led to a decision to either trust someone and pursue a potential relationship, or end it.

"What do you want?" she asked.

"Your cooperation."

She stared at him perceptively and then reached into her purse for her notepad.

"You're not a very good liar, Tom Ross. But that's a plus with me. You want my silence, and you probably want me to stay where you can keep an eye on me."

"Just until we can get ahead of this thing. You need to act as if nothing unusual has happened. File your crash story normally and inform your station's management that you've asked for and received permission to become part of our team as an embedded reporter, just like those who travel with the military during combat."

She took all this in. "For how long?"

"I don't know. It could be a couple of days or a couple of weeks. Maybe longer."

"So, I keep quiet, and you give me exclusives," she summarized. "I'm not a prisoner, though, right? I mean, you don't expect me to stay locked up?"

"You are not a prisoner. Neither the FBI nor Homeland Security could enforce that. They just want your assurance that your reports won't compromise the investigation. Neela, you can't tell anyone about that message. Not yet. In return, you'll get information that no other news reporter will. Riley and I have agreed to merge investigations. If he can swing it, I'll be reporting directly to him. You'll be traveling and working with us hand in hand. We'll arrange a private workspace where you can assemble your stories. Consider it a special assignment. You'll attend strategy meetings and have access to frontline discoveries. You'll know the facts before any other media. Riley needs your silence about that message, and he'll feel more comfortable if you stay close. So would I."

"Riley," she snarled. "I don't trust him."

"Jack's an intense guy. He's doing what he thinks is best for the country."

"You're willing and able to do all this for me?"

"It won't be easy. I'm talking hotel rooms, long hours, and probably spur-of-the-moment travel. We have to exercise some editorial prerogative over what you release, but you have my word it'll be fair. Besides, NTSB's investigative process has a life of its own. It'll move forward with or without me. I can clear just about anything. That's not the problem."

"Then what is?" she asked.

He returned her cell phone. "It looks like someone has found a way to bring down passenger aircraft. If they did it once, they could very well do it again."

OVAL OFFICE, THE WHITE HOUSE
WASHINGTON, DC

A FORMER senator and Naval helicopter pilot, President of the United States Cale Warren was best described as a tempered moderate. His tendency to lose his temper was an admitted personal flaw, but one that had seemingly faded with age. Friends believed that he had simply learned to harness his anger with little internal harm. To a certain extent, it was true. At sixty-eight years-old, he still had all his hair.

Chief of Staff Andrew Bard had served Warren for five years as an underling and political advisor. An unremarkable yet loyal aide, Bard spent a minimum of twelve hours each day keeping the president up to date on current events and ensuring that his schedule carried a balance of recreational activities. Right now that meant preparing for the upcoming presidential election, which was just eighteen months away.

"Andrew, this isn't Hollywood," the president said, pacing while sipping fresh juice. "Does Samuel know the impact of that?"

"I would certainly hope so," Bard replied. "He's not one to overreact, but without solid evidence of this so-called premeditated act, I suggest prudence, sir."

The president placed his glass on a napkin and sat down. His mind raced with emotions that swelled between rage and grief, controlled, but powerful. Levels he'd not felt in years. Next came a flurry of distasteful decisions he knew might be required. Distasteful because they would involve the entire country and impact the lives of millions of Americans. He drew a breath.

"I want to hear it myself. Irrefutable, clear, and correct facts. We cannot bring the air transportation of this country to a standstill without cause."

Secretary Bridge and Jack Riley entered the Oval Office.

It was Riley's first time in the famous room. He was, like all other virgin visitors, immediately mesmerized. A week earlier, Riley and his wife had met with an interior designer to discuss swags and fabric-covered cornices for their living and dining rooms. The designer recommended straight-boarded window treatments that, while offering simple elegance, still carried a hefty price tag. Riley stared in awe at the signature cornice on the windows behind the president's desk. It followed the building's contour.

"Morning, Mr. President, Andrew." Secretary Bridge nodded politely to both men.

The president rose from his desk and eyed Riley suspiciously. It took a few moments to make the connection.

"Your theme park scenario was interesting, son," he said, putting his hand on Riley's shoulder. "What was that name again? Ah, yes, Komodo. But I'm afraid you give terrorists too much strategic credit. One would hope that we'd have enough intelligence foresight to identify a group of over one hundred individuals intent on shooting up roller coasters and baseball stadiums. Before long, every public venue will have solid security measures in place, especially sporting events. Don't you agree?"

"I hope you're right, sir," Riley softened his answer. He wanted to say that there was no way private businesses or professional or collegiate sports organizations could afford such measures, and even if they could, they wouldn't work, but he decided it wasn't the right time or place to spar with the leader of the free world. The man would have enough on his plate after this briefing.

The men took seats on a set of parallel sofas. The president preferred a stiff wingback chair. His facial expression revealed nothing.

"Gentlemen, there's a rather large group of reporters gathering on the other side of this building who thinks that something big and breaking is coming. Furthermore, my staff is violating every traffic law in DC's books to get in here this morning. I understand you believe a terror act has been committed against a US airline on US soil. Is that true?"

"Yes, sir," Bridge responded.

"And you want me to do something about it, up to and including alerting the nation and perhaps even clearing the skies."

"Yes, sir."

"Very well, Samuel," the president said matter-of-factly. "For how long?"

"One week," Bridge ventured, looking to Bard for support. None was forthcoming.

The president nodded thoughtfully, weaving a subtle trap—not to purposely entwine his Secretary of Homeland Security but to simply arrive at a good and right decision. Warren was a man who liked to do that. Not one given to snap judgments, he was known for baiting his senior advisors, pretending to favor one position and then turning 180 degrees for the other. He referred to the process as "reaching factual equilibrium."

"Does that include domestic and international flights?"

"Yes," Bridge responded at once. "Passenger and cargo."

The president turned to Bard. "Andrew?"

"Mr. President, if we do that, then the terrorists win. We should consider the Madrid and London subway bombings in '04 and '05. Over two hundred people were killed and fifteen hundred injured. They didn't shut down their entire transportation systems."

"The Spanish authorities didn't have a recorded message announcing the threat either," Bridge shot back but he quickly corrected himself. "The voice evidence they found was nothing more than mindless chanting."

"True, but I still think a shutdown is far too drastic," Bard argued. "You say someone gave two minutes of warning? For all we know, it could be anything from a hoax to misinterpreting a wristwatch. Whenever there's a major tragedy in the world, I can name at least four terror groups that always try and claim responsibility. This administration would look like the biggest fool of the twenty-first century. I can't agree."

"Options, Mr. Riley?"

"I see three, Mr. President. There's no evidence to support it, but we must assume that an explosive was involved, probably smuggled on board that Delta flight. If we do nothing but step up preflight security and it happens again, the lives of those passengers are on our hands. Our first option is to physically search all commercial aircraft. That would be a nearly impossible task because we have no idea what we're looking for. It could be a ready-made device or the result of post-flight assembly. Option two, we continue to fly, but under severe restrictions. We hand search all passengers and baggage and stop all carry-ons. Unfortunately, those actions place a tremendous burden on TSA resources, not to mention the airlines."

"That's not realistic, Mr. President," Bard said firmly. "We need confirmation."

"Like what?" Bridge asked angrily. "Another crash, perhaps in Lake Erie? If we don't act, then we are potentially exposing the citizens of this country to murder. And I, for one, am not a murderer."

Bard stood. "Just who are you calling a murderer?"

"Gentlemen, please," the president calmly interrupted, then turned back to Riley. "Your third option?"

"Ground all carriers," Riley said, his voice steady and reasonable. "At least until we find an answer. A similar order was issued nationwide for the first time in history after the Pentagon was hit on 9/11. No aircraft were allowed to move anywhere in the country. The FAA term for the event is 'full groundstop,' and it means just that—everything heads for the ground and stops. The FAA and TSA would have more insight into the logistics, but generally speaking, some 5,300 mainland airports under their jurisdiction literally freeze. All personnel are then dedicated to bringing airborne flights down to the nearest available runway. On September 11, that meant 4,600 planes."

"Mr. President, think about the impact to the nation," Bard warned. "It would be another ground zero."

"What are you talking about?" Bridge asked, displeased with the choice of words.

"The economy of the United States of America," Bard said. "Every sector you can think of is touched by the airlines: tourism, inventory and equipment, mail, food supplies . . . the list is endless. The losses would start with coastal fishermen who'd have to eat their daily catches or serve up a free smorgasbord. It simply snowballs inland from there. Airlines need regular income—lots of it, or they'll all be bankrupt." He shifted toward the president. "Sir, I don't need to remind you that this is an election cycle, and the labor market is one we cannot afford to weaken. We've built a fragile credibility with the unions on job creation. The economy is rebounding. A shutdown of the airlines would be absolutely devastating. The Russians lost two planes to terrorism in 2004 and didn't shut down their air travel because they couldn't afford it. Neither can we."

"We are not Russia, Mr. President," Bridge said. "And we cannot take the chance that another aircraft with crew and passengers might be at risk. Jack is absolutely right. If we do nothing and it happens again, the retribution from the American people would be unimaginable. It would be criminal. I cannot stress more firmly that we must shut the system down."

"What have we put in place up till now?" the president asked Bridge.

"We haven't made any formal announcement, but all law enforcement agencies are expecting an elevated alert status, requiring the flying public to arrive at departure airports three hours in advance. That alone would mean substantially longer passenger lines. The airlines are prepared for that kind of slowdown. Unfortunately, we still don't have everyone up and running with the right chemical isolation or scanning equipment."

"Andrew, I suppose we should move next door," the president said, referring to the Cabinet Room. He was anticipating Bard's next question and weighing the need to bring in all fifteen of his Secretaries plus the vice-president. There was no official schedule, but Warren generally tried to meet with his full Cabinet on a weekly basis. Calling an unscheduled meeting was doable; it would simply take time. "Where's my Attorney General?"

"Sir, Mr. Broderick is recovering from his surgery, but he's reachable. National Security Advisor Wright is in Tel Aviv. She'll cancel if you need her. The vice president is leading that nuclear conference on Iran."

"I want you to get the CEOs of American, Delta, United, and Southwest on a call in half an hour. No foreign carriers yet. And get Norman and Elizabeth in here," the president ordered. He looked at his watch. "We'll reconvene in one hour. I'll make a decision then."

26

CLEAR SKIES, calm winds. It was a perfect day to fly.

Akil pulled into the north parking lot of the three-building, horseshoe-shaped office complex at the intersection of Lawrence and Scott Street on O'Hare International Airport's southeast perimeter. Access on the north, south, and west perimeter was especially strict and virtually impenetrable, protected by mounded embankments, heavy foliage, and regularly patrolled fence lines. Wedged between I-294 and Highways 45/12, the Aerospace Center's runway views and accessibility along the southeastern perimeter, especially for a maneuverable drone, were wide open.

Akil punched in the current numeric month and year, and the lobby door popped open. He perused the wall directory. Ironically, one of his new neighbors was FAA's O'Hare District Flight Standards Office.

Akil boarded the elevator and checked his watch. The sun would rise in three minutes. The doors opened to a dark reception area. He walked past a row of offices, stopping at one with a magnetic sign on the wall that read "Computer Doctors, LLC." He entered his personal code on another keypad. At only 283 square feet, the room had basic office furniture and décor. There was a welcome packet on the desk as well as fresh-cut flowers, and a gift certificate from the nearby Rose-mont Embassy Suites.

He raised the aluminum mini-blinds and opened the window. His distance-reading binoculars said 307 yards. The air traffic was moving steadily, and he judged the departures on Runway 22L at eight-minute intervals, each plane timed to the inbound approaches on Runway 4R. He scanned the surroundings, visualizing the drone's flight path in five segments: vacant land, highway, fence, grass, and runway. Across Scott Street, beyond the first airport fence, stood a sprawling Federal Express distribution building and concrete parking structure. He panned the binoculars north to where Scott Street dead-ended into secured airport property. An unmarked, dark-gray sedan sat there idling. A single occupant was reading a newspaper. Akil noted a flock of starlings methodically searching the grass next to Runway 22L's departure point. Considering that O'Hare was the second-busiest passenger airport in the United States behind Atlanta's Hartsfield-Jackson, everything seemed to be running smoothly. One by one, the morning flights ferried from the terminals. His target, hopefully on schedule, was due at 6:00 a.m.

Akil turned on his laptop and propped an assembled drone on the window ledge. He rubbed a soft cloth over the camera lens. He snapped the fuel cartridges into place and launched the unit out of the window. It quickly rose to seventy-five feet and headed north. He spotted a clear flight path and angled the drone west, crossing over the sparse traffic on Mannheim Road. Gaining confidence, he played with the toggle stems and observed the drone respond with near bird-like flight. He felt a strange euphoria in the effortless manipulation. It was satisfying to know that he possessed both superior ability and raw power. He was a predator with ultimate control.

Something else also pleased him. It was the ability to kill without having to sense or witness the results. The prey was nothing more than a target to be eliminated—a culture target. This was not real killing because it was not observable. It was simply meting out Allah's judgment on those who deserved it. It was all too easy. His targets were lambs or rabbits resting in some open meadow, wandering about their daily lives with no reason to fear that which stalked them. A few would be taken, but no matter; there were many others. The predator would feast and rest, and then the pursuit would begin again.

The drone continued onto airport property, lowering to the grass and pacing alongside an Air France jet. A United flight was next in line, just another of O'Hare's 1,500 daily departures. But it was his flight.

Eyes fixed on the laptop screen, Akil guided the drone into position. The starlings scattered into the air. He smiled at the drone's color—red. He imagined the worst: a passenger in a window seat of a taxiing plane who just happened to be facing at the right angle, scrutinizing the perimeter grass edging at a brief moment in time. The passenger would then have to be savvy enough to notice something unusual, recognize it as both a drone and a threat to the aircraft as opposed to the blurred image of an early-morning cardinal, and raise enough concern to actually halt the flight.

It was a perfect day to fly.

—

THE WHITE HOUSE
WASHINGTON, DC

JACK RILEY was sitting alone in the corner of the Cabinet Room, next to a marble bust of George Washington. It seemed like the only place in the West Wing that offered some semblance of calm. He figured the wait would be brief.

He stared at the room's signature mahogany table, a gift from President Nixon. Each Cabinet member had an assigned seat according to the date the department was established. Members also had the option to keep their chairs after leaving office as a memento of government service. The president's was in the center.

Riley knew that the commander-in-chief was sworn to protect American lives and therefore had the authority to shut down the nation's air transportation. There certainly was 9/11 precedent. But even the president had to realize that it was easy to talk about such action in the quiet confines of the White House but completely gut-wrenching to actually give an order for the second time since flying was invented in 1903. Riley felt a mild throbbing in his temples from thinking about the logistics of just one airline carrier telling their in-flight pilots to bring their planes down ASAP. Then the real fun would begin.

The hapless passengers, the mega-congestion, the angry vendors, the scheduling chaos, not to mention refunding all those prepaid fees charged to customer credit cards and zero income for the airlines and their employees. The list was huge. *Does a carrier contract's fine print contain force majeure language shielding it from terrorism?* he wondered.

On 9/11, stunned pilots frantically prepared to land at the nearest airport. Passengers desperately needed transportation and lodging. In some cases, school and city buses were used. Then came the psychological hits, not only to passengers but also to an oft-forgotten group who probably felt the impact of a shutdown more than any other—the flight crews.

After 9/11, airline unions worked tirelessly to provide support for workers concerned about their futures. When flights resumed three days later, some crews refused, not confident of airport security. Those who did return faced a new threat—layoffs.

Continental quickly cut 12,000 jobs; United and American cut 20,000; Northwest, 10,000; US Airways, 11,000; and Delta, 13,000. If the president issued that order again, he might as well bring in Donald Trump to speak his famous catchphrase to the airline workers.

Riley's cell phone chirped. The caller's ID said "FBI Command Center." Riley answered.

"Sir, I'm Communications Specialist Marten," the voice on the line said. "Special Agent Ford wanted you to know that a second message just came across that Milwaukee news station's tip line. It was an interstate call and lasted approximately seven seconds. It appears to be the same voiceprint. Male, foreign accent, same cryptic reference to devastating wind and Allah. The flight number he mentioned this time was United 605. Agent Ford said that there's been no reports of any incidents from the airlines. In other words, nothing's blown up. What do you think that means, sir?"

Why ask me? What am I supposed to do? Riley thought. "Did you trace it?"

"Yes, sir. It came from a cell tower owned by Nextel. FCC structure registration number 1207758, file number is A0121446. The FAA study is 99-AGL-4202-OE, issue date 10-25-1999 constructed 04-07-2000. Structure type is a building with antenna. Lat-long is 41-59-58.6 north—"

"Never mind all that," Riley said impatiently. "Give me a location. What's the tower's address? What state? What city?"

"It's 6600 Mannheim Road, Des Plaines, Illinois. That's north of Chicag—"

Riley hung up as he bolted upright from the chair. He hurriedly scrolled through his phone contacts, found the one he was looking for, and dialed.

"O'Hare Airport Operations. Rebecca Marsh speaking."

"This is a Homeland Security emergency. Get me Air Traffic Control manager Harold Flynn. Tell him it's Jack Riley. And I mean *now!*"

"Yes, sir. Right away, sir. Please stand by."

Riley could feel the blood pulsing in his neck. He knew Flynn. He was a thirty-year veteran of Chicago's Department of Aviation and a stalwart supporter of O'Hare's multibillion-dollar modernization plan. Sadly, the sequestration crisis had forced them to periodically close their new northern control tower. Flynn was recently given a special assignment to help area residents understand and accept plans for new runway expansions. He was strongly considering retirement.

"Jack Riley? You picked a heckuva time to chat," Flynn's voice said. "If this is about Flight 605, we're already on it. I'm in the main tower, and the FBI is swarming all over the place. What's going on?"

Thank God, Riley thought. "We don't know, Harold. Just get everybody off that plane *fast.*"

"It was logged as an Airbus A319, westbound to Denver, Runway 22," Flynn explained. "Jack, it left an hour ago."

Riley let out an audible curse. "Where is it?"

"ATC Command has them at 450 knots and 34,000 feet. They're approaching western Iowa."

The FAA's Air Traffic Control System Command Center was located in Vint Hill, Virginia, forty miles southwest of Washington, DC. The center monitored the nation's air traffic control towers, approach and departure facilities, and high-altitude control centers. The facility also supported all electronic navigation. The center didn't directly control air traffic, but it monitored and coordinated with other air traffic facilities and system users including the airlines, the military, and business aviation groups. The center's main mission was to balance demand with capacity and to deal with weather and other potential disruptions. If the entire air traffic system in the United States was an orchestra, then Vint Hill was its conductor.

"Jack, I need to know," Flynn said, his tone near pleading. "My assistant tower chief's wife is on that plane. She's taking their only granddaughter back to Taos, New Mexico. They could've booked Southwest through Albuquerque, but decided United to Denver at the last minute. You probably can't tell me, but I'll ask anyway—is this a hijacking?"

"We don't know," Riley repeated, feeling his throat constrict. A wave of nausea rolled through his stomach. "We need to get them down, Harold. And then pray."

DECATUR, GA

STUART ROBERTSON shuffled into the kitchen, stood on a chair, and poured Honey Nut Cheerios into two bowls. He flipped through the channels on the TV and then abruptly hurried to his parents' bedroom. He knocked once, twice, and then waited patiently until someone gave permission. That was a new rule.

He peeked his head inside.

"Mommy, where's Dad?" he asked, his voice weak and fearful.

"In the shower," Linda answered, rising from her dressing table and rolling a lint brush over her skirt. She eyed her son suspiciously as he burrowed into the newly made bed and pulled a sheet over his eyes. Linda froze. Her mind instantly filled with words every working parent feared when faced with a sick child: fever, pediatrician, pharmacy, vacation day. One word collectively summed things: juggle. She sat on the bed and placed her hand against her son's cheek.

"Don't you feel well, honey?"

"A deer got dead on the TV," he said softly. "There was a fire."

Atlanta's surrounding suburbs were overrun with whitetail. In Georgia, drivers had a 1 in 151 chance of a deer-vehicle collision. She assumed he'd seen a news broadcast.

"Oh no. That's so sad. Was it a baby?"

"No."

"Was it hit by a car?"

"Mommy? I don't ever want to fly on an airplane."

—

THE WHITE HOUSE CABINET ROOM
WASHINGTON, DC

A THRONG of bodies burst through the doors. Senior staff and aides hurriedly upscaled the room's functionality with lighting, documentation, office supplies, and communication access.

Secretary Bridge bent next to Riley. "New York's circuit breakers just kicked in."

Riley gave Bridge a confused look and then incorrectly assumed that the city's electrical grid was somehow under attack.

"From the air?"

"Wall Street," Bridge replied. "The stock market's been open for eleven minutes, and it just shut down."

The president entered the room last. Most of the chairs at the conference table were empty. For a moment, Riley thought he might be asked to move up and join what was arguably the single most powerful group of government officials in the nation, sans the Secretaries of Defense and State. Riley noticed FAA Administrator Elizabeth Slavin sitting well behind her boss, Secretary of Transportation Norman Minka, and figured no such invitation would be forthcoming.

Secretary Bridge began. "Mr. President, I'm sorry to confirm that a second commercial aircraft, United Flight 605, has gone down in Bellevue, Nebraska. Debris is scattered across the Fontenelle Forest Nature Center between I-29 in Iowa and Nebraska's State Highway 75. It missed residential neighborhoods in South Omaha by four miles. There were one hundred and eight people on board. All are feared dead. The circumstances appear similar to those in Milwaukee."

The president sat quietly with his hands folded. He was trying to muster the strength to speak the inevitable—a decision perhaps equal in gravity to approving a major military strike. A domestic order affecting the entire nation immediately and with severe economic consequences, it was a decision unlike any other.

"What is happening to our country?" the president said soberly.

"Sir, it has to be done," Bridge gently prodded, careful in his tone so as not to appear to be ordering the president, although that's exactly what he was doing.

"Tell me again . . . are there no alternatives?"

Slavin quietly handed Bridge a folder entitled: *National Security Plan for Air Traffic Shutdown*. It had been prepared for this precise situation.

"Mr. President, with all due respect, two planes and a total of 260 people have been lost. We are, for all intents and purposes, under siege. Both flights appear to have been deliberately targeted with warnings announced beforehand. We were powerless to stop them. However insidious, someone, somehow, has devised a way to carry or plant explosive devices on commercial aircraft and presumably detonate them at a time of their choosing. It is unbelievable. And if such devices have somehow managed to elude our detection capabilities, for all we know there could be tens or even hundreds poised for similar detonation. It is my duty to now admit the possibility that the prior London aircraft bombing attempts and even the mysterious downing of TWA Flight 800 may have shared circumstances. That plane, in particular, could very well have been the first test. We may be facing a perfected tactic so revolutionary that none of our security systems can pick it up. Donaldson is in his grave, but I believe he was dead right."

Bridge had wanted to get that out for years. He never had a good enough foundation. Commander William S. Donaldson III was a United States Navy pilot and Vietnam War veteran with more than twenty-four years of experience in nearly all phases of naval aviation. He challenged the US government's conclusions on what caused Flight 800 to crash into the Atlantic Ocean on July 17, 1996. The Boeing 747-100 literally exploded in midair shortly after takeoff from JFK International Airport, killing everyone on board. Hundreds of witnesses reported evidence of offensive targeting that originated from either the ground or the water. There was also an indisputable presence of the explosive compound PETN around a gaping hole in the plane's fuselage.

"It's got to be attached to a passenger who is somehow getting on board. What if we simply disallowed all carry-on luggage or hand searched each and every pers—"

"Mr. President," Bridge interrupted. "You once told me that I could speak my mind with you as long as it was respectful and from my heart. I hold you to your word. You're micromanaging. There are no alternatives. You have the authority and more than enough evidence. Shut it down."

The president bristled at the public rebuke, but he knew that Bridge was right. He'd been in office over three years. His party had held Congressional majorities for six years. His record on fighting terror was solid; his foreign policy was both prudent and effective, and his domestic agenda was on the rise. The cyclical economy had shed all signs of recession and was showing steady growth. The decision he faced was akin to disciplining a child with a dangerous weapon. Not to mention that this child could vote.

"How long was air traffic stopped after 9/11?"

"Three days," Slavin spoke up.

The president digested that.

"Three days, and the economy went into recession for two years. What's first?"

"A threat announcement," Bridge replied. "There are two choices. Since we've abandoned the color-coded severity levels and created the National Terrorism Advisory System, we must issue either an elevated or imminent alert. Unfortunately, we're trapped either way, sir. Elevated suggests we may or may not be attacked. Imminent implies that real and credible evidence exists that an attack is forthcoming. With neither being true, we must assume the worst case. The question is for how long."

"Thank you, Thomas. Andrew, have Mr. Dorn join us," the president requested. He turned to his Secretary of Transportation. "What can we expect and when? I want to know the immediate ramifications for the airlines and our citizens."

A short Native American with no formal education, Norman Minka's tribal mediation skills had helped avoid a nationwide Teamster's strike last year. His face carried a permanent grimace forged by the fierce winds in Chignik Bay in Alaska. When he spoke, passion often trumped grammar. He and the president regularly hunted together, and he had already alerted his state's network of bush pilots. An airline shutdown would strand their customers on remote fly-ins.

Minka opened an inch-thick folder. "Well, right now there are 147 domestic air operator certificates in use and 170 foreign carriers allowed to fly in the United States. This includes commercial passenger and cargo. There are 7,000 carriers for hire and 223,000 general aviation planes operating at 19,500 airports. A nationwide ground stop would halt 24,000 departures and 1.7 million enplaned passengers per day. The airlines employ 486,000 full-time and 98,000 part-time people. At this time, there's no way to know or predict how many would be laid off. That would be based on the length of the stoppage and each airline's cash position. About 49,000 maintenance personnel might still be able to perform their jobs, but 71,000 pilots and copilots won't. Stopping the airline business sector is a momentous undertaking in itself, but the short- and long-term ramifications to down range sectors dependent on flying go on and on. At ground level, major cities will face massive gridlock. Rental car stations, subways, bus lines, railways, and even taxis will become lifelines. We must deal with the ten largest first: New York, LA, Atlanta, Chicago, Philadelphia, Boston, Dallas/Fort Worth, Miami, Washington, and Baltimore. People need to get back to their homes. We have two things on our side: it's early in the day, and there are no active threats. Carriers should be able to bring down flights in an orderly manner. Some will be near enough to destinations, but many won't. So we're back to severe inconvenience."

"International flights en route over the Pacific and Atlantic will be turned back unless they've passed midpoints or are low on fuel," Slavin added. "Our neighbors will cooperate with whatever we decide."

Minka continued. "That covers the first few hours. After one day, business sectors must brace for the worst. Cargo and intermediary suppliers who don't or can't keep inventory and depend on timely imports will be hurt. The trucking and rail industries will be overwhelmed with the increased volume. I won't get into minutia here, but please know that the financial consequences of stopping operations for the airlines alone are simply devastating. I have preliminary figures on the economic imp—"

"Thank you, Norman. Not now."

"Mr. President," Bard spoke up. "Sir, there is no such thing as an orderly shutdown. You heard the airline CEOs admit that their companies would be thrown into immediate and utter chaos."

"Yes, and they also admitted that they understood the reasoning and would support the decision. They also have no choice."

"Still, I'd like to suggest that we all take a step back for a moment and consider the catastrophic burden that we are intending to place on this country and its economy should you take this course of action. Might we at least consider announcing a delayed or phased approach, say forty-eight hours? Certainly that would give people time to prepare for and even avoid those inconveniences that Norman outlined. Perhaps twenty-four hours, or even twelve or eight? I don't believe that any of us in this room fully appreciate the gravity here. This isn't some restaurant or shopping mall down the block that we're intending to shutter, this is an entire economic sector—one that reaches so deeply into a myriad of others that the full weight of the consequences cannot possibly be known."

The room fell silent. The president's eyes observed every face. He wanted reaction. Eye contact, a twitch, a nod, or even a head shake—something that would indicate a position, pro or con. There was none.

"Thomas, do we need input from Commerce, Health and Human Services, or Defense?"

"No, sir," Bridge answered quickly. "I honestly don't know what value they could add to the up-front decision. They'd be more concerned after. This is my recommendation and mine alone."

"Mr. Riley, do you agree with my Chief of Staff?"

"Mr. Bard has some valid points."

"But do you think he's right? Do you think we should wait?"

Riley thought for a few seconds. *Watch your language, Jack.* "May I clarify those . . . inconveniences?"

The president nodded approval.

Riley stood. "Mr. Bard, you have no idea how much I hate waiting in lines. And you're absolutely right. This country would be turned upside-down in utter chaos for the foreseeable future, especially if the president pulls a hard lever today. Passengers who are stranded in some strange city or airport would be furious about having to find another way home to friends and family. Or worse, spending a night in some flophouse with six other people. I mean, I'm pretty resourceful, and I know I'd be upset. When even one airline stumbles, people suffer. Let's face it—travel inconvenience is a major hassle. Now think about airline layoffs, ruined vacations, deferred business meetings, or even cancelling that special family reunion. Who knows what'll happen to all that luggage? But in my opinion, Mr. Bard, before you curl up for the night on some uncomfortable airport bench and curse at the inconvenience, ask yourself this question: who's more inconvenienced? You, watching a line of stranded people inch forward to order a cold chili dog for dinner in some airport food court, or O'Hare's assistant tower chief watching a line of people inch forward at the wake of his wife and granddaughter, who died today on Flight 605? Mr. President, I wouldn't give these terrorist bomber cowards a second to rest or an ounce more satisfaction. No more flights; no more body counts. Not on our watch."

Riley sat down. His point hung in the air like a clarion call bellowed by Winston Churchill.

The president lowered his head and smiled briefly. He was first and foremost a naval officer who took deep pride in making decisions based on principle and integrity. Nothing riled him more than bending with the winds of election-year politics, which was Bard's real motive. He had simply drifted too far into overprotective waters. This was a textbook example of misguided loyalty.

Jeffrey Dorn, the White House press secretary, entered the room. "Sir?"

"I'll speak to the nation," the president announced, glancing at his watch, "in fifteen minutes. Andrew, please handle the courtesy calls with Norman's staff. Keep things brief. Domestic airlines first, then foreign. Don't forget Senate and House leaders." He took a deep breath and turned to Bridge. "Are we prepared to issue a nationwide terror alert?"

"Yes," Bridge confirmed. "Down to the local levels. They know something's coming, but not the specifics."

The president kept his eyes on Bridge and pointed at Riley. "I want him in charge."

Riley placed his hand on his chest. "Sir, with all due respect, I'm not . . . I don't work for Justice. This is the FBI's juris—"

"I'm not going to get into that," the president said firmly. "I don't care about jurisdiction. I've already spoken with the Attorney General. He understands my reasoning and has pledged his full support. You're it, son."

"He accepts, Mr. President," Bridge spoke up. "I'll inform Director Colmes."

The president rose from his chair and gave Riley a direct look. "For America's sake, find out how they're doing it." He turned to Minka. "Shut it down. Everything."

Minka sat stone-faced. Then he turned and nodded at Slavin.

All eyes in the room watched as she calmly lifted her phone and dialed the number for Vint Hill. A team of senior air traffic managers was already alerted and on standby. From there, emergency advisories would be issued to all regional centers, who in turn would relay the order to local hubs. In less than two minutes, all air and conveyance companies and carriers, airport towers, traffic control centers, and federal transportation facilities across the country would receive the message. In two more minutes, it would be global.

All scheduled departures within or bound for the United States on all flight display boards in all airports across the world would show the word *cancelled*. All US airborne flights were to find the nearest emergency landing field large enough to accommodate the weight of their aircraft and land immediately. Once on the ground, passengers and flight crews were to exit as quickly and as safely as possible. All aircraft were to be quarantined, searched, and cleared. No exceptions. No aircraft would be allowed to fly. Medical air transport requests would have to show life-threatening urgency and be cleared by the FAA's National Operations Manager. A separate call went out to all airfreight carriers.

—

WHITE HOUSE PRESS ROOM
WASHINGTON, DC

SECRETARY BRIDGE strode onto the stage, followed by a mix of newly briefed Cabinet staff and members. At that instant, the networks interrupted their regularly scheduled programs with this breaking news coverage.

President Warren appeared, and the room instantly fell silent.

He approached the podium, pausing to inhale deeply.

"As you know, there has been a second airline tragedy southeast of Omaha, Nebraska. At this time, we are unable to positively confirm whether it or the Milwaukee incidents were caused by mechanical failure, operator, or other human error or via acts of domestic terrorism. In order to take every possible protective measure to safeguard the citizens of the United States, and until we can ascertain cause, I have ordered that an imminent terror alert be issued per the National Terrorism Advisory System. That was initiated just moments ago."

The room erupted in camera clicks and shouts.

"Please, I'm sorry, but I'm not going to answer any questions. Mr. Dorn will hold a follow-up briefing within the hour." The room quieted. The president paused again. "Coincident with that order and in keeping with the spirit and severity of that alert, effective immediately, all motorized, floating, or gliding domestic and international passenger, commercial, cargo, recreational, or other airborne craft inside the borders of the United States will be grounded. Those aircraft approaching our borders will be turned back, if possible, or rerouted to Canada, Mexico, or the Caribbean. The airspace over the United States will be under a complete no-fly zone indefinitely. Make no mistake—there will be extreme delays in general transportation across the country as these actions are set in motion. Please bear with us. I ask for your patience, your cooperation, and your prayers in seeing these events to a rapid and safe conclusion. We will work tirelessly to bring this nation and its air transportation and subsidiary industries back to a level of confidence and security for all. The no-fly zone does not apply to law enforcement. It will be enforced by the military. Thank you."

28

US NO-FLY ZONE, DAY 2
WEDNESDAY, MAY 20

THE NEW YORK Stock Exchange had suspended all trading until some semblance of calm could be restored. Unfortunately, no one on its Board of Directors knew what that meant. They were simply trying to stop the largest volume stock loss in US history, surpassing the previous record set in October 1987 when one *trillion* dollars evaporated into thin air.

Even the sophisticated computer programs put in place to buffer such tsunami-like selling were overwhelmed. The current trading curbs, a.k.a. "circuit breakers," called for an hour-long pause in trading at a drop of 1,450 points in the Dow before 2:00 p.m. Eastern time. A decline of 2,900 points before 1:00 p.m. halted trading for two hours. A decline of 4,350 at any point halted trading for the day. Before the president's announcement, the skittish Dow had lost 1,600 points. The market reopened three hours later but quickly closed again as declines approached a record free fall of 33 percent. Worse, none of the usual liquidity rescuers were forthcoming. They were still trying to digest thirty-day market bottom forecasts flirting with losses of *six* trillion dollars.

Precious metal current and future orders skyrocketed.

—

MILWAUKEE, WI
COURTYARD MARRIOTT
7:00 A.M.

JACK RILEY didn't follow the financial chaos. He was too busy trying to manage his own. He knew the sword of Damocles was hanging over Homeland Security's head—no, that was a dodge. It was *his* head. With his appointment, he immediately ordered the NTSB and the FBI to maintain a central investigation point in Milwaukee. That way, they could all track this mysterious bomber-terrorist on the first of two trails. Per the president's directive, Riley needed to reinforce the fact that, in no uncertain terms, he was in charge. Not the FBI, not FEMA, not state or local authorities, and certainly not the NTSB. It came down to him, period. Riley believed that a good leader should use methodical means and feather ruffling, especially with investigative legwork. Criminal science and theory were fine, but nothing could beat the kind of information a tough, smart cop could squeeze from witnesses and suspects.

The government had commandeered nearly the entire hotel, and Riley had a suite transformed into his personal workspace. With respect to décor, he ordered that a 20 x 24 inch framed photograph be brought in from his Washington office. Captured off Duck Key, it was a photo of the ocean's glass-like surface at slack tide. He had been about to snap the sunset when something made a noise on the side of the boat. A tail-flapping, taunting noise. When he peered into the water, he saw Shaitan looking up at him in some sort of direct challenge. The photo clearly showed the size and ugliness of the monster—complete with its gaping, hook-lined mouth. Each time Riley looked at his nemesis, it renewed his determination to have the ultimate fish fry.

Riley's cell phone chirped.

"Jack, I just want to recommit my support," Secretary Bridge's voice said. "If you need anything from any department or agency within the US Government, you've got it. If anyone balks or says the word *no*, then I want a phone call, understood?"

"Sir, I'm still not convinced that I'm the right person for this. I don't think that the president realizes what's involved. I'm not exactly comfortable telling seasoned federal agents how and when to do their jobs. The FBI is funny that way."

"Since when is Jack Riley uncomfortable with anything?" Bridge asked. "Director Colmes was kind enough to suggest a good right-hand man, someone who can help you keep the investigation on track."

"The investigation or me?"

"Whatever the reasoning, he's supposed to be one of the Bureau's best, not to mention you could use a good sounding board. He's from their Investigative Training Unit at Quantico. But more important, he knows agency politics. His name is David Cheng."

"We've already connected," Riley said. "He's agreed to head up the ground investigation in Milwaukee."

"You'll do fine, Jack. Use your instincts."

"I still don't understand why the president wants Homeland Security in charge of such a high-profile investigation. I can name at least a dozen senior FBI people who could handle it. I'm missing something."

"Precisely because you *are* Homeland Security," Bridge answered. "The president wants to show the country and the world how effective his administration can be in combating terror on America's soil. He has the utmost faith in you because of your outstanding qualifications. He's told me more than once that he likes you, and—"

"I don't buy that," Riley interrupted the patronizing. "Tell me the truth."

There was silence. "It's a prelude."

"A prelude to what?"

"Consolidation."

Riley shifted the phone. "I'm not following."

"Jack, remember Hurricane Katrina? What were the lessons we learned?"

"Not to build cities below sea level," he answered flatly.

"I mean relative to the federal government's structure and culture, particularly in a national crisis. We exposed the worst of ourselves, and I want to see if you agree."

"If you're talking about selective response and rescue based on ethnicity or race, then I don't agree."

"Jack, no informed person believes that. It's bureaucracy. We showed the world how miserable we were at coordinating and communicating with our own internal agencies. As a direct result of that exposed failure, the president developed a plan that will shake the federal government to its foundations. It'll involve the largest single reorganization in US government history. Agencies that have existed for over a hundred years will be eliminated, and their functions will be merged. The code name for the new singularity is DNS, Department of National Security. Anyone in the federal government who carries a weapon, investigates a crime, or defends our nation against an enemy or threat will be impacted. And by the way, threats include man-made terrorist acts and natural disasters like hurricanes.

"During Katrina, FEMA and especially Homeland Security looked like bumbling idiots. The media filmed human horrors that we never knew existed. While people were literally dying in the streets, our fire and rescue teams were sitting in diversity sensitivity meetings. We don't want anyone to put us through that kind of embarrassment again.

"Your appointment on this case is simply a prelude. The president wants to use the outcome of your actions—the *successful* outcome—to serve as a showcase on how multiple agencies can and should work together permanently, not just during a crisis. In other words, it's a working model that paves the way for interagency cooperation."

"You mean kills it," Riley said.

"That's a true statement, Jack. There won't *be* interagencies. They'll all be the same organization."

Riley shook his head. Senior government managers were always reorganizing something. All federal law enforcement personnel working in one seamless entity? It made too much sense. It also placed an even greater burden on him and his investigation. He didn't like being a public guinea pig. He knew what was coming next. He even mouthed the words.

"Do you have any leads?" Bridge asked. "Anything at all?"

"No, sir. The FBI . . . er, my teams are still forming up here."

"What about resources? Do you need any more bod—?"

"Thank you, but we have enough people. I'm about to have a kickoff session. We'll be covering every possible avenue."

"Do you need anything? Anything at all?"

Riley paused. "I want someone from NTSB on my lead team. I wanted you to know up front in case it causes any problems over there."

"It won't," Bridge assured. He didn't know Tom Ross, but it didn't matter. "What else?"

Riley took a deep breath. "I need to bring someone from the media inside. A reporter." He held the phone away from his ear.

There was extended silence. "For what reason?"

Riley explained.

"Good thinking, Jack," Bridge agreed. "Is that all?"

"If you said a few introductory words to my teams, it might help reinforce the fact that we're in charge of this thing and not the FBI."

"You can handle it. I like your idea of splitting things by airport, but I still want all reporting to come through you."

"Thanks. I'll keep you informed. There is one more thing. I'm curious about the president's singularity plan. What happens to the military?"

"Simple. The first and foremost question that will determine if you belong in the Department of National Security is . . . do you carry a weapon? Obviously, the answer is yes. All four branches of the military will integrate. Common commanders, common bases, perhaps even common uniforms. Everything is on the table. I'll bring you up to speed on some other facets, but we need to get through this first. Good luck, Jack."

"I'll do my best."

"That's my boy." Bridge clicked off. He was under as much pressure as Riley, if not more.

Riley collected a set of papers. *The Department of National Security,* he thought, smirking. *The president has gone crazy.*

For a moment, Riley actually felt equal measures of calm and confidence. Then something slapped the back of his head. It was a wake-up slap given by someone who wanted his full attention. His father, Robert Jackson Riley, had passed away five years ago. A high school business-education teacher and wrestling coach, Robert had left an indelible mark. Though he was a stern disciplinarian, the rap to his son's head wasn't meant to hurt; it was meant to remind.

Don't let anyone ever call you "boy."

Riley walked into an adjoining room where the Homeland Security and FBI senior team leads were seated. A simulcast teleconference on an eighty-inch flat screen linked the room with an FBI site at the Hilton next to O'Hare's main terminals.

Riley spoke into the camera. "Good morning. I don't need to remind everyone that the president and America are depending on us to make a rapid impact in finding the perpetrator or perpetrators who committed these vicious acts. To say that we're in the spotlight is an asinine understatement. I'll reiterate what Secretary Bridge told me a few moments ago: if you or any of your agents encounter resistance from either a private or a governmental jurisdiction, I want to know. And I mean that. You can contact me anytime, day or night, with anything of interest or relevance, or to report roadblocks to these investigations. With respect to chain of command, my personal likes and dislikes, and my leadership style, let me say that I hold each of you and your people in the highest professional regard. I expect progress, and I like to see things for myself. Be advised: I will take a hands-on approach. That simply means I'll be on-site whenever I can. I dislike weasels, blamers, excessive paperwork, good ol' boy cliques, and people who don't take responsibility. And if you ever lie to me, I'll throw you out on your tail. I expect cooperative teamwork. Special Agent Cheng will cover for me when I'm unavailable. Treat him as you would me.

"One more thing regarding my position here before we get started. The president appointed me, and I realize that it may rub some of you the wrong way. I have one thing to say about that: this is an interagency mission, so get over it. It's not about you or me or careers; it's about freedom. Whoever committed these crimes will be found and brought to justice. I will work tirelessly for this country, and I expect that same energy and ethic from you. That said, let me share our strategy."

Tom Ross entered the room. Riley whispered a few words before continuing.

"I expect each of you to read and become fully aware of the tactics used in the 2006 London transatlantic aviation terror cell operation. It includes twenty-one background dossiers and the types of accelerants they planned to use to destroy ten aircraft. London's Anti-Terror Branch calls it a summary, but it's still four hundred pages. Pay special attention to sections ten and eleven, 'In-Flight Pre-Detonation Placements' and 'Explosive Containers.' The summary is a separate and accessible module that has been added to your Virtual Case File Network. And speaking of virtual, we're going to establish coverage zones for the Mitchell International and O'Hare Airports respectively and then assign teams. The first zone is the inside perimeter. Both Delta and United's CEOs have personally assured me of total cooperation from their employees. Let's start with Mitchell's team structures. Checked baggage. I want a face matched to every piece. Who's reviewing security videos?"

"I am," FBI agent Derrick Gale spoke up from across the room. "We already have Mitchell's tapes. I'll have O'Hare's by this afternoon."

"Who's handling carry-ons?"

"Will Clark."

"Perimeter security?"

"Nelson Bennett."

"Customer service personnel?"

"That'd be Agent Cortez. His teams are covering rampers, agents, baggage tugs, wing walkers, fuelers, and caterers. If he needs help, my people can assist."

"Good." Riley nodded and returned to his list. "Anyone else?"

"Mechanics."

Riley thumbed through a Delta contact list. "John Louter, VP of Maintenance Operations. Has anyone contacted him?"

"Patricia Creed. She's one of the NTSB's investigators. She's started an interrogation list and has already had some problems."

"What problems?" Riley demanded, vaguely recalling the name.

"Some of the mechanics have a real attitude about talking to the government. They've got an inherent fear of having their tickets . . . er, licenses pulled. They're afraid of being thrown in airport jail. It's some kind of union thing."

"You tell Ms. Creed to keep pushing. I want hard interviews with every one of the people who either touched that aircraft or were on duty at Mitchell preflight. If anyone acts suspiciously, mentions constitutional rights, or balks at questioning, I want to know. Anything else?"

"Sir, with respect to reporting hierarchy, what exactly is the FBI's role here? I'd rather not have any conflicting orders from our side of the chain."

Riley's first instinct was to slam his hand on the table, but he caught himself.

"There won't be any conflicts. I know this is new, and you may have to shift your thinking. This is, first and foremost, a national security investigation headed by the Department of Homeland Security. The FBI is taking the lead at O'Hare, and their progress will be reported to me. That goes for the NTSB too. The gentleman sitting next to me is Tom Ross, their man in charge. His findings at each of the crash sites will also become instantaneously available to this team. We'll have centralized, accessible information—no overlap, no confrontations, and no media leaks. Everything comes through me. Let's move to the outside perimeter. Mr. Cheng?"

A lean Chinese-American with a drawn face and a marathon runner's physique strolled to a whiteboard. He inserted a marker into an electronic sleeve and drew out a rectangular sketch. The image was visible on a receiving board at the O'Hare site.

"Mitchell International Airport covers seven square miles. There are 274 private businesses operating on the perimeter. The investigative boundaries will start at the airport property and stretch outward one mile in all directions. Our objective is to literally flood the area with bodies and interviews.

"We have confirmed that our perpetrator was in the area when he made that the cell phone call. My people will visit every building, restaurant, gas station, office, and residence within two square miles of the originating cell tower. If our caller was sitting in a car on a side street along an airport boundary, then someone saw him.

"We have seventy-three federal agents assigned to the street. Milwaukee's mayor has offered as many local detectives as we need to supplement the ground coverage." Cheng sat down.

Riley nodded. "I want the local and national media to see us tripping over each other. We need to scare up some information. Okay, personnel assigned to Mitchell International are released. Let's move on to O'Hare."

29

WEST BARABOO, WI

AKIL PLACED his ID back in his wallet and recited a reference number to a young female clerk in a Check Advance Service Center.

"You can have a seat, sir, while I process this. How would you like the cash?"

"Hundreds and twenties, please," Akil said, easing into a club chair. Even the interior air smelled like manure in this unremarkable Midwestern farm town of 1,400 people just south of Wisconsin Dells. He thumbed through a stack of reading materials, bypassing *People* and opting instead for a cattle disease article in *BEEF* magazine.

"You a gambler?" an elderly Native American man asked from across the lobby. He wore a bright-red, leather-fringed trapper costume and a red felt cowboy hat adorned with silver, turquoise, and bright-red feathers.

"I do my share," Akil said. He knew that for him, gambling was strictly forbidden:

> *In them (wine and gambling) is great sin and their sin is greater than their benefit. (2:220)*

> *You who have believed, intoxicants, gambling, and divining arrows are but defilement from the work of Satan, so avoid it that you may be successful. (5:90)*

Akil also knew that his participation was perfectly acceptable and allowed in the course of deceiving his enemies.

"They call me Wanig-suchka, the Red Bird," the old man said. "My ancestor was a war chief who always wore a red coat and called himself English. He was born in 1788. Ho-Chunk Casino is four miles north on County Highway BD. I give local tours, and I drive a shuttle, if you need a ride. You staying around here?"

"Nah, not today," Akil said. "I don't feel real lucky. Besides, I'm heading south. Gotta get back to Cincinnati by tonight."

The old man shrugged. "Too bad. Ho-Chunk is one of six tribal casinos in Wisconsin. We are also known as the Winnebago, a Sioux-speaking tribe of Native Americans from Wisconsin, Minnesota, and parts of Iowa and Illinois. We have 2,500 slot machines now, but everything started with bingojack."

"Bingojack?"

"That goes way back," Red Bird said. "When it first opened, there was nothing on this land but a pole barn. Bingojack was the only game we offered. All the employees were tribal volunteers with no gaming experience. Even I was a dealer. Some of us barely knew how to read." He laughed. "We miscounted so many hands it's a wonder we stayed in business."

"I've never heard of bingojack," Akil said.

"Tens and face cards were white, with a pink ball in the center. That way nobody could say it was blackjack, a game prohibited by Wisconsin state law. When a player got dealt an ace and a pink ball card, someone shouted bingojack." Red Bird waved his arms theatrically. "The rest is Indian history."

"Is the casino crowded with the flying ban?" Akil asked.

"There could be a nuclear war and people would still come here and gamble. Las Vegas might be dying, but nobody flies to Wisconsin Dells. They all drive.

"This area is one of the most beautiful and scenic locations for Midwestern tourists to pack up their rug rats and spend a summer vacation. Where else can you find majestic views of the Wisconsin River and giant roller coasters within five square miles? The water parks here rank among the best in the country, especially the indoor ones. Our casino and hotel rival any operation anywhere.

"We may not be the Bellagio, but give us time. If we forced Donald Trump's casinos into bankruptcy, then we're doing something right. All the Indian revenues in the United States are more than Las Vegas and Atlantic City combined. I can remember when the Ho-Chunk Nation used to raise money selling caramel apples to tourists every night at the Indian Ceremonial Dance north of town. Not anymore. Now we own the town. Tribes all over the country lobbied state governments for the right to gamble on sacred land and provide for our people. What a crock! Hardly any of the profit goes to poor and under-privileged tribal families. It all funnels back to the original investors. And many of them already own shares in the Nevada and New Jersey operations. One of the wealthiest lives in Singapore."

The cashier appeared at the counter window.

Akil gave Red Bird a cordial nod and strode outside to his car. He tucked the seven thousand dollars into his jean pocket along with a new prepaid cash card. The MoneyGram transaction amount was well below the ten thousand dollar limit that would alert Financial Crimes Enforcement. The drive to San Diego would take at least twenty-four hours.

—

COURTYARD MARRIOTT

TOM ROSS was curled up on a folding cot in a laundry room next to the NTSB's communication center. A row of industrial clothes dryers gently hummed through their cycles.

Ron Hollings noticed his boss sleeping lightly and had no choice but to wake him. He knelt on the floor near the cot.

"Ross? Ian Goodman is here. We're trying to patch in the live underwater video feed from the cockpit. It should take another twenty minutes or so, if you want to watch. It looks like it's in decent shape."

Ross sat up and let out a huge yawn. "Did the Fontenelle team form up yet?"

"Uh-huh. About an hour ago."

"That was quick," Ross said, inhaling deeply. "How many people did we have to give?"

"Just three. There was a contingency list of retirees willing to come back in an emergency."

"Retirees?" Ross said incredulously. "Heaven help us."

"Yeah. Nobody even knew there was such a list, but multiple airline crashes tend to gobble up resources. I guess they had to create some kind of backup plan in case of another 9/11."

"My back is killing me," Ross said, stretching for his toes.

Hollings shook his head. "You look awful, Tom. Why don't you just sleep in your room? We can handle things here. Besides, it wouldn't look real good if the media found the NTSB's investigator-in-charge napping in the laundry."

"Call me when that film starts. And by the way, I'm not in charge anymore," Ross said matter-of-factly. "You are."

"What?"

"Don't worry and don't ask. You probably wouldn't believe me anyway. Suffice it to say that I'm going on a special assignment. I just need you to cover things. I have a one-on-one interview in fifteen minutes. Where's Neela?"

"In her room with her cameraman. She's been there all day. Tom, this is crazy. Are we really supposed to start approving news stories? We're investigators, not editors."

"I'll handle that," Ross assured.

"Fine with me. Nobody in our office has any experience with TV reporting. It's so early in the process that we don't even know the topic of the news story."

Ross stood up and looked Hollings in the eyes.

"The topic is me."

30

OVAL OFFICE, WHITE HOUSE
WASHINGTON, DC

CHIEF OF STAFF Bard fingered through several folders, trying to determine which crisis to bring up first. With an ever-slanted eye on election politics, he decided on economics.

"Mr. President, six major airlines are planning a joint statement at 1:00 p.m. I'm afraid they're going to announce a drop-dead date for a bailout. Their cash reserves are already on fire. Secretary Minka hasn't had time to consolidate all the carrier numbers, but he did manage a rough estimate of Delta's—one without the accounting hocus-pocus. He looked at it from a daily revenue intake of zero. From here on, it's all about cash flow. One thing's for sure: they're in pre-panic denial. Delta's VP of Finance, John Jacobs said they have six billion in cash and could survive a shutdown for two to three months, maybe longer. Minka thinks they only have three billion in cash and the rest due from receivables."

"What about fuel savings?"

"Already factored in, as are the effects of an unprecedented layoff of nonessential employees and union workers. They can also reduce contract maintenance work, but they still owe nearly a billion a month in short-term debt payments alone. Sir, Minka believes these companies will be on life support in twenty-five to forty days."

"What about other assets?"

"Of course that's an option. They all have short- and long-term investments along with credit lines, but no business wants to start raiding those just to make payroll. And it gets worse. In addition to losing three billion dollars a day in revenue, initial forecasts suggest that the fear alone generated by airline terrorism could result in a forty to fifty percent decline in passengers if and when service resumes. And that decline could last for six months or more. That spells more than bankruptcy; that spells ceasing operations. I have to admit that I never realized how fragile that industry is. The unions are already planning mass protest rallies. I'm afraid this is just horrid. The airlines, hotels, restaurants, resorts, and all the travel and business-related sectors could also lose 1.1 million jobs in just two months. One year after 9/11, domestic and foreign air travel were down 15 percent and 25 percent, respectively. After just three days of shutdown, the airlines needed ten billion dollars to survive. If this thing runs for ten or even fifteen days, I'm afraid they'll need upward of seventy to eighty billion dollars to keep operating . . . maybe more."

"Then it's our job to get it for them," the president said firmly. "Andrew, please stop saying you're afraid. We're all afraid. It is what it is. The fabric of our very economy is unraveling before our eyes, and we're powerless to stop it. This is a living economic and political nightmare. No—it's more than that. It's economic terrorism and extortion rolled into one. Whoever did this planned it beautifully. Think of it. They've placed the responsibility for the economic impacts right in our laps. We don't know the terror method, and therefore we have no choice but to injure the economy. All the blame shifts to us until we figure out how it's being perpetrated. Meanwhile, we have to be the bad guy. And we certainly can't go to the American people with two anonymous phone calls. On the other hand, if we allow air traffic to resume, knowing that more attacks are possible, it would be criminal." The president glanced at his flag. "One nation under God . . . one nation held hostage."

The president's phone chirped. "Yes?" he said.

"Mr. President, I wanted to remind you that we're giving the first interview via our embedded media relationship," Bridge said on the other line. "It's scheduled to air on all networks later this evening. Hopefully, it will—"

"Excuse me?" The president shifted the phone. "Our embedded what?"

"Cale . . . er, Mr. President, we talked about this," Bridge gently reminded. "Jack Riley was forced to make an arrangement with the news reporter who received the initial terror warning. She's the only non-governmental person who's heard it. We've given her access to certain investigative information and have allowed her to do some on-site broadcasts in return for her temporary silence. Thankfully, she's agreed. I'm uncomfortable with it too, sir, but if Jack says it's for the good of the investigation, then that's good enough for me."

"Her silence," the president muttered. "Why would anyone agree to that? Is Riley involved with her?"

"Absolutely not," Bridge assured. "I think he's smarter than that."

Too bad, the president thought to himself. He was almost disappointed. A tawdry personal scandal might divert the nation's attention elsewhere. He thanked Bridge, hung up, and turned his attention back to Bard.

"Has Congress approached us?" he asked.

"Not officially," Bard answered. "There's an army of airline lobbyists working on a taxpayer bailout. United's CEO, Jeffrey Smirtek, said that without it, the airlines would become a major casualty of war. And he also stated that his company would not agree to a single concession attached to such a bailout by their security holders, creditors, or employees."

"I wouldn't either," the president admitted. "I don't know if airline shares can possibly decline any further."

"Senator Benvenito is resurrecting his draft of the Airline Recovery Act to get a jump on the loan guarantee requests. He's also broached the subject of going national again. He said he's got people willing to form up in committee to create the framework. He wants to know your reaction."

The president rolled his eyes. "Those socialists and their knee-jerk ideas. For the life of me, I'll never understand how such highly educated politicians can be so dumb. Can you imagine the US government operating what is arguably the world's most service-oriented business?

A national airline would be an unmitigated screw-up, even worse than government-run health care. Do you know what the real problem is? Some people in Congress need a good, old-fashioned history lesson. In a socialistic society, government controls business. In a communistic society, they own it. In other words, there is no difference."

"Is that an official or unofficial reaction?" Bard said, collecting his folders.

The president slumped into his chair and gazed out the windows.

"I should have stayed in the Navy, or maybe on our farm. You know, for all his military heroism and political savvy, George Washington was a farmer—and an extraordinary one at that. He always wanted to be at his Mount Vernon plantation, tending his land and horses and sitting on his porch overlooking the Potomac. The man loved horses. He even built a sheltered manure pit right off the main house because he knew the value of fertilizer. I'd like to send a wagon of it up to Capitol Hill. How's that for my reaction?"

—

COURTYARD MARRIOTT
MILWAUKEE, WI

"TOM ROSS, this is my cameraman, Terry Lee," Griffin announced, collecting her purse. "I'll be right back. If Terry tells you that he's my protective little brother, don't believe a word of it." She winked and closed the door.

Ross took a seat on the sofa. He eyed Lee warily. "So, are you her brother?"

"Depends," Lee replied, tightening the legs of a tripod. "Why? You interested?"

"I might be." Ross narrowed his eyes. "Are you?"

"I'm just a friend who wouldn't want her to get hurt again. I guess you could say that I'm a little brother and chaperone rolled into one."

"What do you mean 'again'?"

"I take it you don't know about Skip." Ross shook his head. "Liar, drinker, and wife beater—three separate times. Skip's a remodeling contractor. He's a tough guy with an attitude and an alcohol problem.

Neela knew it and still married him. She thought he'd change. Right after she signed on with Fox, Skip went on one of his binges and smacked her around pretty good. Her first week on the job, she wore an eye patch. She blamed it on a bicycle accident. The second time, she stayed home. Even then she still wouldn't report it. When it happened a third time, she had the sense and the guts to file charges. It was a big day for the Milwaukee news media. All Skip got was probation while Neela got publicly embarrassed. It hurt her reputation real bad. I don't think she'll ever let a man get close to her again. So, Mr. Ross, if you're into physical violence or alcohol addiction in a relationship, then I suggest you look elsewhere. She doesn't need another Skip. But be warned, she's taken enough self-defense classes to handle most men no matter how big they are. Trust me, you don't ever want to get her mad."

"I've never hit a woman in my life," Ross said adamantly. "I'm not that way."

"Neither was Skip at first, so consider yourself warned."

"Fair enough, Mr. Lee."

"Call me Terry."

The door opened, and Griffin walked in with a bag from the hotel gift shop.

"Are you sure this is a good idea?" Ross asked. "With me, I mean?"

"Yes," Griffin said matter-of-factly. "It'll give the segment instant credibility. Don't be so shy."

"I'm not shy," he huffed. "I've given interviews before."

"Then you know the routine." She turned to Lee. "How does he look?"

"Camera ready," Lee replied, adjusting the lighting. He casually motioned to the top of Ross's head.

Griffin reached into the bag and produced some extra hold mousse. She gave Ross's hair two squirts and brushed the mousse through it.

She caught Ross staring at her in the wall mirror.

Griffin smiled and faced the camera.

"We're coming to you from the Courtyard Marriott on Layton and 5th Street in Milwaukee, Wisconsin, where the National Transportation Safety Board, or NTSB, has established its temporary headquarters. I'm here with Thomas Ross, the man in charge of the NTSB's vaunted Go

191

Team, which is investigating the airline tragedies that occurred here on Monday morning and in South Omaha, Nebraska, on Tuesday."

She turned. "Mr. Ross, what can you tell us about the black boxes that have been recovered? Will they provide any clues to what caused these incidents?"

"Yes and no," Tom replied. "We've recovered two CVRs, or cockpit voice recorders, and two flight data recorders, or FDRs. Both sets are in good condition. We've analyzed the Delta boxes, and preliminary results have shown that the flight controls and instruments were functioning normally during the plane's takeoff. But shortly after that, there was an indication of a problem with two of the major systems: maneuverability and thrust. The data indicated that—"

"Excuse me, could you explain that?"

Ross noticed Griffin's perfume.

"Um, sure . . . um . . . I'm sorry . . . er, yes, we found that one engine had lost all capability to produce turns due to compressor failure. In layman's terms, a jet engine does four things: suck, squeeze, burn, and blow. Something literally stopped the air from being squeezed or compressed—something very violent.

"Second, we know that shortly after takeoff, the aircraft started turning and lost its ability to straighten its nose. The pilot's best recovery reaction, given the time frame involved, would have been to control that movement by the rudder on the plane's tail. It appears that something dramatic happened to Flight 771's rudder, and that meant the pilot was unable to bring the nose back to the original flight path. Then it went into an uncontrollable roll.

"We also know that the loss of control happened at a specific point in time. The data shows that it was instantaneous. What we don't know is how or where the problem originated. It could have come from a variety of places, including something as simple as a stripped screw that allowed the rudder to move back and forth. That's only a theory right now, though. We're still recovering the physical pieces."

"Correct me if I'm wrong, Mr. Ross, but that sounds similar to the accident that happened in the Belle Harbor area of Queens, New York, two months after 9/11. Wasn't that also a rudder problem?"

"Yes, unfortunately, that's true. American Airlines Flight 587 took off from John F. Kennedy Airport and lost an entire section of its tail. We concluded that it was caused by a combination of improper pilot pressure on the rudder pedals and a concentrated vortex of air created by the jet wash of an earlier departure. It was both operator and manufacturer-related. At this time, we're not ruling that or anything out."

"In his press conference on Tuesday, the president would neither confirm nor deny any terrorist linkage. Is that still true?"

"I certainly can't speak for the president, Homeland Security, or the FBI, but at this time there are no indications that these crashes were caused by anything other than mechanical failure. The Delta flight's voice recorder supports further evidence of that. Conversation between the pilot and first officer is relaxed and normal up to the point where they discover something is wrong. Sadly, the time element between that discovery and the actual crash itself was very brief. There simply wasn't a lot of talk. That's strong evidence, though, that there was no pilot duress and no unauthorized persons in or trying to gain access to the cockpit."

"What can you tell us about Flight 605?"

"Oddly enough, the engine failure appears to be identical to that of Delta's except that both of United's engines lost power at the same moment in flight."

"Doesn't it seem incredible that two different aircraft have crashed under circumstances exactly like those of two Russian planes in 2004?"

"I wouldn't say it's incredible, but it is highly unusual," Ross clarified. "Those things just don't happen. Flight 771 was a Boeing MD-90 and Flight 605 was an Airbus. However, it's important to understand that while the aircraft are different, their flight control systems and mechanics still have many similarities, especially in physical components and parts. Those similarities are then vulnerable to similar failures. If it is a mechanical or physical defect in a common component, then I'm confident we'll find it."

"How long would it take for a mass replacement of such a defective part?"

"Good question. It would happen airline by airline. I can't begin to estimate the time frame. I do know that the maintenance staffs in the entire industry would work day and night to correct such a defect. I don't want to speculate, but it would take a while."

"Thank you, Mr. Ross." Griffin turned to the camera. "Incredible or highly unusual? We'll have to wait and see. In the meanwhile, stay tuned for regular updates. Reporting from NTSB investigation headquarters in Milwaukee, this is Neela Griffin, Fox 6 News."

Lee turned off the camera.

"Nice take, Neela. This is sweet stuff. The other stations know we're here, and they're really ticked. How come Fox gets such preferential treatment?"

"Never mind about that." Griffin turned to Ross. "Do you want to edit this?"

"It's fine; let it go."

Griffin ushered Lee to the door. "There's a deadline in four hours," she said to her cameraman. "There'll be more to come. I'll call you."

Ross rose from his chair. "I'm impressed. A lot of people are uncomfortable with our findings on Flight 587. And you did your homework on those Soviet flights. How has reaction been at your news station? Are you still a problem child?"

"Are you kidding? They're treating me like I'm Ann Curry, Megyn Kelly, and Diane Sawyer rolled into one. It's been a complete turnaround. I can do just about anything I want with segment topics and time slots. They did think it was a little unusual that I was given private access to such a sensitive investigation, but everyone in this business realizes that's where the media is heading. It's certainly a good way to present the truth. My colleagues did wonder why I'm staying here when I live just ten miles away, but other than that, it's all good."

"I see you're hosting a fund-raiser tonight for some of the families," Ross said, reaching out and gently grasping Neela's hands. "How are you holding up? I mean, can I help with anything?"

"I'm a little tired, but other than that, I'm okay." She gave a quizzical look and then smiled. "You're even busier than I am, but that was really sweet. Thanks for asking."

Ross pulled her closer. Neela's expression fell somewhere between interested and shy. She didn't resist. She lowered her eyes briefly, then raised them to meet his. Ross placed his hand under her chin. His kiss was ultra-soft, barely touching at first, then grew firmer.

Warmth rippled through her body, and her cheeks flushed pink.

Ross pulled his lips away slowly.

Trancelike, the couple stood an inch apart, eyes closed. The moment was interrupted by vibrating from Ross's pocket.

Griffin swallowed hard, catching her breath.

"What was that for?"

"Your perfume does something to me. I can't think straight." Ross ignored his phone. "I just want you to know that this is something that I'm not used to. I've never been through anything like this before, at least in a while. And I feel good knowing that you're the person I'm involved with. I mean, that you're the person who's involved with me. I mean, the one working with me on this investigation. I'm glad I met you."

She held back laughter. "I'm glad I met you too."

Ross was noticeably relieved. "We never really had the chance to . . . well, if both of us could find the time, would it be all right if we had dinner?"

"Are you asking me out on a date?"

He paused thoughtfully. "I want to be sure that I thoroughly researched the issue using approved NTSB procedures. Let's see . . . a subject male has just invited a subject female to partake in the consumption of nutrition at a public establishment that serves such nutrition. Personally, I told myself that I would never become involved with anyone at work, but that referred to employees within the same company. And finally, the subject female is kind, intelligent, caring, and very attractive. Yup. I'm asking you out on a date. For the second time. And I really hope you'll accept."

She smiled sympathetically. "I'm sorry, but someone called me earlier. I've been invited to do something special."

Ross's heart sank. "Special?"

"Uh-huh. The Fox News Channel. The cable people in New York," she clarified. "I think they're going to offer me a position."

"That's wonderful," Ross offered weakly. He was comforted by the suitor's name but not the location.

"I have to drive out there, but I'll take a rain check on dinner, okay? I promise I will when I get back if you let me listen to that CVR."

Ross cocked his head suspiciously. His phone buzzed again.

ROSS HURRIED downstairs to an NTSB staffing room.

Ron Hollings was talking with Ian Goodman from the Association of Retired Aviation Professionals. On the surface, such a meeting would seem like an unholy alliance based on the grief Goodman had caused the NTSB and the FBI on prior investigations—namely his theory that a SAM-6 missile brought down the infamous TWA Flight 800. But Ross didn't care. Goodman was an expert in jet armaments, including handheld surface-to-air weaponry.

Hollings turned off the room lights and clicked on a TV monitor.

The video showed an FBI diver descending into Lake Michigan just two hours earlier. Armed with a JW Fishers DHC-1 handheld camera, the diver straightened a tangle in his one-hundred-foot cable and drifted down forty feet, to the right side of the Delta fuselage. As with all underwater filming, the light conditions tended to filter out yellow and red, thus giving images a bluish-green tint. The lake's maximum visibility at that depth was less than twenty feet.

The camera revealed that the main wreckage was contained within one square mile. The diver fanned his spotlight and caught the silvery flash of a Coho salmon cruising past, following the oxygen-rich layer of the lake's thermocline. He concentrated the light beam at a large piece of wreckage in the distance. The cockpit was on its side.

Incredibly, there didn't seem to be much damage until the diver spotted a black, starlike streak. He swam closer and ran his hand along the exposed edge of a large gaping hole where the nose landing gear used to be. He panned up to the roof.

"Pause it right there," Goodman requested. "I think I'm wasting your time, gentlemen. This was definitely caused by an explosion, but based on the apparent direction of the blast, I think it came from inside the plane. There's not a single impact point or trauma anywhere else. It's all on the bottom side of the hull at the gear."

"Is there any possibility that internal sparking ignited the fuel?" Hollings wondered.

Goodman crossed his arms defensively and shook his head. "You and your sparking. Is that all the NTSB ever thinks about? Let me be frank: there's no way. Jet fuel vapors are not explosive until the temperature reaches 185 degrees. Even then, it's not enough for a violent explosion. And really, Ron, this plane was full of fuel. Certainly, anything set off inside the wiring or air conditioning compartments or even the center tank would have taken out that entire section, but it's all still there. And you can unequivocally rule out a missile."

"How so?" Ross asked

"A blind man could see it in a minute," Goodman said confidently. "First, the roof. A missile would've blown right through the cockpit, windshield and all. There's simply too much of it intact.

"Second, stingers—the most common weapon to use here—are heat seekers. Not super-efficient, but enough to do the job, especially at low altitudes, slow target speeds, and *defined heat sources*—and that's the clincher. There's no heat anywhere near the point of impact, and this jet certainly wasn't taking any evasive maneuvers. Besides, witnesses would have seen a vertical smoke trail from ten miles away. Gentlemen, you've got a real problem on your hands. It almost seems as though something was *placed* in there."

"Placed there?" Ross asked.

"I bet the physics would support it," Goodman said.

"Inside the cockpit?"

Goodman shrugged. "It's as good a place as any to start investigating. If I were you, I'd tell your FBI friends to take a hard look at two groups of people in particular."

"Who?" Ross asked.

"The flight crew and the mechanics."

—

US NO-FLY ZONE, DAY 3
NEVADA DESERT
THURSDAY, MAY 21

AKIL WAS westbound on Interstate 15. He lowered his eyes and squinted into his dashboard at the Camry's odometer. He'd recently had it repaired, but it was stuck again.

In daylight, the Nevada desert was hauntingly colorful. The sun had nearly disappeared below the horizon, and the scenery reminded him of Al Khadra, Saudi Arabia. The desert east of Mecca also radiated black from the rocks that littered the landscape. They were rocks with imprints of strange fossilized animals. On their first pilgrimage, his father told him that the desert was once an ocean, but some animals had lost faith so Allah dried the water and turned them into stone. His father said that would happen to anyone who lost faith.

Akil noticed the distant glow of Las Vegas. He would stop there for the night.

—

O'HARE AEROSPACE CENTER
SCHILLER PARK, IL

ROSIE BURKE locked the wheel brake lever of her cleaning cart and then pressed numbers on Suite 200 West's door keypad. She paused at the signage and the letters *LLC. Probably some legal mumbo-jumbo,* she thought.

"Not that one," a supervisor shouted from the other end of the corridor. "Computer Doctors never signed up for cleaning."

She glanced around the room briefly, curious at the fact that there was nothing there. Nothing on the desk—no computers, no pictures, no papers, no sign of use or occupancy at all. Just a vase of wilted flowers and an empty office that someone rented for the next twelve months.

She closed the door and moved on.

32

JACK RILEY paced the floor in his command center office, cell phone at his ear, impatiently waiting for his home answering machine to beep. His daughter had recorded the announcement and was into long-winded greetings. She'd make an excellent lawyer.

Agent Cheng appeared in the doorway.

Riley waved him in.

"Kissi, it's me. I'll try and sneak away tomorrow afternoon. I should be home around four. Call if you can. Love you."

Cheng smiled. "If I don't call mine every day, I catch heat too."

"Kissi is short for Bhekisisa," Riley said, feeling the need to explain. "I can deal with heat. Once, I was gone for five days and never called. When I got home, our horse stable population had increased by two occupants, and our savings had decreased by $18,000."

Cheng approached the wall behind Riley's desk.

"So this is the famous ocean picture I've heard about. Looks like someone's reflection in the water. Is it you?"

"Look closer," Riley said, printing an email message. "Below the surface."

Cheng stared deeper. "Oh, it's a fish. Wow, it's a huge fish. His mouth looks big enough to swallow someone's head."

"Someday it'll be the other way around, pal," Riley said. "How's the investigation?"

"Progressing."

"Anything strong?"

"No. One of the Milwaukee detectives reported that there was a death at a local bar on the north side of the airport on Layton Avenue. It happened just before the Delta departure."

"What kind of death?" Riley asked, his interest piqued.

"Don't know the details other than it was apparently a male with a heart condition," Cheng answered. "I only saw a summary report. I'm heading over there myself to follow up. It's an American Legion Post."

"Does Mitchell International record its departure gates?"

"Every one. So does O'Hare. Inside and out."

"Tell Mr. Cortez that I want all videos of Flight 771 the whole time it was parked," Riley ordered, "from the security checkpoints to the ramps. I expect them in one hour."

"What is it, Jack?" Cheng wondered.

"NTSB thinks someone might have placed an explosive device inside the cockpit, in a box or some type of container that wouldn't arouse any suspicion—something that had the ability to force an explosion downward. We need to check it out."

"That's interesting," Cheng commented.

"No, it's not. It's scary."

"Why is that?"

"Read Cortez's status." Riley reached for the printer tray and gave the document to Cheng. "A Delta gate agent said she saw the captain carry a metal container on board. She said it looked like a kid's lunch box."

—

US NO-FLY ZONE, DAY 4
PORT OF LAS PALMAS, GRAN CANARIA ISLAND
CANARY ISLANDS (SPAIN)

"ENTER." PROFESSOR Faiz Al-Aran acknowledged the knock on the door of his Q5 luxury suite on board the Cunard Line's flagship, the *Queen Mary 2*. The ship was docked just one hundred miles off the African coast.

He closed his laptop and rose from a desk that was positioned between two balcony doors. He'd chosen not to use the room's desktop PC because the ship's IT staff monitored the network, and any emails with system, server, or transmission failures would appear in paper copy outside his cabin door.

A steward appeared with a food service cart.

"I'm terribly sorry about the regulations, sir," the man apologized in a stout British accent. "We've slid into port so quickly I'm afraid the luncheon grill had to be turned down. We couldn't manage your pancakes. We did find a bit more fruit. We know how you enjoy the papaya."

"Thank you, Kerry," Al-Aran replied, peeking under one of five silver-capped lids. "What is the weather forecast?"

"Oh, I suspect another day of sun as usual. The Canaries are known for it. Will there be anything else?"

"I was thinking of sport fishing—something large and aggressive."

"Very good, sir. I know an Australian gent who runs a reliable business out on Lanzarote. He charters the Ana Segundo, a deep boat sixteen meters long and four or five wide. He rents a variety of smaller craft too. He's a gruff little chap but he's honest and very knowledgeable. He'll put you on tuna, marlin, wahoo, and several species of shark. Mako, blue, and hammerheads rule these waters. The locals say you can't even dangle your legs overboard. We'll be pulling in there tomorrow, so you'll have a good ten to twelve hours free. It's on the north end of the big island near Orzola. I'll send someone 'round with a map."

Kerry nodded graciously and closed the door.

Al-Aran returned to his laptop.

> **PartyLuvr30308:** Greetings from the Atlantic. It looks like I'll be able to fish for a trophy after all. I've always wanted to catch a shark.
>
> **Toothdoc2b:** I'm glad to hear that you're enjoying your cruise. Tell me more.

PartyLuvr30308: Big time! Stayed out late last night. So much so that I haven't paid much attention to world events. In fact, I've never even picked up a newspaper. Too busy enjoying the ocean views. Of course, we've all heard about the airlines.

Toothdoc2b: It's a mess. Seems everyone here is upset. A real pain to deal with.

PartyLuvr30308: Any idea on when things might get back to normal?

Toothdoc2b: I don't think anyone knows.

PartyLuvr30308: Too bad. Any upcoming vacation plans?

Toothdoc2b: Think I'll check out California. Maybe LA, San Diego, or even San Fran. I hear the food is great.

PartyLuvr30308: San Diego is really nice. The weather should be warm and dry this time of year, if you can handle it. Take care.

Toothdoc2b: I can and I will.

—

AKIL LOGGED off and drew open the window curtains. At 3:00 a.m. it was still eighty-seven degrees in Las Vegas. The Strip had been deserted all evening: the flight ban had definitely made an impact. Akil noticed something on the room table. Gaudy red with metallic gold lettering, a business card advertised a variety of female escorts.

Akil tore the card in half and opened his Qur'an.

—

US NO-FLY ZONE, DAY 5
SATURDAY, MAY 23
BELLEVUE, NE

THE AIRLINE crash had been both a human and an environmental disaster. Rival groups argued about which was worse. A quiet and peaceful respite threatened by suburban growth, the Fontenelle Forest

Nature Center was a two-thousand-acre oasis of forest, prairie, and wetlands. A peaceful home for contented wildlife and lush, varied vegetation, the preserve was dually referred to as a very rare ecosystem and the largest deciduous forest in Nebraska.

The animal losses were difficult to tally. The loss of trees was not. The sight of huge sections of disease-tolerant American elm raised by countless hours of nurturing now flattened or burned by Airbus debris, was especially sad. Most of Flight 605's wreckage was scattered in a quadrant just beyond the Missouri River in an area framed by the Chickadee, Hickory, and Linden Trails on the northwestern edge of the forest. The plants that managed to avoid the initial heat and flames ultimately died from the residual chloride left by six thousand gallons of diluted, aqueous, film-forming foam.

NTSB investigator Scott Hoover, a member of the debris recovery team specializing in hydraulic and power systems, waded through a creek in Childs Hollow. He stopped to examine a piece of round metal tubing half-buried in muck. Using a small shovel, he carved away a top layer and exposed what appeared to be a piece of nose landing gear. He spotted the charred remains of the piston shaft covered in black melted rubber, presumably from one of the tires. Something caught his eye.

He could barely see it, but it was there: color. Like a skilled archaeologist, he scraped further with his hand and stared at the red feather-like object. He used a pair of padded tongs to grip an exposed corner. Remarkably, whatever it was peeled away from the rubber intact. He laid it into his gloved palm.

There was a rigid, notched t-stem at one end that appeared to be made from some sort of hardened plastic. The other end was flexible. The curved, thin object was six inches long, with an intricate design of leaf-like filaments. It reminded him of an elongated ear or some type of insect wing.

He drew out an evidence bag from his jacket kit and placed the object inside.

33

MITCHELL INTERNATIONAL AIRPORT
DELTA AIRLINES MAINTENANCE HANGAR

PATRICIA CREED lifted her briefcase onto the conference room table. She opened her laptop and reviewed her notes on Flight 771's captain and first officer, including their licenses, ratings, experience, and any indicated limitations. She also completed a brief picture, using the best available witnesses and associates, of each man's actions seventy-two hours prior to departure, including drug, alcohol, or prescription usage.

Both pilots checked out beautifully.

Creed checked her appointment calendar. She glanced through the doorway at a man pacing in the outer hall, and she waved him in.

Matt Driesen closed the door and took a seat.

Thin and fit in his mid-thirties, he wore a set of deep blue coveralls with a pair of airman's wings sewn on his chest. The palms of his hands were clean. His fingers were lightly crackled in something black.

"Mr. Driesen, I'm Tricia Creed. I understand that you just had a company service anniversary. Congratulations."

"Fifteen years," he acknowledged warily. "I don't even know why I'm here, ma'am. I worked my shift on the eighteenth, but I never went near that plane. I don't want anyone blaming me for something I didn't work on."

"Matt, just relax. We're not here to blame anyone." She casually touched a button on a small tape recorder. "I'm with the NTSB, and I'm assisting the FBI's investigation of the Delta 771 incident. We're interviewing everyone who was on shift that day.

"I'm going to ask you some questions related to your work responsibilities. This is nothing more than a general interview. It's routine, and I want you to feel comfortable. You won't need any Union representation because this is just an investigative inquiry. You're not being accused of anything."

That was a complete—albeit legal—untruth by omission. NTSB interviews were evidentiary interrogations. Interviewers never advised subjects to have an attorney present even though statements were absolutely presentable, binding, and often damaging in court.

Driesen's face was taut, but he managed a nod.

"What's your official title and primary responsibility at Delta?" Creed asked.

"Technical Line Maintenance. I do everything from routine turnaround and overnight checks to nonroutine aircraft log entries. I can also handle complex in-service repairs. I do whatever it takes to keep an aircraft flying."

"How long have you been assigned to aviation maintenance?"

"All fifteen years."

"Have you ever received a warning for improper procedures on maintenance that you performed?"

"Never."

"Ever receive a security reprimand?"

Driesen folded his arms. His leg started bouncing repeatedly. "I got my first one last month. I walked outside through one of our hangar exit doors and didn't close it tight enough. The wind was blowing hard that day. One of those TSA guys was sitting in the parking lot over at UPS, eating his lunch. He saw the whole thing and wrote me up on the spot. It cost me one hundred fifty dollars."

"How did that make you feel?"

"Take a wild guess," he snapped. "Especially when he gave me this big lecture on how we all need to watch out for terrorists and everything. We started shouting at each other. The guy was a real jerk."

"Did you feel the fine was justified?"

Driesen shifted uneasily and then looked over his shoulder. "Between you and me, most of those federal guys just walk around thinking that they're better than everyone else. Just because they work for the government, they think they can stop you anytime and ask if you've seen anyone or anything suspicious. I guess it's their job or something, but it's a joke.

"And I'm not the only one who thinks that. They check some workers over and over, and forget about others. I mean, they'll look to see if the person is wearing a badge but never real close. One of my buddies cut out the president's face and taped it over his ID. He wore that for a whole month, and nobody ever noticed. They just get used to seeing the same people. But the worst thing is that no one checks us when we come in and out of the building at shift change."

Creed sat forward. "Can you be more specific?"

"Sure, I can be *really* specific, but not while that's on." He nodded to the recorder. Creed clicked it off. "Over three hundred people work in this building on two shifts, mostly mechanics and their supervisors. Nobody ever checks us when we come in. I could bring a thermos full of gasoline in my lunch pail and stick it any place on any aircraft, and nobody would ever know. Nobody.

"I know these planes inside and out, and I have access to every inch of every system. Sometimes, during routine maintenance, I get into places that hardly anybody has ever been to or even knows about.

"One time, I accidentally left an extension drill next to the hydraulic pump shafts. If that drill rolled, we'd be talking serious damage to rotating parts with the potential for a complete loss of fluid and pressure. That plane left Milwaukee and was gone for a whole weekend. Needless to say, I didn't get much sleep, because guess who was on it? The St. Louis Cardinals baseball team. Luckily, they were playing the Brewers again, and it came back around. I found my drill and got it out of there.

"But you see what I mean? That could easily have been a bomb. Nobody checks us for anything. It's really scary to think that there might be mechanics or techs on other airlines all over the country or even the world who could hide something in a hundred different places."

Creed closed her folder and handed Matt a business card. "Thank you, Mr. Driesen. I think we're finished. If you think of anything else that might be relevant, please call."

Creed studied him as he left. She remembered what Jack Riley had said at that NTSB conference center presentation about critical thinking and raising a brief terrorism eyebrow. It certainly applied to this witness.

She found it fascinating that the FBI's seventeen-year search for Theodore Kaczynski, a domestic terrorist-bomber who killed three people and injured twenty-three others, actually had a connection to Driesen. In that investigation, the FBI's Behavioral Sciences Unit issued a psychological profile of the suspect, describing him as someone with above-average intelligence and connections to academia. The profile later said he was a technology-hater with a science degree. A third and final revision said that the infamous Unabomber was most likely a blue-collar airplane mechanic.

AMERICAN LEGION POST 154
MILWAUKEE, WI

THE FIRST thing Agent Cheng noticed as he entered the unfamiliar bar was that at 11:00 a.m., every seat was filled. The second thing he noticed was the reason why.

The only bartender, twenty-eight-year-old Marianne Alby, had a model's physique, and a dangerously short skirt. She always made good tips.

"I'll need to see a membership card," Marianne said matter-of-factly, setting two mugs on the rail and pulling a draft spigot. Cheng produced his ID. She glanced at it briefly, topping off the second mug. "What can I get for you, sir?"

Cheng didn't drink. He searched around for an option. "How about a bowl of that?" Cheng said, nodding to a sign on the wall.

"One turkey and dumpling soup. Anything else?"

"Thank you, but I just have a few questions about a Mr. Jerry Watts." Cheng fingered his notes. "I understand he worked here and passed away on the morning of the Delta crash. He was also known as 'Chief.'"

Conversation throughout the bar stopped.

Marianne pressed a towel into her eyes. She quickly composed herself.

"You feds already came through here the day after that plane went down," a long-haired patron in a metal neck brace shouted from across the room. "They interviewed everybody. The government's got no respect for people in mourning. We all know it was a suicide passenger whacked both those planes, so why are you hassling us?"

"Sir, I'm not hassling anyone," Cheng calmly responded. "I'm simply revisiting the area. I have a few more questions. Is this a private post for military veterans only?"

"You got a problem with that?" the man hissed.

"No problem at all," Cheng said calmly, stirring his meal. "Thanks for your service. I guess you probably see a lot of friends and strangers come and go."

"If you're asking what I think you're asking, then hang on." The man stood up from his barstool. "Anybody seen any terrorists in the neighborhood?"

"Yeah, there's one down at the 7-Eleven," a man sang out.

"Go get 'em, Stan," someone else shouted.

"That's Stanley Wosniak," Marianne whispered to Cheng. "Wisconsin's most decorated Vietnam vet. He had 380 confirmed kills. He doesn't like too many outsiders. Sorry."

"I can see that," Cheng whispered back. "So, no new faces or suspicious people hanging around? No new war buddies that just happened to show up? Nobody asking questions about airport security or bad-mouthing the US government?"

"Nope. Nobody new around here except Mikey." She gave a distant look. "Chief said he was related to Sean Penn the actor, but that was probably a lie."

Cheng pushed his soup aside and opened his notebook.

"Don't bother about him," she assured. "He just rented the apartment upstairs for the summer. Nice college kid. He's supposed to start bartending: we need the help."

"Which school?"

"Beats me," Marianne answered. "I think he's trying to be a dentist."

"Is he here?"

"He's never here. He's always running back and forth to Minnesota to see his girlfriend. He seems pretty whipped."

"What's her name?"

Marianne pursed her lips. "Good question. I've only met him a couple of times myself. He never talked much about anything."

"You said he lives in back?"

"Upstairs. I suppose I could let you see the place, but your people already did that. They searched every building on the block."

She plucked a key from the register. They walked upstairs.

Cheng saw an unmade sofa-bed, fast food wrappers, a sink full of dishes and a floor strewn with empty soda cans. Video games were piled inside cardboard boxes along with several textbooks:

Journal of Craniomandibular Practice
Contemporary Dental Practice
Effects of Mechanical Vibration on Orthodontic Tooth Movement

A typical college student.

Cheng opened the refrigerator. It was empty.

34

US NO-FLY ZONE, DAY 6
SAN DIEGO, CA
SUNDAY, MAY 24

AKIL PULLED off Kettner Boulevard into one of five empty parking slots and turned off the Camry's engine. He yawned deeply. He approached the side entrance of the Russian Star Tattoo Parlor, walking past what he thought was old bedding strewn next to a blue recycle dumpster. An arm suddenly rose up, holding a filthy styrofoam cup. Akil ignored it.

Inside the Parlor, a young woman appeared. She was a heavyset Mexican-American with long black hair and a deep brown complexion. She wore a white frilly top and designer blue jeans.

"Do you need a tattoo, *señor*?"

Akil was mesmerized by the wall photographs of prison inmates displaying their ink.

"Thanks, but I'm actually just looking for Viktor Karkula. My name is Eddie."

She contemplated that for a moment. "Are you the Eddie who keeps leaving messages so early on our answering machine?" Akil nodded. She glanced at a clock on the wall. "I'm glad to meet you. Viktor is in the back. He's usually up by ten, but now that the airport is closed, he can sleep a little longer."

A name was tattooed on her arm. "You're Marissa," Akil announced, extending his hand and noticing her finely manicured nails. Each featured shimmering metallic polish. "I knew it. I could tell by your voice that you were a nice-looking lady. Who's Alejandro?"

"A mistake," she answered unapologetically. Her smile returned. Compliments were rare here. Most clients were from eastern Europe, and they seldom spoke English.

Two faces peeked through thin bamboo strips hanging in a rear doorway. Marissa whispered something in Spanish, and the strips split open.

"My kids," she said sheepishly. "Viktor doesn't mind as long as they don't bother the customers."

The children filed into the room and stood politely.

"This is Amber. She's seven. And this is little Jo-Jo. His real name is Jeremy. He just turned five." Marissa combed the boy's hair with her nails. "Say hello to Eddie."

Amber blushed. Jo-Jo lurched forward and hugged Akil's leg tightly.

"He likes you," Amber announced. "He only does that to people he likes."

Akil whisked him into the air. "Hey, little dude. How old are you?"

"We live next to McDonalds, and we have a swimming pool," Jo-Jo said, pressing five fingers against Akil's nose. They were sticky and smelled sweet. "It's called a Travel Inn. Are you going to marry my mommy?"

"Jo-Jo," Marissa called out a mild reprimand.

Akil smiled and lowered the boy.

Marissa clapped her hands twice. The children scurried away.

"I come from a big family myself, and I love kids," Akil remarked, noticing the sound of a musical toy in the background. "I guess I just haven't found the right woman."

Marissa's smile faded, and she actually took a step back. Too many men appeared in the neighborhood under court-ordered placement.

Akil sensed her wariness. "I'm sorry; I'm from Minnesota. I'm finishing up my degree. I'll be living in the apartment upstairs."

"A degree in what, *señor*?" Marissa's smile returned. So did her interest.

"Business, actually. Someday I want to open my own music store. You know, sell instruments and equipment, give lessons." He smiled. "And you are Marissa . . . ?"

"Sanchez. It's good to have goals," she said. "Amber likes music too. She got a keyboard organ for her birthday. She takes it everywhere. Maybe she could play it for you sometime?"

"I'd like that," he said. "I don't know much about San Diego. I wish I could find someone who could—"

"I would be happy to show you around," she quickly offered. "I've lived here all my life. Seaport Village is really nice, because you can walk along the ocean. There are lots of shops and restaurants. And our zoo is one of the best."

"That sounds great, Marissa. I really appreciat—"

"What you want?" a deep male voice interrupted. "Tattoo special, sixty dollars. No stars. Stars only for Russians. You pick from book. Cash or credit card. No checks."

"Hello," Akil said. "I'm Eddie Ginosa. I rented the apartment."

"You pay for whole May and now show up?" the man said, extending his hand. "Viktor Karkula."

A thick-necked Russian in his mid-fifties, Karkula had unkempt hair, and a face covered in gray stubble. His stained T-shirt exposed a carpet of body hair. His eyes were thin slits, and his face was puffed and round, which made him seem almost teddy bear–like. His disposition was grizzly.

He let out a resounding belch.

"You're such a pig," a woman's voice sang out from another room.

Karkula moved closer to Akil and lowered his voice. "My wife, Tamara. She crazy in head and pain to my neck. She just get out of hospital. It was actually nuthouse, but I no can say that. If she act crazy, you let me know, okay? I send her back."

"I'll try and remember that," Akil said, dodging the man's foul breath. "Did you get my money order?"

"Sure, I get it. I cash it; I spend it. But first I make copy, so I know who to throw out on street if you make damage like last pigs. I sleep late. You break window, you pay. No drugs, no parties." He noticed Marissa in the next room. "Hey, you got no customers, you clean. And tell your little mice to make quiet that TV."

Karkula produced a key.

"Door is outside. Keep locked or street pigs find your bed. You no touch Marissa; you can do better. I don't move your stuff; don't try sell me anything because I don't buy nothing. You pay first of month, not after. Don't ask for loan and don't ask for ride—I no do that. Call taxi. If you have car, park in back, or a pig steals it tonight."

"Thanks, I'll be fine," Akil assured. "Some friends from school might come by later this week to help me move in. I just wanted to get a few things settled before—"

"Ya, ya, ya," Karkula said, turning away. "No parties."

"Pssst." Marissa appeared with a scented candle. "You might need this. Don't worry. Viktor calls everyone a pig. If someone steals your car, then I'll give you a ride. Nobody bothers my minivan."

Upstairs, a stained uncovered mattress reeked of urine. Akil lit the candle and slid a window open. He smiled at how effortless it was to entice and befriend seemingly helpless American women living in poverty. Unmarried and vulnerable, they were raising fatherless children who were also starved for the affection and companionship of a caring man. He shook his head. One compliment, one simple hint of caring or politeness, and a small amount of concern for the well-being of their children, and these women would do and believe anything. They were like puppies craving affection and direction. They were eager to follow their new master, ready to do his will—and Allah's.

Akil lifted his binoculars. He had a clear view of deserted San Diego International Airport Runway 27, three hundred and sixty yards away.

US NO-FLY ZONE, DAY 7
COURTYARD MARRIOTT
MILWAUKEE, WI
MONDAY, MAY 25

RILEY WAS sitting in his office, free-throwing Shaitan into a large makeshift net rigged to the wall behind his desk. It was Memorial Day, and his phone messages had dropped dramatically. He actually felt a small amount of respite. The president was busy performing his annual duties at Arlington National Cemetery. Those duties consisted of a wreath-laying at the Tomb of the Unknowns followed by a speech at the adjoining Memorial Amphitheater. Earlier in the year, Riley had several meetings with the US Secret Service regarding a credible foreign terror threat/assassination plot set for this very day. With help from the NSA, an Embassy liaison—a.k.a. a CIA section operative in Madrid—has uncovered a plot involving a vacuum bomb of nitrogen octaiodide complete with metal shards soaked in dimethylmercury.

Set to explode on contact with air, the device would have been encased in a meter-long rectangular box that perfectly matched the Arlington Amphitheater's marble façade and placed on an overhanging ledge ten meters above a central walkway.

The assassins had discovered a potentially fateful security weakness in the president's itinerary—a weakness called repetition. The president

214

always conducted the wreath-laying directly in front of the Tomb of the Unknowns, a lone bugler *always* played Taps thereafter, the president *always* crossed that center walkway en route to the Memorial Remembrance Ceremony in the Amphitheater, and the wreath-laying event *always* occurred on the last Monday in May between 11:00 a.m. and 11:05 a.m. EDT.

Placed twenty days beforehand, the device was set to awaken via a simple mechanical timer, and then roll forward and fall to the walkway below just as the president was within both the scheduled time frame and the blast radius. According to several senior members of the president's personal protection detail, the device was extremely lethal and perfectly capable of taking him out and killing or injuring many of the five thousand onlookers.

The assassins, needing just a few minutes to physically lift the bomb to the ledge, had even devised a brilliant late-night mugging-distraction of the lone Tomb guard as he paced back and forth. The tactics forced wide-scale reviews of all presidential schedules and physical surroundings.

There was a gentle tap on Riley's door. Tom Ross peeked inside.

"Where have you been hiding?" Riley asked, banking Shaitan off the ceiling and missing the net completely.

"Neela and I have been analyzing the cockpit voices from Flight 771. Neither of us can figure out the relevance of the captain's last word. It sounds like he was trying to say *Starbucks*. As far as I know, it's not an aviation term or code word. She wants to do a human interest piece on it. Have you ever heard it before?"

"Yeah, whenever I need caffeine," Riley quipped. "You like her, huh?"

"I do," Ross admitted, pausing thoughtfully. "I like her a lot. We've become friends."

"And what about your tenant friend?"

"Funny you should mention that." Ross took a seat and crossed his arms. "Neela and I have had some heart-to-heart conversations, and we both enjoy each other's company. It's amazing how much we have in common, especially with bad relationships. Your marriage is obviously successful. What's the secret?"

Riley shrugged. "There's no single recipe, pal. And I'm certainly not an expert. But if I had to narrow things, then I'd say hard work and honesty are at the top of the list, along with faith, morals, and traditional values. The usual stuff. The question is, can a news reporter have morals?"

Ross rolled his eyes. Riley picked Shaitan up from the floor and slammed him into a drawer. "Does she like kids?"

"She loves kids, but she can't have any," Ross answered. "It's a shame."

The conversation abruptly stopped. Riley stared out his window.

"How could they do it?"

"Do what?" Ross asked.

"Kill kids. It just doesn't make sense. Did you know that there were fifteen high school drama students on board that Delta flight? They were headed to Atlanta to research *Gone with the Wind*, their fall play. They raised the production money themselves through car washes and bake sales. Terrorists are more cowards than anything else. What I don't understand is how they can live with themselves afterwards. Indiscriminate subways, buses, marathon races, and all those restaurant and hotel suicide bombings in Israel . . . then there was that Russian-Chechnyen school hostage situation a few years ago. When some of the terrorists balked because kids were involved, their compatriots shot them. Talk about deranged. And speaking of Russia, remember those two Tupolev airliners that crashed south of Moscow? Both were confirmed as coordinated terrorism."

"Impossible to determine," Ross said flatly. "The wreckage was scattered over thirty-five kilometers. That was nothing but a guess."

"Who needs wreckage?" Riley asked smugly. "You've got to give the Russians credit. Their Federal Security Service—formerly the KGB—made that call based on a single circumstantial fact, but it's one great fact: a RESURS-DK-R imagery satellite owned by Sovinformsputnik Company in Leningrad detected dual heat fluxes from the Tula and Rostov-on-Don crash regions at precisely the same instant. That, my friend, was coordinated."

"Are you thinking that our terrorist is Chechnyen?"

"I'm not sure what to think, other than that there's a timing element involved."

"You seem pretty confident," Ross observed.

"I'm confident of two things in life: I'm going to catch that mystery cell-phone terrorist, and I'm also going to catch my fish."

"You and that fish," Ross chided, removing an evidence bag from his briefcase. "What did he ever do to you? Speaking of confidence, we found traces of potassium in the burn residue off of Flight 605's gear piston."

"Potassium? Did you do a lab test?" Riley asked.

"There was no need. Our portable scanner took accurate measurements at the scene. It uses an ion spectrometer to spot TNT, Semtex, PETN, and a whole range of nitrates. Potassium is one of the major flags for unstable explosives not common to the elements you'd expect to find on or near jet fuel burns."

Riley lifted the evidence bag.

"We also found some type of a wing," Ross noted. "One of our techs picked it up from the Fontenelle crash site. It's made from a molded composite. Nothing unusual: it's probably from a kid's toy. The configuration doesn't fit with any known explosive model because it's too thin. These are sketches of what it might look like if it were whole."

Riley frowned at the drawings. They ranged from an oversized ear to a six-inch bat wing. He set the bag down. "Excluding the passengers, a total of twenty people had contact with Flight 771. One fueler, three baggage handlers, two mechanics, two caterers, two maintenance workers, two rampers, three agents, and, of course, the crew. None fit any obvious profile. One technician replaced a brake temperature fuse, and we've got a copy of his log. Do you have anything else?"

Ross produced a set of colored computer drawings. One showed remarkable detail of Flight 771's fuselage cut away to expose the cockpit section.

"My team has concluded that both planes crashed due to a dramatic loss of power, hydraulics, and pilot controls. The Delta flight data recorder showed evidence of a shutdown that originated here."

He used a pencil-thin marker to connect the nose landing gear with the vertical tail fin. He fingered through the drawings.

"Here's a closer look at a potential point of impact. It was in our preliminary opinion, by an explosive. Notice the direction of the outward burns. This was further evidenced by the distortions in the hinges and riveting on the gear bay doors. Everything was forced outward."

"What's your conclusion?" Riley wondered. "How did it happ—?" Ross cut him off.

"You can conclude whatever you want. In this case, an aviation action. I've just told you what we believe happened. The facts support damage caused by an internal explosion. Unfortunately, that opens an even bigger box of unanswered questions."

"Such as?"

"I'm sure you know that people are screaming 'cover-up' on TWA Flight 800 and the NTSB's theory of sparks or electrical shorts igniting fumes. There's a truckload of speculation and witnesses in that case, especially with regard to missiles. I simply can't afford to go into why it happened. And I won't cross the line between pure investigation and criminal intent. That's your job. But I do have my own theory."

"Fine, it's not a missile." Riley was frustrated. "So give me your opinion."

Ross lifted a bag of pumpkin seeds to his mouth. "This was criminal. On the Delta flight, someone planted a bomb inside or underneath that cockpit, a radio-controlled or a timed device with enough power to rupture the flight control cables. The airborne debris got sucked into the engine. I didn't mention it in my public interview with Neela, but the United flight was even worse in that the voice and data recorders showed that things were running smoothly and operating normally. Three seconds later, everything was gone—controls, hydraulics, voice, electrical, and *all* backups. It had to have been a massive in-flight explosion. Things simply don't go from normal to dead in three seconds."

"Aren't modern jets supposed to be able to handle foreign material being pulled into the engines?" Riley asked. "Didn't Boeing prove that by heaving a bunch of frozen turkeys into the fan blades?"

Ross wanted to laugh. "Jet engines are machined so perfectly that their tolerances are measured in thousandths of millimeters. A couple of seagulls can ruin a pilot's day. Those turkey tests were done to prove that the engine cowling itself could withstand an explosion and not damage the fuselage in-flight. Trust me, the engines would lose power. My opinion on this is that it was criminal. It's your job to find out how."

36

NAMED *PUNTA de los Muertos* for early Spanish scurvy victims, Seaport Village consisted of seventy shops, galleries, and restaurants set on a ninety thousand square-foot landfill. The Point of the Dead had four miles of tourist walkways.

Kevin Jones set his guitar case on a tiled bench seat across from a seawall that overlooked San Diego Harbor. He lifted the guitar to his lap and strummed through C, D, and G chords—his favorite way to verify tuning. The air smelled deliciously of fresh-baked pretzels. He set the guitar down and pulled one pretzel apart. He thought he could eat, but he was simply too nervous so he tossed the piece onto the sidewalk. In a scene straight from Hitchcock's *The Birds*, wings and beaks instantly appeared. The seagulls were remarkably bold and fought angrily over the morsels. One bird hopped onto the guitar case. When Jones tried to pet the seemingly friendly visitor, he was given a nasty warning. It was all about the dough—literally.

Behind him, a crowd gathered in the open food court. Music pumped through two amplifiers. The musician at the microphone had a smooth voice, and his guitar playing was crisp. Jones froze. He instantly recognized the classic Travis-style, finger-picking chord bounce from C to G. The song's melody and lyrics were especially familiar.

219

"Laying low, seeking out the poorer quarters, where the ragged people go, looking for the places only they would know. Lie la lie . . . lie la la la lie la lie . . . lie la lie . . . lie la la la lie la lie la la la la lie."

He's singing Simon & Garfunkel, Jones thought. *"The Boxer." Why can't I do that? I can. I know I can.* He eased closer, checking his watch. He was next.

"This guy's good, hey?" a bystander commented to Jones. "I dig that song."

"Me too," Jones remarked. "Paul Simon wrote it way back in 1968. He recorded it with four guitars and a piccolo trumpet. It took six weeks. It's amazing that it's still so musically pleasing after all these years."

"I've always wanted to play the guitar," the young man admitted, noticing Jones's case. "But I'd be totally freaked if I had to sing in front of anyone."

"Playing is the easy part," Jones noted, checking his watch again. "Unfortunately, not everyone can sing."

"That's the truth. When I sing, foxes start to howl."

The song ended. The crowd responded with loud applause.

Jones's eyes grew wide, and he turned to the man. "Fennec foxes?"

"Yeah, when I was a kid under a bright desert moo—" Akil turned warily. "I'm sorry, were you talking to me?"

"Omar? Omar Yassin? I'm Kevin. Kevin Jones." He pumped Akil's hand vigorously. "The Entomopter drone—remember? You called me about performance in sand and maximum leg grip pressure. I can't believe it. How weird is this? What are you doing in San Diego? I thought you were beta testing on a project with Dr. Al-Aran in some Saudi Arabian oil field. Are you finished?"

"Kevin . . . um . . . what a surprise," Akil stammered. "Of course. My profound apologies. Dr. Al-Aran's project. A funeral . . . my . . . um . . . one of my dearest relatives passed away. My aunt. She lived here . . . north of here. She had pneumonia. In Romoland. It's in Riverside County. I am actually on my way there now. We . . . my family is extremely saddened by the loss. It was a long illness."

"Oh man, I'm sorry," Jones offered, sensing something odd in Omar's manner. Somehow the slovenly look didn't match his demeanor. "But how did you get all the way to California with the flight ban?"

"Mexico. I flew into Tijuana. If you've never done that, it's indeed an interesting experience."

"I bet," Jones agreed. "This whole country's gone scary, especially the economy. Can we do dinner later or something? I'd love to hear about the drone's test results. I've been so busy that I've lost touch with my old project team. How long are you in town?"

"I am truly sorry, Kevin, but it's not possible. There are pressing family duties that I must attend to. Then I return home tomorrow."

"That's too bad," Jones said, glancing at the time. "So, tell me, how did the drone perform?"

"Well, to be honest, it was rather disappointing. Average at best. The initial flights looked promising, but I'm afraid we simply expected a little too much. The device did not hold up very well in sand. The wings kept dislodging. It could only travel a few hundred yards before becoming uncontrollable."

Jones's reaction fell somewhere between surprise and embarrassment. Then it turned defensive. "That's bizarre. What exactly were you trying to accomplish? You shouldn't have had any problems."

"Our team documented everything, so we do have a record for any required enhancements. I would be more than happy to provide you a copy."

Jones reconsidered. "Nah, don't bother. I've got enough on my plate."

"It was nice meeting you," Akil said, cutting the conversation short. He extended his hand. "Perhaps we can play music together sometime."

"Sure," Jones said with a puzzled look. "I've got a condo two blocks from the beach. Gotta keep up my image."

Akil gave Jones a limp handshake and awkwardly turned away.

He spotted Marissa and the kids waving to him from the seawall walkway. He waved back and gestured toward the parking lot.

"Who was that you were talking to?" Marissa asked when they met up at the minivan. She was fairly certain it was a man, but the person did have a ponytail. She helped Jo-Jo with his seat belt and then slid into the front passenger seat.

"Just a guy I knew in high school . . . in Minnesota," Akil answered, starting the engine. "We were on the gymnastics team. He was a year behind. Why?"

"I'm just jealous," she admitted. "You've been to so many places, and I've never been out of San Diego."

"I know how to fix that."

"What do you mean?"

"Feel like getting away?" he suggested. "The kids would love a vacation."

"So would I." Marissa looked at him oddly. "But I just met you."

"Did you hear what I said? Don't think, don't worry, and just do it. There's nothing for you here, especially living in a motel and earning commission from a loser like Viktor. We'll take a nice long trip and then maybe find a new place to live—somewhere that's not so crowded. Maybe we'll come back or maybe we won't." He lifted her hand. "Don't tell anyone about us, okay? Especially Viktor. I'll handle him."

"Eddie, please, he's mean," she warned. "He's the reason that his wife, Tamara, had a nervous breakdown in the first place. He always complains about other people, but he's even worse. She keeps a gun in the house and said she would use it if he hurts her again. I think she's serious."

"In the house where?" Akil asked sternly.

She hesitated. "Her laundry basket. Under a towel."

"Is Viktor right- or left-handed?"

"Left, I think. Why do you want to know that?"

"In case he ever swings at me," Akil answered. "It's always good to be prepared."

Marissa felt her heart race with excitement. Hope was something she rarely experienced. She had dreamed of a better life but had never had the financial means or opportunity. This was a complete whirlwind. She could easily pack up and leave. She had no real assets except her minivan, and no close family ties. Her children could adapt to anything.

"What about you?" she wondered. "You just got here. What would you do about school and your apartment? Viktor would really be—"

"I have a confession to make," Akil interrupted. He lifted her hand to his lips and looked into her eyes. "There's something special about you. I've always said that when I found the right girl, I'd know it. Someone who's kind, beautiful, and who'd make a good friend and partner. Maybe even a wife. I know it sounds crazy, but I'm telling you the truth from my heart. Something happened the first time we talked on the phone. Let's just get away. Your kids are awesome. I want to be a part of their lives. Please let me prove that I can be a good role model to them, maybe even their father. I can finish college anywhere. I only need a few more credits. It doesn't have to be here. My parents left me a lot of money. You'll never have to worry again. If you want, you can put your things in storage; I'll pay for everything. Just take what you and the kids need. You won't have to work another day, and you can have anything you want. We'll find out about ourselves. I mean, if there's really something there. I promise I'll take care of you and your family, Marissa. A couple of weeks and a nice long vacation. Trust me, okay?"

"Eddie? I have a confession too," Marissa said, smiling. Tears streamed down her cheeks. Akil wiped them away with his thumb. "Viktor just left me a voice mail. He said business is bad, and he has to let me go."

Akil cupped his hand gently around her head. "Forget him. It's fate, and it's a good thing. I'm here for you, Marissa, and I'm going to take care of you. We're going to be a family. Come with me, okay? A nice, relaxing, fun vacation. Who knows? Maybe we'll find a new place to open my music store."

Marissa composed herself and turned to her kids.

"Who wants to go on vacation?" They cheered. She nuzzled Akil. "I could really use some new clothes. Would it be okay if we stayed here? Maybe half an hour?"

"Shop as long as you want." Akil smiled broadly, checking the time and opening his laptop. He reached in his pocket and peeled off five hundred dollars. "Buy some ice cream for the kids and something nice for you. I'm going to check out car top carriers and then work on our business plan."

Akil watched her stroll out of sight.

He signed into Gmail.

Toothdoc2b: What's up, dude? Catch any sharks?

PartyLuvr30308: Not yet. Still hung over. How is Southern California?

Toothdoc2b: Awesome. Things are working out great. I think I'm in love! Any other suggestions for a nice vacation?

PartyLuvr30308: New York's a fun town. You should check it out.

Toothdoc2b: Dude, I live there! Stop in when you get back and we'll visit some cool places. My address is 0112 18th Street in West Pinehurst.

FROM HOT air balloon rides in Santa Fe, New Mexico, to the
biplanes that usually trailed advertising banners along New Jersey's
boardwalk, not a single private or commercial aircraft appeared in
the skies. And the American people weren't stupid. Polls showed
that 85 percent believed this was the direct result of a terror attack.
Divergent special interest groups swarmed to Washington. Many
camped in the National Mall. Fringe environmentalists claimed
the lack of commercial jet contrail vapors that normally reflected
the sun's heat would raise the Earth's temperature by a stagger-
ing two degrees. Another group claimed that the shutdown had
already caused over one thousand new driving deaths due to the
increase in vehicular travel. Worst of all, United and Delta Airline
stocks had fallen 78 percent, double the plunge they had taken
after 9/11.

"I want you to listen to something," the president said, opening a
window. "Now I know how Lyndon Johnson felt during Vietnam."

"There's another protest rally tomorrow," Transportation Secretary
Minka said soberly, flopping the Washington Post onto the president's

desk. "American Airlines Group is laying off another ten thousand machinists. We may have to reconsider."

The president stared at the Washington Monument, hands clasped behind his back.

"You mean end it, don't you?"

"Sir, I took the liberty of projecting some numbers. If the airline shutdown were to last thirty-five days, aviation bankruptcy filings would reach their highest levels ever. All US carriers would seek protection. As you know, filing bankruptcy just means that creditors are held at bay until a company is better positioned to repay. Unfortunately, we're at the point where even that is becoming impossible, even with loans. People are losing confidence. If something isn't done, the sheer weight of the economics might not support a recovery. I know how you feel about polls, but the latest show that 78 percent of Americans believe that we should lift the flight ban regardless of the potential for additional loss of life via another crash. Of those, only 6 percent said they'd personally take that risk. That tells me that air freight should be allowed to resume immediately."

"Tell me how we frame it," the president asked.

"We frame it by telling the truth."

"The truth? The truth is that we don't have a clue about what or who killed 260 people?"

"Well, sir, not exactly like that. We say that we're doing everything possible to prevent further attacks. That's number one. Second, we inundate the major airports with visible military. Every bag is opened and scanned, every passenger is questioned and searched, every plane is inspected before it leaves the ground, and everyone who comes in contact with an aircraft is monitored visually. That will get us flying again with credibility. Passengers need to feel safe. And when I say 'inundate,' I mean it. We'll get state governors to mobilize National Guard units to stand side by side with federal forces. You have the authority to do it."

The president felt a tickle in his throat and coughed slightly. He knew where Minka was heading. The Federal Posse Comitatus Act was created to limit the powers of the federal government in using US armed forces to enforce state law. Congress had since revised similar insurrection and national defense legislation for natural disasters, terrorist attacks, or other conditions that civilian authorities were unwilling or unable to handle.

Minka filled the president's water glass.

"My father taught me a simple lesson about a wolf and a bear. If you are in a terrible position with no way out, it is better to fight like a wolf and lose with honor than to cower. If I come back to my den and find a bear eating my pups, then I'll fight to the death. Sitting here doing nothing is like planning a Haida hunting party day after day and never going out after the grizzly. We need to get back in the air."

The president smiled at his friend. "You speak as eloquently as always, Norman. Give me a few moments alone."

Minka left. The president folded his hands and prayed silently. He repeated the ending out loud.

"But deliver us from evil."

—

ATLANTA, GA
GEORGIA TECH RESEARCH BUILDING, TECHNOLOGY SQUARE

PROFESSOR MICHAEL Robertson stared in disbelief at his appointment calendar. It resembled a crossword puzzle of inked-out meeting dates that were scheduled, cancelled, and then rescheduled to coincide with the potential for flying again. He pasted a sheet of blank paper over one three-day period and jotted down yet another entry:

International Aerial Robotics Exhibition—EPCOT Center Pavilion

Disney's animatronics engineers wanted the drone to fly up to the tip of the Magic Kingdom's castle vis-à-vis Tinker Bell during the evening Parade of Lights. The event would bring drone competitors from schools all over the country. He was the master of ceremonies and overall program coordinator.

His phone chirped.

"Michael, thank heaven you're there." Dr. Garton's voice was frantic. "I just spoke to Milt Vandenbaum in the Treasurer's office. He has no record of that Saudi check. Apparently, no deposit was ever made. We've already contacted the Bank of Riyadh, and they're in the dark too. I knew we should have used a wire transfer. Michael, we need those funds. We're already drawing against the balance. Where is Dr. Al-Aran?"

"Faiz has been on vacation since the fourteenth, and I have absolutely no idea where. He was handling everything, including the funding. I never even saw the check."

—

SAN DIEGO, CA
FRIDAY, MAY 29

AKIL SAT patiently at his window above the Russian Star, binoculars in hand, eyes trained on the south end of San Diego's Airport. He opened the drone's case and set the two remaining frames on the sill—midnight blue and black. He hadn't decided San Diego's color. One block away, Amtrak Intercity commuter trains linked communities and travelers from as far away as Los Angeles and Orange County to downtown San Diego. Amtrak's Pacific Surfliner and the COASTER that carried travelers to and from the airport were empty.

He leaned forward intently. Something about those trains and the airport proximity triggered his memory. His mind flashed back to the O'Hare Aerospace Center and another train that he watched roll south on O'Hare Airport's western perimeter. It was a freight train, and he remembered it slowing dramatically as it pulled open gondola coal cars around a curve in the tracks. Departing aircraft were flying right above. He surmised that a soldier could easily climb into one of the train cars, assemble a weapon, time an aircraft's departure, and then attack it. *But how?* he wondered. There was plenty of room to fire a weapon, but it would have to be powerful enough to both reach and disable the plane. A high-powered rifle with a heavy six-hundred-grain bullet might do the job, but it might not. The velocity of such a projectile would easily tear through an aircraft's aluminum skin, but creating enough damage to actually bring it down was questionable. *How high would a plane be as it passed over the train?* he wondered. *Two, three hundred feet? Perhaps a rocket launcher or heat seeker? No. The beauty of such an attack would be four-fold*, he reasoned. The sound of the weapon would be masked by the jet engines, no witness would see the projectile, the escape would be effortless and automatic, and the investigation of the crash would no doubt focus on the aircraft itself. No one would suspect it came from the train.

Akil booted up his laptop and brought up Google Earth. He donned a set of earphones and focused intently, toggling back and forth between satellite views of the target area and United Airline's and Union-Pacific's operating schedules. Forty-seven minutes later, he outlined a summary of the terror attack.

> *CRITICAL SUCCESS FACTOR: Find a high-powered weapon with some type of exploding round. A Powerful, Accurate Weapon! Code name PAW.*
>
> *Select a Monday afternoon. Commence in Palatine, IL. Park and leave a disposable vehicle at Hotel Bollero (vacant??) parking lot. PAW must be concealable. Collapsible? Two pieces? Place PAW in a special harness underneath a loose-fitting jacket. Cross Northwest Highway. Head south along three railroad tracks managed by the Union Pacific. Use tree line for concealment from afternoon traffic. At 4:01 p.m. freight train XX approaches from the north. Count the open coal cars. At car number 50, pace and board car 65 via the rear ladder. Climb over railing and drop to floor. Assemble and load PAW. Set ranging for XX feet. Use train car hopper braces for aiming stability. At 4:34 p.m. the train will slow. CRITICAL SUCCESS FACTOR: Disable the aircraft's flight controls. Fire multiple (2–3) rounds into cockpit of United Airlines Airbus A320 Flight 672 to San Francisco departing on O'Hare's Runway 22L. CRITICAL SUCCESS FACTOR: Collect spent shell casings. After impact, **DO NOT EXPOSE POSITION!! DO NOT PEEK!!** over the car railing. Rising smoke will confirm the kill. Escape on the train as it continues south through the Proviso Rail Yard at Melrose Park. At 5:11 p.m., count off seventeen seconds. Heave PAW and case over the top car rail and into the center of the Des Plaines River. Verify center water depth XX. Count thirty seconds. Exit train. Backtrack one-half mile to McDonald's Restaurant on Illinois Highway 171 and 64. Exit to ?? partner?? in waiting vehicle. Escape to Indiana border, then southbound on I-65.*

Akil closed the Google Earth application and casually clicked on Google News.

His pulse quickened at the breaking headlines:

FLIGHT BAN LIFTED—AIRLINES ALLOWED TO RESUME OPERATIONS

Reuters—14 minutes ago

WASHINGTON | Fri May 29 (Reuters)—At midnight on Saturday, ten full days after instituting a nationwide No-Fly Zone, the US Department of Transportation will allow the nation's airspace to reopen.

According to the statement released by Secretary of Transportation Norman Minka, "I must caution everyone that a system as diverse and complex as ours cannot be brought back up instantly. We will reopen airports and resume flights gradually on a weekend, with stringent levels of security. The first flights to operate will be cargo. This phased approach will assure the highest levels of safety, which remains our primary goal. For passenger travel, anyone planning on flying should check with their airline regarding the level of service and flight schedules, and be sure to allow plenty of time to deal with security procedures. There will be inconveniences, but safety will be the first element in restoring our system. Despite the reopening of the skies to commercial carriers, travel will likely be difficult for the foreseeable future. It will be some days before air travel returns to full operation. Information from airports, airlines, and government agencies continues to change frequently. If you must travel within the next forty-eight hours, contact your travel agent, customer service department, or the airline representative where you bought your tickets. If your plans are scheduled beyond forty-eight hours, hold off calling so that others with more immediate concerns can get through to overburdened call centers. Expect to spend time waiting on hold, as call volume will be heavy."

The decision, announced just moments ago by the White House, was met with resounding support from labor and business groups all across the country.

—

SUNDAY, MAY 31
7:10 A.M.

AKIL CLOSED his apartment window and returned the black drone to its case.

He deactivated one cell phone and dialed another.

"I'm on my way. Do me a favor and get me two Egg McMuffins and two hash browns, okay? I'm starved."

He clicked off, gave the room a cursory look, and then went downstairs.

Out on the street, he loaded his luggage into Marissa's minivan. He double-checked the firmness and lock on the X-Cargo car top carrier on the roof. Next, he unlocked his Camry's doors and placed the keys conspicuously on the dash.

He glanced at the darkened windows of the Russian Star Tattoo Parlor.

Viktor and Tamara had had a rough night. They'd both be sleeping in today.

Akil made his way south on I-5 toward Chula Vista and pulled into the Travel Inn Motel on Broadway and G Street.

Marissa and her children were waiting, luggage and breakfast bags in hand. They filed inside the minivan. Akil drove to the I-805 freeway and merged into the northbound traffic. He checked the rearview mirror and then turned on the radio.

Marissa immediately turned it off.

"Why did you do that?" he asked. "I wanted to hear the news."

"I want to hear about us," she whispered seductively, placing her arm around his neck and toying with his ear. "Did you miss me?"

"Of course." He smiled, setting the cruise control for five miles over the posted limit. They kissed. "Where would you like to go?"

"Any place you want as long as it's out of California. I hate this state," she said, resting her head on Akil's shoulder and gazing through the windshield. "I've always wanted to see the Statue of Liberty. How about New York City?"

Akil bit into his sandwich and checked the rearview mirror again.

"New York sounds like a winner to me."

38

THE PRESIDENT had finished his remarks and was sitting with leaders from the Urban League and the National Council of Churches. The Umbato Choir from Uganda had finished a second set of hymns.

Eerily reminiscent of a scene that occurred on the morning of September 11, 2001, in the Emma E. Booker Elementary School in Sarasota, Florida, Chief of Staff Bard hurried to the table and bent next to the president's ear.

Guests were riveted by the action.

The president nodded twice and made it a point to examine a fork before calmly setting it on his plate. His face had turned ashen. He neatly folded his napkin and then rose from the chair.

"Folks, I apologize, but something has come up."

By the time he reached the Oval Office, he was shaking with anger.

"California? Federal Express?" the president shouted into the speakerphone. "Samuel, this is indiscriminate anarchy. Do something!"

Bard entered the room with a handful of faxes. The president covered the mouthpiece with his hand.

"Mr. President, the airports are in panic. You need to reverse

232

your position. Someone is killing our citizens. Flight crews and passengers across the country are already refusing to board planes. The American people think that you're putting the economy ahead of their lives by keeping the airspace open. They're blaming you for the deaths."

The president strained to make sense of what he had just heard. He swallowed hard, forcing himself to stay calm. He lifted the phone. "Get Minka to reinstate the no-fly order, please. Do you hear me, Samuel? Back to nationwide groundstop—*do it*."

The president hung up the phone. "Get me Jack Riley. Then the Secretary of Defense and General McFarland."

"Sir, please, you cannot deploy the military on US soil without declaring a state of emergency," Bard warned. "And even then, you need explicit requests from state governors. It would be viewed as a severe intrusion into—"

"I don't care about states' rights," the president shot back. "And you're wrong. I have the absolute power and authority to deploy federal troops anywhere in the country in a national crisis, and I'm going to take action. I want a presence. An overwhelming presence at all airports. We need to screen everything and everyone."

"Sir, there's no need," Bard said calmly. "The airports will shut down per your order. That will show you're in charge."

The president glared at him. *In charge of what? An incompetent Department of Homeland Security that can't stop aircraft from crashing to the ground like paper toys?*

"I want a thousand soldiers patrolling every airport. I want them hand searching every single passenger and opening every piece of luggage." He nodded confidently. "The military will assist the airlines. They'll board every aircraft just like the Israelis. Soldiers, scanners, even polygraph machines if we have to. Everything. We'll open every single piece of luggage on every single plane, then put it through the scanners, and then let the canine units have their way. Or better yet, we'll simply disallow all luggage. That'll work. It has to."

"Mr. President," Bard interrupted the tirade, "two pilots and two technicians are dead. This was a cargo jet flying from San Diego to San Francisco for routine maintenance."

The president looked at his chief of staff quizzically. "What's your point?"

"There was no luggage, sir. It was empty."

—

COURTYARD MARRIOTT
MILWAUKEE, WI

"YOU SMUG idiot. Are you insinuating that I need counseling?" Ross's ex-wife yelled through the phone. "Don't you *ever* suggest that again. We may be divorced, but I'm still the tenant, and you're still the landlord. I demand to be treated with respect. The weeds in the front lawn look like a jungle to the point of embarrassment. The railing in my hallway is loose, and so is that same piece of carpet on the stairs. I came home the other night with a friend and nearly fell. Oh, and by the way, Brad is twice the man you ever were. When are you coming home?"

"I don't know," Ross answered, shifting the phone. "We've got three major investigations running simultaneously in three major cities. This is entirely different than 9/11. At least with those crashes, we knew the cause. We don't have enough people to support the work on this one. I can't just up and leave."

"I despise you and your misguided loyalty. Can't you even answer a simple question?"

"I'm sorry," Ross said evenly. "It's the best I can do."

"The best you can do," she said disgustedly. "Did you know . . ."

Marcia continued to talk, but Ross wasn't listening anymore. A sudden realization had come to him. He wasn't angry; he wasn't frustrated. In fact, he actually smiled before hanging up. As he did, he felt a sudden euphoria. This was an opportunity for a clean break and a fresh direction. She'd receive the move notice at her office via registered mail in a few days. For the first time in months, he had clear insight into who he was and what he wanted from a relationship. Good riddance.

There was a knock on the door.

Riley stormed in and clicked the TV remote. "I've been calling. Who have you been talking to?"

"A bad connection."

The breaking news showed a helicopter's view of San Diego's Mission Bay, six miles northwest of the airport.

"The media know what's happening even before we do," Riley observed.

Ross's face was drawn, the pain obvious. "Whoever's doing this has us running all over the country. The NTSB can't handle it anymore, Jack. We need help. It's gone beyond our ability."

"It's about to get worse," Riley said, reading a news scroll announcing expected financial market futures. "Bridge said the president is ordering another nationwide shutdown until the military can put armed soldiers on all commercial flights. One more thing: congress is in emergency session, and your organization is on the agenda. They're thinking that the NTSB can do more good in this crisis by assisting law enforcement task forces than by staying so isolated. If the recommendation is accepted, then you and your teams will be reporting to me until further notice. All other investigations and work efforts will stop, and resources will be redirected and made available to Homeland Security. We need the expertise, pal."

"Firearms on aircraft is a horrible idea, Jack. Is that even legal?"

"Nobody knows anything. The whole country is in chaos."

"What do you need from me?" Ross asked.

"Physical evidence." He snatched the plastic bag on the tabletop containing the mysterious red plastic wing. "The president's coming down on me—hard. At this point, I'll take anything. Is there any way this thing has significance?"

"I don't know what to think anymore," Ross said. "One thing's for sure—it came from somewhere or something. We need more time."

Riley's cell phone chirped.

After a brief conversation, he raised his arms. "There is a God, after all. A webcam operating in Fiesta Bay Park in San Diego captured the whole flight path on film. We've got live video of the explosion. It came from under the cockpit."

RILEY SUCKED the last of the liquid from a plastic water bottle and neatly replaced the cap. Numb from hours of nonstop video meetings with field teams, he sat on the floor, staring dejectedly at a stack of unread investigation progress summaries. He yawned at the television. The sound was barely audible, but he managed to hear a cable news roundtable guest claim that the airline crashes were caused by shoddy maintenance and that the president was culpable for not adequately funding the FAA and its inspectors.

Riley tossed the bottle across the room at Tom Ross, who was curled up on a sofa. It landed directly on top of his head, giving off a loud but harmless bonk.

"Turn that idiot off," Riley said with considerable annoyance. "News commentators who allow people to bloviate without supporting facts should find another job."

Ross snorted and reached for the remote.

"When can I go back to my old job?"

"When the skies are safe, and not a minute before," Riley said, rubbing his eyes. "Did you ever have that pain in your side looked at?"

"It hasn't bothered me lately, but I gave up the pumpkin seeds." Ross stretched. "I'll be in my room. I need two hours."

Riley turned his head suspiciously. "Your room or Neela's?"

"Mine," Ross answered firmly. "Besides, she's still in New York. She's driving back Wednesday."

"That job offer?"

"Uh-huh. And get this—she's supposed to be interviewed on Fox's national morning news show. They want to hear about her embedded assignment. She's really getting popular. Unfortunately, I'm not real keen on long-distance relationships. We'll have to see."

Ross pressed what he thought was the TV remote's *ON/OFF* button. Instead, it was the "favorites" button, and the screen flipped to the Discovery Channel. He found the right button, and the screen went black.

Riley was in the middle of a deep yawn when he suddenly leaped to his feet.

"Did you see that?"

"Huh?"

"Turn that TV back on."

Ross complied and raised the volume.

A narrator was standing inside a sports stadium underneath a football goalpost. He was holding some kind of mechanical, bird-like creature.

". . . the Mars project due to severe federal budget cuts. It's the brain-child of Professor Michael Robertson, who designed the flying insect for Georgia Tech here in Atlanta. As you can see, it actually looks and feels like a toy with wings. That makes the Entomopter quite different from traditional unmanned military drones. It has a built-in camera, and thanks to its pincer-like legs, can carry up to double its weight in rock samples from the Martian landscape. Unfortunately, even the best inventions never get off the ground. Next, we'll look at some of the military's high-tech land robots."

Riley's eyes and mouth couldn't grow any wider. By the time he turned to Ross, his face resembled that of some wild, raging beast. The TV screen showed a commercial touting Taco Bell's late-night drive-through. Neither man heard a word. They spoke in unison.

"Drones."

—

DECATUR, GA
4:30 A.M.

LINDA ROBERTSON sat up in bed, awakened by what sounded like voices and radio static. She fell back to the pillow, wondering why the boys would be up so early. The bedroom door cracked open, and she heard the sounds again. She nudged her husband.

"There's someone in the house. It's your turn. And don't pull my covers off this time."

"That's far enough, buddy," Michael groaned, rising on his elbows. "You're gonna need more than a Nerf gun. I'm serious. If you come in this room, I'm going to tie you to a tree outside and squirt you with the garden hose."

There was silence.

The door burst open.

Seven federal officers armed with AR-15 assault rifles surrounded the bed.

A second team swept onto the premises.

Linda pulled the covers up to her face, gasping in disbelief as they whisked her pajama-clad husband outside and into a waiting vehicle.

A young, clean-shaven Abe-Lincoln-ish man strode into the room and gently laid an envelope on the bed.

"Ma'am, y'all need to be advised that this is a federal warrant served by authority of the US attorney's office to detain a Mr. Michael C. Robertson," FBI Special Agent Harlan Ellis said in a soft Southern drawl. "Your husband will be at the FBI offices on Century Parkway in Atlanta. If y'all have a lawyer, then you can call the number on the back for further information. Y'all need to get up and get dressed, ma'am. We need to search this room."

—

ATLANTA, GA
10:30 A.M.

RILEY STOOD outside the secure detention cell, peering through its thick glass window and studying his prisoner's physical appearance.

He opened the cell door and nodded to the two agents inside. They removed Robertson's hand and leg restraints.

"I sure hope you're in charge, mister," Robertson said, rubbing his wrists.

"My name is Jack Riley, and as a matter of fact, I am."

"Well, you're going to pay, Mr. Riley, because I demand to call my lawyer. You had no right to do what you did to me. You had no right. Why won't anyone tell me anything? I'm going to sue you and your whole department, whatever it is."

"Homeland Security," Riley clarified, pulling up a chair.

"I want a phone and my lawyer. His name is Ray Mills."

Riley produced an evidence bag and slid out a piece of red plastic. "Do you know what this is?" Robertson glanced at it briefly, then turned away. "I don't have time for games," Riley said sternly, repeating the question.

"Of course I know what it is. It's a wing. A drone wing. I want a phone. I won't say another thing to you or anyone else."

Riley moved closer. "Sir, this wing was recovered from the wreckage of United Flight 605 in Bellevue, Nebraska. It was stuck to one of the landing gear tires. We believe it had something to do with the crash. We also presume that someone smuggled it aboard or otherwise placed it on that plane. Trust me, you'll feel a whole lot better if you tell us how it got there."

Robertson pointed his finger. "Mister, you storm into my home, place me in handcuffs in front of my wife and my boys, and then cart me off to jail like I'm Timothy McVeigh. I'm a decent, God-fearing man who's lost every ounce of patience. I've been sitting in this stink hole for over five hours, and no one has said a thing to me about why. I demand to be released, I demand a public apology, and I want my lawyer."

Agent Cheng cracked the door. "Jack, could I see you a minute?" Riley stepped into the corridor. Cheng opened a notebook. "This guy's a professor. He works downtown at a Georgia Tech research extension on Fifth Street. He's in charge of some kind of remote-control drone project. He's got a list of accomplishments on Wikipedia a mile long. He has an exemplary academic record and recently received worldwide attention in the scientific community for inventing some kind of a flying insect. I've got one right here. It's called an Ento—"

"Mopter." Riley examined the device.

"Uh-huh. Entomopter. According to his wife, he hasn't been out of Atlanta since they got back from Italy. He won some prestigious science award there. She's a high school teacher and seems credible. She's really furious. Maybe they're both in on it?"

Riley gave Cheng a doubting look. "We need to be smarter. Why did Ellis have to drag him out of his house like that? All we need is a front-page photograph of federal agents manhandling an innocent citizen. If he's not involved, then we're going to be up to our ears in lawsuits. Do me a favor and have Ellis track down a local attorney named Ray Mills. He'll want a piece of us too."

Cheng jotted the name. "There's one more thing. His wife is on her way down here with a bus load of students. The media is already setting up outside."

Riley returned to the cell with the drone and a paper cup of water.

"Professor, I just wanted to tell you that we probably could have brought you here in a more respectable manner. I'm sorry. And if you're not involved, then I'll give you your public apology. It may take a while. Please try and be patient."

Robertson slammed his hand onto the table. "Involved in what?"

"The loss of three aircraft and the death of 264 passengers."

Robertson choked twice. "You think . . . the airline accidents . . . that I . . . seriously, do I look like some Arab terrorist?"

"Looks can be deceiving, pal. They're not all Arabs."

"All right, that was inappropriate," Robertson admitted. "I'm sorry, but truly, the drone is nothing more than an exploratory tool. I built it exclusively for NASA. It was supposed to be part of the manned mission to Mars until it got cancelled. That's all there is. I have absolutely no idea how a piece of one ended up in Nebraska. These drones aren't secret, and neither are the components. Anyone could've picked one up and walked off with it."

Riley sipped his water. "This can really fly?"

"It can fly."

Riley felt his leg twitch.

"For carrying tools or rocks," Robertson said. "They can also hold it in position—on the roll bars of a moving Mars rover, for example."

That roused Riley's curiosity even more. "Anyone else make these?"

"I can name hundreds of universities and corporations all over the world working on aerial robotics. For its size, ours was the first of its kind. We had high hopes until—"

"Mars got cancelled. You mentioned that before." Riley set the drone down. "So, if this can carry a rock, then why not something else?"

Robertson knew what Riley was thinking. "I'm sick and tired of people assuming that my invention can instantly adapt to all these bizarre commercial or military applications. It wasn't built for that. It's not a guard dog, and it certainly can't launch Hellfire missiles."

"What do you mean bizarre applications?"

"A pie-in-the-sky security monitoring venture that has some people at Georgia Tech blinded by dollar signs."

Riley leaned forward. "What kind of monitoring?"

"Oil rigs and other fixed assets. One of my colleagues is in charge. I don't care to even bring it up."

"Oil rigs where?"

"In the desert outside Dhahran, Saudi Arab . . ." Robertson's mouth simply stopped working. He swallowed something rising in his chest. Deep lines appeared on his forehead. He closed his eyes.

Riley rose from the table, tipping his chair. "What did you say?"

Robertson's mind raced. He mumbled something, shaking his head repeatedly.

"I asked you a question," Riley pressed impatiently. "What did you just say?"

"Saudi Arabia," Robertson answered softly. "We gave six drones to someone from Saudi Arabia."

"Who did?"

"The university . . . my project . . . my colleague . . . no, it's not possible."

Riley leaped for the door. "His name. What is it?"

Robertson sat quietly, his hands folded in his lap.

"Professor Robertson! What is his name?"

"Al-Aran. Faiz Al-Aran."

40

ATLANTIC OCEAN
QUEEN MARY 2

"WOULD YOU repeat that, please?" Captain John Francis asked the caller on the other end of the telephone. He calmly walked across his cabin and touched his finger to a computer screen's navigational icon. He perused his ship's course and speed.

"The *Centro Nacional de Inteligencia* orders you to return to port, *señor*," Alberto Tadich spoke in broken English. "Immediately."

Spain's National Intelligence Center (CNI) had responsibility for all international terror threats. Domestics were handled by their Spanish Interior Ministry.

Francis had served in Britain's Royal Navy and was a NATO strike force commander before an arrogant German general relieved him. He'd carried a grudge against foreign authority ever since. He bristled at the Spaniard's tone.

"Orders me? On what grounds? Good grief, man, that's completely off our itinerary. Do you really expect a ship of our size to simply up and turn around without any explanation? We're on an extremely tight schedule."

"It is my duty to inform you of this instruction, *Capitán*. Return to Las Palmas."

"Then you've done your duty, sir. I'll take the request under advisement. Good day." Francis hung up. His face had a smug expression. The ship had already reached international waters.

Chief Officer Clifton Remmers knocked on the cabin door. "Captain, sir, we've just gotten word from MI5 in London. It seems they'd like us to detain one of our passengers. A fellow named Al-Aran. They say it's urgent and to use extreme caution."

"This is absolute madness," Francis grumbled, snatching the dispatch from Remmer's hand. "Send a detail at once."

"Right away, sir." Remmers reached for his radio. "I think it's something about the US flight ban, but I'm afraid they wouldn't let me in on the details."

Francis touched his computer screen's security icon and scrolled through the passenger list. Al-Aran's name came up highlighted and flagged by the ship's SmartCard System as a non-returning passenger on embarkation.

"Belay that, Clifton."

"Sir?"

"The chap never reboarded. He's still in the Canarys. It's their problem now."

———

NORTH LANZAROTE ISLAND
CANARY ISLANDS
GREEF'S CHARTER FISHING

"AL-ARAN, AL-ARAN. Yeah, I've seen him. A tall, dark-skinned fellow," Rollin Greef recalled. Dressed in dock shorts and knee-high rubber boots, Greef carried a filet knife slung over his back. "He's out on one of my runabouts. He took a tub full of squid and half a dozen rods. I thought he was a bit of a dill to go shark fishing alone with nothing but a fancy briefcase. But he kinda persuaded me, if you get my meaning, eh?"

"In other words, he gave you money," Cheng clarified.

Greef winked. He reached in his pocket and pulled out a tin container. "You look a little knackered, mate. Where did you say you lit off from?"

"Atlanta."

"This Al-Aran must be in some big trouble if the American FBI sets off on a four-thousand-mile walkabout. Drug runner?"

Cheng shook his head. "How long has he been fishing?"

Greef craned his neck at the boathouse clock. "All of five hours now. I'd say he's due back this way anytime."

———

ATLANTIC OCEAN
28° 47'04.80"N 13° 12'52.58"W
THIRTY-THREE MILES SOUTHEAST OF ORZOLA

FAIZ AL-ARAN removed a handheld GPS receiver from his briefcase and verified his position. He checked the time and peered through his binoculars. To the south, a freighter appeared on the horizon. Its silhouette grew steadily larger until gray-white lettering was visible. He flung the receiver and binoculars in a wide arc and watched them plop into the water, narrowly missing a curious pilot whale. Next, he heaved the squid overboard and churned the runabout's propeller through the blood-soaked entrails. The first shark appeared in less than a minute. Finished, he stripped off his clothes and laid them in a neat pile on the floor. He slipped into a swimsuit and slung a backpack over his shoulder. He pressed the engine's throttle.

The freighter had slowed to four knots.

Al-Aran brought the runabout alongside the big ship and leaped to the portside boarding ladder. Three crew members watched with mild amusement as this odd tourist-seafarer scrambled up to the main deck.

The runabout puttered away aimlessly.

A man in a white turtleneck sweater appeared on the freighter's bridge and eyed Al-Aran suspiciously. He lit a cigar as he walked down the metal steps, a bundle of clothing tucked under one arm.

"Why do you board the *Abuzenima*, the finest ship in the National Navigation Company? And why are you so far from shore in the trade lanes? Surely you have had bad luck, but I'm afraid you will be with us for a while. Rabat is another five hundred miles. Do we know each other, *señor*?"

"My name is Faiz Al-Aran," he said, shivering. "I am a friend."

"I am Captain Riad Naimi, and I choose my friends carefully."

"I have a message from your brother, Ali Naimi," Al-Aran announced. "The animal that visits your garden each night is not a mongoose. It is an Iberian lynx."

The captain smiled broadly, offering Al-Aran a towel and a set of workman's overalls.

"Come, we will dine together. You must tell me of the interesting life you've had in Ameri—" Riad lifted his binoculars. "Your run-about, *señor*. You left something aboard on the console—a briefcase. Do you wish to retrieve it?"

Al-Aran tightened his belt. "Your brother is well and sends Allah's love."

NORTH LANZAROTE ISLAND
CANARY ISLANDS
GREEF'S CHARTER FISHING

LAS PALMAS authorities and curious locals crowded the dock watching Rollin Greef secure his recovered runabout. In the Canaries, the drowning of one cruise ship passenger carried more significance than a capsized migrant raft from sub-Saharan Africa. Tourists meant money.

Greef scampered up the dock steps, carrying what were presumably Faiz Al-Aran's clothes along with a brown leather briefcase.

"Not one sign of him," Greef announced. "If he jumped in that water, the poor bloke's a shark biscuit by now. I've never in my life seen anyone try and swim with man-eaters as if they was dolphins. That's like ringing a dinner bell."

Cheng took the briefcase and attempted to flip the latches.

"Whoa now, mate," Greef said, bending next to Cheng's ear. "There's one heckuva camera mob watching. We need to think about this. There's something weighty in that case that I wager you want. Problem is, if this Al-Aran rigged up a nasty surprise, then I don't fancy having your or my face blown off. Not to mention scrubbing all these sticky beaks off my dock."

"Good points," Cheng whispered. "I need to get off this island and back to the States quietly. I don't have time for the media here or the hassles of evidence protocol. Is there a back road to the airport?"

"Hmmm, it's possible, mate," Greef answered quietly. "Lanzarote or Arricife?"

"Lanzarote."

"Any brass headed into my pocket?"

"Fifteen hundred dollars, US."

Greef pursed his lips. "The FBI keep its word?"

Cheng offered his hand. "And I was never here."

"A tidy sum, but these Las Palmas bullymen could have a say. Some might even go berko wanting their own investigation." Greef's eyes narrowed. "I was a fair truckie in my younger days, but if we could just take my water tinnie, everything would be ace. That way nobody'd know where we was off to. All we need is a little misdirection. You run these blokes off my dock, mate, and we've got a deal."

Cheng flagged a young policeman in front of the crowd.

"*Hablas* English?"

"*Si, señor.*"

"There's enough high-explosive in this briefcase to blow up all of this crowd and half this island," Cheng advised. "Where's the nearest law enforcement headquarters with x-ray capability?"

"Las Palmas," the policeman answered, nervously backing away. Cheng followed him. The man stumbled slightly. "Please, *señor*, be careful. We must ask everyone to—"

Cheng lifted the briefcase high in the air. "*Bomba.*"

The crowd scattered, and as they did, Cheng and Greef sprinted to the waterside docks. In a flash, Greef had the lines untied and the engines started. He flattened the throttle on the twenty-one foot Cobia 211 Bay Skiff, and the hull planed out for the open ocean. Top speed was fifty miles per hour. Lanzarote Airport was twenty-seven miles away.

"You can open that briefcase anytime," Greef shouted over the wind and spray. "It's safe enough for a $1,500 peek."

"How do you know?" Cheng shouted back.

"I already looked."

—

WASHINGTON, DC
OVAL OFFICE

"NOW WE'RE getting somewhere," Secretary Bridge announced to the president. "We have a laptop computer, names, and a possible method. We've been concentrating on the interior of these aircraft when all along the threat's been outside. It's a flying bug."

The president nearly laughed. "Have you lost your mind?"

"A remote-control drone capable of carrying who-knows-what kind of explosive and attaching it to the plane somehow—an engine or wing near a fuel tank or some other vulnerable position." Bridge rifled through a folder. "Here. This is your aircraft killer."

"Entomopter?" The president strained to make sense of the term. "What on Earth is an Entomopter, and what maniac designed it?"

"He's no maniac," Bridge assured. "He's a well-respected professor at Georgia Tech. Believe it or not, this drone was built for your Mars mission. It was supposed to help survey planetary landscapes and carry rock samples."

"Are you sure you have proof?"

"Riley has a name, address, and description of a potential conspirator. He's an Egyptian-American named Faiz Al-Aran. We think he's on the *Queen Mary 2*. At least, he was registered as a passenger. He may have temporarily disappeared somewhere in the Canary Islands. Riley's working with the Spanish authorities. They'll find him. The State Department also has a request in to the Saudi embassy for sight detainment of another individual named Ibrahim Al-Assaf who supposedly works for their oil ministry. He arranged to acquire these drones from Georgia Tech. That's the good news.

"Unfortunately, there are some unconnected dots. A man fitting Al-Aran's description was on that ship. But if that's true, then it's unlikely that he personally triggered any detonations. And that means he's working with unknown accomplices inside the United States. Second, we still have no idea on the method used. We're confident that the drone is involved, but we don't know how. Riley wants a visual of it in flight."

"What's the bad news?" the president asked.

"We've had three crashes," Bridge said. "Before he left the country, Al-Aran walked off Georgia Tech's campus with six drones."

"Did you say six?"

"Yes. Six."

COURTYARD MARRIOTT
FBI COMMAND CENTER
MILWAUKEE, WI
TUESDAY, JUNE 2

RILEY SET Shaitan on the conference table.

"One good-guy professor, one flying bug, and one bad-guy professor who for some strange reason decided to backstroke with man-eating sharks. There's no way this Al-Aran could have acted alone. I want his conspirators—names and descriptions. They had to have been somewhere with a clear view of the departure runways. We haven't come up with a single airport lead in this investigation, and I'm sick of it. I want a suspect list, and I don't care how it's done or who is on it. How many interviews have we completed?"

"We have Al-Aran's laptop," Cheng said. "It's in New York, where our best people are looking at it."

"Yeah? And who is the FBI's best?"

"Bruce Baltis. He works in the Bureau's Cyber Security Division. I'm sure you've heard of him. As an intern, he wrote an integration program that connected state fingerprint identification systems to the FBI's national system. We think he was involved in that Siemens thing."

Riley's head turned fast and he gave a painful look. Cheng couldn't tell if that meant "shut up" or that Riley really didn't know. Cheng thought about ending the topic, but he finally decided to share. After all, it was never proved.

"Supposedly, a supervisor found and read a folder in Baltis's office. When he questioned it, the supervisor was immediately reassigned. Like, that day."

"What kind of folder?" Riley asked.

"From Siemens."

Riley had a vacant look. "So?"

"It was a System Controls portfolio," Cheng announced. "The supervisor thought that Baltis was simply leaving the Bureau for a job there, but nothing ever happened. Things just went back to normal. The folder also contained a list of Israeli contacts. I thought that at your level at DHS, you'd have been briefed."

"What are you talking about?" Riley asked incredulously.

"Siemens? Iran? There was speculation that Baltis was working with Israel during that time. Some thought that he was *that* guy. He's that good."

"Wow," Riley said after a moment. Now he understood. He remembered the terrorism briefing, and it scared him. Governments were the prime suspects. "Are you telling me that the guy looking at Al-Aran's laptop designed Stuxnet?"

"I never said that." Cheng raised his hands. "I said there was speculation."

Stuxnet was a devastating computer worm that had secretly infected thirty thousand Iranian PCs, including those running uranium enrichment processes at the Bashir and Natanz facilities. The worm caused centrifuges (machines that spun and separated Uranium-235 weapons-grade) to increase their normal operating speeds of 1,064 hertz to 1,410 hertz for fifteen minutes before returning to normal frequency. Twenty-seven days later, the worm slowed the centrifuges down to a few hundred hertz for a full fifty minutes. The stresses from the faster, then slower speeds effectively destroyed one thousand machines. The United States and Israel denied any responsibility.

"You're sure Baltis is on our side?" Riley quipped.

"Ask him yourself," Cheng responded. "You'll get along great. He's no-nonsense and very direct. Almost bordering on rude, but I guess it's expected. His mind doesn't think like yours or mine. The laptop has become the focal point of the investigation. He's analyzing the hard drive as we speak. If there's anything there, he'll find it. And if I might make a suggestion . . . I don't think we should give any of this to that Fox woman."

Tom Ross entered the room and caught the end of the conversation. He glared at Cheng. "Are you talking about Neela?"

"I was just saying that I'm uncomfortable sharing too much information, especially from Al-Aran's computer. I think some things should be kept confidential." He turned to Riley. "As far as names, first you need a list of suspects, and right now that's impossible. All we've got is raw data. There are no suspects."

"Then I want numbers," Riley demanded. "How many?"

Cheng exhaled and reached for a stack of papers.

"Mitchell International has a ten-mile perimeter bordering 118 military, civilian, and commercial structures. So far, our agents have interviewed everyone who lived, ate, worked, or touched those structures—truck drivers, delivery personnel, transients, renters, and old and new homeowners. We even tracked down customers who were filmed by restaurant security cameras, just like you requested. Any one of them could have had access to a rooftop or vantage point from which to maneuver and guide a drone onto a runway. Take your pick. There are over two thousand names."

Riley turned to Ross. "Okay, Mr. NTSB, start thinking of how we can use Neela to our advantage. Perhaps even a little disinformation?" He approached a magnetic dry-erase whiteboard and lifted a thick black marker. He drew five columns.

"Mr. Cheng, do we know how many businesses around Mitchell's perimeter are foreign-owned?" Cheng shrugged. Riley labeled that as column one. He labeled column two as *High Vantage Points*. "I want names of anyone who had access to an area that overlooked a runway. Does anyone fit that?"

"We never looked at it from the perspective of a flying drone."

"Number three, a link to the military. I want a sorted list of people we interviewed who are currently or have been in the service. Number four is"—he turned and wrote *Unusual Circumstances*—"strange behavior, a practical joke, an accident, or an injury. Anything that could be attributed to a terrorist training mishap. Even a suspicious or untimely death."

Cheng dug through his notes. "A Milwaukee detective reported some commando activity in the woods south of here."

"Say again?" Riley perked up.

"A paintball tournament," Cheng said straight-faced. Riley was not amused. "I'm sorry, Jack, but I'm punchy, and this is impossible. We need at least two or three input days so we can do some system searches. Poring through all this paper will just bog things down. Where do we even start?"

"We start with Mitchell International," Riley said. "Our perpetrator was in the vicinity somewhere, and then he vanished. Something tells me that the observation area on the north side of the airport is hot. That Professor Robertson said his drone operated from a laptop. Maybe our suspect just sat there and controlled the whole thing from a vehicle right out in the open."

"No way," Ross observed. "He would've been spotted by security cameras."

"Who covered the north side perimeter and associated buildings?"

Cheng straightened in his chair. "I told you that one of my agents ran into some disgruntled military personnel at an American Legion Post, so I went back there myself."

"And?"

"Nothing. They're disgruntled, all right, but other than a bad case of racism, it was clean. One of their employees did pass away recently on the premises. I guess you could consider that an 'unusual circumstance.' His name was Chief . . . er, Watts. Jerry Watts. A Vietnam veteran who managed the place. He was well liked. His friends said he drank too much even when he wasn't celebrating his birthday. They found him behind the bar on the morning of the eighteenth. He's suffered a massive heart attack."

"His birthday?"

"Uh-huh. He turned sixty. Talk about bad luck. It was his own party. He and his buddies played cards until around 5:30 a.m. He died just before the Delta crash."

"Hmph," Riley said, drumming his fingers. "Anything else?"

"Not really. We interviewed all the regulars except for some kid who lives above the bar in an efficiency apartment—a Marquette dental student. Their admissions staff is running him down. He was out of town."

"What's his name?"

Cheng rifled his notes. "Waleu. Mike Waleu."

Riley wrote the name under *High Vantage Points*.

"That's one. Who else?"

"Jack, don't do this," Cheng pleaded. "We're talking two thousand names attached to the Milwaukee investigation alone. The follow-ups could take weeks."

"We don't have weeks," Riley said angrily. "I need a conspirator, and I need my fish. I think better with my fish."

Riley retrieved his stuffed toy and noticed Cheng's eyelids drooping slightly. He launched Shaitan across the room. It sailed past Cheng's head and skipped off the whiteboard, erasing the I in Mike Waleu's first name.

"David, wake up. When's the last time you had any rest?"

"Not since I got back from Lanzarote," Cheng admitted sheepishly. "I can't sleep on a plane, especially over water."

"Go get some. We'll finish up here. Mr. NTSB and I will run out to New York and meet with this Baltis character. Where is he exactly?"

"The Manhattan field office," Cheng responded. He collected his materials and started for his room.

Tom Ross picked Shaitan up off the floor and set him on the conference table. He uncapped a marker and rewrote the missing letter I on the whiteboard. He walked toward his seat and then suddenly froze in mid-step. He turned back to the board and used his finger as an eraser.

HIGH VANTAGE POINTS

M KE WALEU

Ross easily recognized MKE as Mitchell International's three-letter FAA airport designation code for Milwaukee. He put the I back on

254

the board and wrote another word below, matching letters to Waleu's name like some federal Wheel of Fortune.

"Uh, Jack? You might want to look at this. Can I go back to my old job now?"

HIGH VANTAGE POINTS

MIKE WALEU
MILWAUKEE

Riley took a moment to compose himself.

He turned to Ross. "I want you to call your reporter friend and tell her to meet us at the Javits Building, 26 Federal Plaza in New York City. Mr. Cheng? I'm afraid you're not going to get any sleep in the foreseeable future. Find this Waleu kid, *fast*. Have all Milwaukee, O'Hare, and San Diego personnel lock down any airport perimeter building space that has recently been rented or has reported a missing person or a fatality of any kind. Top priority. Seal off entire blocks if necessary. Go."

Riley took the eraser and swiped the whiteboard clean.

43

BURLINGTON, WI
FRIDAY, JUNE 5

A PINK neon vacancy sign burned brightly against the predawn backdrop.

Akil eased the minivan off of County Highway 36 and pulled up to the office of the Lakeside Motel.

He gently shook Marissa's shoulder. "We're here."

She yawned. "What time is it?"

"Five thirty in the morning."

"Is this New York City?"

"Wisconsin."

"I've never been to Wisconsin." She opened a window and peered outside. "How long have we been sleeping?"

"Since Iowa."

"It's so quiet and cold," she observed. "I think I can see my breath."

"This isn't California. It's a farm town," Akil said. "I used to stay here when I visited friends at the University of Wisconsin-Whitewater. It's only an hour away." He popped the rear hatch. "Do me a favor and check in. We should be in number twelve."

"Okay, Eddie, but I don't have a credit card."

"You won't need one."

Marissa ran a brush through her hair and then shuffled into the

256

motel's office. There was a handwritten note and a room key taped to the counter:

> *Sanchez family—*
> *We open at 7:00 a.m. Please fill out the guest registration*
> *card and leave it on the counter. You can pay later.*
> *Thank you!*

Marissa collected her children and walked to the room.

The interior was spartan clean and smelled of northern pine. The walls were painted gloss white. There were two queen beds.

"I didn't have to pay," she said, shivering. "Someone will rip them off."

"People aren't like that here," Akil yawned. "They trust everybody."

Marissa tucked Amber and Jo-Jo into bed and covered them. "Eddie, do you think we're a family?"

"From now on, we'll always be a family," Akil assured, sliding a suitcase against the wall. He turned on the wall heater and draped a blanket over Marissa's shoulders, rubbing her arms vigorously.

She leaned into him appreciatively. "I love the way you say that to me."

"I love to say it." He kissed her cheekbone and then her lips. "Are you hungry?"

"Sure. How long are we going to stay here?"

"Just today," he said, checking the time. "Go back to sleep. I know a little restaurant. They should be open. I need to get gas and check the tires."

Akil drove north on Honey Lake Road and then east on Academy Road to Annie & Angel's Country Café in Honey Creek. The restaurant was slammed.

A silver Ford Taurus sat idling in the rear of the parking lot.

Akil saw it and instantly became furious. With a single brief glance, he immediately recognized the male driver as a soldier. He sported a beard with a thin mustache, deep-toned skin, tight black hair, thick extended eyebrows, and an overall suspicious, even guilty visage. The man was as out of place as a fire hydrant in the desert, a

JOEL NARLOCK

Middle-Eastern male stereotype whose face would match half of those on a terror watch list.

Akil backed the minivan alongside and lowered his passenger window.

The man sat motionless, staring straight ahead.

Frustrated, Akil finally tapped his horn. The man lowered his window. Akil smiled pleasantly. "Do they serve barbecue?"

"Only if it is halal," the man replied with a distinct accent.

Akil drew his Glock and unlocked the passenger door. The man slid inside.

"Lift your shirt, slowly," Akil said, instantly serious.

The man complied, twisting sideways, exposing his waist and back.

"What's your name?"

"Abderouf Jdey. Allah has sent me to help—"

"Put your hands down," Akil ordered. "From where?"

"Gafsa, Tunisia."

"A long way from home," Akil observed, carefully feeling the man's thighs and ankles. "Where do you live now?"

"New York City."

"Where do you work?"

"Hunt's Point Cooperative Meat Plant. It is in the Bronx."

"Why are you here?"

"You called me."

"Wrong answer," Akil said, his jaw muscles flexing. "One more and you die."

"I am on orders . . . to assist you and your operation."

"What operation?"

"I do not know."

"Who am I?" Akil asked.

"I do not know."

"What's your skill?"

"*Yudammir.*"

"Destruction, huh?" Akil said doubtingly. "How?"

"I am expert with explosives," Jdey answered. "Plastics, nitrates, powders. Concealed and timed. I have much experience."

Akil studied Jdey's face. "What ratio of RDX and PETN will make Semtex 1A?"

258

"Four percent to seventy-six percent."

The RDX ratio was actually four-point-six. The rest was binder and plasticizer.

"What's the molecular formula of PETN? Don't guess."

"C5, H8, N4, and O12," Jdey recited confidently. "I serve you and your operation."

"And so you shall, my friend," Akil said, relieved. He eased the Glock back into his waistband holster. "Dude, this isn't Tunisia. You need to relax in public. You look like you're waiting to be arrested. And lose the beard. Try and look more . . . like a student. No more sport coats or expensive shoes. Wear old jeans and a cap with a college or sports logo. Nothing that draws attention. Find some lady to hang with, preferably with kids."

"What do I call you?" Jdey asked.

"Kenny," Akil said. "And you, my friend, will help me finish destroying America's airline industry."

"Praise be unto Him," Jdey said, bringing his hands together almost gleefully. "I knew it was of our doing."

"We're going to kill one more plane," Akil said matter-of-factly. "Correction . . . *you* are going kill one more. I will teach you. But first, I need you to gather information about your company's beef operations. Processing, distribution, stockyard access, and security."

"Three soldiers and I have worked at Hunt's for two years," Jdey explained. "We have earned their trust. All this information is accessible. What kind of stockyards?"

"Feedlots." Akil yawned. "Particularly in Nebraska and Texas."

Jdey turned to Akil, a question in his eyes. "The planes . . . how are they—?"

"An explosive killed those aircraft. Attached to the landing gear and then lifted inside."

"Attached how? What type?"

"A stable mix of potassium chlorate. It works fine. But you need to listen carefully and do exactly as I say. It was placed on the landing gear by a flying drone that operates from a laptop computer. It sees with a small camera. Everything is radio-controlled."

"Fascinating," Jdey mused. "Think of the power of one thousand such drones. We could attack one thousand targ—"

"*Halast*," Akil rebuked him in Arabic. "We're not interested in attacking one thousand anything. There's a plan in place, and we need to follow it. And that plan says one remaining aircraft."

"Where will we strike?"

"I have an apartment in East Elmhurst, directly across the street from LaGuardia Airport," Akil explained. "I need you to take the drone there and study it. In exactly sixteen hours, I'll join you. Together, we'll wait for the US president to open the skies."

"Friend, I am overwhelmed," Jdey admitted. "This is truly a gift from Allah."

"It's more than a gift," Akil advised. "Our work can no longer be carried out indiscriminately. There's a saying in America that suggests change is inevitable. It's true. We must change to survive. Our fight must be guided by new technologies—technologies that we will pass to the next generation and beyond. Remote-control devices are a solution to many problems. Do you know American history?"

Jdey pondered the question, proud that someone of Akil's status would ask for his opinion but embarrassed that he couldn't respond.

Akil checked his watch. "The native tribes early in America couldn't compete with their invaders because they lacked technological skills and abilities. And their culture died because of it. They couldn't adapt and thus were conquered. The day will come when great numbers of Allah's people will come to America. We are the new invaders, and we will learn and master technology. We will live among the infidels, we will conduct business with them, we will gain their trust, and then, if they still choose not to believe, we shall kill them wherever they are. It is written in our Holy book. Allah is great. He has designed our destiny."

"Allah is great," Jdey repeated.

"Take these," Akil said, placing a key and a cell phone in Jdey's hand. "My landlord lives next door. Don't let her see your face. She's harmless but nosey. If she bothers you, do what you have to without killing her. You must keep her alive."

Akil reached in his pocket and fished out something the size of a pack of cards. It was tightly wrapped and addressed to Mrs. Timmons.

"Place this in her mailbox. It's a payment. In sixteen hours, if Allah is willing, another infidel plane will fall from the sky."

"Sixteen hours," Jdey confirmed.

"You're a good man, and I trust you," Akil said, squeezing Jdey's hand. "Faiz Al-Aran mentioned that you have information about a cache of weapons?"

"Yes," Jdey said excitedly, proud to have gained Akil's confidence. "There is a man. His name is Denman. I work with his brother at Hunt's. He is licensed in federal firearms and operates in a cabin behind his home less than a mile from here. He boasts of one weapon in particular that can burst concrete blocks at three hundred meters. I believe it is a Barrett M82A1 sniper rifle complete with an optical ranging system that mounts right on the scope. It lets a shooter focus on the thrill of putting lead on a target. All you do is turn the elevation knob until the LCD displays the target's range. Three internal sensors automatically calculate the ballistic solution. It compensates for temperature, changes in barometric pressure, even aiming at an upward angle. He also stocks shotguns, pistols, fully automatic machine guns, black powder, scopes, ammunition, accessories—supposedly more than three hundred pieces. The Barrett can fire tracers, incendiaries, and even exploding rounds with tungsten penetrators that can punch through armored vehicles and destroy anyone inside. If we can gain access to such a place and such weaponry, we can arm many soldiers inside the United States and also avoid the dangers of international imports."

Akil leaned forward and kissed Jdey's cheek. He glanced at the time. "Show me this cabin."

———

DENMAN PROPERTY
BURLINGTON, WI

AKIL FOLLOWED Jdey's Taurus down County Highway W and onto a deserted access road. They parked. Akil fitted his Glock with a Silencero .40 Osprey silencer and gently closed the minivan's door. He motioned for Jdey to wait. Akil carefully followed a tree line toward the back of the property. The cabin was off to one side at the end of a long driveway. A Chevrolet pickup truck was parked in front. The cabin's windows were lined with steel bars. The heavy metal gate that usually protected the front door was unlocked and swung to one side. The interior lights were on. Someone was inside. Akil crouched low beside the porch railing. He peered through a crack in the window blinds at an obese, bearded man with a camouflaged Bass Pro cap sitting at a desk, eating something and tapping on a calculator. Akil waited and watched. After another minute, he twisted the door handle.

Denman froze.

Akil instinctively moved to a corner. He raised his pistol.

"Stand up and show me your hands."

"Okay, sir, just relax. You can have anything you want. There's no need to go crazy. I have the most expensive stuff in the back."

"Don't speak unless I ask," Akil warned. "How many concealed weapons?"

"I have two on me, sir. One in my right pants pocket and another under my shirt on my belt. I have no intention of reaching for them, sir. I don't want any trouble."

"Nothing behind your back?"

"No, sir. I never thought that was very comfort—"

"Be quiet," Akil snapped. "The Barrett."

Denman thought for a few seconds and then nodded to his left. "Brand-new in the case."

"How does it assemble?"

"Umm . . . with two pins. A mid-lock and then the rear receiver."

"Cartridges?"

"In the middle cabinet. I have two hundred standard rounds and—"

"No. Explosive armor piercing."

"On the top shelf. The ones with green tips and gray rings. The boxes are marked with blue tape. You can have them all."

"Is the weapon sighted?"

"Yes, sir. It's dead-on at three hundred meters."

"Who has access to this place?"

"No one but me. Keys are on the wall. Take my truck, wallet, anything you—"

One round pierced Denman's forehead. His body collapsed behind the desk.

Akil collected the Barrett and the exploding ammunition. He had found his perfect, accurate weapon. His PAW. The perfect system for destroying a departing aircraft's cockpit from inside a moving freight train car. He locked the cabin and flung the keys into heavy foliage. He calmly walked to Jdey's vehicle and placed the weapon inside. He tapped the roof twice.

Jdey headed east.

Akil drove the minivan west. He typed into his portable GPS. A female voice responded, "Destination Lakeside Motel, 920 Jefferson Street, Burlington, Wisconsin 53105, 5.4 miles. Recalculating."

———

JAVITS FEDERAL BUILDING
NEW YORK CITY

COMPUTER TECHNOLOGIST Bruce Baltis was ensconced in a glass office in the FBI's Information Technology Center. A hulking man with a baby's face and an oversized head, Baltis had dainty fingers that were expertly now typing on three separate keyboards. He finished his input and then tilted one monitor. The screen showed a mass of numbers and cryptic program language.

Riley tapped the window and walked in. He extended his hand.

"Bruce? Jack Riley. I've heard a lot about you, pal. I'm glad you're on our tea—"

"I'm running dual but parallel environments," Baltis interrupted rudely. "Faiz Al-Aran's laptop had an older version of Windows 7. I found retained dialogues in both the cache indexes and files. Whoever used it left a cyber-trail that a blind man could follow. There's also a ton of cookie history. See for yourself."

"The English version, mister. I'm not Bill Gates."

"Sorry. Every email sent or received on this laptop is still identifiable. No data, no secret terror plans, no hidden files or evidence of hard drive erasure—just two people chatting. Someone calling himself *Tooth-doc2b*, and the other one is *PartyLuvr30308*. That's probably Al-Aran."

"How do you figure?"

"Well, the number sequence 3-0-3-0-8 is also the zip code for the Technology Square Research Building in Atlanta, so it's a logical assumption. Other than that, there's not much else—just partying, vacations, and shark fishing. I started wondering if you got the right people. But the more I reread the conversations, the more it seemed like the two parties were *trying* to sound like a couple of good ol' boys. It was a labored deception, but not too labored. Do you get what I mean? And then there's this squirrelly address one of them mentioned right here in New York City. That's what my systems are chewing on."

"Squirrelly how?" Riley asked.

"Well, *Toothdoc2b* said he lived at 0112 18th Street in West Pinehurst. I was born and raised here, and I can't picture West Pinehurst. There's no such place."

Riley flopped into a chair and scratched his head. "Then it's got to be some sophisticated signal or code. How long will it take you to crack it?"

"I don't think it's a code, at least in the normal sense. These two are definitely playing word games, but they don't seem that smart. Then again, they do. Something just feels odd."

"That's great," Riley said dejectedly. "Talk to me. Odd how?"

"For one thing, no physical mailing address starts with a zero. And anybody can create an anagram like Mike Waleu for Milwaukee if you start with a city's name. The difficulty comes into play when you first try and identify all potential names. There could be thousands, and the only limitation is the number of letters."

"You're losing me," Riley said.

"Think about it. There are no rules for a person's name. It can literally be anything, especially a phony one. This guy may be slick, but so am I," Baltis said with a sly grin.

He rolled his chair across the room and tapped a keyboard. The screen saver disappeared and a status bar said 9 percent completed. "This is a simple program that takes a city crash site name, like San Diego or Chicago, and crunches out all possible words and names. Then it compares the results to names found in US databases. If we don't get any American hits, then we'll go international."

"Criminal databases? What if he has no record?"

"Criminal files are only the tip of an information iceberg," Baltis explained. "Don't get me wrong—the US government has a ton of data at the IRS and Social Security—but I'm talking all data and databases. The kind that's harvested, stored, and managed by the monster of monsters, Acxiom. The biggest data god in the world. Scary big. They peer deeper into American life than the FBI, IRS, or even those prying digital eyes at Facebook and Google. If you're an American adult, then, quite frankly, they know more about you than you do. And right this second, 23,000 computer servers in Conway, Arkansas, are processing more than fifty trillion data transactions a year. They have double the databases of any competitor, and they're particularly good at focusing on personal human habits. It's all about marketing. Their search programs are the most sophisticated and intuitive anywhere. That means they'll help you even if you screw up the input. Instead of returning *not found* errors, they'll flip data around and make suggestions. Their financial credit databases alone have over two billion accounts."

"Do we have access?"

"Sure, the FBI has access." Baltis gave an evil chuckle. "But most normal users don't have the navigation skills. Only the most sinister users do."

"I see." Riley smiled. "How long will it take you?"

Baltis moved to yet another PC and brought up a logon screen. He entered a user code, company ID, user ID, a mandatory 16-character password, and finally a series of security answers. He filled in the address blocks, leaving the zip code field blank.

"Let's see if we get lucky."

> 0112 18th Street, West Pinehurst, NY appears to be incorrect. Did you mean 2110 81st Street, East Elmhurst, NY 11370?

"*Si, señor*," Baltis responded. He clicked "OK."

The program continued searching for approximately twenty seconds and then produced several lines of data along with a MapPoint location.

"Gotcha. One of Acxiom's marketing databases tracks automobile registrations and vehicle repairs. They provide that data to companies who sell repair warranties and roadside protection. Follow? If you take your car in for service, somebody somewhere knows about it. It's all about keeping track of customers and their personal preferences. Let's see what we have . . . on Saturday, April 11, Queensboro Toyota in Jackson Heights repaired the odometer on a 2003 Camry. The owner listed 2110 81st Street as his home address. Someone by the name of Kenneth Wory."

"Gotcha," Riley whispered to himself. "Ken Wory . . . New York."

Baltis drilled further into the selection and brought up a Google Earth satellite view of the surrounding neighborhood.

The residence was located across the street from LaGuardia International.

CHENG NAVIGATED his vehicle around a series of police barricades and pulled up to curb on Kettner Boulevard.

"Am I glad to see you," FBI Special Agent Ben Jeffers said, straightening his necktie and extending his hand. "San Diego PD isn't very happy about us roping off this whole block and barging into the middle of a double domestic homicide. Their assistant chief, Cheryl Bryden, wants answers. It's one thing to take over an investigation, but to simply lock down a crime scene and not let anyone in or out?"

"Did you tell her it was a Homeland Security priority?" Cheng asked. "If she'd talk to her own DHS Liaison, she'd know this might be connected to the airline crashes."

"Things are moving so fast that I'm not sure I know what's going on," Jeffers admitted, handing Cheng a charcoal-lined dust mask.

They walked inside the building to a rear bedroom. The odor of human decomposition was strong.

Cheng knelt to the carpet.

"Who found them?"

"A utility meter technician had a key to the rear entrance," Jeffers said. "The victims are Karkula. Viktor F. and Tamara L., ages fifty-four and fifty-five. The medical examiner said they've been here nine, maybe ten, days. Apparently, the husband killed his wife and then himself. She was shot once through the chest. He was in the kitchen. Powder burns on his left temple. Textbook murder-suicide. The gun was still in his hand. According to police records, this place had its share of violence. There are Russian gangs, and neighbors said they were always screaming at each other."

"What's upstairs?" Cheng asked.

"A vacant apartment and bathroom for the homeless. Pretty bad."

"Employees?"

"None on record. They come and go—part-timers who work a few days for cash and then leave. Hard to keep track of the movement."

Cheng drifted into the kitchen and spotted a file cabinet next to a desk. He slid out the top drawer and casually fingered the folders. One was curiously labeled "Pigs". Inside, there was a copy of a money order. The signature was sloppy but readable. It was issued by a bank in Milwaukee.

—

JAVITS FEDERAL BUILDING
INFORMATION TECHNOLOGY CENTER
NEW YORK CITY

RILEY PUT his cell phone on speaker so he could write.

"Okay, I'm ready."

"Jack, it's the same MO. He rented an upper-level apartment with a clear view of San Diego International's Runway 27. The name on the money order is Ginosa," Cheng spelled it. "First name, Eddie."

"E-D-G-I-N-O-S-A," Riley translated the letters. "San Diego."

"We also struck gold on someone who recently leased an office at the O'Hare Aerospace Center on the airport's east perimeter," Cheng explained. "You can clearly see Runway 22. The building's access logs showed that the tenant was there early on the morning of May

19 and then never showed up again. The time slot dovetails with the Airbus departure. The lessee is Ghoacci, an anagram of Chicago. First name, John."

"That's some beautiful work, David," Riley said. "You get two out of two. Now all we need are descript—"

"We've got one," Cheng said. "He was caught on a lobby security camera. Medium complexion, male. Medium height and build with long brown hair. He's young. The image is a little blurry, but enough for a bulletin. He fits the description from the American Legion witnesses in Milwaukee. One more thing: there is no Michael Waleu registered in Marquette's Dental School. Jack, I think we're dealing with the same person in all three cities."

"We've got him," Riley whispered to himself. He pumped his fist once and made a kissing sound. Then his eyes narrowed and his face grew stern. "That's for you, mister."

"Do you want a nationwide alert?" Cheng asked.

"No," Riley said smugly. "I think I know exactly where he is."

Riley clicked off and headed for the door. He turned. "No offense, Mr. Baltis, but you can unplug your programs. We've got the names."

"Mr. Riley?" Baltis stood. "I'm paid to use my head and to give opinions, so here goes: this was too easy. I mean, just flipping an address around? It doesn't make sense. These people are either really careless or they've worked things out so perfectly that they're leading us down this path."

"Too easy for you may mean too hard for someone else," Riley countered. "Why do you feel this way?"

"I won't get into details, but I *am* experienced in 'sinister.' You should trust me on that. Call it a gut feeling."

"Point taken, pal," Riley said. "And thanks for your . . . sinister service."

"Sir? My cousin lived in Queens just two blocks from that address. She died on 9/11. She never made it out of the first tower. I hope the guy you're looking for is there, and I hope you nail him."

—

FBI OPERATIONS CENTER
7:30 P.M.

THE TWENTY-THIRD floor was buzzing with staff agents and members of New York's Joint Terror Task Force. Riley took a seat in a large conference room next to the man in charge of the New York field office. Special Agent Robert Farino bore the striking, albeit hairier, resemblance to his second cousin, ex-Mayor Rudy Giuliani. He also shared a family trait for tenaciously prosecuting of evil.

Farino began the briefing with introductions.

"You all know Jack Riley from DHS. The gentleman in the back is Tom Ross from NTSB, and next to him is Ms. Griffin from Fox News."

Heads turned.

"She's with me and has complete authorization," Riley added matter-of-factly. "It's about time we got some positive press for a change."

Farino continued. "Okay. We have information that our suspect is at an address in Queens, holed up in a flat in the middle of an upscale residential neighborhood—quiet, connected older homes. People keep to themselves. We, along with NYPD, have had the area and the flat under close surveillance since we got the notification. No one goes in or out without us seeing. There are seventy-five officers and an armored personnel control carrier staged and waiting three blocks from the premises. We're receiving radio updates from two tactical officers who are inside the adjoining houses."

Riley winced. "I thought we agreed not to do that. I don't want to spook him. Why'd you have to get that close?"

"I gambled, Jack," Farino admitted. "Both of those officers are carrying handheld G-rays. I figured we'd want to know how many perpetrators we're dealing with."

"Excuse me," Griffin interrupted from the back of the room. "What's a G-ray?"

Farino looked at Riley. He nodded.

"Gigahertz radiation, or G-ray, is an experimental radar flashlight that shoots a pulse of radiation at a target location and receives a digital image in return. It's like an x-ray that can see through fog, smoke, and even solids. It can detect drugs or explosives through walls up to ten inches thick. But it's currently limited to just seventy feet."

"How long have you had the ability to . . ."

An agent entered the room and bent next to Farino's ear.

"Okay, people, listen up. We've confirmed not one, I repeat, not one but two suspects inside that flat. One appears to be inactive, possibly asleep, and one is active. He's been in a sitting position for the past twenty minutes."

"Doing what?" Riley asked.

"Unknown. The frames only show that the subject's hands and arms are repeatedly moving to and from different positions. He could be sitting at the kitchen table reading a newspaper, petting a cat, or simply eating."

"Or arming more drones."

Farino nodded. "Or arming more drones."

45

EAST ELMHURST, NEW YORK CITY
8:15 P.M.

THE ORDER was for quiet transport—flashing lights, no sirens—during the NYPD escort from downtown Manhattan to LaGuardia. Twenty-two minutes later, Farino's Ford Expedition and fifteen other assorted Terror Task Force vehicles pulled off Grand Central Parkway and into the staging area.

Technically, Riley was in charge of the assault plan, but he deferred operational authority to Farino, provided everyone understood that intelligence gleaned from live terror suspects was far more valuable than any physical evidence. All personnel were to do everything possible to capture them alive. The use of lethal force was discouraged.

Ross cracked the SUV's door. "What should we do?"

Riley slid into a Kevlar vest and handed Ross a pair of binoculars.

"Stay inside, out of harm's way, and guard my fish," Riley ordered, nodding toward Shaitan, which was propped up in the front seat. "It's the brick two-story next to the corner. Both suspects are upstairs. We don't know who they are, we don't know their firepower, and we don't know what's going to happen. That said, I want both of you to stay here where it's safe. Neela, still photos only. No video. I'm already second-guessing my decision to bring you two out here.

272

These people don't care about human life. This could get public and loud real quick."

"We're in position," Farino announced.

"Do we have an interpreter?"

"He's standing by," Farino confirmed. "His name is Rooze—Agent Firooz Ghanbarz. He's fluent in thirteen Arabic dialects. We need to move. Is there anything else, Jack?"

Riley took Farino by the arm and gently walked him behind the SUV. Riley sat on the vehicle's bumper.

"I'm not a very sensitive man, and I'm not prone to drama," Riley said. "But I'll never forget September 20, 2001, when president George W. Bush gave a speech to a joint session of Congress. 9/11 was nine days old. This city was still in shock, and the world was gripped with fear. And he stood in that Chamber and talked about Todd Beamer and the rest of those American heroes who died on Flight 93 over Shanksville, Pennsylvania. They bull-rushed those hijackers to save lives on the ground. Todd's wife, Lisa, was in that audience. She was five months pregnant. Man, I wanted to hug her so bad. Before he said good-bye, Todd said the Lord's Prayer and two other words that I'll never forget. Bravery like that shouldn't be so rare, especially when it's about freedom." Riley gazed heavenward. "Todd, this is for you, pal. 'Let's roll.' "

Vehicles, agents, and officers in full tactical gear converged from three directions, forming a skirmish line across 81st Street. Two helicopters with thermal imaging capabilities focused spotlights onto the suspect's roof and upper windows.

The interpreter, Ghanbarz, lifted a bullhorn. "Attention, you are surrounded. Show yourselves with your hands in the air. We are authorized by the United States government to use deadly force if you do not comply."

No response.

He spoke in Arabic. "Allah is a peace lover and will look upon you with forgiveness. Show yourselves, and he will be merciful."

Nothing.

Farino put his radio to his ear and then turned to Riley. "Something strange is happening in there. The north G-ray officer is still reporting two suspects. One is reacting and the other is in a prone position with no movement at all. We may have a victim."

A face appeared in the window.

Riley reached for the bullhorn. "This is Jack Riley, United States Homeland Security. Step outside with your hands up, and you will not be harmed."

Incredibly, the window slid open. A hand drew the curtains back.

A few seconds later, a small, black object slowly fluttered through the window toward the staging area.

Barely visible, Riley followed the drone with binoculars. His stomach sank as it circled with pinpoint precision and disappeared under Farino's SUV.

—

Griffin opened the SUV's side door and focused her binoculars. "I can see Jack. It looks like he's on the phone. Do you think it's over?"

Ross cleared his throat. "Neela, before this comes to an end, I just wanted to say that I had hoped . . . um, if there was a way that we could work something out and still see each other even if you relocated to New York. I really enjoy being with you."

Something chirped once, then twice, then a third time.

She reached for his hand and smiled. "Are you going to get that?"

Ross finally realized the chirping was his phone and thought not to answer, but then he did.

"*A drone!*" Riley's voice screamed. "*Underneath you!*"

Ross didn't think, didn't hesitate. He snatched Shaitan from the front seat, swept Griffin into his arms, and, sprinter-like, propelled himself through the door. He scrambled a few precious yards before stumbling to ground. His body weight slammed onto Griffin's abdomen, forcing the air from her lungs like a hit from an NFL linebacker.

The detonation easily ruptured the SUV's plastic fuel tank, shredding the vehicle's undercarriage. A millisecond later, the vapor from thirty gallons of fuel unleashed a horrific secondary explosion that sent hardened chunks of debris and shrapnel spraying laterally.

The last thing Ross remembered was shielding Griffin's head with Shaitan, to the peril of his own.

—

Hurtling airborne end-over-end like a child's toy, the Ford Expedition landed on its roof, spinning and engulfed in flames. Black smoke mushroomed skyward. A few seconds later, fiery droplets pelted down like some spring rainstorm from hell.

There was momentary quiet, and then a barrage of tear gas and stun grenades launched from the middle of 81st Street, shattering the flat's windows. Seconds later, smoke illuminated by muffled explosions billowed through the interior.

The assault lasted just thirty seconds and then stopped.

The front door opened.

Two arms appeared first, then the head of a youthful-looking adult male. Barefoot, he wore blue jeans and a Milwaukee Brewers baseball cap. A Boston College sweatshirt hung below his waist. He raised his arms and stepped off the concrete stoop.

A chorus of metallic assault weapon breeches clicked in unison.

"Do not shoot; it is over," he coughed in broken English. "Allah is our judge."

"Get down on the ground!" a bullhorn voice echoed.

The man dropped to his knees and placed his hands behind his head.

No one went near him.

From forty feet, one of the G-ray officers initiated a scanning sequence. A black-and-white video screen showed the outline of a spaghetti-like mass of wires and four gray rectangular lumps strapped to the suspect's torso.

"*Wired!*"

Riley had wandered too close.

The suspect stood, arms outstretched like Frankenstein's monster, his legs repeatedly kicking at the cyclone fence gate in the front yard. He stopped and zeroed in on Riley, the closest enemy, and made eye contact. The moment froze in time. The man's stare was lifeless and cold. Then he smiled. A split second later, he detonated.

The Semtex blast wave rocked the vehicle skirmish line, shattering windows in a five-hundred-foot radius and sending a swath of collateral and human debris as far as the airport's noise abatement wall across the street.

—

RILEY'S FOREHEAD felt as though it had been split by an ax, and his pummeled eardrums translated only muffled sounds. His face and his eyelids were painfully singed, and when he opened them, he realized he was lying on his back on a stretcher. He vaguely remembered the detonation and the sensation of his body somehow being lifted off the ground. He remembered nothing about slamming back to the pavement, apparently knees and head first. When he gently turned his neck, the blurred images of three emergency medical technicians cleared. They were lifting a motionless body into an ambulance. Griffin was seated inside, sobbing.

"Oh no!" Riley wailed, trying to rise from the stretcher.

"Sir, he still has a pulse, but we need to go now," a technician said, pushing Riley back down. "They're waiting in the ER."

The ambulance pulled away.

Riley lay on the stretcher, holding his hands to his head.

Farino appeared and bent to one knee. "Are you all right, Jack? You should lay still."

"I take it we lost our suspect?"

"Yeah. He's all over the place—literally. And there were no other perpetrators. The second body inside that flat was Mary Timmons, the landlord who lived next door. She was blindfolded and tied up in the bathtub. She's on her way to a hospital in Queens. They think she'll be okay." Farino winced as he put his hand on Riley's shoulder. "We found something else."

"Will this ever stop?" Riley asked bitterly. "Please tell me it's the missing drones."

"A Barrett .50-caliber sniper rifle. Fully loaded with explosive-tip rounds. Jack, it was for another aircraft."

Where did he find that? Riley wondered, gently fingering his ear. "How do you know?"

"There was a note inside the case. He wrote the tactics down on paper. He planned to hop a freight train and shoot at the cockpit of another runway depart—"

"Don't," Riley choked, nearly breaking down. Farino helped him to his feet. Riley filled his chest with air and exhaled deeply. "I'm tired, and I've had enough. I'll call you. Get me some ice and some Tylenol. I need to speak to that landlord."

46

NEW YORK HOSPITAL QUEENS
FLUSHING, NY
EMERGENCY CARE
11:40 P.M.

WAITING AREA patients and staff crowded around television screens that showed breaking news of an FBI drug siege.

Griffin was sitting on a sofa, holding hands with a beleaguered young mother whose four-year-old daughter had accidentally fallen on the sharp end of a pencil.

Derek Feldman, one of seven board-certified trauma center physicians on staff, surveyed the room briefly and made his way toward the two women.

"Chandra? Your daughter is very lucky, ma'am," Feldman announced. "The pencil missed her eyeball and punctured the area next to the bridge of her nose. She'll need a patch bandage, but she's going to be fine."

He turned to Griffin and sat down, flipping a page on his clipboard. "Ma'am, is your name Neela?"

"Tom Ross," she choked. Her eyes welled up instantly. "Is he . . . ?"

"Why don't you ask him yourself?" Feldman smiled. "He's got a nasty wound just above the left temple, but he's stable. He's going to be okay. It's a good night for near misses. We'd like to keep him for a while. He's mildly sedated, but he's been asking for you. He's in Number 3 South. Follow me."

—

JACK RILEY arrived at the hospital and managed to limp his way to the second floor. The nurse in charge kindly directed him to a room. He peeked inside. A patient was lying in bed gazing blankly at the ceiling.

"Mary, my name is Jack," he announced softly. "How do you feel?"

"Fine." Timmons smiled, the diazepam taking hold. "Are you a policeman?"

"Sort of, ma'am," Riley answered, gently lifting her hand, careful to avoid the deep purple wrist bruises. "Mary, I need to ask you some questions about Kenneth Wory. It's important." She nodded once. He leaned closer. "Can you tell me what happened?"

"For the life of me, I don't know," her voice cracked. "I went next door to see if Kenny was hungry, and when I walked in, he came up behind and pushed me to the floor. He tied a rag over me eyes and dumped me in that tub. He never said a word. I couldn't believe it was happening. Then he taped me up. It was all I could do to breathe. Is he . . . gone?"

"He's dead, ma'am," Riley said. "Would you describe him for me?"

"Why would Kenny do such a thing?" she whimpered, tears drizzling down her cheeks. "Such a handsome, nice lad. Always so neat and polite. He used to show me that trick with those coins."

"Coins?"

"They was in me mailbox. Now they're in me sweater." She turned her face toward the closet. "Kenny always said he'd bring them home. I knew he would."

Riley rifled through the pockets and found a small plastic case.

Amaze your friends
with
Scotch and Soda

"Ma'am, did Kenneth ever have any visit . . . ?"

There was no response. She had drifted asleep.

Riley made his way to Ross's room and found Griffin at his bedside.

"They say you're going to make it, pal," Riley said. "How's the head?"

"It feels as if I've been kicked by one of your wife's horses," Ross managed weakly. He noticed the dried blood below Riley's ears. "Are you okay?"

"My knees are banged up, and I can't hear so well, but that might be a blessing."

"Can I go back to the NTSB now?" Ross spoke louder.

"Be my guest. I'm finished with you."

"Jack? That night at the Outback, you refused to tell me what goes on in the Florida Keys. Would you reconsider?"

"He's all drugged up, right?" Riley asked Griffin.

"A little bit. But now I want to know too."

"Paradise goes on," Riley said matter-of-factly. "Come see for yourself."

Ross struggled to sit up. "The terrorists. Did you get them?"

"Him," Riley corrected. "It was one person using multiple false names. I doubt if we'll ever know his real identity. We'll have a composite sketch drawn up and share it with known witnesses. He was pretty much blown to pieces. Can't say that I'll lose any sleep over it."

"Jack? Something else got blown to pieces," Ross admitted. "Your fish."

Riley's face darkened, then brightened again with a shrug. "You did good, pal."

"What's that?" Griffin asked, noticing something in Riley's hand.

"A coin trick. Apparently, our terrorist was into magic. It's a circumstantial link, but right now it's further proof that it was him. We'll have it analyzed."

Griffin placed her hand in front of Ross's face. "How many fingers?"

Ross smiled warmly. "Are we ever going out on a date?"

She kissed his cheek and gently adjusted his pillow. "I've accepted a job with Fox's DC bureau. Who knows? You might even get your shirt back."

"I guess I'll leave you two alone." Riley winked at Ross. "I've got to tell the president that his country can start flying again."

47

PORT OF RABAT, MOROCCO
CARGO VESSEL *ABUZENIMA*
CAPTAIN'S QUARTERS

"WE MUST part ways, Faiz, but only for a short time. I assume your struggle is over?" Captain Riad Naimi said, handing Al-Aran an envelope. "You are now Habib Saloume, named from the rural village of your birth in Senegal. The real Habib served on my crew and was lost in a storm three years ago. He had no friends or family. You could be his twin. Do the authorities know you?"

"You might say that I managed to avoid the bureaucracy and fingerprinters." Al-Aran set his pipe down and examined the documents. "Is Aljezur safe?"

"My friend, I am a man of faith, and I support your work, but I do not wish to know the details. I will provide everything that you require in life as a service to my brother, Ali. You will lack nothing. You may help raise my vegetables and assist with my animals. I have a small but reliable servant-staff. On my land, your time is your own. The town of Aljezur is filled with tourists who mind their business. No one will ask anything of you. You may walk among the stores freely or browse the world's information in our Internet cafés. We have some of the most beautiful beaches on the Western Atlantic. Praia de Monte Clérigo has a fantastic view of the coast and a convenient lay-by where

281

you may stop and admire the sea. The cliff tops are a mass of color in spring. The region is completely uneventful. It will be as if the old professor no longer exists."

Riad glanced at his watch. "The *Abuzenima* sails for Lisbon today. After some business in Antwerp, I will return and we will both rest. Perhaps the time may come when you admit you have done enough for Allah."

"Perhaps," Al-Aran agreed. "But only Allah can determine that. In twenty-one days, I must travel to London. My work begins again."

"As you wish," the captain said, extending his hand. "May I ask you a question? The crew has noticed you in your cabin studying some-thing late into the evenings. A large winged insect made of plastic. Perhaps a toy? You disassemble it and then reassemble it over and over. A hobby, *señor*?"

Al-Aran turned for the door, then paused. "Your farm, *Capitán* . . . what animals do you raise?"

"Goats and a small herd of livestock. A plentiful and local source of meat."

"You are a fortunate and prosperous man," Al-Aran praised. "You may take comfort in the fact that your meat does not come from America."

———

DUCK KEY
TOM'S HARBOR INLET

RILEY DIALED his cell phone.

"Tom Ross."

"I can't believe you're back to work," Riley chided. "Tell the NTSB you need more medical time."

"I did, and they went ahead and promoted me anyway." Ross laughed. "They took the word *acting* out of my title. How's paradise?"

"Congratulations, pal. I'm sitting under a tiki hut with a mango smoothie. Kissi's flying down tonight on a private jet, compliments of the Secretary of Homeland Security."

"That's not enough. For what you did, it should be Air Force One."

"I suppose," Riley said halfheartedly.

"Jack, what's wrong?"

"Mixed emotions. I just feel empty about the way things turned out falling into place the way they did. It seemed too perfect."

"Do you have sunstroke?" Ross asked. "What's wrong with perfect? You led a successful investigation that identified and tracked down a terrorist who killed Americans. You stopped a real threat that almost brought this country to its knees."

"He did bring the country to its knees."

"You know what I mean. It could have been worse. A lot worse."

"Frankly, I wanted more," Riley admitted. "Like a name, for instance. We never even knew his real name, not to mention where he came from or how he was able operate those drones so freely right under our noses. And there's still two more unaccounted for. Think about that. How many more are out there? It reminds me of when I was a kid in Georgia. We used to play in the woods near a creek. One day, a cottonmouth snake bit my friend, and the next thing you know, the whole place was roped off. He lost his right leg. They found and killed a snake, but we never knew if it was *the* snake or if there were others. They simply assumed. They hung signs and told us not to play there anymore, just to be safe. Something bothers me about that Saudi professor. The one who supposedly swam with the sharks. I can't put my finger on it. Something keeps buzzing around in my head. A little voice keeps telling me that he played us. What if he set the whole thing up?"

"You have absolutely no evidence to support that," Ross said. "And for the sake of argument, if Faiz Al-Aran *is* still alive, he'd be a marked man all over the planet with no place to run or hide. Someone would pick him up."

"But it proves my point that there might be a heckuva lot of snakes out there," Riley quipped. "Poisonous snakes. Tom, I fear this is only the beginning. We have no idea what the world is about to experience in a new drone age."

"All right, I order you to snap out of this cynical funk. Get your butt into your boat and go catch your fish."

"Already on my way," Riley said. "I'll call you when I'm back in DC.

When you're one hundred percent, we'll have you and Neela over for a horseback ride."

Riley finished his drink and gazed north to Tom's Harbor Bridge, which separated the Gulf of Mexico from the Atlantic Ocean. A light breeze gently tickled the US flag above his pier. He turned the handle on his elevator boat lift, and the L-shaped aluminum beams lowered *Just-Duck-Key* onto the water. The boat's engine started faithfully, and he eased the craft forward. It took only minutes to reach his fishing hole. It was just off a deep-water canal halfway between his dock and the open ocean. He swung the bow into the tide flow and dropped anchor. The iron flanges gripped the bottom and held firm. He methodically rigged three lines with chunks of fresh mullet and set each rod in a holder. Just as he sat back in a padded captain's chair, his cell phone chirped. It was his home number.

"Good morning," Kissi Riley's voice sung. "What's the temperature?"

"Eighty and sunny. There's a nice breeze off the Gulf. I miss you. Are you packed?"

"Yes. Are you sure about this?"

"Trust me. All you have to do is show up at Dulles. The Secretary's jet will be fueled and ready to go. It's his way of saying thanks."

"How long is the flight?"

"A little over two hours. It's exactly one thousand miles. You should arrive in Marathon Airport around six. Don't eat. We're doing something special."

"Aren't you the romantic one?"

"Hey, you deserve it. We both do. I'm looking forward to some nice time off—" A fishing line twitched. "Kissi—I'll call you right back. I gotta go."

Riley clicked off and set the phone on the console.

He gripped the rod, and as he did, the line instantly went limp. He counted to ten. Nothing. False alarm. His phone chirped before he could redial. He brought it to his lips and spoke seductively.

"Sorry, honey. I almost forgot . . . be sure and bring that black see-through thing I bought for your birthday. Tonight, you're going to live up to your name. You've got a great body, and I want it all."

There was silence.

"I don't know about great, but I have been working out," the president's voice finally spoke.

A series of waves bounced off the canal seawall and rolled the boat sideways. Riley dropped his phone but quickly retrieved it. "Mr. President, geez . . . I'm sorry. I thought you were . . . I didn't know it was you."

"No harm done, son," the president said, laughing. "I just wanted to offer my personal thanks for what you did for the country. You made us proud."

"Thank you, sir. I appreciate that, but I had a lot of help. It's bittersweet, though. I mean, I wish we could have discovered and prevented those attacks beforehand. It would have . . . well, the economic problems and all. I hope you know what I mean."

"I do, Jack, and I tend to agree. Sometimes victory is bittersweet. I pray that the American people can think in those terms. It'll help us all recover."

"Yes, sir."

"Jack, how old are you?" the president asked.

"Forty-four."

"That's a good young age, son. It's rather comforting to know that you'll be around a bit longer. I suspect that we'll need all the sharp minds we can muster if we expect to win the war on terror. Anyway, thank you again from my heart. Have a good vacation and enjoy your . . . birthday present."

Riley set his phone down and noticed his line move again. This time it was different. It was straightening. He gently lifted the rod from its holder. He lowered the tip and heaved backwards.

The fish nearly pulled him into the water, and Riley could hear the rod's graphite filaments cracking. In an instant, the air was filled with the reel's high-pitched buzz. The line peeled out toward a deep hole next to the seawall.

It was him.

The line went limp, and Riley quickly reeled in the excess. The monster on the other end wouldn't budge. After ten minutes, Riley's arms ached from the stalemate, and he felt rather stupid just standing there. Something had to give. He had no choice. The pressure would either force the fish out of its rock sanctuary or snap the line.

He gathered his strength and pulled.

Something actually moved.

A wave of excitement ran through Riley's body, so strong that he felt like shouting. He knew he had a chance. His equipment was in top shape, he had a stiff piano-wire leader and a new stainless steel hook. That fish was *not* getting off.

Twenty-five feet away, Shaitan's massive body broke the surface like some steel barrel. The giant black grouper fanned its tail slowly, and the movement brought it closer.

Riley spied a net on the boat's canopy but decided to use a six-foot gaff hook instead. He wrapped his hand through a thick leather loop on the handle and leaned over the water.

"Come to papa!" he shouted. "I'm gonna grill your fat hide."

The fish would have none of it.

With one strong flap, Shaitan turned back for the seawall. Riley managed to alter the path slightly, and as he did, the monster headed straight for a docked forty-eight-foot Sea Ray Sedan Bridge. The name on the stern was appropriate:

DEVILFISH

Riley couldn't see below the surface, but he knew that the fish had circled the yacht's propeller. Strained beyond its limit, the line suddenly gave off a firecracker-like snap, and the momentum sent him backward onto his butt on the deck. His head smacked into the console. He gave out a loud curse.

A little girl wearing oversized sunglasses and her mother's floppy straw hat appeared on the Sea Ray's bridge.

"You said a bad word, mister," she scolded. "And you're not a very good fish catcher. He got away."

——

A US INTERSTATE HIGHWAY

"I NEVER knew this state had so many cows," Marissa said, observing a large herd grazing in the flat grassland.

"It ranks eleventh in the States," Akil noted. "Most of the beef cattle here are from a Brahman strain. They can handle the heat and humidity. Now I can too."

"I like it." Marissa smiled, rubbing Akil's newly shaved scalp. "It feels so sexy."

"Eddie said we could visit lots of places where cows live," Amber announced from the backseat. "He said that Kansas, Nebraska, and Texas have the most cows and that I could even feed some."

Marissa looked at Akil oddly. "How come you know so much about cows?"

"I dunno. I guess I read it somewhere."

"I'm hungry," Jo-Jo whined impatiently. "Are we almost there yet?"

"Mommy, listen," Amber said, bracing the toy organ on her lap. She pressed out the tune perfectly with two fingers."

"Amber, that's beautiful. Who taught you that?"

"Eddie did," she said, beaming. "Mommy, does McDonald's turn cows into hamburgers?"

"Well, yes. Some cows are used for meat, and also milk and butter."

"Does McDonald's kill them?"

"No, I think someone else does."

"Mommy, is the world big?"

"It's very big."

"Is it a world of fear?"

"Of course not, sweetie," Marissa assured, frowning at her daughter and giving Akil a confused look. "Why would you say something like that?"

"Because that's what the song says. Eddie even sang it with me."

"Amber," Akil scolded. "That's not what it means. The world is nice. Especially America. We're going to a special place with lots of animals and friendly people from all different countries. There'll be lots of fun things to do and see. It's not a world of fear, okay?"

"Can we stay there for this many days?" Jo-Jo begged, raising four fingers.

Akil checked the rearview mirror and eased the minivan into the right-hand lane. He turned his head and winked. "If you're a good boy, we'll stay there for twenty-one days—uh-oh, look who I see."

Jo-Jo's eyes grew wide. He covered his smile with both hands at the sight of a large billboard. Two symbols represented a simple but universal code that every child could decipher. One was a large, black arrow that pointed south. To the right of that arrow, three circles formed the distinctive ears and face of Florida's most famous mouse.

Amber set her organ aside, rested her head on a pillow, and gazed out the window. She sang the words softly from memory.

"It's a world of laughter, a world of tears. It's a world of hope, it's a world of fear. There's so much that we share, that it's time we're aware, it's a small world after all."

ABOUT THE AUTHOR

JOEL NARLOCK thrives on asking "what if." He has interviewed the US Secret Service, top commercial airline pilots, and FAA and military officials about drones flying where they shouldn't. He was given a private tour of Andrews AFB specifically to evaluate an unmanned drone penetrating its perimeter. He walked the rooftop of Camden Yards Stadium in Baltimore specifically to evaluate a drone's ability to target the pitcher's mound. He predicts that drone technology and usage in America will increase dramatically, hopefully to benefit mankind. *Drone Games* is a realistic story about using drones for evil. By raising drone awareness, perhaps others will ask "what if" and be prepared to stop those who might actually try similar tactics. And that's a good thing. Joel is the author of *Target Acquired*. He took first place in Key West's 2013 Mystery Fest Short Story Contest.